Tales of the Were

Inferno

BIANCA D'ARC

DEDICATION

This book first released in 2009 – a time when my life was still reasonably carefree, and my mother was still alive. She died at the end of that year and things will never be the same. I'd like to dedicate this second edition to her, for her love, guidance, understanding and support. She was my biggest cheerleader though she never read a single one of my books. She was simply...the best.

And the original dedication from the first edition still stands...

Thanks to my family, first and foremost, as always.

And to my Aussie friend, Megan, who unknowingly lent her first name to the heroine in this book.

Thanks also to my friends and "helpers" Valerie and Jambrea, who were kind enough to offer their time to act as beta readers on another project. Also to Peggy, who assisted in fact gathering—an invaluable help to my forgetful self. You guys are the greatest!

PROLOGUE

"I have one final task for you. Do this, and your family's blood debt will be repaid."

Megan knew, whatever the task, it wouldn't be easy. Nothing about the *Altor Custodis* had turned out to be easy since they'd come into her life.

She knew better than to ask questions. This man would not be rushed. Igor Poferov was not one to take interruption well. An immigrant to New York from some Baltic country, he took old world charm to the extreme.

"It will not be easy," he continued in his deliberate way.

Big surprise there. She kept her expression carefully blank and stifled an ironic chuckle.

"But it is a task that needs doing. Strange things have happened among the *were* and all is not as transparent to us as it should be."

Megan didn't like the sound of this, though working among her own folk was no real hardship. True, she didn't associate with many *were*, preferring to be a lone wolf. Still it wasn't so hard to fit in among them for short periods of time.

"Reports have come from the Northern Territories of an unholy alliance between the current Lords of the *Were* and a certain vampire we've been watching for centuries."

Her ears perked up. Vampires were tricky creatures. Most *were* had an instinctive distrust of the bloodletters and would have nothing to do with them. If the current leaders of all *were* in North America were suddenly allying themselves with a vampire, it was big news indeed.

"His name is Dante d'Angleterre. The last report I have on him regarded an agreement to work with a human mage named Patrick Vabian. The mage disappeared. I need to know what happened to Vabian and the exact nature of the alliance between *were* and vampire—and any others that might be involved."

When the old man finally wound down, she waited just a few heartbeats to see if he had anything further to add. Then she sprang.

"So you want me to spy on the *were?*" It wasn't her favorite thing to do, but she would do it if it meant clearing her family's debt of honor. Spying on other *were*folk wasn't so bad. They were her kind, after all. She understood them, even if she'd never lived among them. She owed them no loyalty. Not after the way they'd treated her family in the past.

"No."

She waited, dreading what the old man might say next.

"I want you to spy on the vampire. I want you to infiltrate his inner circle. Get close to him. Bed him if you have to. I want to know what happened to the mage. D'Angleterre's powers might be greater than we believe, and he may have other allies. I want to know everything there is to know about Dante d'Angleterre. Everything."

Megan felt the blood drain from her face and knew she was probably white as a sheet. She did *not* like vampires. Not one bit.

"I won't whore for you." Her voice was a cold as a Montana winter.

The old man laughed. It was a brittle, almost evil sound. "It probably won't come to that. You've got something the vampire will want more than sex."

She waited for him to elaborate, knowing the coy expression on his weathered face meant he had more to disclose.

2

"*Were* blood is like a drug to his kind. Offer him your blood and he'll keep you around. Guaranteed."

CHAPTER ONE

Debauchery wasn't something Dante indulged in very often anymore, but when Duncan suggested a night of revelry with a select few mortal playmates, Dante didn't object. He knew it had been a long time since the fey knight had had his choice of women. Being kept prisoner in the fey realm for centuries hadn't been easy on the half-mortal knight. Dante felt it only fitting they celebrate Duncan's newfound freedom with a little indulgence of the flesh.

In his case, Dante drank of his partners as well as fucked them, and they didn't seem to mind one bit. The vampire Glamour had that effect on most beings—mortal and supernatural alike. It was a rare creature that could resist his brand of mojo when he chose to use it full force.

And Dante knew Duncan had some interesting fey powers of his own. Still, the knight hardly needed magic to conjure a bevy of bed partners. The man was charming enough to acquire them without much effort, without tapping into his considerable magic.

It had been a few weeks since the adventure in Montana had uncovered a *Venifucus* plot to destroy the current Lords of the *Were*, the *were*wolf twins, Rafe and Tim, and their new mate, the priestess Allesandra. Dante had been sucked into that intrigue on the wrong side, before he had realized exactly what was going on. That he'd been so easily led still grated on his nerves. Never would he knowingly help the *Venifucus*. Not even to finally achieve vengeance on the *weres* who had so wronged him in the past.

Dante remembered the *Venifucus* as an ancient, evil sect devoted to the restoration of the *Mater Priori*—the sorceress Elspeth—also known as the Destroyer of Worlds. Though he wouldn't have believed any of it just a few weeks ago, he'd heard the human mage, Patrick Vabian, speak of their plans to restore the banished sorceress and rule this realm with an iron fist. Dante had recently discovered the *Venifucus* had worked in secret for many centuries to bring this about, and no one really knew how close they might be to achieving their goal.

It was a frightening thought to contemplate. Even for an immortal.

Thankfully, tragedy had been averted for the time being. The current Lords of the *Were* were enjoying an extended honeymoon with their new mate as she learned how to use her magical powers. Dante had more than made up the debt he owed from helping Patrick Vabian get close enough to attack them in the first place but was still annoyed by how easily he'd been duped by the mortal mage.

Sure, he'd held a grudge against all *were* for over a hundred years. An old set of *werelords* had sanctioned the death of his friend, Erik the Firewitch. The battle that had ensued as Erik tried to defend himself had burned half of Chicago. In the end, Erik had died at the hands of the *were*. And they owed Dante for that.

Erik had been like family to him. In fact, Dante often thought Erik had been the reincarnation of his younger brother, Elian, who had been murdered by the *Venifucus* centuries before. Both young men had been torn from him. Only now had the plot come to light that the *Venifucus* might have orchestrated both tragedies in an effort to turn Dante to their side.

But it would never work. Dante was many things, but he

was not evil. He wouldn't bestir himself to help restore an evil bitch to some kind of imagined throne from which she could rule mortals and immortals alike. No, he wanted no part of that.

He only wanted justice for Erik and Elian.

To that end, he'd become embroiled in the dust-up with the current *were*lords, Tim and Rafe, and their new mate, Allie. Somehow Allie had managed to summon Duncan from Underhill, rescuing the knight from his imprisonment in the fey realm. Dante and Duncan had been friends centuries before and it was the half-fey knight who tested Dante's mettle by tempting him with the amazing power of his blood.

Fey blood would kill most vampires outright. Half-fey blood, however, was diluted enough to pose a temptation most bloodletters could not refuse. With the ingestion of half-fey blood came power. There were few half-fey in any of the inhabitable realms, and they had quite enough power to stave off almost any vampire's attempts to subdue them. No, the only way a vampire could get a taste of half-fey blood was if the half-fey allowed it, and since most supernaturals didn't get along as a general rule, it rarely happened.

Yet Duncan had given Dante his blood—although it was bespelled at the time to poison him if his intentions were truly evil. Duncan had tested him. It had been a hell of a risk. A poisoned vampire is a crazed vampire, and Dante could have killed Duncan long before the bespelled blood would have disposed of Dante.

Luckily—or perhaps, it was fate rather than luck—Dante's heart had proven true. He had passed Duncan's little test and gained immense power, for a time, from the half-fey knight's blood. Enough power to help the *were*lords trap Patrick Vabian and bring him to the justice of the Lady.

Allie had done that. Smashingly well, Dante thought, by dispersing Vabian's magic to the farthest realms and leaving it up to the Lady she served to exile Vabian—now powerless—to some forgotten realm. It was likely they'd seen the last of Patrick Vabian, though his allies in the *Venifucus* were still enemies to be reckoned with.

But that battle was for another time. For tonight, there were women to bed and blood to be savored. Dante followed Duncan into the nightclub, well aware they would find more than a few willing mortal women inside. Dante paused to sniff the air, satisfied for the moment with the ripe scent of humanity that assailed his sharp senses. He also noticed some other, more subtle scent lacing the air.

It was off to his right.

Dante opened his eyes and looked around, only to meet the gaze of the most alluring woman he'd ever seen in all his long centuries. Lustrous, mink brown hair framed her face and swayed gently with her movements. Snapping hazel eyes fringed with thick, dark lashes batted at him with come-hither motions.

She was sitting on a bar stool, surrounded by mortals, but she shone as if she were the only being in the room. She was not human.

Dante sniffed again.

Were.

And she was looking directly at him, meeting his eyes boldly while she raised a glass of red wine to her lips. He followed the curving line of her luscious throat as it flexed in a swallow, and his cock went hard. Just like that.

This woman was potent.

And she held knowledge in her eyes.

Silently, she stood and stalked toward him. She moved like a predator, sinuous and sensuous as she held his attention and his gaze, mesmerizing him. He got the feeling he was definitely *her* prey this evening and not the other way around. It was a novel experience for him. Never had a woman enthralled him so quickly or so completely.

And they hadn't even touched.

That would soon be remedied.

"She's a fine looking woman, but beware my friend," Duncan said in a low voice, "she is not what she seems."

Dante nodded, his gaze glued on the woman as she

approached. "I know what she is."

"But do you know why? Why would such a creature seek you out?"

Dante shrugged. "Probably for no good reason, though I find it hard to resist the puzzle she presents."

"Just be certain this puzzle doesn't get you staked out in the desert at dawn." Duncan laughed as he moved off, two women already in his sights. "I'll be near if you need backup."

*

She hadn't realized he would be so handsome. Of course bloodletters were said to have a Glamour all their own. She didn't think she was close enough to feel his magical influence, but she didn't have any personal experience with his kind. Their powers were said to grow with the centuries, and Dante was an old one.

There was something about the tall man at his side too. Something that gave Megan the heebie geebies. She couldn't quite put her finger on what the deal was with him. He wasn't a bloodsucker. His scent was different but very, very magical. Not human entirely, yet not anything else she recognized. She would have to tread carefully—very carefully—until she knew exactly what she was dealing with.

Still, the ball was in play now. She'd have to see it through and play the game she'd planned. Just this one last task, and she'd finally be free of the meddlesome *Altor Custodis*. She would do just about anything to clear her family debt of honor, but she had to be careful. This Dante fellow was more than likely the deadliest being she'd ever meet.

Squaring her shoulders, she walked up to him and shifted her weight to one foot, letting the opposite hip jut out toward him provocatively. Dante was certainly a tall drink of water, almost a foot taller than her own five foot four. Of course, she was petite for a wolf shifter. She was only half *were* by blood.

She didn't speak, just looked him over and let him look in

return. She saw the flare of interest in his eyes before he banked it to something less obvious. She was close enough to scent his magic though well protected—she hoped—against his vampire mojo by her shifter nature. Still, he certainly did have an effect and she had to admit—mojo or not, this man was potent with a capital P.

"Do you like playing with fire, little one?"

His voice wafted over her like dark silk, caressing her pelt in the most sensuous way. She had to suppress a shiver of pleasure at the tone and timbre.

She struggled for nonchalance. "I know what you are."

"And still you came to me? You're a brave little shifter. Does your pack know what you're up to?"

"I have no pack. I'm a loner." Her chin rose defiantly.

"Ah, a lone wolf out on the prowl." He made the words mocking. She squared her shoulders and stood her ground. "You are a foolhardy youngster, out to test her limits."

"No doubt I'm younger than you but by no means a child." She thrust out her chest and was glad to see his gaze snagged by the motion. "I'm curious, I'll admit. I've heard your kind has certain abilities for pleasure."

Dante leaned back, studying her from under hooded eyes. He was a seducer of the senses in every word, every motion. It would be hard not to fall under his spell—magical or not. Everything female in her wanted to be with this male, regardless of his species or his power.

He watched her, seeming to come to some kind of decision. "My name is Dante."

She laughed. "Playing with fire indeed. I get the literary reference, *Dante*." She grinned at him. "My name is Megan."

"Well then, Megan, can I buy you a drink?" He ushered her toward the bar where two chairs opened up for them as if by magic.

She knew darn well he'd used his influence over mortals to make the others move. It was a casual show of power that scared her. Without the protection of her shifter blood, would she be as powerless against him as other mortals? And how could she be certain she was protected? Would she even know if she was being influenced by his vampiric powers?

It was a worrisome thought. This man was more than she'd been led to believe. She could tell from the few minutes she'd been in his presence. And his friend was troublesome too. What *was* he? Megan feared she'd suddenly been thrust into the deep end of the pool with no warning, and she'd have to learn to swim. Fast.

"So what brings you here tonight?" Dante asked, turning back to her after ordering wine for them.

"Just on the prowl."

"Ah." He nodded knowingly. "Something your kind enjoys, from what I hear."

"How do you know what we enjoy?" She tried her best not to sound suspicious but feared some of her wariness showed through.

He leaned back as the bartender returned with their wine. "Contrary to popular thought, I actually do have some friends among the *were*tribes." He kept his voice low so that only she could hear him. Her hearing was better than any mortal's and he definitely knew the scope of her abilities in that area at least, proving his shocking words might hold some truth.

"It thought your kind didn't like *weres*."

He sipped his wine before answering. "It's not that we don't like you. It's more that we don't like how resistant you are to our power. Bad blood in the past has made all the various supernaturals distrust each other over the centuries. Yet I have a feeling that will soon come to an end."

She was shocked. "Why?"

He shrugged. "You're a loner so you probably haven't heard. There are certain bad elements returning after many generations. I was around the last time we fought them, and we all worked together. Seems to me we might have to do so again."

"What are you talking about?"

He shook his head in the negative. "Not here. No matter how good your hearing, there may be others listening as well.

If you really want to know, I'll tell you in private."

"I want to know." This was her chance. Even if he was leading her into some kind of weird vamp trap, she needed to get close to him. That was her mission and she wouldn't shrink from it. She was also curious about his hinted knowledge. She really was a lone wolf. She hadn't had interaction with her own kind in a long time. If there was something going on in the supernatural world, she didn't trust her contacts in the *Altor Custodis* to tell her. They were too damned secretive and their policy of non-interference went way too far in her opinion. She'd like to know what Dante thought he knew.

"All right then. Later." He drained his glass of wine and set it on the bar. "For now, will you dance with me?"

She noted the sudden change from house music to a slower tempo that allowed couples to move close. His influence again? She had little doubt such was the case. Lowering her half-finished drink to the bar, she took his hand and felt an immediate awareness of him shoot through her skin. It tingled where they touched, sparking with magical energy. It didn't hurt. It felt more like tiny bubbles popping against her skin. Almost tickling and definitely happy.

It was a strange, unexpected sensation. It was as if their bodies recognized each other.

He took her in his arms, and it was as if they'd been made to fit together. Their bodies moved in rhythm to the slower music, his strength countering hers in a way she'd never experienced. As a *were*wolf, Megan was stronger than most human males. As a lone wolf, she'd never really consorted with her kind. She'd never been this close to a vampire before and taken all together, she'd never felt so feminine or sheltered in any man's embrace.

She closed her eyes, enjoying the feel of his strong body against her. For just a moment, she let thoughts of her mission and the debt of honor owed by her family fade from her mind. She let herself revel in the feel of him and the way his strength complemented her own.

And he was one hell of a dancer. She never danced much, but as a wolf-shifter, she had a certain amount of natural agility. She followed his lead with pleasure, liking the way he commanded her movements with a sureness she was unused to encountering in the human males she'd dated from time to time.

"You're very good," she whispered, trying to suppress the growl of pleasure that wanted to issue from her throat.

Dante laughed low, his breath whispering past her ear in a way that made her shiver. "So I've been told."

"I meant you're a good dancer." She pulled back to meet his gaze, grinning in what she hoped was an inviting way. Banter was good. He was responding well to her flirting. So far, her mission was on track.

"Once upon a time a man's status in life was judged on such things as how well he danced."

That comment took her aback. This man—this vampire—had lived for centuries. He must have seen and done a lot of things she could only dream of in those many years.

"You're an old one then?" She had to play coy. He couldn't know that she already knew his background—at least as much as the *Altor Custodis* file about him contained.

"Old enough to remember when the waltz was considered a scandalous dance. And now look at us." He chuckled as his gaze roved down her body to where they brushed together intimately, only the fabric of their clothing separating them. "All in all, I think things have changed for the better. Still, there was something charming about those days."

"It must have been beautiful." She'd read her share of Jane Austin and dreamed of beautiful ball gowns twirling around the floor of some grand ballroom to the strains of a string quartet. It was a far cry from the pounding bass of this club's sound system and the whirling neon lights.

"I see you're a romantic at heart, young Megan."

She shrugged, noting the way his gaze fell to the upper swells of her breasts, visible in her low-cut blouse. Things were progressing according to plan. He seemed attracted. Of course, for all she knew, he was leading her on for his own amusement. She had no basis to judge her progress when it came to vampires, having never dealt directly with any before.

"I think I'm like most women. We all yearn for romance at some point in our lives."

"Ah, but shifter women yearn for their one true love. Their mate. Do they not?"

"I've heard that your kind do the same. Is it true that most of you search for centuries until you find that special One?"

Dante's eyes grew dark as he held her gaze. "It is true, though most are unaware of our plight. How do you know about it?"

"My mother knew one of your kind in her day. Pretty much all I know about your kind comes from her." She'd almost blown it. At least her excuse was mostly true. Her mother *had* had dealings with a vampire once upon a time and had told Megan about it. It was also true Megan's meager knowledge had been duly supplemented by her keeper at the *Altor Custodis.*

"Do you know his name? This one that your mother knew?"

"What makes you think it was a male?" She gave him a saucy look, hoping to get back to the flirtatious banter they'd been sharing before she misstepped big time.

"All right then, who was it? There are few unmated females among us, you know."

"Her name was Esmeralda de Young, though she was going by Mira when my mother knew her. She was a healer of sorts, and my mother sought her help when I was still a pup."

"Ah." Dante pulled her in close once more, and she rested her head on his shoulder. "I know Esmay has always had a soft spot for strays. I guess you come from a line of loners, eh?"

Mutely, she nodded against his chest and felt his muscles relax just a fraction as her story reassured him. It was the truth after all, just not the full truth. For a flicker of a second, she felt bad about lying to him. Then she remembered her family and realized she had to stand firm against the vampire's allure. She had a mission to complete and her family honor depended on it.

"Is it true you'd get a rush if I let you drink from me?" She hadn't meant to ask that question. It just slipped out, something that had been preying on her mind.

He looked at her strangely for a moment, then nodded. "*Were* blood is more magical than human. Only mage blood can match it and there's only one thing more powerful."

"What's that?"

"*My* blood."

Duncan joined them on the dance floor, grinding against Megan's backside as Dante dominated her front. She'd jumped when Duncan snuck up on her, but recovered well. All in all, Dante was quickly becoming fascinated by the lone wolf pup.

She turned in the small space they allowed her, to face Duncan.

"And exactly what are you? You're not all human, yet you're nothing I've ever sniffed before."

"Good nose." Duncan bent down to kiss the tip of her nose, and Dante felt himself repressing a growl. That surprised him enough to make him back off a bit and let things unfold. Duncan undoubtedly knew what he was doing. Or so Dante hoped.

She pulled away, clearly uncomfortable with the way Duncan had just invaded her personal space, though they were dancing scandalously close to begin with. Dante supposed dancing the bump and grind was accepted behavior these days, while kissing without prior contact was still something a little unexpected.

"So what are you?"

"That's for me to know and you to find out, my dear. Suffice to say, I'm older and more magical than either of you, so you'd both best behave." He winked and left her with a smile, seeking his mortal female companions elsewhere on the dance floor.

Dante pulled her back against him with an arm around her middle and they danced like that for a while, his aching cock pillowed by a round, tight ass that made his mouth water. Before he could get too carried away, she turned again in his arms to face him.

"Did your friend just warn me off?" Her expression was one of disbelief.

Dante smiled. "I think he was warning both of us. He's become my keeper in a way. A thorn in my side, though we've been friends for centuries. I'll be glad when things return to normal."

"And when will that be?"

He didn't see any harm in answering her truthfully. Change was coming and the more *were* who knew about it, the better. Even lone ones could be of help in the coming struggle if what they feared came to pass—if the *Venificus* were successful and brought the Destroyer of Worlds back to this realm.

"When our enemies are defeated. Again."

"Who's your enemy, Dante?" She looked confused, alarmed and suspicious all at the same time.

"Like I said, I'll tell you all about it. Just not here."

"How can I be sure you'll tell me the truth? You might be one of the bad guys, after all."

"Am I? Wouldn't your highly trained nose be able to tell?"

She seemed to consider that, then moved in to take a delicate sniff of him. "You're right. You don't smell evil at all. Not entirely good, but definitely not evil. You'd have to be a hell of a mage to hide that kind of thing from me."

"It's good you realize that. Mages can fool us all. However, I am not a mage. I am what you see."

"Your kind and mine don't get along all that well." She seemed to be having fun playing devil's advocate with him. "So how do I know I can trust you?"

"Because all creatures on the side of light should be warned."

BIANCA D'ARC

"And how do *you* know *I'm* one of the good guys?" She fingered his lapels, regaining some of her composure as the music changed and they moved more slowly. He edged her toward the outer ring of the dance floor, into the shadows.

"You're not the only one with a good nose, sweetheart." He dipped his head, daring a kiss. He licked the seam of her lips, coaxing them to open. When she let him in, he wasted little time, taking full advantage of her yielding lips to stake his claim on her mouth, on her very breath.

She tasted divine. Wild, free and of the earth. Temptation made flesh. Dante had never fucked a *were*. He'd been around them from time to time—more so in the far past when they'd fought side by side. He'd not had much exposure to them in recent years except for his adventure with the *were*lords. He hadn't known they were so full of life and light. He hadn't known their females contained such passion in their lithe, lovely bodies.

She pulled away with a little moan of delight and a teasing smile. He wasn't quite ready to let her go. He grew aware of their surroundings and knew this was not the place for what he had in mind.

"Come back to my place." It wasn't much of a question, more like an order. Luckily, she seemed to be on the same page.

Her head tilted in a cute way as she thought about it. "If I do, will you want to bite me?"

"Undoubtedly. I'll make you come so hard, you won't even feel the prick of my teeth. And I'll only take a little. You have my word of honor you'll come to no harm."

"Your word of honor, eh?" She seemed to consider that. "I suppose you're the old-fashioned type to whom his word really is his bond, right?"

He dipped his head in acknowledgment of her words. "Not only that. Duncan will be watching both of us for the slightest misstep. Believe me, you do not want to mess with a knight."

"He was a knight?"

16

"Was and still is," he confirmed. "And that's all you'll get from me on that subject unless and until he chooses to let you in on his little secret. It's his call and I respect that, but surely you can sense the power around him. It's so pure, it's almost kind of pretty."

She chuckled as she looked over at Duncan dancing across the room with two lovelies.

"I smell it. I don't see it as clearly as you apparently do. To me he smells like pure fresh air. Like the full moon on a sabbat. Like everything good in this world and beyond."

"Yeah, that kind of sums him up in a very *were* way. To me, he looks like a mixture of remembered sunshine and blessed moonlight, the rarest of vintages and the hum of angels singing. Damn, I need a drink if I'm waxing poetic about Duncan." He laughed at himself, though every word he'd spoken was true. Duncan's power was all these things and more and it would keep him on track while he learned his way through this new crisis.

"All right. I'll go home with you, but you should be warned—" she stepped back from him and trailed her finger down his chest teasingly, "—I bite back."

They left the club shortly thereafter. Dante couldn't wait to sink his teeth into Megan. He had to get her home and in his bed in the shortest amount of time possible. He ached to be inside her. His fangs dropped just thinking about tasting her blood while he possessed her body, making her scream in ecstasy as he drank from her.

Distracted by his unusual desire for a mortal, he wasn't as attentive to his surroundings as he should have been when they exited the building. A car screeched around the bend of the parking lot as they headed for his vehicle parked in a dark corner of the lot.

In a fraction of a moment, Dante caught the flash of peroxide blonde hair as a woman's arm shot out the window of a gleaming black, late model Porsche. What set his internal alarms to clanging in warning was the fireball poised in her hand.

She was a mage and a powerful one at that. She lobbed her missile at his head, and Dante ducked for cover as streaks of sickly ochre fire rained down around him. He didn't understand. It should have dealt him a glancing blow at the very least.

The woman in the Porsche called her magic and launched once more. Dante was pinned between two vehicles and the brick wall that ran along the back of the parking lot. He'd stared death in the face before and knew this time it would claim him.

Then, in an unexpected blur of motion, a *were*wolf in the dangerous and magical half-shift form bounded between him and the female mage. The blast hit the wolf square in the chest. Dante heard himself shouting as he raced to catch her, even as the Porsche squealed away.

Megan fell into his arms, singed fur covering her muscular body. She was unconscious but breathing as he cradled her to his chest.

A shadow fell over them, and Dante bared his fangs in a fierce snarl. No one would touch her again. No one.

Thankfully, it was only Duncan.

"Ease off, friend. Mortals are coming to see about the commotion. We must leave. Is she...?"

"She lives." Dante's voice rasped out over roughened vocal cords and fangs lengthened in preparation for battle.

"Let's get her someplace safe then."

Dante wouldn't allow Duncan to touch her. It was unreasonable, he knew, but his fragile temper wouldn't allow it at the moment. He stood with her in his arms. Her body shifted to human form, even as he rose, her pale flesh gleaming in the moonlight. She was hurt badly. He would see to her survival if he had to move heaven and Earth to assure it.

"Open the car door. You drive." The terse words were all he could get out through his elongated teeth and fierce anger. The anger wasn't directed at Duncan. Rather, it was meant

18

for the woman who had done this—and himself.

There was little doubt in his mind that Megan had deliberately intercepted a strike meant for him. The little fool. She'd probably saved his life, but at what cost?

CHAPTER TWO

"I know it's bad when you allow me to drive." Duncan tried to make light of the serious situation as he ushered them into Dante's car. Luckily they'd taken the big Mercedes tonight in anticipation of having a few ladies with them later. How differently things had turned out from their original plan.

All they'd wanted was a night of carousing and good fun. It had changed in an instant. Two instants, actually—the first being the arrival of the sexy little *were*wolf and the second, the subsequent attack by a mysterious blonde in a hot car. Duncan wondered if the two events were somehow related. He wasn't a big believer in coincidence.

The wolf girl had secrets. There was no doubt of it in his mind. Was she in league with the woman who'd just lobbed killing blows from fifteen yards out? That was powerful sorcery, and it had been aimed directly at Dante.

If the two women were working together, why would Megan put herself in the path of danger to save his life? Or was a more elaborate ruse yet to unfold?

Duncan would keep watch, as was his duty, and try to keep an open mind. Dante was more special than anyone knew and it was Duncan's task to keep him safe for the battle ahead. If the other side managed to take him out in the early rounds—or worse, to turn him to their cause as they'd been trying to do for centuries—it would be a tragic and dangerous turn of events.

"Where are we headed?" Duncan asked once they were out on the open road. It was essential to put as much distance between them and the threat of danger as possible. The girl was in bad shape. She needed medical—and magical—attention.

"Home." Dante was growling. Something Duncan had never heard him do before. Come to think of it, he'd never seen Dante react so strongly to a female of any kind before. Something was definitely strange with this situation, yet Duncan would be damned if he could put his finger on exactly what it was.

"Are you certain that's wise?"

"Home, Duncan! Fast."

Well, that was clear enough. Duncan applied his foot to the gas pedal, watching the mirrors carefully for any sign of pursuit. He also kept a magical eye out. He'd arrived in time to taste the flavor of the blonde's magic. If she was anywhere near them, he should be able to tell, regardless of how strong she was.

Duncan's magic was of the fey realm. No mortal mage should be able to fool him once he'd identified a unique magical signature.

"She'll be all right, Dante. Her light is strong and pure." Duncan spared a moment to reassure his old friend about the wolf girl's chances of survival.

Since Duncan's release from the fey realm, Dante had proved himself a man of honor, once again fighting on the side of light. Duncan respected that. He respected the man Dante had become, though he hadn't trusted him at first. Duncan had laid a trap for Dante, feeding him his potent half-fey blood to both heal him and test him. Duncan held the key to Dante's continued existence. If he ever stepped over the line into darkness, Duncan could destroy him.

They'd left Montana together, both aware of the need to renew their bonds of friendship. Trust would come in time and in fact, Duncan was already far down the road to trusting

Dante. The bloodletter hadn't changed much over the centuries. He'd been a good man before he'd become immortal, and his basic goodness had never been suspect.

He might have become more dour—more introverted and solitary—but that was to be expected when one lived so long and so alone. Dante had no mate. He'd never found the fabled One most of his kind searched for. The One woman who, legend said, would be able to share his mind and complete his soul.

Duncan had seen it a few times during his last sojourn in the mortal realm. There was nothing more beautiful than the magic of two souls joined in love. He hoped one day Dante would find that.

Hell, if he didn't know better, he'd wonder if the woman lying injured in his arms wasn't the One. Dante's reaction was certainly violent enough. He was uncharacteristically possessive and quick to anger, and he wouldn't let anyone near her.

Weres and bloodletters didn't mingle. Oh, *weres* and immortals had worked side by side in the distant past to defeat the armies of darkness. However, these days they kept themselves separate and distinct.

So it was unlikely he was witnessing such a true mating. Still…Dante's unreasonable reaction gave him food for thought.

Dante had always been something of a rebel. He never seemed to do anything the easy way. His life had been one crisis after another. Not an easy road and not one of his making. Only now did it come clear—there had most likely been *Venifucus* infiltrators behind most of the tragedies that had followed Dante d'Angleterre throughout his long life.

They'd killed his beloved brother. They'd been behind the death of a mortal mage who'd been a close friend and tricked Dante into a vendetta that lasted to this day. Most recently, the mortal mage named Patrick Vabian had tricked him into helping hunt down and attack an innocent young Priestess. Vabian had preyed on Dante's simmering need for revenge against the *were*wolves that had killed his friend. Thankfully, Dante had come to his senses in time to foil Vabian's plot and prevent her murder.

Dante fought against the *Venifucus* at every turn, yet they continued to pursue him, hurting those he befriended and those he loved. It was no wonder he'd become a hermit, not allowing anyone to get near him.

Duncan had vowed to look after him while the half-fey blood Duncan had given him still enhanced Dante's already formidable power. Duncan wouldn't let darkness overtake Dante d'Angleterre. Not while there was breath in his body.

He drove directly to Dante's brownstone. It was one of many residences Dante owned and maintained for his personal use and it had every protection an immortal could wish for. Duncan was certain no one had followed them the traditional way and fairly certain no magical means had been able to track them. They'd be safe here while they sorted out what to do with the woman.

He pulled the car up to the curb, and Dante was out like a shot, the wolf girl held close in his arms. Duncan shut off the engine, secured the vehicle and followed close on the vampire's heels. But Dante wasn't waiting for anyone. He used his powers to fling the door open before him as he stalked through the house to the bedroom directly above his subterranean resting place. It was the master bedroom. The one he kept for show. It was decorated to his tastes and contained some of his belongings. He used it and the attached master bath when he came upstairs after dark. It helped maintain the fiction that he was just a regular guy should anyone come to call.

Not that he let just anyone inside his home. No, Dante was a regular hermit, holed up alone the majority of the time. Duncan was changing that. He didn't think it was good for Dante to be so solitary.

Oh, he went out to hunt every once in a while. A man had to eat, after all, but he didn't linger. He barely even talked to his prey anymore, he'd confided to Duncan after one particularly long night spent reminiscing and drinking.

Dante had an extensive wine cellar, stocked with the finest vintages from all over the world. He also had an excellent selection of wines from California and preferred the burgundies of Atticus Maxwell's winery in particular. Duncan knew Maxwell was also a vampire, though he'd never met the man. Wine was their last link to the sun and one of the few substances they could consume. It had healing properties for them and many of the greatest vintners in the world were secretly immortal.

Duncan watched Dante place the girl on his king sized bed as if she were made of glass. She was mostly naked. Her clothes hadn't survived her partial shift to *were*wolf form very well. She was in bad shape at the moment. She hadn't regained consciousness, and her breathing was shallow.

Dante removed the remains of her clothing and checked her for injuries, cursing under his breath.

"She's got at least two broken ribs and her left wrist looks bad." Dante held her hand gently, probing the joint tenderly.

"May I help?" Duncan didn't want to approach without Dante's knowledge. He was focused on the girl and had been unpredictable since she'd taken the hit meant for him. It was best to tread lightly.

Dante looked up, and Duncan was struck by the emotion in his eyes. He hadn't seen Dante really *feel* in far too long. There was an ocean of guilt swimming in his eyes along with worry, fear and something that looked like longing, but Duncan would worry about that later. For now, he had to help set this little mortal wolf to rights. He didn't think he'd get anything resembling sense out of Dante until she was on the road to recovery. And that was something else he'd have to ponder...later.

Duncan moved closer as Dante nodded his consent. Duncan put one hand over her brow, closing his eyes as he sent out magical tendrils of his power, seeking her mind and her consciousness. She was hidden deep within herself, hiding from the shocking blast that had caused her so much pain.

She was cuddled with her wolf, the animal spirit wrapped around her mortal soul, protecting it. Duncan had never seen the like, though he'd heard stories. It was beautiful and strange. They were separate and yet one.

He'd been inside *were* minds before, but none had ever looked like this. This girl was different.

She became aware of him. The wolf looked up, recognizing his light. She nuzzled the girl's spirit encouragingly while Megan's human side looked at him with wide, frightened eyes.

"Fear not, Megan. We're trying to help you. Can you speak? Do you have the energy?"

"We? Is Dante all right?"

Odd that her first thought would be of the bloodletter. Duncan filed that away in his mental "things to ponder" file.

"He is well. He's seeing to your physical injuries. I'm more concerned about your spirit. Will you come back to us or do you seek the light? I think your wolf spirit would prefer you to stay in the mortal realm, don't you?" He sought to engage the wolf in helping to coax the injured spirit back to the surface where it should be. Only then would Megan regain consciousness in the mortal realm.

As he hoped, the wolf agreed, nudging her toward him in the space of her soul.

"This is gonna hurt, isn't it?" She had enough moxie to smile at him, one eyebrow raised mischievously, though he could see her fear.

"I'm sorry, Megan. I won't lie to you. You were injured by the blast, but you'll recover. Especially with Dante watching over you like a mother hen."

She giggled. There was no other word for the pure sound of enjoyment that issued from her lips. She was enchanting, and now Duncan knew for sure that her heart of hearts was pure and true. There was no darkness in her tender spirit, only honor, duty, loyalty and love.

All in all, if she'd been completely human, Duncan would have thought her a great match for Dante's warrior soul. She was something he'd never personally encountered. The wolf inside her was strong, separate in a way he didn't quite understand, but would like to discover. This strange phenomenon deserved further study.

"All right. Let's get this over with." With a last caress to the fur of her wolf spirit, she stood on her own, the wolf walking beside her to the boundary separating her unconscious mind and the waking world.

Duncan retracted his mental probe when he saw her step over the line. She would wake and need their help getting through the wrenching pain of her injuries—both physical and magical.

She gasped as her eyes opened, her body trembling in reaction. Dante's hands went to her face, cupping her cheeks gently as he soothed her. Duncan watched the uncharacteristic tenderness from his old friend with a worried sort of interest. Dante was behaving out of character, but then, nothing was normal about this situation—from the girl to the attack to Dante's reaction.

"Son of a bitch!" she sobbed aloud as consciousness returned. "That hurts!"

"Where does it hurt, baby?" Dante questioned, moving his hands lower, to cup her bruised ribs and injured wrist. "You've got two broken ribs and a few snapped bones in your wrist."

"Yeah, that's what hurts." She gasped once more as she tried to get up and failed. Dante pushed her back, making soothing sounds.

"Stay put, little wolf. I'll take care of you. Is anything else bothering you?"

"Besides the fact that I'm naked in front of two strange men and can't really move?" Sarcasm dripped from her terse tone.

Dante actually blushed. If Duncan hadn't seen it himself, he wouldn't have believed it.

"I had to check for injuries," he explained. "And your clothes didn't make it through your partial shift." His tone went from chastised to serious in less than a second. "You shouldn't have jumped in front of that fireball."

"You'd rather I let you get killed? Fine. Next time I'll just mind my own business."

He stroked her hair back from her face. "You saved my life, sweetheart. Thank you. But I couldn't have lived with the guilt if you'd died to save me."

Duncan wondered if Dante realized the serious nature of that statement. It sounded almost like a declaration of...something. Still, there was no way they could be mates. They weren't even close to the same species. *Weres* hadn't mixed with immortals since the Dark Ages.

It was one thing for a bloodletter to find his One among mortals. Humans could be turned to become like their mates. *Weres* were already magical in quite a different way than vampires. There were tales of *weres* who had been turned to vampires back during the black times of the *Venifucus*, but such power hadn't been needed—or wanted—in the peaceful times since Elspeth, Destroyer of Worlds, leader of the *Venifucus*, had been banished to the farthest realms.

Dante tugged the blanket from under the girl, jostling her as little as possible. It was as he rose to lift her legs and slide them under the cover that he stilled. Duncan sensed something amiss and froze as well.

Dante's eyes rose to his and back down to Megan's thigh. There was a mark there, and it was obvious Dante wanted Duncan to see it. He moved closer, noting that Megan was likely in too much pain to tell that something was up. He stared at the smooth flesh of her muscular thigh and had to stifle his reaction.

There, clear as day, was the ancient mark of the *Altor Custodis*. It wasn't a tattoo in the traditional sense. It was a magical mark they sometimes used on creatures that owed them allegiance for one reason or another. It was a rare thing, but Duncan had seen it once before. Many years ago.

Yet another piece to the puzzle that was Megan.

He nodded to Dante and left him to settle her beneath the

blankets. He had a lot to think about.

*

"She's sleeping." Dante strolled into the living room minutes later heading straight for the sideboard that held a large decanter of his favorite wine. He poured two glasses, bringing one to Duncan as he claimed the opposite chair.

"That's good to hear. With her *were* constitution, she'll most likely be up and around sometime tomorrow. I'll keep an eye on her during the daylight hours."

"Much appreciated, my friend." Dante toasted him with his glass before drinking the deep red burgundy with a modicum of relief. "What I still can't figure is how that first fireball missed me. I felt it brush by, and saw the remnants of it drip past me—right in front of my face. It didn't even singe a single hair on my head. I just don't get it."

"That, perhaps, is due to me. Or at least, the remaining power of my blood in your system. I believe it deflected the worst of that magical blast, though I don't believe it would have protected you from the second one. You have your lady wolf to thank for saving your hide from that one."

"I just don't understand why she did it."

Dante was filled with residual anger and frustration that hadn't left him. It had hurt more than he expected to see the girl go down in a fireball that was meant for him. It was too much like his past. Too much like the tragedy that seemed to follow everywhere he went. If he didn't know better, he'd think he was cursed.

"You should know something. She isn't entirely *were*." Duncan sighed and placed his wine glass on the table in front of him, looking troubled. "When I was coaxing her back, I saw inside her soul. The wolf was there, but it was very separate from Megan herself. I've never seen that before."

"What do you think it means?"

"I've been sitting here pondering that as a matter of fact."

"If she's not fully *were*, what's the other part?"

"Human, most likely. Though, as you well know, when *weres* mate with humans, the *were* side usually wins out in the offspring. I've never seen a half-*were* before. Not like that."

"Neither have I. But the new Priestess—"

"Yes, I thought about that too. Her situation is different since there is quite a bit of magic involved, not to mention the Lady Herself."

Dante realized the Goddess might very well have intervened where Her newest Priestess was concerned. Therefore, any comparison to Priestess Allesandra probably wasn't an accurate one.

"So what do you make of what you saw in Megan?"

Duncan reached for his glass. "I just don't know, Dante. She's special. I can tell you that. The wolf lives in her and protected her mortal spirit from the blast of that fireball. It would have killed you. It would probably have killed any other *were* as well. I think it was her dual nature that saved her."

"So we have a unique lone wolf sporting an *Altor Custodis* mark of obligation on our hands. None of this is the usual course of business, Duncan."

"She is an enigma, I'll give her that," Duncan agreed.

"So where does that leave us? What do we do with her?"

"We watch her. She came to you—or was sent—for a reason. Whether of her own making or directed by someone within the *Altor Custodis*. We need to find out who and why. Until we do, I must caution you not to partake of her blood if she offers. It could be some kind of trap. The surest way to harm one of your kind is to bespell blood, as you learned firsthand when I did it to you."

"Agreed." Dante wanted to growl at the half-fey warrior. That had been a dirty trick, but he supposed in hindsight it had been necessary. Duncan had needed to be sure of him after all the time that had passed since they'd last fought side by side.

He thirsted for a taste of Megan, but he firmed his resolve. He had to stand strong against the almost unreasonable attraction that drew him to the small wolf nestled in his bed.

"There is also the possibility that the taint in the *Altor Custodis* has reached whoever pulls Megan's strings. That kind of mark means she owes someone within the *AC* allegiance—maybe even a blood debt. We can only hope her patron is someone on the right side of things and not a *Venifucus* infiltrator."

"I promise you this—" Dante felt the power of his conviction, "—if the one who marked her is an infiltrator, he or she will die by my hand and Megan will be freed of the obligation. Even if it is the last thing I do on this Earth."

Duncan was silent as Dante's words reverberated through the room. Both men realized how much the girl was already affecting Dante. The situation demanded caution. Dante's volatile emotions were already getting the better of him. His unthinking words had proved the point eloquently.

"Let's hope it doesn't come to that, my friend." Duncan drained his glass and placed it on the table. "It's a few hours until dawn." He yawned and rose from the chair. "I'm going to catch a little sleep. I'll take the day shift. I assume you have the wee hours covered."

Dante raised his glass in agreement as Duncan headed for the hall that would lead to the guest room he'd been using. He paused on the threshold.

"Be cautious, my friend. I don't fully understand what we're dealing with here and that hasn't happened to me in a very long time."

Dante laughed. Duncan sometimes said the funniest things without even meaning to. His consternation at encountering something he'd never seen before was laughable, though the half-fey warrior no doubt didn't see it that way. He just shook his head and left the room, muttering as he went down the hall.

*

Igor Poferov looked at the head of the Vabian Dynasty

over the tips of his steepled fingers. He'd called Viktor Vabian and his wife, Una, in to see him as soon as he received the surveillance report on his minion, Megan.

"You need to control your daughter Siobhan. She almost cost me a valuable agent last night."

"What can I do?" Viktor made an unconvincingly helpless gesture. "She's a grown woman, and you know she took her brother's disappearance to heart. She worshiped Patrick."

"He was as bad as she's turning out to be. Nobody authorized him to go after the *were*lords' new mate. He was foolish to try and worse, he may have compromised our position badly. That's what I sent my pet wolf to find out. Your daughter interfered with my plans last night, and I do not take that...kindly." He lowered his hands allowing his power to tingle through the air, snapping viciously at his guests' exposed skin.

To his satisfaction, Viktor sat up straighter in the ornate chair, trying hard not to show his discomfort. Igor looked to Una, watching her carefully. She'd always been the stronger of the two. She didn't allow the pain to show, but Igor saw a subtle tightening of her red-painted lips that gave him immense satisfaction. He was the most powerful in this room, though both Una and Viktor had challenged him from time to time. Still, he was in charge here. The Vabians, "dynasty" or not, had to learn their place.

"Really, Igor," Una spoke, saccharine dripping off her every word, "you're far too fond of the creature. Our Siobhan didn't do much more than take a bite out of your wolf. She'll live. Thanks to the bastard who hurt my boy." Her eyes turned deadly cold. "I will have my revenge on Dante d'Angleterre, Igor. It is my right."

"And you will, Una, but you forget who is running this show. It's my call as to when and how Dante will meet his fate. First, I need to know more. Even an ancient bloodletter should not have been able to counter the Elspian Ring. That spell was handed down from the *Mater Priori* herself. Its magic comes from another realm entirely. No mere vampire—

31

regardless how old—should have been able to detect it. Dante is running with some strange characters, and we need to know more about them before we act."

"But—"

Igor cut off Una's words with an angry sneer. "We also need to know what your useless son divulged before he disappeared. If he compromised our plans, the entire Vabian *dynasty* will pay. Mark my words. Or perhaps," Igor said as he tilted his head to give them a quelling look, "that was your plan. Maybe you wanted to do away with the bloodletter before Patrick's failure is fully known?" He rubbed his chin as if considering. "The plan has merit, I will admit. It's a good way to cover your asses. However, you should know this, if Dante or those around him so much as catch a cold in the next two weeks, I will have all of you Vabians up before the *Priori*. I've been tasked to find out what happened to Patrick and how badly he damaged our plans. That will come out no matter what you try to do to block my agents. Harm my wolf and I will kill you myself. She's been far too valuable a tool to lose now. She's mine and only I will decide when to put her down like the dog she is. Is that clear?"

Una hesitated, and Viktor looked at her for guidance. The so-called leader of House Vabian was weak, just as he'd always been. It was Una who wore the pants in the family. Of that Igor was certain. And her daughter Siobhan was turning out to be just like her, the bitch.

"Bottom line, call off Siobhan or you will all pay the price."

Una stood, huffing in outrage. She bit back her words before she could speak the treason that would give Igor reason to smite her where she stood. Too bad. She stomped out the door, leaving her henpecked husband to face the music.

"We'll do what we can, Igor, but Siobhan is a grown woman who makes her own decisions."

"Is that your way of hedging your bets, Viktor? It won't

work. If your daughter continues pursuing d'Angleterre, you will all pay the price. Have no doubt about that."

Sadly, our Siobhan is a lot like her mother." Viktor stood with stooped shoulders and followed his wife.

CHAPTER THREE

Megan was up and around by the time Dante rose the following day. She looked a little worse for wear and was moving cautiously, but she was clearly in better shape than a mere mortal would have been, given the extent of her injuries the night before.

She sat with Duncan in the living room. She'd taken over the couch with a pillow tucked behind her back and her legs stretched out on the cushions, covered by a blanket. She was wearing a sweatshirt and pants that were too big for her, most likely pilfered from Dante's closet while he slept below ground. The sight that touched Dante most, in the oddest sort of way, was her dainty feet peeping out from under the edge of the blanket, cuddled up in a pair of his fluffy white gym socks.

It didn't make any sense that a little thing like that would capture his attention. Somehow, it appealed to his sense of the ridiculous and also warmed something inside him that had lain cold and lifeless for centuries. She was cute though ferocious in her own feminine way. He'd been impressed by her half-shift, which wasn't an easy form for even the strongest of shifters to hold for long. He had no doubt she was fierce. Which was probably why he found it so charming that she needed to roll his socks into donuts around her ankles because they were too big for her petite frame.

Every article of clothing she'd borrowed from his closet was too big, and he thought she looked adorable. He liked the idea of her wearing his clothes. That the softness of the shirt that he'd felt many times against his own skin was now caressing hers.

Dante shook off the uncharacteristically sappy thoughts with some difficulty as he entered the living room.

"Good to see you looking so well, Megan." He smiled as he joined her on the couch.

There were other chairs in the room, including another wing chair like the one Duncan occupied, but there was enough room for him on the couch, down at the end near her dainty feet, and he was drawn to it. He wanted to be near her. He didn't look too closely at why.

"I feel much better, as I was just telling your friend Duncan here." She smiled at him, and he felt it like a sucker punch to the gut.

"When did she wake?" Dante turned his attention to the half-fey knight who currently shared his home.

"Not long ago," Duncan answered with an elegant shrug. "She wanted to leave but I talked her into resting on the couch for a bit until you rose. I think we have a lot to discuss before anyone talks of leaving." Duncan sat forward, and his words came down heavy in the space between him and Megan, as if he'd been making this point for some time already.

"You can't keep me here against my will." She sounded like a recalcitrant child. Of course, the way she filled out his sweatshirt reminded Dante that she was definitely all woman.

"Try me." Dante recaptured her attention, his tone brooking no argument. "Last night you took the full force of a magical blast that would have killed anyone else. How is it you survived, Megan? And why did Duncan see two distinct entities in your soul? You are *were*, but you are also something more. That's what saved you. Isn't that right, Duncan?"

"That's my theory, and I haven't come up with anything better while you were below. So how about it, Megan?"

Duncan turned the force of his question on her. Between the two men bearing down on her in concert, she began to fidget.

"I'm only half *were*." Her voice was as soft as he'd ever heard it, as if she was embarrassed by her origins.

"Nothing to be ashamed of in that," Duncan softened a little. "I'm only half human myself. What's your other half, lass?"

"Human…as far as I know. My mother was *were*. I never knew my father."

Dante shifted on the couch, raising her legs, blanket and all, to rest over his lap as he moved closer. She needed the warmth of another being right now. Touch was something all *weres* needed—or so he'd believed. He rubbed her legs through the blanket, giving her reassurance with his gentle movements. At least he hoped that's how she'd see his actions. He didn't fully understand it himself.

"You'd best not be spinning tales to try to gain our sympathy, lass."

"Duncan." Dante's growl was a warning not to push her too hard.

"It's no lie. Nothing I've told you has been a lie. I wouldn't do that."

Duncan answered with one eloquently raised eyebrow, but Dante let it pass.

"The fact remains, you can't leave, sweetheart." Dante tried to bring the conversation back to the point. "Remember what we talked about last night before all this happened? Remember I told you there were things going on that I wouldn't talk about in public?"

"Yeah, so what? Are you going to tell me now that some crazy woman wants you dead? That's not exactly news." Sarcasm was thick in her voice, and Dante didn't like it one bit.

"I don't know who that woman was or why she targeted me in such a public way. I can only guess at her motivations."

Duncan picked up the narrative. "For centuries, Dante and people around him have been targeted by agents of the

Venifucus."

"*Venifucus?* I thought they were ancient history. Right?"

"I thought their days long over as well." Dante ran a frustrated hand through his hair. "However, your current Lords have had dealings with one of them in recent weeks, as have I. They're back. The threat is real. Whether it is imminent or not, remains to be seen."

"So this affects me how?"

"It affects all *were*. All supernaturals for that matter," Duncan said. "If the *Venifucus* are back, and Dante and I both witnessed one of their mages confessing some of their plans, then all creatures of good conscience need to know and prepare."

"All right." She leaned forward confrontationally, toward Duncan. "You told me, and I'm prepared. Can I go home?"

"Absolutely not." Dante's words were iron.

"You're too much of a mystery for us not to want to keep you around for a little while, lass." Duncan eased back in his chair, a cunning smile playing about his lips.

"I'm no mystery at all." She sounded defensive to Dante's ears.

"Allow me to be the judge of that, my dear." Dante resumed stroking her legs, slower now, with a more seductive purpose.

"Now that you're up—" Duncan rose from his chair, nodding toward Dante, "—I'll see about making some dinner." The half-fey knight beat a retreat toward the kitchen at the rear of the house, leaving Dante and Megan alone.

"Won't you stay a while? At least to heal. And perhaps to pick up where we left off last night before we were so rudely interrupted?" He poured on the charm, knowing his usual tricks with mortals probably wouldn't work on her.

For one thing, her mind was half-*were*. She'd likely be immune to his ability to cloud mortal minds, just as she was somewhat immune to magical attacks like the one they'd lived through the night before. *Weres* had a special kind of protection against magic. Or perhaps it was the nature of the animal spirits that shared their souls that protected them against most kinds of mortal magic. Dante didn't know for sure, but either way, it was likely what had saved her.

Megan couldn't believe her good fortune. She'd been ordered to find a way to spy on the vampire and had been prepared to do almost anything to accomplish this final mission that would free her from the debt her family owed the *Altor Custodis*. This was almost too easy. She made a show of reluctance, but inside she was overjoyed by his invitation.

She could use the excuse of her injury to keep some distance from the attractive bloodletter. Last night, she probably would have shared his bed. He was handsome as sin and she'd been too weak to fight the need he stirred in her body, regardless of her distaste in associating with another supernatural of any kind.

She was clear headed now. The pain of her injuries was a grim reminder of the danger of her mission. With any luck, she could accomplish it without succumbing to the temptation he represented.

"All right." She sighed, trying not to look as pleased as she felt. "I'll stay a few days. Until I'm fully healed. But I won't promise anything more."

This was the perfect setup. She could nose around his house all day while he slept. The only sticking point in the plan was Duncan. Whatever he was, he was formidable. He'd said he was half human, but what in the world was the other half?

"Understandable. Let's just take it one night at a time for now." His big hands stroking her legs through the blanket made her feel distinctly warm. She tried to shift away, but he wouldn't let her go and she refused to engage in a childish tug of war with him.

"So tell me more about this threat." She tried to get him back to his earlier conversation. Without Duncan in the room as a buffer, the atmosphere felt too intimate.

Dante sighed, looking away from her for a moment and

she felt some relief from his intense regard. His dark eyes were so compelling. When he looked into her eyes, it almost felt like she was falling into them, drugged by his presence, and she feared she'd give him anything he wanted. She had to be on guard. Of course, the handsome bastard made that nearly impossible just by breathing. He was too damned sexy and too distracting.

"I was approached by a man several months ago. He said he had information on how I could avenge a wrong done to me by the *were*lords who were in power in 1871." Megan didn't like the sound of this. "They had sanctioned the murder of a close friend of mine. An unjustifiable act of evil that destroyed a promising young man and most of the city of Chicago."

"The Great Chicago Fire?" She *really* didn't like the sound of this.

Dante nodded. "That is the sordid history. What matters most now is the fact that I felt the *were*lords owed me a blood debt. Like an idiot, I went haring off across the country on this man's information. What I didn't know was that he was a magic user, bent on murdering the new Priestess and mate of the current Lords of the *Were*. I helped him get close to them and made it possible for him to attack them. Once I realized my mistake, I changed sides and tried to help them, but it was already too late. One of the twins was grievously injured and it required a great working of magic to save him. That's how Duncan was brought back into this realm. But that's another story for another time." He turned to her, his dark gaze zeroing in on her. She could see as well as feel his very genuine regret. "We eventually captured the mage, and he confessed to being a *Venifucus* agent. He spoke of their plans to return Elspeth to this realm."

"Elspeth?" A chill of fear trembled through her. "Isn't she the one they call Destroyer of Worlds?"

"The very same," Dante agreed. "So you see, we have to be on guard. None of us can afford to let that happen. Not *were*, not immortal, not fey. If she regains power, we're all in danger."

"Bright Lady, I had no idea. They've got to be crazy to want to bring that kind of evil back into the world."

"Crazy and power hungry." He resumed stroking her legs through the blanket absently, as if to comfort himself with the repetitive motion. "Duncan thinks they've been behind all the evil that has followed me most of my life."

"What kind of evil?" She was afraid to ask but needed to know.

"The murder of my brother and the beginning of my immortality. The death that started the fire in Chicago and my vendetta against the *were*lords. All that and more. Evil has followed me at every turn, tempting me to turn against what I know to be right and good." His expression was tormented, spurring her into motion. Despite the pain in her side and wrist, she moved next to him on the couch, reaching out with her good hand to take his.

"Why?" She searched his bleak gaze, offering her warmth when she saw the cold pain there. "Why would they do this to you?"

"To try to turn me to their side. Or so Duncan believes. Personally, I don't see why they'd target me, but it sure feels like they have. There's no other explanation for all the bad things that seem to follow in my wake."

She put her hand on his shoulder. "I'm so sorry, Dante."

She was drowning in his gaze, mesmerized by his regard as he moved closer. She met him in the middle and their mouths touched, igniting a fire to rival the one that had consumed Chicago so many years ago. This fire however, wasn't destructive. It was *seductive*. It flamed within them both, drawing them near, binding them together in the moment.

He deepened the kiss and she was right there with him, pushing herself into his arms, into his body, despite the pain in her ribs. It was nothing compared to the pleasure to be found in his embrace. He moved over her, setting her down on the couch beneath him as he held himself above, keeping the majority of his weight off her smaller body. He was careful with her, and she liked that. In fact, she liked everything about his possession. Here was a man who knew how to make a woman feel cherished. Even with something as simple—and as overwhelming—as his kiss.

Dante's hand skimmed under the loose hem of the borrowed sweatshirt to ride up the bare skin of her midriff, grazing lightly over the area that hurt like the dickens and upward, to cup her breast. She sighed into his mouth when his big hand took possession of her sensitive skin, his fingers going right to the hard peak that so wanted his attention.

She wanted more. So much more...

The sound of a throat clearing rather loudly at the entrance to the living room interrupted. Dante pulled back first, frustration and chagrin clear on his handsome face. Megan was still in a fog of desire that he'd created, unsure of her surroundings.

The sound came again as she shook herself, and Dante's hand slipped from beneath her shirt. He helped her sit up.

"Dinner is served," Duncan intoned with clear amusement.

Megan looked at the doorway in shock to see the other man there. He winked at her before turning to leave, and she felt heat flood her face. He'd seen what they were up to and deliberately interrupted. She'd have to thank him, despite her embarrassment. Either that or kill him. She would decide later.

"You'd better go eat. You need your strength." Dante's resigned amusement rubbed her the wrong way. She decided to give him the silent treatment and beat a hasty retreat toward the kitchen.

She couldn't move too fast with her injuries, but she walked quickly, with as much dignity as she could muster. She refused to acknowledge the sexy chuckle that followed her out of the living room.

She found Duncan in a gourmet kitchen that sparkled. She realized that while Dante kept it for show, he certainly didn't have need of a place to prepare food. Still, it was a nice room with comfortable seating. It had a large table and work area and Duncan had something simmering on the stove that smelled wonderful.

Her stomach growled.

Duncan made no comment as he dished up a large plate of thick beef stew for her. He served them both, then took the chair opposite her with a satisfied grin.

"Dig in. I know you *weres* have healthy appetites."

He'd given her almost double the serving on his plate and while she felt hungry enough at the moment to eat the entire thing, mass quantities of food wasn't her normal routine.

"I'm only half *were*," she said quietly as she began to eat. "I probably eat more than the average girl, but I don't think I'm up to full blood status."

He looked up at her, tilting his head to the side, considering. "As I told Dante last night, you're an enigma, Megan. I've never seen a soul like yours."

"Seen many, have you?" She decided to fight him with humor if possible. He was getting close to subjects she'd rather not discuss.

"More than my share." He sat back and seemed to concentrate on his meal.

"If I'm an enigma, what are you? I'd say that's a bit of the pot calling the kettle black, don't you think?" Offense was sometimes the best defense.

"*Touché*, my dear." He sent her a small smile. "I suppose you've earned the right to know who you're dealing with. I'm half-human and half... Come on, won't you even try to guess?"

She liked a challenge. "Well, you're not *were*. I'd recognize that right off. And you're not like Dante. So that leaves a few other possibilities, all of which seem *im*possible."

"When you've exhausted all the possible answers, you have to start looking at the impossible ones. Come on, what's your best guess?"

"Well, I've heard stories about...um...fey. Though it's

said they rarely visit the mortal realm."

"True," he said, beaming at her. "Still, your instincts are good. I'm half-fey."

"No way."

"Way." His grin teased her.

She sat back, her meal forgotten. She was sitting at the table with a real live elf!

"No wonder you're so magical. Even Dante seems a little in awe of your power."

"*Och*, he'll get over that soon enough and revert to our old relationship. He was injured, you see, during the battle with the *Venifucus* mage. I had to give him a little sip of my blood to save him, and it's left him a little…weird."

"I heard that!" came Dante's shout from down the hall. Duncan chuckled.

"Mind your own business," Duncan called back.

Megan felt like she was in a fraternity house with two overgrown frat brothers lobbing insults at each other. The very idea of it made her laugh. Frat boys with ramped up supernatural powers. Too funny.

"No wonder he's so compelling. He got a dose of your magical whammy when he drank your blood, huh? I thought fey blood could kill a vampire."

"Right you are about that. Full fey blood is too strong even for our immortal friend, but I'm a cat of a different color. I'm only half-fey. To a bloodletter, my blood is a rare delicacy. It gives them too much power, so as a general rule it's not done to give them even a taste. This was a special circumstance. I knew Dante years ago and have always known him to be a man of honor."

"You're watching him, right? I mean, that's why you're here. Isn't it?"

He saluted her with his water glass. "You think on your feet. I like that in a woman. To answer your question, yes, I'm keeping an eye on him until the effects wear off, but I would probably be here anyway. As I said, Dante and I knew each other long ago. I've been away from this realm a long time and now that I'm back, it's time to catch up with old friends. If war is on the horizon, you can be sure that Dante d'Angleterre will be on the front lines, as he was in the past."

"And you'll be right beside him, won't you?" She could almost see the glow of power as a golden light around this strange half-fey warrior. It drew her, calling to her sense of honor, of what was right. She had to resist. She had a mission of her own, a chance to finally clear her family name, and she had to see it through to the end no matter the cost.

Dante sauntered into the kitchen, a large box in his hands. It tinkled as he moved, telling her there was glass inside. The faint odor of fermented grapes and alcohol reached her sensitive nose. It was wine.

"I haven't forgotten that you called me weird, fairy boy," Dante muttered under his breath as he headed toward the largest wine cooling unit she'd ever seen. He opened the glass door and began placing bottles from the box into the cooler.

Duncan answered with a mock growl and launched a cloth napkin at Dante's back. It slid off and hit the floor.

"I'm not picking that up." Dante pointedly ignored the scrap of white fabric at his feet. Megan couldn't help it. She giggled.

Dante turned and favored her with a wide grin. "I'm glad you find us amusing," he said, and the funny thing was, she believed he meant it.

"Sorry. You two just don't act like I'd expect two powerful supernaturals to behave. Remember, I'm a loner. I don't have much experience hanging out with your kind—or even my own kind."

"Why?" Duncan asked softly, reclaiming her attention. "Why do you walk alone, Megan? Where's your family? Your pack?"

"I have no pack. I never have. As for my family...they're all gone. I'm the only one left of my line. After me, it will be no more."

She didn't tell them that she thought perhaps that was a good thing. After all, the twin wolf *were*lords who had caused her line so much shame were long gone, but their descendants still paid the price. Megan would end it. She would repay their wrong and restore her family's honor. Then the line would die out with her. It was sort of poetic really.

"It's not natural," Duncan said quietly. "*Were* place great value on their family units, packs, clans and tribes."

She shrugged. "What can I say? I'm only half *were*, and I've never known what it was like to be part of something like that."

"And you never knew your father?" Finished stowing the wine, Dante moved to stand beside her. "Was it just you and your mother? No siblings?"

"No. No brothers or sisters. Just mom and me. And now she's gone."

"I'm sorry." Dante crouched at her side, cupping her cheek in one warm, powerful hand. "I know what it is to lose loved ones and to be alone in the world."

"It isn't so bad, really. I like my freedom. I get the feeling pack life would be too restrictive for me."

"Perhaps," Dante agreed. "But you should have had the opportunity to find out. It's one thing to choose to be alone. Another to have a solitary existence thrust upon you."

How well her ancestors knew that truth. They'd been ostracized from all *were* society for what they'd allowed to happen. Bad decisions and bad information had led them to a heinous mistake that could never be fully recompensed. For over a century, they and their descendants had worked to right their wrong, but the stain was deep and was hard to cleanse.

Megan was almost there. This last mission and she'd been promised absolution for herself and for her family line. Her ancestors were gone. Nevertheless, she knew their spirits watched over her, waiting for the day she completed the task so they too, could be free to move on. It was a huge responsibility to have resting on her shoulders, but she knew no other way. She'd been raised with the knowledge of her biggest task in this life and had worked steadily toward achieving her goal. Now it was almost in sight.

She couldn't let her feelings grow conflicted. She couldn't get attached to Dante d'Angleterre. He was a job to her—a means to an end. He had to be. She couldn't allow it to go any deeper, no matter how tempting he was.

She drew back from him, taking her empty plate in hand and standing. She moved toward the sink. Duncan rose and intercepted her, taking the plate out of her hands.

"I'll wash up," he said gently. "You still need to be careful of your injuries."

"Thanks." She didn't know where to go, but she needed space. "I'll be in the living room if that's okay."

Dante watched her as she left. She could feel his eyes on her all the way down the hall, and she didn't breathe freely again until she was out of his view.

"She's running scared," Dante said quietly after he'd closed the swinging kitchen door. "But from what?"

Duncan turned from placing the clean plates on the draining board. "From you, I think. At least at the moment. You're overwhelming the poor lass, my friend, and I have to wonder why. She's *were*. She's not for you."

"She's only half *were*, Duncan," he argued before he thought better of it.

"And what's her other half? Human? Or some mongrel mixture of human and something else? Even I can't tell yet." Duncan sighed. "It'll come clear in time, I think. In the meantime, we need to keep an eye on her."

"Agreed." He ground his teeth in frustration. "Can you sit with her for another hour or so? I have to check a few things."

"Sure. I'll catch a nap later. Take all the time you need."

"Thanks." Dante stalked from the room, avoiding the living room, and headed for his office. He had work to do.

CHAPTER FOUR

An hour later he was no closer to discovering where Megan had come from or exactly what she was. He had checked his messages however, and discovered he'd been summoned. A summons from the Mistress wasn't something he could ignore. He RSVP'd for himself and Megan. Maybe taking her out in public would rattle a few cages and elicit more information. It was worth a shot.

He put out feelers with a few old friends, but it would take time to get a response. For now he was at a dead end. He could find no record of Megan anywhere. That in itself was suspicious. Then again, the few lone wolves he'd known in the past had been good at covering their tracks and hiding their presence from affiliated *weres*.

He placed a few calls and ordered some items to be delivered. An hour later, his plans were set, and he had only to collect his date for the evening. He swept into the bedroom after only a perfunctory knock, a bulging garment bag in one hand, another bag containing matching shoes and accessories in the other.

"Put this on. We're going out." Dante opened the garment bag and a swirling mass of fabric drifted out over his arms. It spilled to the foot of the bed where he spread the fabric before setting it down. When it settled, Megan realized it was a deep emerald ball gown—the kind she'd imagined in fairytales but had never seen in real life. It was something out of another era.

"You're kidding, right? Where do people actually wear something like that?"

"At an honest-to-goodness vampire ball. I hope you know how to waltz." The devilish smile that accompanied his words made her tummy flip.

"No way."

"Way. Get dressed, tiger. If you're good, I'll teach you how to promenade old school." He went out the door, grinning as he closed it behind him.

Megan wouldn't miss a chance like this for the world, regardless of the miserable duty she had to fulfill. She'd always been fascinated by the gentility of past centuries and couldn't pass up the chance to dress in a silk gown and go to a ball with a man who had probably waltzed in the ballrooms of the *haute ton*.

The dress was a dream, and it fit her like a glove. Dante had no doubt guessed at her size, and he was a very good guesser. Of course, a sexy man who'd lived for centuries no doubt picked up a thing or two along the way about women's clothing. She'd bet he'd undressed more than a few women in his many years.

The thought rankled but nothing could dampen her spirits once she got a look at herself in the gorgeous silk gown. She felt like Cinderella at the ball. She'd never worn anything so exquisite. She twirled and giggled like a schoolgirl only composing herself before she went out the door and descended the grand staircase.

Dante waited for her at the bottom, a long, slim, black velvet box in his hands. Her breath caught at the look in his eyes when he saw her dressed in the gown he'd selected for her. She floated down the stairs to stand before him.

"You are a vision, my dear." He bent over her hand, kissing her knuckles. "It only needs one thing to complete the look."

He opened the box, presenting her with it. She gasped at the rainbows of light twinkling in reflection off a myriad of diamonds and emeralds. There was a necklace, earrings and a bracelet. The exquisitely matched set had the look of antiquity.

"They're beautiful." Her voice was breathy and hushed as he lifted the bracelet from the box to drape around her wrist. He fastened the catch and then moved behind her to do the same with the necklace.

She'd put her hair up for the occasion so only a few loose tendrils of her hair teased her neck. Dante blew them out of his way with a soft breath that made her shiver. The platinum of the necklace was cool against her neck but warmed rapidly, as did her entire body with Dante so close.

"Put on the earrings." He handed her the old fashioned dangles as he stepped around to look at her. She complied while he watched, the fire in his eyes making her breathless. "I was right," he said as she fastened the second earring and faced him. "Emeralds suit you, Megan. You'll be the belle of the ball."

She didn't argue though she was certain she didn't look *that* good. Oh, she admitted she looked better than she ever had. She cleaned up well for a half-breed wolf. There was no doubt in her mind though, wherever he was taking her, other women would be lined up for his attention.

He was dashing in white tie and tails. He looked as if he'd been born to model formal wear, and she had to keep reminding herself that he was just a job. There could be no future in anything between them. She had to do her work, report back to her keeper and then she would be free to go on her way.

"So where exactly are we going?" She needed to bring this dazzling moment to an end and focus on her objective.

"Even I have to dance attendance on the Mistress from time to time. She rules this area and when she issues an invitation, it is always wiser to accept than to decline."

"Mistress? Not Master? I thought your kind had Masters

in every region."

"In rare instances, women hold the office. Because the position is won by prevailing in combat, few women have the stomach for being constantly sized up and challenged at the first sign of weakness, or the desire to even try to keep the rest of us in line."

"So what is this Mistress like?"

"The New York Mistress is an exceptional female with a keen mind for political intrigue. I'd say she thinks her job is fun, having met her a few times in the past. She has a somewhat perverse sense of humor." Dante seemed amused by his own words.

He let her precede him out the door to a waiting stretch limousine. Duncan was nowhere to be seen, so she assumed he hadn't been invited. For that matter, she hadn't been invited. She surmised from their clothing that she was the obligatory date for whatever social occasion demanded formal attire from a century past.

The limo took them to a downtown edifice that had once been a church. Not just a church but something only a little less grand than a full-fledged cathedral. This place had gargoyles on the battlements and carvings of all kinds gracing its stone walls. Even from a distance, Megan could sniff out the fact that not all the gargoyles peering over the crowd were made of stone.

Shivers coursed over her spine when they entered through massive carved wood and steel doors into a cavernous vestibule. They didn't get far before an officious man with a list spoke to Dante. He looked down his nose at Megan until he got a good look at her, then his expression changed. It was almost comical how he reacted once he realized she was *were*.

The majordomo—that's what she assumed his function was—was a vampire. The shiver returned when Megan realized she was literally surrounded by vamps of every description, all staring at her as they paused in the vestibule before being announced. The majordomo's counterpart stood at the entry to the main room, announcing each couple or singleton who passed under his watchful eye.

It was like something out of a novel. Megan had never seen the like before, and she marveled at the way these vamps revived the traditions of a century ago and made them seem perfectly normal. For many of them, she realized, this was once the way they had really lived. It boggled the mind.

Dante kept a tight hold of her hand, secure in the crook of his arm as they moved closer to the herald who would announce them to the larger room. Megan could hear the sound of many voices, the clink of glasses and the low murmur of stringed instruments being tuned to concert pitch at the far end of the massive structure.

"What is this place?" she dared whisper to Dante as they waited to be announced.

"Well, as I'm sure you can see, it used to be a church, but even houses of worship fall on hard times once in a while. The Mistress bought it and renovated it, removing most of the pews and polishing the marble. She apparently got the idea from a nightclub in the Village. The owners of the nightclub gutted the old church they bought and put in separate floors for different kinds of music. This place is pretty much the way it was, except for making room for dancing and removing the altar, replacing it with a much larger stage area. That's where the orchestra for tonight will be seated I believe."

They neared the door, and she got her first look inside. Vaulted ceilings capped off a truly magnificent structure that still held all the trappings of a house of worship. The Stations of the Cross graced the walls, and the stained glass windows depicted various scenes in the lives of famous saints. The pews were mostly gone. The only wooden benches left were along the sides and back of the room and had been polished until they shone with a high luster. At the front, there were luxurious tables set up with cushy chairs. In front of that, on the raised area where the altar would have been, there was a full orchestra seating arrangement with a few musicians already seated, tuning their instruments.

Behind the tables was a large open area with polished marble floors that gleamed in the gently flickering light of chandeliers that had candles in them, floating overhead at intervals. Servants in livery stood here and there around the walls, ready to assist with whatever the revelers might want. Wine flowed in fountains on several tables, but only a token display of finger food graced one table near the back.

"It's magnificent," she breathed as they stood in the center of the great arched doorway. The herald announced them and many heads turned. Megan felt conspicuous and very, very mortal all of a sudden.

"Be brave little wolf," Dante murmured just within her range of her hearing. "I'm a newcomer. It's only natural they're curious. Especially when I bring such a lovely *mortal* companion into their midst. Trust me, you'll come to no harm tonight. Not if I have anything to say about it. On that you have my word of honor."

He squeezed her arm reassuringly and she felt better, though she would have been loathe to admit it. Dante was a job to her. That's all he *should* be, but things were getting very complicated very fast, and he was too appealing for her peace of mind.

They walked into the room and Dante snagged two glasses of wine, giving one to Megan. She took a bracing sip, noting there were no other refreshments being offered. Why would there be? The majority of guests didn't eat or drink anything except wine and blood. Megan would pass on the latter, though her inner wolf had never turned up her nose at the blood she shed while hunting.

Megan looked around the room, impressed by the opulence they'd managed to reproduce in what had once been a more utilitarian building. The arched ceilings lent their imposing height to the grandeur of the place and long silken wall hangings, priceless tapestries and other *objets d'art* turned the former place of worship into a distinctive hall for gatherings and amusement.

The orchestra began to play, and a few couples danced in

the large area set aside for it. More joined in, and they performed dances from another era she'd never seen outside Jane Austen films. The dancers performed perfectly in formations that were too complex for her to follow. The scene fascinated and enchanted her.

"So what do you think?" Dante murmured in her ear.

"It's beautiful. Thank you for inviting me here tonight. This is something I never thought to see."

"It is kind of interesting, I suppose, in a vintage sort of way."

"Oh, come on. This may be old hat to you, but this is like something out of a dream for me. Every girl grows up dreaming about going to a ball like Cinderella." She fingered his bow tie with a challenging smile. "This is my chance, and your ennui isn't going to ruin it for me."

Dante laughed, and she felt it down to her bones. He was so sexy when he smiled. Her heart did a little flutter before she could stop it.

"All right, Cinderella. Tonight's your night. I'll try not to ruin it for you." He took the half-finished glass of wine out of her hands and placed it on the tray of a passing waiter, then grasped her hand. "Would you do me the honor of sharing this dance with me, princess?"

Oh, she wanted to, but the set that was just ending was some old dance pattern she didn't know. She looked with longing to the dance floor and didn't notice Dante swooping in to whisper in her ear until his hot breath blew past her sensitive whorls.

"The next dance is a waltz. You know the steps to that, I'm sure. Don't worry. I'm an excellent lead, or so I've been told."

"I bet."

He tugged on her hand and led her toward the floor, reeling her in to stand opposite him at just the perfect distance. She looked into his eyes, mesmerized by the way he looked at her. The music started and the strains of her favorite waltz—the Blue Danube—wafted to the heights of the vaulted ceiling.

Then Dante began to move. He was a wonderful dancer. Built like a warrior, he nevertheless danced like a prince, guiding her around the room among the swirling dancers, her skirt billowing behind her. Megan noted the attention they drew as they whirled across the dance floor but paid it no mind. This moment was too perfect to ruin with worries about what other people thought.

Dante drew her closer in his arms as the waltz progressed, closing the distance between them in a way that would have been considered scandalous a century past. She finally understood why. The feel of his thick muscles rubbing against her body whenever they touched sent her pulse spiraling nearly out of control. Her steps matched his perfectly. Her panting breath came in time with his. They were one for that short space in time, a matched set, moving together with one purpose.

And then the music ended.

Megan was left staring into Dante's eyes, her thoughts whirling, her senses in an uproar. Dante returned her attention until his elbow was jostled by a couple positioning themselves on the floor for the next dance.

He bowed to her in a courtly way, taking her hand and leading her from the floor. When they reached a spot along the wall where a champagne fountain flowed, he paused to collect two glasses of the sparkling wine, handing her one.

"Thank you for the dance, princess. You are without doubt the most graceful partner I have ever claimed."

Megan felt a flush rising to her cheeks even though she suspected his words were more teasing than truth. She declined to answer, sipping her champagne and looking around at the other people in the room. The abundance of diamonds, rubies, sapphires and emeralds was astounding, not to mention the ladies' beautiful gowns and the men's hand tailored suits. This was the *haute ton* reborn. Or perhaps it would be more accurate to say it had never died. Not for these people.

One woman stood out among the crowd. She wore a stunning silk dress with a slight Japanese air to its lines. Her eyes tilted exotically, displaying bone structure that indicated she was the result of the mixture of more than one race. She was exquisite. From her upswept silky black hair to the diamonds dripping around her throat, she was every inch the lady and Megan found it difficult to look away. She was fascinating.

"Who is she?" The woman drew attention simply by breathing. She was fair skinned despite her clearly Asian traits.

"She is the Mistress of this region, Virginia Dean."

"And the great hulking brute behind her?" Megan couldn't help noticing the incredibly handsome man who stood protectively behind her.

"That would be her father, Sir Heathclif Dean."

"They don't look much alike," she mused aloud.

"Heath adopted her in Japan over a century ago. Virginia is the daughter of a Geisha and an English sea captain. As you can imagine, half-blood children didn't do well in those days. Virginia lived a hard life until she met Heath. He told me she tried to pick his pocket. He caught her, of course. She was just a child at the time and he took her in, raising her as his own."

"She wasn't born a bloodletter then?"

"No," Dante admitted. "That came later. Tragedy visited young Virginia and in a moment of heartbreak, Heath turned her. So he is her maker as well as her adoptive father. Together, they are a formidable pair."

"They'd have to be to rule over all the vampires in New York."

Even as she watched the handsome couple, the woman's gaze moved around the room, finally coming to rest on Megan. An elegant hand rose, fingers beckoning.

"It seems we are summoned." Dante took Megan's arm and led her across the space separating them. "She apparently wants to meet you, Cinderella."

Megan found her lips lifting in a tense smile at his small joke even as she approached the striking woman and her father. Though to be honest, Heathclif Dean didn't look old enough to have fathered an adult child. The man was as handsome as sin and utterly devastating in that same way Dante was, only more refined. Where Dante was a warrior through and through, Heathclif looked every inch the gentleman. A gentleman who knew how to fight and use his brawny body to advantage no doubt but still a gentleman.

Dante had rough edges that showed at the oddest moments. He was more *real*, if Megan had to define it, but she couldn't say exactly how. It was just a feeling he gave her. And it was very attractive.

When they stood in front of the couple, Dante made the introductions. Megan felt like a butterfly that had just been stuck on a pin under a magnifying glass as the Mistress looked her over with assessing eyes.

"I'm pleased to make your acquaintance, Megan. It's not often our kinds mix socially, which is something I regret. It wasn't always that way." She spoke with refined candor, her tone welcoming and polite. Megan wasn't sure what she'd expected, but relief filled her at the Mistress's friendly overture.

"I was honored to be invited, Mistress." Megan hoped she was sufficiently polite yet projected a confident stance. It wouldn't do to be seen as weak in a room full of predators. Especially not by the leader of the pack.

"Dante, I have some news we should discuss in private, which is impossible given our current circumstances." Heathclif Dean spoke to Dante, though he eyed them both. "Come to the house tomorrow night. You are welcome too, Megan."

She nodded politely, unsure what she was agreeing to. She was intrigued by the couple, but she was also very wary of them. It paid to be cautious when dealing with bloodletters and these were two of the most powerful in the New York area. Considering the sheer numbers of rich and powerful vampires in the metro area, that was saying something.

Dante and Heathclif began talking of things Megan had no knowledge of—people they both knew and reminiscences of the past. She tried to listen, but much of it went over her head. She became uncomfortably aware of the Mistress's regard. The other woman was looking her up and down as if deciding what to make of her. Megan didn't enjoy the once over. She'd been getting the same look—only more pronounced—since she entered the hall.

"Are you a student of the martial arts, Megan?" the Mistress asked seemingly out of the blue.

Caught off guard, Megan nodded. "I believe most *weres* find the study of martial arts both soothing and useful. The discipline helps us focus our inner beast, and the skills are always useful whether in the hunt or in self-defense."

"And when you are in the dojo, what color graces your waist?" the Mistress asked with a coy smile.

Megan squirmed a bit, not used to giving out personal information of any kind. "Black."

The Mistress grinned widely, her exotic eyes lighting with excitement. "Which discipline do you prefer?"

"Kung fu, actually."

She laughed. "I should have known. Animal forms would be second nature to one of your kind."

"I've studied jiu-jitsu as well, and a little iado."

"Sword study is a noble discipline, Megan. I'd welcome a chance to spar with you sometime. Perhaps tomorrow while my father is talking business with Dante, we can spend a few minutes in the dojo."

"I'd like that."

She wasn't sure what she'd just agreed to but hoped the Mistress meant her invitation at face value. This was a woman Megan would be a fool to anger.

After that little aside, the men included the women in their conversation again, talking about the excellent musicians the Deans had managed to hire for this party. To her surprise, they talked about other performers, from rock stars to opera companies, that had either played at or been booked to play at future vampire get-togethers. It seemed these immortals liked to party.

Or perhaps the Deans hosted such events in order to keep an eye on their people. Dante had spoken of tonight's invitation as a summons. Maybe the Deans liked to dress up their public audiences in the form of parties. It made sense. People were less inclined to start trouble at a festive event and more likely to attend, even if they understood there was an ulterior motive.

Sort of like a business conference. You went for the food and freebies and tried not to mind the sales pitches that happened along the way. Very clever indeed of the vampires to use that old stratagem. Then again, they might've been the ones to come up with it in the first place.

"Shall we dance?" Sir Heathclif's cultured tones shook her out of her internal musings.

He offered his hand to Megan and it was nearly impossible to say no to the command in his powerful voice. Still, something made her look over at Dante. She wasn't seeking his permission exactly. It was more like a quick check on whether he thought it would be safe for her to go off with this strange man. After all, Dante knew more about these people than she did. The very idea that she would instinctively trust her safety to Dante's judgment was something to ponder at another time.

"I've never waltzed before tonight, Mr. Dean," she said, hoping to find some reason to decline. The hard expression on Dante's face and his narrowed eyes made her want to say no, though the independent lone wolf inside her balked at any restriction.

"Please, call me Heath. I saw you dancing beautifully with d'Angleterre. All that native agility and grace makes you a natural for dancing, my dear. Please, allow me the honor of partnering you."

Once again he held out his hand, and she had no choice but to accept. Heathclif Dean hadn't become one of the most powerful vampires in the country overnight. He'd had centuries to hone his commanding ways and at a mere thirty years old, *were* or not, Megan was no match for the power of his will.

She put her hand in his and was quickly whisked off to the dance floor. The revelers parted almost magically, making way for the important man in their midst and staring at Megan with assessing eyes that made her uncomfortable. She never liked being the center of attention.

All that was forgotten as Heath led her into the whirl of an energetic yet genteel waltz. He was a master not only of men, but of the dance, leading her with subtle movements that positioned her exactly where he wanted her to go. All she had to do was follow and allow herself to be caught up in the swirl of skirts, the swish of silk and the loveliness of the music reverberating gently over the walls of the large hall.

She lost track of time and space, mesmerized by the dance and the compelling man. He looked deeply into her eyes, and she felt the pressure of his magic against her natural *were* resistance. He couldn't influence her, but the dance was dreamy enough, the fact that he was trying to use his power on her didn't alarm her as it should.

The waltz music drew to a crescendo, and Heath dipped her low over his bent knee. He moved closer. She was in no position to move, much less evade him. Her body was positioned in such a way that she had absolutely no leverage and no hope of escaping the kiss she thought he meant to deliver.

Such a public display would be embarrassing, but she would live through it. She braced herself, and when he dipped even lower she realized he was aiming not for her lips, but for her jugular.

She could see the gleam of his fangs as they descended. He struck fast, the fear only momentary before his bite seduced her senses. Vampire mojo was not to be discounted at close range, she learned, even for a *were*wolf. The bite propelled her into a hazy state of mind where she didn't fight, only succumbed to the Master vampire.

Shocked whispers erupted all around them on the dance floor as Heath abruptly let her go with a final lick and raised her to her feet. She was dizzy. His big hand steadied her as he guided her from the dance floor, toward their small group.

Megan was in a daze. A kind of shocking sexual hunger had been aroused in her body but left unfulfilled. She'd never been bitten by a vampire before and was unprepared for the way it made her feel. Being unsteady on her feet was not something she was used to. *Weres* in general had excellent balance. Her balance, of course, was shot to hell by Heath's disturbing influence.

He brought her directly to a seething Dante. The man was so angry he practically bristled. She saw the fury in his eyes even before he opened his mouth to speak.

Heath preempted him. "Come with me, d'Angleterre. We have much to discuss."

Heath turned away abruptly, his hand still firmly grasping hers as he led them toward the door. He stopped only once, to tell his daughter he was leaving and that she should continue to enjoy herself at the party.

Thwarted in his fury, Dante followed. Megan caught a glimpse of his heavy stride as he came down the steps behind her and their host. She was ushered into a long black limousine and guided to the seat behind the driver, facing Heath and Dante. Both men looked angry, but Dante won the award for sheer ferocity.

The car began to move and Dante turned on the man who was, for all intents and purposes, Master of this region, though his daughter carried the actual title.

"You should not have done that." Each word was bitten out between Dante's clenched teeth.

Heath sank back against the plush cushions. "Oddly enough, I agree with you. She is poisoned."

"What?" Megan had no idea what Heath was talking about and was wary of the anger she saw in their expressions.

"Damn." Dante's anger continued but was redirected.

"Why don't you seem surprised?" Heath asked him suspiciously.

"We thought it might be something like that. We weren't sure. Otherwise we'd have done something to prevent this. I've been keeping an eye on her while resisting the temptation of her blood, just in case. It seems our suspicions were valid."

"Who's *we*?" Heath demanded.

"Surely you've heard of the company I've been keeping lately?" Dante reached for his cell phone and flipped it opened. "If you permit, I'll call my friend. If you are indeed poisoned, he may be able to help you."

"Duncan, right? I heard he was back." Heath rested against the cushions, looking paler than he had before. "Been meaning to look him up and say hello."

"You'll get your chance. I'm calling him." Dante dialed the number.

Heath waved one hand negligently in his direction. "Call him. I don't think the fey bastard could hurt anything, and most likely he can help. I feel terrible."

"I'm so sorry," Megan whispered before she thought better of it. She'd drawn their attention back to her. Dante was on the phone so he could only watch as Dean eyed her.

"Who was your target, little one? Surely not me. I doubt you had any idea I would single you out in such a way. Did you intend this deadly surprise for Dante?"

"No! I didn't know. I swear!" Her mind raced, trying to think when or how she could've been exposed to something that would be so poisonous to their kind. It was nothing she'd done on purpose.

Heath leaned forward, pinning her to her seat with his mesmerizing gaze. She could feel the Glamour he tried to inflict upon her, but it wasn't taking fully. Not like it had during their dance when she'd been too close to him to take advantage of her natural immunity. A few feet, it seemed, made all the difference in the world.

Dante flipped the phone shut. "He's on his way to your home. I assume that's where we're headed, right?"

Heath nodded briefly as he gave up trying to cloud her mind. She felt the removal of his energy as a weight lifting off her shoulders.

Within moments they arrived in front of a gorgeous old brownstone. The property had to be worth several million, but Megan didn't have time to fully appreciate its grandeur as she was whisked up the stairs and inside in record time. Dante had one hand on her arm as if he was afraid she might try to take off running at any minute. She was tempted to do just that, but she couldn't leave Heath like that. Whatever was wrong with the man, she'd been the catalyst, and she owed him.

She felt terrible as she watched him deteriorate in front of her eyes. The limo driver had to help him inside and down a flight of hidden stairs to a large master suite below ground. The driver's face was grim as Heath instructed him to go upstairs and await the arrival of Duncan.

As Heath collapsed on the giant bed, the driver cornered Dante and Megan by the door.

"If he comes to further harm, you two will not leave this place alive. Am I clear?"

"I hear you, Hugh." Dante stood up to the other vampire but accepted his words with good grace. "There's little we can do for him without Duncan's help. Bring him directly here the minute he arrives."

Hugh sent a menacing, measuring look Dante's way before heading upstairs.

Megan spared a quick glance at Dante's grim face before turning her attention to Heath. The man was in bad shape, growing paler by the minute as he labored to breathe. He chucked his tie across the room, his suit coat following after.

Megan took the initiative and collected the items of clothing, folding them neatly before placing them on a silk upholstered settee along the one side of the grand room. Dante went to Heath after pouring a large glass of deep red wine. She knew wine had healing properties for their kind, but the vintage seemed to have little effect on him. Although he didn't seem to get worse after he had the wine, he wasn't getting any better either.

Duncan arrived moments later with Hugh as escort. He went straight to Heath, casting his hands out over the man on the bed even before saying hello. A glow of magic entered the room, and Megan bit back her surprise as she got her first real glimpse of Duncan's full potential. His entire being was suffused with a magical aura so strong, it almost hurt to look directly at him.

"How does it look, Duncan, my old friend?" Heath asked with a faint smile as he leaned against the headboard.

"Not good, I'm afraid. This is deep magic, tied to Megan's blood, as I feared." He drew back his power somewhat, turning to her. "Do you like what you have wrought?"

CHAPTER FIVE

"No! I didn't do this." She stepped backward, away from the accusation in Duncan's tragic blue eyes, but Dante was behind her, blocking her way. She felt his strong body caging her from behind as her mind raced. "I mean... I didn't know. I'd never do anything like this on purpose."

Duncan regarded her steadily for a long moment, finally nodding. "I believe you. The real question is, how far are you willing to go to reverse what was wrought with your blood?"

She thought fast. She didn't want Heath to die. If he did, she'd most likely follow. She also didn't want him to die for more than selfish reasons. Despite being born half-*were*, she was basically a peaceful person. She couldn't hurt a fly unless she was in shifted form and then she only followed the instincts of the wolf. She never reveled in her alter-ego's hunts or rare kills.

But this was something else altogether. Though she hadn't known anything about the poison in her blood, this felt like cold-blooded murder. She didn't think she could live with that kind of thing on her conscience. She'd do anything in her power to help Heath survive.

"I don't want him to die. I'll do whatever I must to reverse this."

"I was hoping you'd say that." Duncan stepped closer to her. "Yet I fear you'll balk when you understand what is required."

Her blood went cold. "Do I have to die to save him?"

"No, lass." Duncan was quick to reassure her but his eyes were grave, feeding her fears. "Their kind feeds off blood, sex and psychic energy. Your blood is poisoned, but your heart is not. The combination of your sexual energy combined with your pure heart may counteract the magic that was somehow siphoned into your blood."

"You want me to have sex with him?" She couldn't be sure in the tumult, but she thought she heard Dante growl behind her.

"With him and with me. Together, your good intent and the energy produced in climax, enhanced with my magic, might be enough to give him the strength to overcome your tainted blood."

"Both of you? At the same time?" She couldn't wrap her head around the idea, though if she were being honest, she'd admit it wasn't an altogether abhorrent notion. Both men were handsome and very attractive. She didn't love either one of them, but she had warm feelings for Duncan and her attitude toward Heath was complicated by intense guilt over what he was suffering because of her blood.

She wanted to help him and even though she wasn't a promiscuous woman and had never had two men in her bed at one time, she would do what was necessary to save Heath's life. She owed him that much at least. She was *were*, and even though she hadn't grown up in a pack, she was no stranger to sex, as all children of the Earth were.

"What do you say, Megan?"

"I…I don't know what to say. I don't want him to die because of me." She looked at Heath's handsome face, devoid of color as he struggled to breathe. "I'll do whatever you ask."

"Good." Duncan was brisk as he took her hand and led her to the bed.

"Awkward, is it not, my dear?" Heath sat up as Duncan guided her to sit next to him on the giant bed. Dante prowled in a corner, his eyes flashing. And then there was the silent Hugh, watching like a bodyguard from near the door. Heath put his hand on her shoulder, drawing her attention back to him. "I would have this be quite different if circumstances allowed, but believe this..." He leaned in to nuzzle her ear and spoke in a low voice only she could hear. "I took one look at you in the ballroom tonight and was struck speechless. You are beautiful, my little *were*wolf, and the most mysterious woman I have ever met. I wanted you the moment I saw you."

What woman wouldn't go gooey to have a real, live British nobleman whisper such things in her ear? Megan wasn't immune to the charming rogue's wiles, even depleted as he was. He didn't have to seduce her, and she didn't think he could have forced her by clouding her mind. The truth was, she found Sir Heathclif Dean compelling in a very basic way. While she wasn't easy by any stretch of the imagination, like any *were*, she had a healthy sex drive and not as many inhibitions as most mortals.

She'd had satisfying romps with a few select human men since she'd reached adulthood, but she doubted any of her lovers had ever pushed her to her full potential. These bloodletters though were another story. Ever since she'd first seen Dante, she'd been wondering how far an immortal could take her. Just being around Dante and Duncan had her primed.

She was attracted to the goodness and power in Duncan. She'd heard that fey were close to irresistible. Of course having never met one before, she hadn't known just how big a punch they packed both magically and sexually. Since meeting Duncan, she'd been drawn to him and even aside from that fey attraction of his, she liked him as a person. He was the voice of reason when Dante's temper flared. She liked the way the two friends interacted and how they balanced each other.

If she had to do this—and she was pretty darn sure her life depended on it—she was glad Duncan would be part of it. He would watch over her. She sensed his deep sense of honor and knew he would protect her should something go awry.

She breathed deep, gathering her courage. "It's all right." She blinked at Heath. "I can do this."

He stroked her hair away from her face. "I wish I could cloud your mind to make it easier, but you're strangely resistant."

"I'm glad you can't. I like to take responsibility for my actions, both the good and the bad. Somehow I did this to you, and I will fix it."

"It's better this way, in any case." Duncan sat behind her on the bed, boxing her in between their two hard male bodies. His hands spanned her waist, caressing lightly through the fine silk of her ball gown. "Intent counts for a lot when trying to nullify magic like this. You need to focus on your desire for Heath to be well and free of the taint. And you need to enjoy this, lass." Duncan's mouth nuzzled her shoulder, left bare by the low neckline of the soft gown. "Sexual pleasure is like ambrosia to their kind. It powers them even more than blood in certain cases."

Megan believed him. She felt the tingle of magic trailing after Duncan's touch like little bubbles of champagne bursting against her skin at her back. In front, Heath wasted no time in licking his way down her neck into her exposed cleavage. Duncan undid the tiny buttons at the back of her dress, and Heath assisted in tugging it downward to expose her breasts.

Megan gasped as Heath's fangs trailed down her chest, leaving little marks, though he was careful not to draw blood. She watched him, her temperature rising as he exposed one of her nipples, laving downward until he could latch onto it with his tongue.

Across the room, Dante made a rumbling, growly sound that only carried to her ears because of her sensitive *were* hearing. She doubted the other vampires in the room had picked up on it, but her eyes were drawn to Dante's. His eyes glowed with barely suppressed fire. It looked almost like a mixture of passion and rage. He was really mad and his jealous expression lifted her arousal another notch.

"After this, you are mine," he whispered, just barely audible to her heightened senses. Her gut clenched as the top of her ball gown was pushed to her waist, and Duncan began working on the tiny buttons that held the fluffy crinolines and skirt.

She held Dante's gaze as Heath and Duncan made her body sing. She felt each touch as if it came from Dante and the idea that he watched over her joining with two of his friends made her hot. The kink factor was off the charts. She'd always enjoyed something a little different and chose her few human lovers for their creativity and willingness to experiment since she needed a more earthy experience to get off than a purely human woman.

This was beyond anything she'd ever done or even imagined. She'd never been with more than one man at a time and never had anyone watch. Both were things she hadn't thought of experimenting with but discovered a liking for—at least in this situation.

Dante's presence made this nightmare situation palatable and though she could see he was eaten with jealousy, he was turned on too. His cock tented the front of his dress pants and as she watched, he stripped off his tie and jacket, throwing them on a nearby chair. The first few buttons of his shirt were next and then his cuffs. He rolled them up, the muscles of his forearms making her mouth water as Heath sucked strongly on her breast, then shifted his attention to the other one while Duncan divested her of the skirt and threw her ball gown and the froth of underclothes to the foot of the bed. All she wore was the white lace thong Dante had supplied for under her lovely gown.

She'd blushed when she'd seen the scandalous bit of underwear, knowing he'd picked it out for her to wear. There was no bra. The dress didn't allow for one. All night her nipples had been pressing against the soft silk, rasping as she moved, in a perpetual state of arousal.

It had all been leading to this, she realized. Though when the night started, she thought she would have been in Dante's bed, behind closed doors with no witnesses. All in all, things had become much more complicated than she'd expected. She was relieved Dante hadn't bitten her. She'd have felt awful if she'd poisoned him. It was bad enough Heath had succumbed.

He was a handsome man, and she'd felt something when he bit her. He was strong, powerful and extraordinarily attractive, but Dante was...more. Just more of everything. More appealing, more devastating, more dangerous to her.

Still, it was no hardship to be near Heath. He was a gorgeous man with lots of sex appeal. A woman would have to be dead not to notice him.

Having Dante here in the room, saying things only she could hear added to her excitement. And the generous touches Duncan spiked with little zings of his magic nearly made her swoon. He was bespelling her. She was almost sure of it. It was different from the vampire mojo that took away all independent thought. This was more like a coaxing of her natural response, a heightening of her already sharp senses. He was making this easier for her, and she could have kissed him for the extra effort. In fact, she wanted to kiss him. Desperately.

She tried to turn in their arms and after a moment of struggle, they allowed it. She faced Duncan, staring into his eyes, unable to find the words to voice the thoughts in her mind but he understood. She could see it in his gaze as it softened. He leaned in and kissed her brow.

"You're a beauty, little wolf. I want this to be good for you."

"It is." She sighed as she lifted upward to claim his mouth with hers. She poured all her thanks and attraction into the kiss, hoping to give a little back of the pleasure he was working so hard to give her. She knew he had expended magical energy on her, and no mage did that without some effort on his part. He didn't have to. She'd agreed to do whatever they needed her to do, but Duncan was giving her a little extra whammy that pushed her beyond mere cooperation into the realm of truly devastating enjoyment.

She learned the flavor of him, and it was as magical as the man himself. Duncan was fast becoming a dear friend, someone she could trust with her body, if not her heart. She felt tender toward him, especially for the way he cared about everyone in his realm of friends, which oddly enough seemed to include her. It wasn't a truly romantic sort of love. It was the love of a friend. A friend with some heavy duty benefits at the moment, of course.

She squirmed in his arms as he broke the kiss. Heath's hands were beneath the elastic of her thong, pushing downward. His lips were at her neck, too close to the place he'd bitten her on the dance floor.

"No nibbling, my friend," Duncan reminded the vampire with a teasing but firm tone. "That's what got us into this mess, and you don't need a double dose of poison tonight."

Megan pulled back to look between the two men. Heath looked stronger but his eyes were...scary. She couldn't think of another word for the look on his face. Hunger and desperation mixed in his expression in a frightening way. Duncan's lips firmed as he seemed to recognize the fine edge of desperation on the Master's face.

"Hugh," Duncan called without looking away from Heath's face. "Can you give him a vein while we conclude this?" he asked the silent vampire who came to stand beside them.

Hugh nodded, and Megan could see the fire in his eyes though he clearly did all he could to control it. She was glad he could rein in his instincts. She had more than she could handle between taking Duncan's direction, fending off Heath's desire to bite and Dante's furious whispers and molten gaze.

The room was too crowded. She would have been even more self-conscious if not for Duncan's magic affecting her senses.

"I hate to rush things, darling." Duncan winked at her. "But this is important. I want you to think about Heath. I want you to focus on your desire that he will be free of the taint, healthy and whole. Think good thoughts, lass." He leaned in to kiss her briefly, refiring senses that hadn't yet settled. Her skin was ultra sensitive to the four masculine hands roaming over her at will. Her thong slid down her legs and Heath's hands settled between her thighs, one in front, one in back.

He wasted no time, sliding his front hand into the slick wetness that waited for him, coaxing her legs apart where she sat on the edge of the bed. He teased her clit, sliding his middle finger up into her. She gasped as Duncan's mouth settled on her breast. His touch was gentler than the vampire's had been, more solicitous, and she realized in an instant that he was the choreographer of this entire scene.

Heath was half out of his mind with the magical poison mucking up his system. Duncan was the one who knew how such things worked, and he was the only one who would be able to actually *see* when the poison dissipated. He was their guide in this foray into the forbidden, as well as a participant. She trusted her safety and her pleasure to him.

So far, he hadn't steered her wrong. She wanted more than just Heath's finger in her pussy. She wanted his cock and his come. And she wanted it now.

Whether it was Duncan's magic doing its thing to fire her senses or Heath himself, she had no idea and at this point, she really didn't care. She was hornier than she'd ever been in her life, and she had a gorgeous vampire ready, willing and more than able to satisfy her.

She turned and pushed Heath down onto the bed. He let her do it, smiling as he lowered himself to the soft mattress. She used just a tiny bit of her *were* strength to rip his shirt open, buttons flying everywhere as she growled and sniffed at his spicy, masculine scent. She'd never been able to let her wolf out to play during sex before and was a little appalled by her own actions, as if watching them from afar. But not appalled enough to stop.

No, she wanted more and Heath didn't seem to mind at all. She ran her hands over his muscular chest, pleasantly surprised by the rippling muscles of his abdomen. He was built solid, brawnier than she'd expected and just slightly taller than the other men, like a weightlifter with an eye for symmetry. He wasn't too bulky anywhere, in fact, he was just right to her painfully aroused *were* senses.

She licked over his pebbled nipple, nibbling on his pectoral muscle, and was gratified when he actually trembled for a moment. She worked her way over his well-defined abdomen, pausing to unbutton his trousers and pull the tab of the zipper with her teeth. She tore his tighty whities in her haste, but he didn't seem to care.

His aroused cock sprang into her hand, and she didn't waste any time. She wanted a taste. She licked the head, loving the feel and salty taste of him, pausing to go down on him, taking him as far as she could for just a moment before slurping her way back. She left him wet and heaven knew she was wet too. She wanted that thick cock inside her.

She tried to climb over him, but Duncan's hands on her waist stopped her from mounting Heath completely.

"Just a moment, lass. I need to be with you this time. It's the best way to counter the dark magic."

She didn't understand. She was past caring at that moment. Duncan's magic touch had sent her into a nearly mindless frenzy of need, and she didn't want to wait. Then Duncan touched between her legs with that amazing, magical hum in his fingers. She held her position on all fours, hovering over Heath, waiting to see what Duncan would do next.

She didn't have long to wait. She felt a drizzle of warm oil in the crack of her ass and the foreign sensation was oddly thrilling. The oil felt like it had been infused with the same magic Duncan's touch had spread over her body. She wanted it inside her. She wanted him to rub it all over her bottom

INFERNO

and do whatever he wanted. She was open to anything he might demand and totally uninhibited for the first time in her life.

Soft growls issued from her throat as Duncan's fingers spread the oil. He pushed inside her bottom, shocking and delighting her with a sensation she'd never anticipated. She didn't question. She didn't object. She was beyond all that, in a place she'd never been before. A mindless realm where the only thing that mattered was sexual gratification. The sooner the better.

She whimpered when Duncan removed his fingers but strained toward him when he positioned himself between her legs, pressing into her ass with something much larger than his fingers. He was sticking his cock there and she nearly screamed, wanting his possession with a mindless intensity.

He worked steadily, pushing in and then pulling out only to push in a little farther, working his cock into her with the help of the oil and a great deal of patience. She helped him as much as she could without quite knowing what to do. She worked on instinct, wanting his cock up her ass in a way she'd never really contemplated or imagined. All she knew was that at that moment, she wanted his possession with everything in her.

When he was finally seated fully inside, he stilled. She cried out with the need for him to move. He slapped her ass, chastising her into submission. Her wolf whimpered at his mastery, subdued by an alpha male much bigger and stronger than she. It was the wolf bitch's pleasure to submit, and it translated to forbidden pleasure for her human side as well.

"Now, Heath," Duncan instructed, pushing her downward, guiding her body with his strong hands as he maintained his place inside her. She lowered herself with his help, slowly, achingly, onto the widest cock she'd ever had.

Thick, long and strong, Heathclif Dean was masterfully built. With Duncan in possession of her ass, she had to work to take Heath's girth into her pussy. It was worth every sweaty effort. She hovered over him, using her wolf strength

73

to lower herself onto him a little at a time.

The sensations were like nothing she'd ever experienced. She'd never been taken in the ass and never had two at once. And never such well endowed partners either. They were a delight to her hungry *were* senses. Her beast side loved it. They filled her completely and made her want to beg for the fulfillment she sensed would come. If she was good.

Both men were alpha males of their species, and both made her wolf want to submit. It was rare her inner wolf found any man worthy of her attention, but since meeting Dante and his friends, her wolf had been in a near constant state of heat.

Megan needed this. She needed an orgasm almost as much as the vampires probably did, but it was just out of reach. She finally took all of Heath's thick cock. She was filled completely.

Well, maybe not. She looked up to find the silent Hugh staring at her, the flame in his eyes even hotter than it had been before.

Then Duncan gave an imperceptible signal and the men began to move inside her. She moaned, unprepared for the increase in arousal that followed. She was lifted so high, she thought she might die if the men let her crash.

Heath reared up and tried to bite her. Duncan held her out of his reach as his cock stretched and claimed her ass fully.

"Now, Hugh," Duncan instructed and Megan clenched around them when she saw Heath bite into Hugh's wrist, a line of his rich, red blood slipping slowly around his wrist as Heath fed from his subordinate.

The men stroked in counterpoint and soon she was panting, crying out on each successive thrust. She was noisier than she'd ever been, wilder and more needy too. Her mouth was open, her eyes closed, when Hugh's free hand grasped the back of her head, guiding it downward onto his waiting cock.

She took it greedily, beyond caring who fucked her mouth. She was sex incarnate at that moment, every orifice stuffed with cock, not caring who or how, just that she was filled and ready to come—and to bring them with her.

She licked eagerly at the salty essence in her mouth, wrapping her tongue around the long shaft while Duncan orchestrated the movements of all three men. Duncan bore her down onto Heath while he pulsed hard, slamming her pussy with his big body. The violence of it made her want to scream, but the cock in her mouth pushed deep in demand.

Only Duncan's magic and her mindless frenzy kept her from gagging. Instead of fear or revulsion, she was drugged on Duncan's sex magic. She found their harsh possession of her body more than arousing. It was something she needed with every fiber of her being. They pounded into her, using her as they wanted. It was no hardship in her current state of mind. She would have begged to be used if she could speak.

The power was all theirs, yet she felt like the Lady Goddess, giving them the precious gift of her bounty. The moment was beautiful and she felt the magic of it drawing tight in her heart, her soul, the very center of her being and spinning outward to the men who possessed her body.

She came hard, releasing all the power, bathing them in her feminine magic, augmented by Duncan's direction. He took her power and focused it into a cleansing fire that swept over Heath, burning the toxin from his system and partially from her own at the same time.

The mini supernova made them all come hard. The cock in her mouth exploded, sending its come down her throat in a satisfying wave. Heath's cock spasmed in her pussy, filling her with a tide of warmth and Duncan filled her ass with his slippery tribute, soothing her sore muscles with his special magic.

She flew to the stars, then drifted slowly back to Earth. She must have blacked out for a few minutes because she woke on the settee across the big room, Dante's glittering gaze on her. The magic spell Duncan had woven was winding down, though tingling remnants of it still tickled her skin here and there.

Her legs were splayed over the short arms of the wide lounger, her body dripping with other men's come. Dante stalked over to her, standing above her with something that looked almost violent in his eyes. She felt no shame, only a return of nearly paralyzing arousal.

"My turn," he growled. He cleaned her with clipped motions using a cloth he'd gotten from somewhere. His touch was oddly gentle, if possessive in a harshly exciting way. When he'd wiped evidence of the other men away, he ripped his pants open and bent over her on the small couch-like piece of furniture.

His big cock slid into her with no preliminaries and no resistance after what she'd just been through. Her arms went around him, holding him close. She didn't like the fabric of his clothes between them but was so drugged from her earlier climax, she couldn't summon the strength to push them away.

Dante gave her a hard, fast fuck that brought her wolf to growling, biting, playful life inside. The wolf was happier with this harsh sex play than any she'd had before and it barked like crazy to get her attention. The wolf kept saying something but Megan was too drugged from the earlier encounter to really understand, and rising too rapidly toward another huge orgasm to care.

Dante pounded into her, anger and jealousy clear in his expression as his head dipped and his fangs dropped. He was going to bite her. She knew he shouldn't. She was too weak with completion and too distracted by the mounting climax to do anything about it.

A second before he struck, Duncan was there, pulling on Dante's shoulder.

"No biting, my friend. She is still a danger."

Dante turned wild eyes on the half-fey warrior and cursed him, baring his fangs. Finally, after a momentary standoff, he sat back, moving away from the temptation of her neck. He stroked deeper in this position, his hard thrusts pushing her up the settee until she was wedged into the little crevice where the back of the small couch met the wide cushion. Dante thrust a few more times, his fingers tugging on her nipples hard enough to make her cry out but perfect enough to make her tremble as her climax began.

It was a slow build this time that led to an amazing explosion of pleasure. She screamed when he came into her shaking body.

She chanted his name as he groaned above her, coming hard and driving her still higher into the longest series of pleasure spasms she'd ever known.

She blacked out again. The last thing she saw was Dante's fiercely masculine look of conquest. He'd gotten what he wanted and staked his ownership, and she couldn't argue with that one bit.

When she woke, she was covered by a blanket, her legs and arms tucked under it as she reclined on the settee with a pillow from the bed cushioning her head. Someone had taken care of a few things. For one, they'd cleaned her up and tucked her in. She was sore but didn't feel the telltale stickiness she'd expected. She hadn't counted on that kind of caring treatment from a group of bloodletters, one of whom she'd poisoned. Then again, these men had shown her that chivalry wasn't entirely dead. Even if it was undead.

She chuckled at her own small pun. These men were the farthest thing from the monsters in the horror movies she'd ever seen. Who knew vampires could be such gentle and fierce lovers? Not all of it was magic induced. There'd been some serious technique in their possession that any woman would welcome. She felt languorous as she lifted her head to look around the room and get her bearings.

Hugh was gone, and Heath was sitting up in the bed as Duncan checked him. The glow of Duncan's magic was breathtaking and his smile brought one of relief to her face as well. Dante stood at the bedside, apparently waiting to hear the verdict. He was the first to see that she'd rejoined the land of the living.

His gaze locked with hers. She couldn't tell what he meant

by that dark look. Her mind was still fuzzy and her body hummed with residual pleasure.

"Is he all right?" Her voice was hoarse.

All three men looked at her, but it was Duncan who spoke.

"Much better. The poison is gone and any weakness that remains should be gone by the next rising. Your passion restored him and negated the effect of your tainted blood."

Megan blushed at the reminder. Now that her head was clearing, she started to feel embarrassed by what had gone before.

"You'll stay here for the day," Heath said from the bed, his tone brooking no argument. Megan realized it must be close to dawn, so it was safer for Dante to stay here than make his way across town to his own place and face the danger of the sun. "Hugh can show you to a guest suite before he must retire."

As if waiting for just those words, Hugh reappeared in the doorway, holding a woman's silk robe. He delivered it to Megan with a respectful bow of his head.

She slipped into it gratefully, though the thin material did little to hide the lines of her body or the sharp nipples poking at the cool fabric. These men had seen all she had and tasted it too. Just because she'd been under Duncan's spell at the time, she couldn't blame them for the necessary familiarity they now had with her body.

It was a good body. A half-*were* body. And *weres* were invariably well formed and attractive. It was a blessing of the genes. When they shifted, they ran, exercising more than the average person to hone strong, fit bodies and sleek muscles that translated well when they shifted back to human form. She had nothing to be ashamed of and everything to be proud of. She just wasn't used to flaunting herself in front of men who'd given her the best orgasms of her life.

The situation was strange, to say the least. Oddly, she couldn't work up any real outrage over it. Just a little embarrassment. And that was a small price to pay for saving a

Master vampire's life and your own in the process. Megan figured she'd gotten off easy. She'd nearly killed Heath and her punishment—if it could be called that—had been the best sex of her life. So far. She didn't know what Heath had planned for her the next evening when he was back to full strength. She hoped he'd let her go free after the way she'd given over control of her body to save his life.

He was a good man. He'd given her a hell of a climax, but she knew he'd enjoyed it too. A man didn't come that hard without a lot of pleasure behind it. And after something like that, a man like Heath wouldn't subject her to some arcane punishment for an act that had not been intentional on her part and totally out of her control.

She followed Hugh from the room with Dante at her side. He hadn't spoken to her, but she expected he'd have something to say once they were alone. Duncan stayed behind to see to Heath's comfort.

"The three of you will confine yourselves to this suite for the day," Hugh said with great ceremony as he opened the door to a beautifully decorated suite of rooms on the second floor of the brownstone. There was a central sitting room with a couch and entertainment center, a small kitchenette that looked to be fully stocked and four other doors leading off from the main area. "The doors lead to bedrooms and a bathroom. You'll find everything you need within and all is sun-proofed for your convenience, Dante. No exterior windows."

"Thank you," Dante said to the other bloodletter. "This will be fine. I assume you'll come for us tomorrow?"

Hugh nodded gravely. "The Mistress will most likely see you after you talk to Heath." Hugh's blue gaze slipped to Megan, and he stepped closer to her. "Don't worry," he unbent enough to say. "You transgressed, but you also did all in your power to fix it. Heath is not an unreasonable man, and his daughter is fair-minded as well."

"Thank you," she replied in a subdued voice.

"No," Hugh took her hand, surprising her even further as

he brought it to his lips for a gentle kiss. "Thank you for sharing yourself with me. Your psychic energy is unlike anything I have ever tasted before. I'm not surprised Heath bit you out of hand. He can be rather impulsive like that." Hugh's eyes sparkled as the first smile she'd ever seen on his face tilted the corners of his lips.

He was a devastatingly handsome man when he smiled and the faint twang of an Australian accent made him too sexy to be believed. His brooding demeanor made her think he'd known tragedy in the past and her heart went out to him. Suddenly a little of her embarrassment faded. She'd helped this dour man enough so that he could conjure a small smile for her. That was something, at least. A little ray of hope for a man who otherwise was the picture of sadness.

Hugh left without further discussion, leaving her alone with Dante. They hadn't spoken since his tumultuous claiming after what had been the kinkiest sex act of her life. She hadn't thought anything could top being stuffed with cock in every orifice, but Dante had taken her higher than even that amazing scene. He'd rocked her world off its axis, and it was still wobbling out of control.

CHAPTER SIX

Dante busied himself at the small wine cooler in the kitchenette, pouring a large glass of burgundy for himself before turning to Megan.

The moment of truth had arrived.

She fidgeted, fingering the hem of her borrowed robe. Dante's eyes raked her from head to foot, remnants of fire in his eyes reigniting to flame low in the background while he sipped his wine.

"I'm sorry," she began haltingly. She didn't know what to say but felt responsibility for the night's events settling squarely on her shoulders.

"It's near dawn." Dante sighed heavily, moving into the sitting area with his glass of wine. "No doubt we'll talk this over in minute detail tomorrow. For now, I should probably apologize for taking you like a barbarian. In all honesty, I don't understand what came over me."

"It's okay—" she began, but he forestalled her.

"I said I *should* apologize, not that I will. I'll be damned if I'll apologize for something that felt so good...so right. I'm only sorry if I hurt you, Megan." He reached out with one hand to stroke her cheek as his gaze held hers. "Please tell me I didn't hurt you."

"No, you didn't hurt me." She was mesmerized by the tender yet militant light in his eyes. "Actually, I kind of enjoyed it. I've never been able to be myself with a man before. Whatever Duncan did to me let the wolf howl and she really liked it, but she—and I—liked it most with you."

"You're not a foursome kind of girl?" His lips quirked up on one side in a teasing, lopsided grin. His casual manner said without words that he'd seen and done a lot in his centuries. Somehow, that made her feel more comfortable about the whole evening.

"I'm afraid not. At least..." she teased right back, "...not on a regular basis." She stepped closer to him, into his personal space. "I'm more of a one at a time kind of woman."

"That's good." He trailed his hand through her long hair. "That's real good, sweetheart, because I have a feeling we're going to be doing a lot of one on one as soon as they let us out of here."

"Do you think they will?" In a flash, worry returned. "I mean, do you think Heath will forgive me for poisoning him? And what will his daughter say? She's the Mistress, right? So my punishment is up to her. Isn't it?"

"Don't worry," Dante soothed her. "I think you more than made up for the tainted blood with what you did tonight. It's not every woman who could nullify that kind of thing, even with Duncan's help. We talked about it while you slept, and Duncan thinks it's the purity of your heart that allowed the bespelled blood to be counteracted at all. That seemed to be proof enough for Heath, and he'll square things with his daughter. They rule together, despite the title she wears."

"I hope you're right." She chewed on her lower lip in worry.

Dante leaned down and did a little nibbling of his own, tempting her tongue out to play with his as he kissed the worry off her face.

Duncan came in a few minutes later and found them like that, locked in an embrace, mouth to mouth, Dante's hands inside the open panels of the silk robe, cupping her breasts.

"Haven't you had enough for one night?" He chastised

them as he flopped down on the couch in full view of their activities. As Megan turned to look at the half-fey warrior, he winked, giving her an exaggerated once over as she pulled the robe together and retied the belt at her waist.

"How's Heath?" Dante asked as he sank onto the overstuffed chair facing Duncan and pulled Megan onto his lap.

"He'll be fine with a little rest. As will we all."

Dante nodded. "Will you two be all right here today? They'll no doubt lock us in, and I wouldn't recommend trying to break out." He tugged on her hand until she looked at him.

"I'll be okay. I'll probably sleep the day away and if not, there's a television and some food in the kitchen to keep me occupied."

"Good girl." He raised her hand to his lips and kissed each knuckle.

"I'm probably going to sleep this off most of the day," Duncan warned. "I need to replenish."

"Thank you for what you did to make it easier for me, Duncan," she said in a low voice as she met his eyes. "I don't think I could have done...that...without you."

Duncan rose and came over to face her, lifting her to her feet, off Dante's lap. "You're a passionate woman, Megan. I'm not really sorry about what had to be done, only sorry there was no other way. I'll remember your passion and generosity all my days." He leaned down to kiss her cheek with a tender salute. "Thank you."

He stepped away and headed for one of the bedrooms. Dante stood and led her to the doors on the other side of the sitting area.

"You'll be all right?" he asked, holding her gaze.

She nodded. "I need sleep, then some sustenance. I'll see you tonight."

He kissed her deeply before claiming one of the rooms for himself.

Megan took the room beside his, taking time for a long, hot shower before collapsing bonelessly into the soft mattress and silk sheets. She didn't know anything again until just an hour before dusk. She rose, showered again and dressed in clothes that someone had laid out for her. A designer tracksuit that fit her well enough, though it had been designed for a taller woman. No doubt it was one of the Mistress's. Beggars couldn't be choosers, she thought as she examined the rich fabric and eyed the size. She dressed and made her way into the kitchenette to see what she could scrounge for dinner.

Duncan joined her at the small dinner table just before sunset and shared her meal. Dante arrived in the sitting room as they finished eating, joining them in a glass of wine after their meal while they waited for Hugh to show.

He collected them only moments later. Hugh spared a small smile for Megan, and she felt like she was making progress melting the ice that surrounded the stoic man. He led them to a plush living room on the ground floor. Heathclif was there before them and poured drinks for everyone.

When everyone had been served, silence reigned for a moment as everyone present stared at her. She started to fidget.

"What now?" Megan was afraid of the answer but knew the time to pay the piper had come.

"Now it's time for answers." Dante touched her face, guiding her gently to the couch in the living room. Duncan and Heath followed behind.

"I'll tell you anything you want to know."

"Yes you will." Duncan took the place next to her. "I'm giving you no choice, Megan. We must have the truth, and I'm going to bespell you to be certain we have it."

Fear raced through her heart. "I'm *were*. Magic doesn't work on me."

"Some does," Duncan assured her. "The poison in your blood is proof of that. The magic I plan to use on you is not of this realm. It will work. I'm sorry. It has to be this way. What you've done is sanctionable by death under the bloodletters' laws. You need to tell them everything you know, and they need to be certain it is the truth. Only then might you be able to avoid the ultimate penalty."

"Oh Goddess!" She shrank into the cushions, trying to avoid the spell Duncan was weaving. She could feel his magic rising around her, sparking off her exposed skin like static electricity. It grew in strength as tears gathered behind her eyes. She'd never been so frightened in all her life.

"This is interesting." Duncan seemed to redouble his efforts. "She's more resistant to my magic than any mortal I've ever encountered. Ah, so we finally discover another part of your heritage." Duncan shifted closer and suddenly a door opened inside her. She was no longer in control. She was Duncan's puppet, and she would do anything he asked.

The idea scared her to death, but she was powerless against his fey magic.

"Who was your intended target? Who were you sent to kill?"

"No one." Her voice was raspy, as if her body fought every word. She felt compelled to speak by the force of his magic. "I don't want to kill anyone."

"You were sent here deliberately, were you not?" Duncan was relentless.

Slowly, she nodded. "I was sent to spy. Not to kill."

The three men shared significant looks. "Who were you sent to spy on?"

"Dante."

"What did your keepers want to know about him?"

"His habits, his friends, his allegiances. The usual stuff."

"What else?" Duncan's questions came like rapid fire.

"The mage. He wanted to know what happened to the mage."

"Vabian?" Dante's voice reached her from over Duncan's shoulder.

"That was the name he said. Patrick Vabian. They lost him and want to know what happened."

"Who sent you, Megan?" Duncan refocused her attention

on him.

She felt as if she'd hit a brick wall. Duncan's magic was compelling, but there was something stronger at work inside her, preventing her from speaking. The pain caused by the two clashing compulsions made her writhe in agony.

"I can't!" she cried as fire leaped along her veins, burning her from inside out. "Please!"

"All right." Duncan backed off that line of questioning. "Let's examine your intentions. When you approached Dante in that nightclub, what was your intent?"

"To watch him. To see if I could get close to him."

"So you could spy on him?"

"Yes." The pain of conflict had eased, yet Duncan's compulsion held strong.

"Did your keeper tell you to sleep with him?"

Anger boiled inside along with Duncan's magic. "I refused. I told him I wouldn't whore for anyone, and I meant it."

"What was your keeper's response?"

"He told me to offer my blood. He said shifter blood was a delicacy to vampires."

A significant look passed between the three men.

"And what did you think of that?"

"I didn't like it, but I didn't see any alternative."

"Why? What compels you to do what they say?"

"The obligation. I'm the last of my line. I must finish the task and clear my family's name."

"The mark you carry on your thigh. Is that the mark of your family's obligation?"

"Yes."

"And the obligation is to the *Altor Custodis*?"

"Yes." The answer felt like it was being ripped from her as the counter-magic rose once more, preventing her from speaking about her keeper. Duncan must have seen her discomfort, for he changed his line of questioning again.

"What circumstance created the obligation and how long ago did it start?"

"The fire. The great fire. It was my ancestors' fault. They trusted the wrong people. Made the wrong decisions. And people died. Innocent people. Chicago died."

Dante gasped, but Duncan persisted with his questions.

"Which ancestors caused the obligation of your family to the *Altor Custodis*?"

"The last set of twins. The *were*lords."

"And what was the year?"

"1871."

"The Great Chicago Fire?" Heathclif asked from the side. She saw Dante nod, his face grim.

"What happened to your ancestors after the fire?" Duncan reclaimed her attention.

"They were disgraced. When their mistakes came to light, their people threw them out. My line was banished, sentenced to run alone until they could atone for their sins."

"So how did the *Altor Custodis* become involved?"

"They approached the twins after. The *Altor Custodis* offered a way out—a way of atoning by working for them. Somehow, the debt never seemed to be repaid. They were my grandfathers, and they passed the mark of obligation to my mother. She passed it to me. I was told this mission would be my last for the *Altor Custodis*. After this, the obligation would be fulfilled and my family's honor would finally be restored."

Duncan sat back whistling under his breath. He seemed to regroup, collecting his thoughts before he continued the questioning.

"So what about the poison in your blood? Did you know about it before last night?"

"No!" The very idea of it made her shiver. "I didn't know. It's nothing I've done on purpose. You have to believe me. I don't want to kill anyone. Not that way. Not ever. Poison is for the weak. It's not the *were* way." The tears in her eyes began to fall. "I'm so sorry."

"It's all right, Megan, but we have to know what you know. We have to uncover the truth. Such magic workings aren't easily performed on a *were*—even a half-*were* like you.

Someone went to great pains to make you a carrier of something that would kill Dante."

She began to cry in earnest and Duncan took pity on her, handing her a box of tissues that had been on the table beside him. He waited a few moments while she mopped her eyes and blew her nose before resuming his questions.

"Did your keeper work a spell over you at any time during the past year?"

"Not that I know of. He's human—" She tried to say more, but the pain of warring magics inside her stopped her words.

"Well, it's obvious he at least managed to put a compulsion on you not to speak of him." Duncan shot the other men another significant look even as his expression hardened with determination. He tried another tack. "When in the presence of your keeper, did you ever eat or drink anything?"

She thought back. "I don't see him often. We've never shared a meal. The last time I saw him, he offered me a drink. I thought it strange at the time. It was a sweet honey wine and it made me sneeze. I thought it was the flower smell of the honey that tickled my nose, but now that you ask, I remember the liquid tingled in my throat and sparkled faintly in the glass."

"Silver dust?" Heath asked from the side. Duncan nodded at him and resumed his questioning.

"Were there any other times you ate or drank with him?"

"No. Just that once."

"What is your opinion of him? Do you think he's a good man?"

She hesitated. "He's... *Altor Custodis* is supposed to be on the side of light. I...I was never sure if he was or not. He didn't feel right to me, but it wasn't my place to question. My mother introduced him to me. She told me to trust him. She told me it was the only way to redeem our family honor."

"Your instincts said differently, did they not?"

Slowly, she nodded. "I don't know why, but I never liked

him. I never trusted him fully, and I didn't like most of the missions he sent me on over the years."

"What kind of missions?"

"Spying mostly. Or he'd send me as a messenger to places I didn't like the feel of."

"What did they feel like?"

"Slimy. Unclean... Evil." Agony stabbed through her brain as memories of those places surfaced in her mind. She'd repressed those memories and now they were back in full force. She threw her head back against the couch, writhing in pain.

Duncan's big hands cupped her cheeks, stilling her movement as he captured her gaze. "Be at ease, my lovely. Someone has done this to you. Listen to me, and I will free you. I'll free your mind and unleash the memories he has hidden from you. Prepare yourself. This may be difficult at first."

Duncan bore down on her with his power, his hands holding her as he loomed over her on the couch. His magic was awesome in its strength, overwhelming her senses and freeing her mind.

The pain of the returning memories was almost too much to bear. Duncan held her through it. He was her strength for those moments, and she knew he would not let her fall.

Suddenly, things that had been hidden from her clicked into place. She recalled with clarity the horrible places her keeper had sent her, and the horrible people he'd made her deal with, delivering messages and carrying them back. The memories made her feel physically ill. Megan clutched at her stomach as nausea threatened to overcome her.

Duncan's hand soothed her brow, a tingle of his energy easing the pain in her gut.

"Whoever did this to you, he is a master mage." Duncan sat on the couch, looking as drained as she felt. "And it was lucky in a way, that Heath felt the need to bite you first. The poison was keyed to Dante specifically, so it had a less violent effect on Heath. It probably would've killed Dante too rapidly for us to counter it."

The compulsion to answer his questions was gone, replaced by a feeling of freedom and a return of memories she hadn't realized were missing.

"Goddess!" She shuddered to think what had been done to her without her knowledge.

"You're mostly free now, Megan. I'm sorry to say the compulsion against revealing your keeper's identity may last until he is dead. I'm sorry. Some magics work that way and have very few counters in this realm."

She looked over at Duncan, taking in his pale face and faintly trembling hand. He'd given a lot of his strength to free her even this much. She reached out to him, touching his hand.

"Thank you, Duncan."

"The poison in your blood will wear off slowly…unless we make further efforts to nullify it." One eyebrow rose as he grinned, and she had a good idea of how they'd go about *nullifying* the magic. After what she'd been through the night before, she wasn't sure she'd survive another round of sex magic. "It wouldn't be a good idea for any of our fanged friends to partake of your blood again until we're sure the poison is completely gone."

"Agreed," Heath was the first to say, though he smiled to soften his hasty words. He even reached out to pat her head, petting her like a favored puppy. "You're a sweet temptation, my dear. All in all, though, I think we're safer keeping you at arm's length for now."

She laughed, smiling up at him. "Believe me, I'm glad to be off the menu. I couldn't go through another night like the one just past."

Heath's eyes went dark. "I'm sorry, sweetheart."

"Oh!" She realized he'd taken her words as a complaint. "No, I meant I hated the idea that I'd hurt you. Despite being half-*were*, I'm averse to causing pain. Even when I'm furry, I don't torment my prey. I'm more of a catch-and-release kind of girl."

Heath seemed to take her words well, easing back in his chair and smiling kindly. There was knowledge in his eyes— intimate knowledge of her that made her heart thump in an unsteady rhythm.

"My daughter was to have met with you tonight, but I think it better to limit your knowledge of her until you are free of the mage's taint. Under the circumstances, I think it's safe to let you continue to roam our fair city. I'd like Dante to keep an eye on you and, of course, I don't want you reporting to your *Altor Custodis* contact under any circumstances. Not yet." His gaze turned sharp. "We may have a use for that connection later, but we will need time to prepare a battle plan."

She didn't like the sound of that last bit. Of course, it was a relief to hear he wasn't going to put her to death for what she'd done. She knew she'd gotten off easy after what she'd almost done to Heath.

With her memories restored, she had no desire to return to the keeper who had run her life from behind the scenes for so long. She was torn about the need to salvage her family's honor, but vowed to find some other way. She would never willingly obey that evil man from the *Altor Custodis* again.

"I can live with that," she said in a subdued voice. Dante must have sensed some of her dismay.

"You're worrying about your family's debt, are you not? I think perhaps, I can help with that." He stood and began to pace the floor, clearly agitated at what he was about to say. "The debt owed by your family is not owed to the *Altor Custodis*. It never was. Likely, some opportunist within their ranks preyed on your ancestors, making them his pawns. I recognize the events of which you spoke. The Great Chicago Fire was a turning point in my life as well. I had befriended a young man. He was a mortal mage, whom I believed to be the reincarnation of my murdered brother."

Megan gasped. She knew all the particulars of the fire story. Her grandfathers had told her of their terrible mistakes when she was just a cub. *Were* life expectancies were much longer than humans'. They lived harsh lives and most often died well before their time. Her grandfathers had lived to the age of one hundred sixty-seven. They would have lived longer had they not died in a fiery crash. The same crash that had claimed the life of their mate and their only child, Megan's mother.

"The firemage was your friend?" She saw the truth in his eyes even before he spoke.

"He was a kind and gentle soul who would not have hurt a fly. He was in control of his power, but when your grandfathers had their wolves corner him in that barn, he lost it utterly."

"The Great Chicago Fire was caused by a human firemage gone rogue?" Heath asked.

"Erik was not a rogue!" Dante snapped. "He was attacked by a gang of wolves. He was trying to defend himself. The conflagration that followed was a result of his death."

"My God, I had no idea." Heath looked both shocked and sympathetic to Dante's obvious pain.

"I was the one who demanded blood price when it became clear the wolves had killed an innocent man." Dante turned back to pin her with his gaze. "So you see, your family's debt is owed to me. No other. Me."

Megan's mouth went dry as her entire existence to this point came into question. She'd been working for the *Altor Custodis*, determined to erase her family's debt, but if what Dante said was true—and she had no reason to doubt him—then it had all been for naught.

"Well?" Duncan prompted her. "Did your grandfathers say anything about a vengeful bloodletter who demanded their banishment?"

Slowly she nodded. "They never spoke his name, but they knew who was responsible for their fate. They accepted it. Guilt over what they had allowed to happen to an innocent man followed them all their days."

"I'm glad," Dante said harshly. "Erik was..." Emotion clogged his throat as he turned away, and Megan got a heartbreaking glimpse of the pain the human mage's death had caused. "He was my brother all over again." Dante gathered his composure like a cloak around him.

"Dante's younger brother was murdered by agents of the *Venifucus* centuries ago, in an effort to turn him to their side," Duncan picked up the story. "It is my belief that they never stopped trying to get him to turn. For whatever reason, the *Venifucus* have targeted him over and over to this very day. The business in Montana recently was only the latest in a long series of tragedies they have manufactured especially for him."

"The *werelords*?" Heath asked, clearly curious as Dante continued to pace near the fire, his face averted.

"Yes," Duncan confirmed. "The mage who set Dante up was a *Venifucus* agent. We heard him speak of their plans before he was dispersed."

"Then they're definitely back?" Heath looked pale.

"I begin to think they never left. But yes, they are definitely back and a threat to every living being in this realm."

"Good lord," Heath whispered, his eyes filled with a mixture of dread and determination.

Dante, recovered from his emotional storm, turned to face her. "Any debt you owe, is owed to me. Do you agree?"

Megan didn't know what else to do. She knew the stories of her family's past as well as anyone who hadn't lived through it. She recognized Dante's claim and had heard enough of his story to know he wasn't making it up. He'd been the bloodletter her grandfathers had wronged so grievously. She really had no other choice.

"I agree." She stood to face him, then went down on one knee in the formal way. "I swear to do what you say to repay the debt my family owes you."

Dante dragged her to her feet before they could seal her oath.

"I consider the debt ended with your grandfathers. I never intended for it to carry over for generations."

She shook her head. "It must be this way, Dante. It is the *were* way. I'll serve you until the debt is paid."

"We'll discuss this later, Megan." Dante's lips firmed, and his words were clipped. She'd annoyed him it seemed, but she wouldn't let the matter drop. She'd talk more about it with him once they were free of this place and had a moment alone.

"This is all very interesting," Heath spoke into the tense silence. "But we have bigger fish to fry if the *Venifucus* is going to pose a threat."

"Agreed," Duncan said quickly. "With Megan free of the *Altor Custodis* obligation, perhaps she can be convinced to help us fight the good fight, eh?" He grinned at her, trying to lighten her spirits.

"Fighting evil is what my life has been all about. Or so I thought. I don't like being duped. Count me in."

"Excellent." Heath stood as he drained his glass. "Now, much as I'd like to continue this discussion, I have a previous obligation that cannot be put off. I know where to find you, Dante. Keep our little friend with you, but whatever you do, don't bite her." Heath took her hand and bent to place a kiss on her lips, reminding her without words of the night before. "I forgive you since it was not your intent to do me harm. Just remember you owe me, little wolf."

He turned and left the room, leaving her flabbergasted. Hugh cracked a smile when he met her gaze. He'd stayed behind, most likely to show them out of the mansion and make sure they went on their way.

Duncan took her arm and escorted her into the hall. A silent Dante followed behind and Hugh brought up the rear.

"A car has been arranged for you. I'll send a messenger over later with Megan's gown, your evening suits and anything else you may have left behind." Hugh was as efficient as they'd come to expect.

"Thank you." Duncan nodded at the man as he ushered them toward the front door.

Hugh gave Megan a smile and a kiss on the hand by way

of farewell before she followed Dante and Duncan down the front stairs and into the waiting limousine.

The ride back to Dante's only slightly less opulent brownstone was accomplished quickly and in silence. Megan's head was spinning, trying to grasp the idea that much of her life to date had been a waste of time. She'd studiously followed her family's dictates where the *Altor Custodis* was concerned, only to discover it had been for naught. Worse, with her memories restored of some very questionable missions she'd been sent on, to downright scary locations, she feared she'd actually been working for the wrong side all this time.

She felt used. Stupidly duped. Dumb as a stump for taking everything at face value all these years. Why hadn't she questioned anything? Was she truly that naïve?

Duncan must have sensed her mood as they mounted the stairs to Dante's brownstone. He pulled her aside in the foyer with a comforting hand on her shoulder.

"Don't take it so hard, lass. Older and wiser beings than you have been tricked before. That your keeper is part of the *Altor Custodis* only confirms my suspicions that august body has been corrupted far more deeply than we first believed. It's good to know the truth, no matter how painful it may be."

Megan sighed, recognizing the value of his counsel. "You're right, of course. It's just so hard to come to terms with the fact that all my efforts have been wasted."

"Not wasted, my dear. Your path brought you here, and with us, perhaps you can use your knowledge against those who tried to use you. Turning the tables on a foe always brings a good feeling. Try it. You'll see."

He left her with a smile and headed toward the back of the house, where the kitchen was located. Dante stood waiting for her, his expression solemn and dour. He said not a word as he opened the door to the downstairs sitting room and gestured for her to precede him.

He didn't speak as he lit a fire in the grate. Megan could feel the anger he harbored ready to bubble over.

"I'm sorry."

"What?" He whirled to face her.

"I'm sorry for what my grandfathers did. I'll do what I can to make it up to you. For what it's worth, they regretted their actions 'til their dying day."

"For the most part, I have put Erik's death behind me. I will not say it's not a sore point, but time and distance from the event have mellowed my perspective somewhat."

"Then why are you so upset?"

She didn't mean to blurt out the question foremost in her mind, yet that's just what she'd done. Everything had been turned upside down since the last time she'd been in this house, less than twenty-four hours ago.

"That bastard Dean bit you." Dante's eyes smoldered as he looked at her. Megan felt her breath hitch in fear, even as her blood heated with excitement at the possessive gleam in those angry eyes.

"I didn't ask for it. He just did it."

Dante moved closer, cupping her cheek in one large hand. "I know that, sweetheart. I'm not upset with you. Heath trespassed. He's the one I blame."

"He said he did it for my protection."

"Did he?" Dante seemed surprised by her words as he moved closer.

"Right before he struck, he whispered something. He said if I was under his protection, I'd be safe from the jackals gathered all around. That's what he called them."

"No doubt he knows his people better than I do. If he deemed it necessary to put a public claim on you, it must be worse than I thought, but he should have asked first. The bastard trespassed. He had no right."

"You'll get no argument from me."

"Good." Dante moved in until she could feel his breath against her cheeks.

One finger under her chin lifted her face to his and then his lips were on hers, his mouth claiming hers, his tongue tangling with hers in the sweetest bliss she'd ever tasted. This was different than all the kisses that had come before. This was a kiss of homecoming, of claiming, of...caring. She didn't dare think it was anything more.

CHAPTER SEVEN

Dante's hand went under her shirt and lifted. They broke apart only long enough for him to sweep the borrowed top off and throw it across the room. She'd had no bra under the gown the night before and the Deans hadn't extended their loaned clothing to underwear, so she was bare to Dante's touch, the way she liked. The way she was coming to crave.

His lips slid down her neck and lower to tease her breasts while his hands disposed of her pants and thong panty. She kicked off the shoes herself, not really caring where they landed. She just wanted all the fabric gone. As soon as her clothes were out of the way, her hands reached for Dante's. Together they worked him out of his shirt and then the door opened.

"Well, I can see I arrived just in time." Duncan moved into the room, closing the door behind him.

Dante's mouth sucked at the skin of her neck but he hadn't bitten her. At least not yet. But it was a damned close thing, and she hadn't even realized.

Megan jumped away from him with a gasp. He'd been this close to biting her and taking the poison in her blood into his body. She began to shake when she realized how close she'd almost come to hurting—possibly killing—him.

Duncan stepped over to her and held out one hand. She took it, wanting his help to keep Dante safe. She was naked, but nothing else mattered except keeping Dante safe from the taint in her blood. And besides, Duncan had already seen her nude last night. It was her naughtiest memory of all time.

"Come back here, Megan." Dante's tone brooked no argument. She wouldn't knowingly hurt him. She had to stand strong against the desire to comply.

"You can't bite me, Dante. I won't have your death on my conscience."

Dante looked like he was grinding his teeth, and his fists were clenched. Duncan's arms came around her waist as Dante moved closer.

"She's right, you know." Duncan's tone was calm. She felt the tremor of readiness in his hold, however. He was ready for anything an angry vampire could dish out. "There may yet be a way to salvage this situation, my friend."

"I need to feed, Duncan." The admission was ripped from Dante's lips and she could tell he wasn't happy about admitting his weakness. "Whether from her passion or her blood, I need it like I need my next breath."

"I see." Duncan's grip around her eased, and he turned her in his arms. "Our friend Dante is in a bad way, lass. Do you think we can help him?"

"We?" She thought she knew what he was asking. She looked at him with questions in her eyes, to be sure.

"Yes, lass. The three of us. Is that all right with you?" His smile was tender and told her the choice was hers. The real question was, how could she refuse? She felt the need in Dante and if she was being honest, she felt a similar need thrumming through her own body. It was a hunger—not precisely like the one that drove him—but a flaming arousal that must be answered. Slowly, she nodded.

"I think I can do that."

"Good." Duncan leaned forward and kissed her brow. "Now go to him. I'll watch over you both."

Warily, Megan walked toward Dante. He lifted one hand, and she paused for a second before she took it and allowed him to reel her into his hard body.

His lips met hers, and she could feel the sharpness of his fangs. He kept them in check for now. It was clear he was holding back, ruthlessly controlling his instincts. She wanted to make him forget the problems facing them. She wanted him to think only of pleasure, not of the danger. She was certain Duncan would save him from going too far and biting her. Duncan was as strong as Dante in his way and could be trusted to keep them safe.

Perhaps that's why she didn't object to him being part of this new, naughty sexual encounter. Or maybe it was because he was a handsome man who'd been kind and gentle the night before, even as he sent her senses reeling.

There was something vulnerable about Duncan. He was the only one of his kind she'd ever met, and she would bet there weren't many others like him in the world. Yet he was a strong man who appealed to her on a visceral level. She'd never been surrounded by so many handsome men in her life, having spent all of it avoiding supernaturals. *Weres* were hot in an earthy way. Vampires had that magical mojo that made them nearly irresistible—and Dante topped that list, of course—but she was discovering that half-fey had a gentler appeal and a magic all their own.

Dante kissed her and all thoughts fled as his hands roamed over her body. He knew where to touch, how much pressure to apply, to make her squirm in rising pleasure. She barely noticed when he moved her toward the big couch that faced the fireplace. She registered the fact that Dante's fangs had dropped even more as his tongue teased her belly button.

He stood her before him as he sat on the edge of the couch, running his big hands over her ass and farther down her legs. He coaxed her legs apart and insinuated his hands within, using his fingers to good advantage, playing her pussy like a master plays a Stradivarius. She hummed just like that priceless violin under the stroking sweeps of his fingers, keening with each move inside her slick channel, each teasing foray of his thumb against her clit. She would do anything for him at that moment. Anything he wanted.

Dante tugged her forward as his lips descended. His fingers spread her and his mouth moved in. She gasped as his tongue touched her clit, only to be followed by a long swipe down the folds that wept for him.

A mouth at her breast shocked her until she realized Duncan had moved closer, both to watch over Dante's tempted teeth and to join the fun. She welcomed him, needing something to hold on to while Dante's tongue claimed her below. She clutched Duncan's shoulders, tugging at the shirt that he hadn't yet removed. She wanted it gone.

Duncan seemed to understand her desperate movements, breaking away momentarily to tug his shirt off over his head. It joined the other discarded garments on the floor some distance away. Gratified to be able to touch his skin, Megan stroked over his thick muscles as he moved in to kiss her.

He had a talented mouth that was nearly as devastating in its impact as Dante's. Duncan kissed her with a gentle respect and tender longing that made her senses spin. He fingered her nipples while he kissed her, and Dante pulled her closer with demanding hands and his voracious tongue. She jumped when his fingers slid from her pussy to move farther back.

Duncan broke the kiss, looking down at her with an amused gleam in his eye. He looked over her shoulder to inspect Dante's progress.

"Feel good, lass?" he whispered in her ear. "I can tell it does."

"Duncan," she moaned as Dante's finger pressed into her from behind, his tongue flicking over her clit. "I need—"

"I know what you need, Megan." Duncan bent to lick at her breasts again, sucking one nipple deep into his mouth and pulling on the other with his talented fingers.

She came, crying out at the sensations racing through her body. Both men held her up while her knees trembled and her body shook.

When she had settled down a bit, Dante moved back, a devilish grin on his face as he stood. Duncan deferred to Dante in this sexy interlude, watching over them both.

"Bend over, sweetheart." Dante's voice was gruff as he moved her body to his liking. She ended up with her ass in the air, her hands braced on the arm of the couch.

She heard the rasp of a zipper and then Dante's hand was on her ass, guiding her back as he moved forward. She felt the tip of him, teasing the folds between her legs before finding the spot she needed him to go. She was desperate for him, for the feel of him possessing her body as only he could.

Dante slid inside her, stretching her slowly, making her want to move to force him to go faster, but he was in control. He was the master of her body at this moment.

He pulled out, then pushed in a little farther, repeating the process several times before he was seated fully inside her. She growled as he made her wait, but deep down she knew the wait would be worth it. Dante was a fantastic lover.

Dante began a rhythm that made her mouth water. She moaned as he slid home with force, pushing her forward over the arm of the couch.

"Open your eyes, lass." Duncan's voice whispered past her ear as she complied with a start. She hadn't even realized she'd closed them.

Duncan stood in front of her, his hard cock on level with her face and she knew what he wanted. She wanted it too. But this was Dante's show. She turned to look at him over her shoulder and was stirred by the harsh expression of concentration on his handsome face.

"Dante?" She wasn't sure what she was asking. She had his massive cock in her body. Still, she wanted more. More of him. All of him.

It didn't make any sense.

She settled for his permission. His instruction. His dominance.

"Suck him off, Megan." His eyes met hers with a hot, speaking look. She could tell the thought of watching her suck Duncan's cock turned him on as much as it did her.

She licked her lips with a promise in her gaze before turning back to Duncan. He held his thick, hard cock in one hand, rubbing under the head with one finger as he moved closer to her mouth.

"Do you want it, lass? How bad do you want it?"

"Give it to me, Duncan. I want it bad."

He didn't make her wait. He stepped forward and touched the tip of his cock to her eagerly waiting lips. She took him in and licked around the head to tease the spot he'd been stroking, then took him deep as she heard Dante groan.

Both men worked her, sliding into her wet places, making her want to come again even though she'd just had a shattering orgasm only a few minutes ago. She began to tremble and both men were there, holding her steady, helping her keep the rhythm they set. Duncan had one hand on her head, guiding her as he began to thrust into her mouth, fucking it like Dante fucked her pussy.

Dante's hands were on her hips, holding her up. One slipped around to her tummy, supporting her and dipping lower to tease her clit as his pace increased. She felt him bend over her and Duncan's hand shot out.

"Don't do it, man."

"I need..." Dante's voice held desperation. For her part, she was too much on the edge to worry about anything except her need to come.

"Take it from me." Duncan's voice was harsh and commanding. He held out one arm to Dante and it took only a moment for him to snarl and latch on with his teeth. Dante bit into Duncan's wrist near the side of her face, where she could see everything.

Rather than turning her off, witnessing the act of Dante's vampire nature did the exact opposite. She came around his cock as she watched him dine on Duncan's half-fey blood. At almost the same moment, Duncan came in her mouth. She swallowed eagerly as Dante followed only seconds later, coming deep inside her in warm jets of ecstasy.

The three of them remained locked like that for long moments, sharing bliss in a way that was unprecedented in Megan's admittedly limited experience. She moaned as Dante sealed the punctures in Duncan's wrist. Moments later, the half-fey warrior withdrew and sank into a nearby chair.

"I'll be damned," Duncan panted as he recovered. "I forgot the whammy you bloodletters can pack when you feed while you fuck."

Dante pulled out of her body and turned her to sit in his lap as he claimed the couch. She had no energy of her own while her body recovered from the most orgasmic encounter yet. Just when she'd thought there was no way to top what happened the night before, Dante had to prove her wrong in the most delicious way.

She lay across his lap as he reclined lazily, stroking her bare skin absently as he talked to Duncan.

"So why the change in plans? Why did you let me feed from you again, Duncan? I thought the whole reason you were here was to watch over me until the last magical whammy you let me have wore off." His words were laced with satisfaction he couldn't completely suppress and a kind of drunken slur that made her want to kiss him silly.

"I got to thinking..." Duncan began.

"Always a dangerous sign," Dante quipped as he cupped her breast and played with her nipple.

"Quite so, my friend." Duncan chuckled. "After what happened last night I thought you could use a booster shot of otherrealm magic with everything that's going on."

"What? You're not afraid I'll run mad with my new superpowers?" Dante's raised eyebrow was softened by a wry smile.

"If you were going to do that, you'd have done it long before now. Besides, I think stranger things are in store for you both." Duncan nodded at the two of them, and then his expression went fierce. "I want you to be ready for anything."

"Sounds ominous." Megan tried to reclaim the lazy teasing of their earlier conversation, but it was lost.

"I didn't mean to ruin the moment." Duncan stood and collected his clothing as he moved toward the door. "I'll be off. I think you're well enough fed to be trusted not to sip on our little friend now, eh?" Duncan winked at Megan as he left the room, not bothering to dress before he stepped into the hall and closed the door behind him.

Dante was quiet for long moments as he held her, stroking her skin almost absently.

"I almost lost control and bit you, Megan." His voice whispered over her bare skin, chilling her. "I'm sorry, sweetheart. If not for Duncan, you'd have another poisoning on your conscience."

"I don't know how you can be so casual about this." She sat up, facing him as the thought of him being poisoned by her blood sent shivers down her spine. "You can't ever bite me, Dante. I'm a wolf. Just pretend I have rabies."

Dante laughed out loud at her sharp words, and she joined in a moment later, realizing how silly she'd sounded.

"I'd love to see you in wolf form, sweetheart. Isn't the moon nearly full? Don't you have to change on the full moon?"

He sounded eager to see her furry alter ego. It was the first time in her life she could share that wild side of her with anyone outside her family. It went without saying, she'd never changed form with a lover. The thought was tantalizing.

"Honestly I don't feel the pull of the moon as strongly as my mother did. Whatever else I am seems to dull the effect. I do like to run every once in a while and the full moon is as good a time as any, but I can shift easily anytime."

"You are a marvel. Instead of being weaker than a full *were*, in many respects you are stronger." He touched her face with tender fingers, stroking her cheek and the look in his eyes was electrifying.

She blinked and stood, moving back so she was facing him.

"Watch."

Her purred command was sexier than anything he'd ever heard. Her next move came unexpectedly, even though he'd asked her to do it. She was just that distracting.

She began to change. Her body elongated into the fierce half-shift form he'd seen her in once before and stayed there much longer than the shifts he remembered seeing so many years ago. It was as if she was stuck halfway.

He knew many *were* warriors practiced holding the half-shift deliberately. It was their most powerful form and useful in battle, but this didn't look deliberate. It looked more like she was fighting to get to her pure wolf form, not as if she was fighting to hold the half-shift.

Maybe that was natural for her as a half-*were*, but Dante wasn't so sure.

Finally, she managed the full shift and shook her fur as if becoming accustomed to her skin. She padded up to him and licked his hand. He reached out, rubbing her silky coat.

"You feel like mink, sweetheart. You're gorgeous." And it wasn't a lie. She was petite and powerful, soft and sexy in a way he hadn't expected. He'd never really been attracted to a *were* female. He wanted nothing more than to run his hands all over her fur, stroking her softness while they slept.

And then when they woke, and she was back in her human form, he'd make love to her for hours and hours. It was a delicious fantasy. One that he might be able to make reality, given a little cooperation.

She stepped back and shifted again. Once more she paused a painfully long time in that difficult half-shift form until she retook her human shape.

"Does it drain you?"

"The shift? No, not at all." She rejoined him on the couch, sitting at his side.

"You hold half-shift a very long time. That's difficult even for the *were* warriors I used to know. It drained them to stay in that form. They used to practice maintaining it and even for the most gifted alphas, it was difficult."

"It is?" She looked honestly surprised. Yet another thing to marvel about her.

He drew her close. "It is." He kissed her shoulder. "You are a beautiful wolf, Megan."

"I've never shown anyone before. Well, except my mom when I was first learning."

He pulled her more securely into his arms and rose, taking her with him. He left the room, using his mind to open the doors in his path and strode toward the center of the house, where he kept an aboveground bedroom to maintain the illusion of normalcy. It was sunproofed and contained a hidden passage that led to his domain belowground. He knew it would be easier for her to accept him if he didn't go out of his way to point out their vast differences. At least for now.

"Where are we going?"

"All the way to heaven and back if you'll let me have my way." He smiled at her and was rewarded by her look of desire.

"You have to promise me one thing."

"Anything. Within reason, of course," he added in a teasing tone.

"You can't bite me. If you try, I'll scream bloody murder until Duncan comes to stop you. I may even bite you myself."

He liked that she was worried for him. He saw under her fierce façade to the very real fear she had that he'd lose control and poison himself on her blood.

"Don't worry. Half-fey blood is like a drug to my kind. I'm sated for a good long while with Duncan's help. I think I can control myself."

"You'd better do more than *think* it!"

He bent down to kiss her as they entered his bedroom. "I love your concern for me, sweetheart. It's been too long since anyone cared if I lived or died."

"I care, Dante. Probably too much, given the circumstances."

He kissed her then, slamming the door shut with a stray thought as he laid her on his bed. He only used this bed once in a while. He kept his wardrobe here, and there was a luxurious bathroom that he loved attached to the bedroom. He'd show her the delights of his tropical bath paradise later, he promised himself. She'd love it too, he was sure. It would, no doubt, appeal to her wild side.

Dante settled over her on the soft mattress, glad of the chance to finally fuck her in a bed. He'd take his time—what time he had left before dawn—and make love to her slowly. He wanted to savor every taste of her skin, every gasp from her lips.

"If you didn't realize it before now," he whispered against her skin as he nipped his way down her body, "you're very special to me, Megan." He paused to look up at her and grin. "Even if you were sent here to spy on me."

"Oh, Dante, you'll never know how much I regret the things that led me here." Her eyebrows drew together, her lovely face frowning with worry as he soothed her.

"I don't regret your being here for one second, Megan. I haven't had this much fun in centuries."

"Fun?" She sent him a puzzled look. "You have a strange definition of the word fun."

"Believe me, you are fun of the most pleasurable kind, my dear." He returned to nibbling her body, teasing her with his sheathed fangs as he trailed them lightly over the skin of her belly. Her muscles clenched as he moved lower. He parted her legs with gentle hands, feeling satisfaction as she shivered under his touch.

"Dante?" She sounded delightfully unsure.

"Don't worry, sweetheart. I'm right here, and I'm going to take my time showing you everything I've been dreaming of doing to your delectable young body."

He moved in closer then, trailing his fingers across the insides of her thighs. Puckering his lips, he blew a soft breath across the delicate folds of her pussy, spreading her nether lips with his fingers and teasing within. He kept his touch as light as a feather, his warm breath visibly exciting the small nubbin at the apex of her thighs.

With a satisfied smile, he lowered his head, his tongue searching for and finding her tight little clit. She moaned as he licked, teasing the aroused nub until she was shuddering in his arms.

He wanted more.

Dante reached down and slid one finger through the slick folds to rim her opening, seeking her warmth and wanting to feel the inner clenching of her muscles as he excited her beyond all reason. His finger slid inside while his lips closed around her clit, sucking lightly. He used his teeth gently, just enough to let her know who was in control of her pleasure and was rewarded with her pussy contracting in rapid motions around his finger.

He added another finger, twisting as he used his tongue to zero in on her clit. His other hand moved lower to tease her back entrance, shoving in with careful movements until he was fully inside.

She came like a rocket, clenching around his hands and nearly bucking him off the bed, much to his amusement. She cried out, moaning his name, music to his ears.

He didn't give her time to regroup. Instead, he rose to his knees between her legs, taking just a moment to stare at the bounty before him.

"You're beautiful." He leaned over her, cupping her luscious breasts and taking time to kiss each turgid peak, using his tongue on her until she began to squirm under him. He knew the signs of her pleasure now, and he knew she was ready for more.

Lifting away only enough to guide himself into her tender pussy, he slid home with a satisfied groan. He stayed there, looking into her eyes as they joined, feeling the electricity of the moment fill them both.

"God, you feel good around me." He leaned in to lick a path up her neck then nibbled on her earlobe until she giggled.

"You feel good too, Dante. Make it even better. I dare you." Her teasing words brought him up to meet her gaze. The devilish light in her eyes warmed him.

"That's a dare I'm more than happy to take. What do I get if I win? Besides the obvious, of course."

She pretended to think it over, her smile widening. "How about more of the same? I'm discovering I'm a sucker for you, Dante d'Angleterre." Her expression grew serious at her soft words. "I've never felt like this before."

"Good." He kissed her lips just once, drawing back to meet her gaze. "Neither have I."

He began to move, recalling his plan to draw out their time together. It was a good plan, and he'd do his damnedest to see it come to fruition. He stroked gently at first, long drags out and even more deliciously slow thrusts in. She was whimpering in need long before he was ready to let them both come.

"Stay with me, my dear. We have a long way to go before I'll let you off the hook."

"Now that's…" she panted, "…a new word for it."

Her humor startled him into chuckling as he paused just for a moment in his sensual torture.

"You seem to like my hook—" he pushed into her with more force and held there, "—rather well."

"I *love* your hook, Dante."

He could see she was on the brink, and he decided to give her a little more. He withdrew, grinding home in three quick, hard strokes. That's all it took for her to reach another bright climax, shuddering around him as she cried out and shivered.

He wasn't through with her yet. Not by a long shot.

He kept himself relatively still inside her while she quieted. He knew she was only on a plateau of pleasure. With a little enticement she could be coaxed to an even greater peak than those that had come before. And he was just the man to do it.

With great deliberation, he began to move again. The slow strokes built up to harder, more rapid pulses within her until she was crying out on every short thrust. He was adamant that they would come together this time. He used all his finesse as he pulsed his hips into the cradle of her soft thighs. When he felt the crisis approach, he spared only a moment to kiss her, wanting to capture her screams of delight as she came with him in the most delicious orgasm he'd ever beheld.

Her psychic energies bathed him in her feminine power. Already sated by Duncan's magical blood, he found room to drink in her sexual ecstasy, wanting more of her with every pulse of his cock inside her.

He came as she did, emptying his balls into her waiting womb, glad this woman—this special woman—shared this moment with him.

He drew back from her lips, wanting to watch her face in the aftermath of the greatest orgasm they had yet shared.

"You are beautiful, *ma cherie.*"

"*Mmm.* French?" Her eyes were half-closed, her voice weak with pleasure, a smile playing about her luscious lips.

"I spent some time in Normandy once upon a time." He bent to kiss her lips gently. "Thank you for this, Megan. I have not enjoyed something—or someone—as much in too long to recall."

"Me neither." She smiled at him, pulsing her hips upward as if trying to capture this moment for all time. "You're one hell of a lover, Dante."

"I aim to please," he joked.

"Your aim is dead on, cowboy."

He chuckled, rolling so they stayed entwined, but his weight was off her. He wanted to stay within her warmth as long as he could. He could see she was worn out. He'd done that to her. Megan's eyes closed and within moments she was asleep, leaving him to marvel at her petite body and beautiful face. She was lovely in sleep, so innocent, yet so alluring. He could stare at her for hours.

And that was the thought that made him get up.

He had no claim to this woman. In any case, she'd been sent to him as a spy and her family was one that had done him personal harm and caused great injustice. He'd have to tread carefully until he was absolutely certain of her.

He left the room quietly, letting her sleep. He had a few more things to get done before dawn. First on the list was a talk with Duncan.

CHAPTER EIGHT

"She shifted in front of you? Why?" Duncan looked concerned.

"I asked her to." Dante shrugged, knowing Duncan would probably read something into his actions, but not really caring. "It was as if something was blocking her from merging fully with her wolf side. Something weakened her shift."

Duncan contemplated his words. "That's not good. I think her keeper's hold over her is stronger than we thought."

"As I feared." Dante hated that she was under the influence of someone so evil. "Is there any way to break his hold? I'll be happy to kill him when we find him. I know the magic will end with him, but it's going to take some time to get the bastard. What can we do before then?"

"You're not going to like it." Duncan made a pained face as he sighed.

"But I suspect you will." Dante managed to make a joke though he thought he knew what his friend was talking about. "I, of all people, know the power there is in sex. The energy of the act is sustenance to my kind, and I've heard you fey practice a different sort of sex magic. You've already been treating her with it."

"Not in concentrated form. I didn't know the problem extended to her wolf. For any shifter, that is a very serious symptom. More serious than I thought the problem was, I'm sorry to say."

"I didn't suspect either until I saw her shift." Dante thought about what she meant to him and the hot way she responded to both him and Duncan when they'd taken her together.

"She'll have to accept me in every way. Can you deal with that?"

Dante tried to be casual but the truth was, the idea of Duncan fucking his woman mattered more than it should. He wasn't sure when he'd started thinking of her as his woman. The thought wasn't as startling as it should have been either. Dante was in deep, but he didn't see any way out. He'd have to play the hand he was dealt and do the best he could with it.

"I don't think she'll mind."

"But will you?" Apparently Duncan saw through his casual words.

"I want what's best for her. Right now she is a danger to all of us—herself included. The longer her keeper's control lasts, the stronger it is. We've already begun the process of weakening it with good results. Until we can find the bastard and free her completely, logically, we should continue to try to weaken the magic he used on her."

"Logically yes, but what about emotionally? I know you're more attached to her than you expected. I suspect there are reasons for that. However, until the threat of her keeper is removed and the taint in her blood gone, you will never be free to pursue the attraction between you fully."

"Then lessening and ultimately removing the threat will have to suffice for now. It's a sound strategy."

Duncan didn't look happy with his answer, but Dante was too raw emotionally to start discussing his feelings. He, who had steered clear of emotional entanglements for centuries, had a hard time with emotions of any sort and wasn't ready to start talking about them to anyone. Not even Duncan.

"We'll start in earnest tomorrow night then. When necessary, you will continue to snack on my blood. The stronger we both are, the more chance we have of nullifying her keeper's hold."

"Aren't you worried about the power I'll gain by drinking from you?"

"I meant what I said before, Dante. Trouble is brewing and about to bubble over. I fear you'll need every advantage you can get, and if my blood saves you—and others, myself included—from the *Venifucus* threat, then it's worth the risk. Besides, I trust you. I've always trusted you to do the right thing, my old friend, but I had to reassess your character after all those years Underhill. I was glad to find that you're the same man of honor I knew before. If anything, you've only improved with the trials placed in your path."

Dante moved uncomfortably under Duncan's praise. Dante knew he was nothing special. In fact, he'd made more than his share of mistakes—the most recent almost cost the *were*lords their lives and that of their new mate. That wasn't just a mistake. That had been a huge blunder, and Dante still felt remorse over what he'd done and the things he'd allowed to happen on his watch. He'd been a fool to trust Patrick Vabian as far as he had.

"I hope I can prove worthy of your trust, old friend."

"You already have, Dante. Never fear." Duncan's fey smile held more knowledge than it should have. Then again, the magical bastard had always seen things Dante had no way of knowing. It was annoying but could also be very helpful, so he let it slide.

It was settled. He'd continue to allow Duncan to make love to Megan. They'd continue in their triad relationship until she was free of her keeper, and Duncan would continue to feed him his half-fey blood. While the power of Duncan's blood was delicious, Dante was shocked to realize all he really wanted was a taste of Megan. She was fast becoming an obsession.

Any bloodletter would be thrilled to have a half-fey willing to supply them with more power than any immortal should rightly have. Yet it paled in comparison to the thought of feeding from Megan. That's what he truly wanted—and it was forbidden until she was free of the poison.

Maybe it was just a case of the forbidden apple seeming the sweetest. Dante wasn't so sure. He also wasn't so sure about continuing the ménage relationship between himself, Megan and Duncan, but there really was no alternative that would be as safe for all concerned, magically speaking. He had to allow it. It rankled more than a bit. Still, it had to be done. For Megan's sake.

The part that annoyed him most was that he didn't think she'd mind one bit. He knew she'd enjoyed the three-way they'd already shared, and even the four-way with Heath. Of course, that would never happen again. It was bad enough he had to share her with Duncan. Heath had tasted her forbidden fruit for the last time, Dante vowed.

And as soon as she was free of her keeper, Dante would claim her, body and soul.

The thought should have surprised him. Instead it just made him feel warm inside his heart, in places that hadn't been warm in centuries. He didn't examine it too closely. It was enough to have made the decision.

Once she was free, she would be his and his alone. For as long as it lasted.

*

Just after noon on the following day, Megan was taking it easy, reading a magazine while she sat on the couch in the front parlor of Dante's gorgeously appointed brownstone. It was one of the public rooms of the house, with long old-fashioned windows that let in the golden sunlight. The entire house was beautiful, but this room held special appeal. At night, the windows afforded a lovely view of the small park across the street and by day it was a warm, sunny spot in which to curl up and read.

With no warning, a window shattered and a flaming bottle landed in Megan's lap. She fumbled the Molotov cocktail, thanking the Goddess that it hadn't shattered all over her. Using her native *were* agility, she raced for the kitchen sink, dumping the flaming torch into it as quickly as she could.

"Duncan!" She screamed his name through the house, knowing he'd be awake at this hour and able to help her. She reached for the fire extinguisher kept next to the stove and wasted a few precious moments trying to figure out how to operate it.

By the time she had it going, Duncan raced into the room, wet from a shower with a damp towel wrapped hastily around his hips. He took in the scene with a quick glance.

"This extinguisher isn't doing any good," she cried as the café curtains on the window above the sink caught fire and began to glow with an eerie green flame.

"Get behind me." Duncan's commanding voice carried over the increasing roar of the fire.

This wasn't a normal fire. It spread quickly and more voraciously than any regular flame, snaking over stainless steel and granite in search of something flammable.

Water began to spit from previously hidden fixtures in the ceiling. Dante had zoned fire protection equipment throughout the house that had finally kicked in, but it did no good against the green flame. Megan peered over Duncan's shoulder as the flames spread.

"Cover your ears," he instructed looking back at her only once. "This could get loud."

It already was. Something about the green flame wasn't right. It was louder than regular fire, creepier and seemingly alive. It was magical, and it wasn't a good kind of magic. Its smoke smelled foul, like rotting flesh and it scorched everything it touched in the once beautiful kitchen.

She felt a shift in the energy of the room as Duncan did something. He was summoning his magic, she realized a split second later, when she saw him clad not in a skimpy bath towel, but in full plate armor that gleamed from head to toe. He faced the flame, his magical self—his true self—girded for battle against the foul sorcery of the green fire.

116

Megan staggered back as the room erupted in a whirlwind. She grabbed on to the doorframe, her hair whipping around her head as Duncan called the element of air to him to snuff out the fire. That, combined with the water still raining down, whirling in the tempest Duncan created, made it feel like a hurricane inside the kitchen as the rumble of magic reached a crescendo that was near deafening.

She held on to the doorframe with one hand, covering one ear with the other. She smashed the other side of her head into her shoulder to try to shield that ear as best she could while struggling to stand against the tempest Duncan had created in the kitchen.

The fire roared in one last attempt at life, reaching for Duncan. His armor repulsed it as the wind howled and the rain beat down upon it, stamping it out for good. Little by little, the tempest receded. Duncan's glowing silver armor disappeared as if it had never been and he turned to her, still wet, wearing the bath towel, his hair twisted in every which direction and a fierce grin on his face.

"That's one way to wake up."

Megan was forestalled from answering as the door to the wine cellar opened, and Dante stumbled into view. He looked terrible, weakened by the sun that streamed in the kitchen window. She noted he was careful to stay out of its path as he hung back in the dark space behind the doorway, peering out.

"What happened?"

Megan went to him, practically running into his arms. "Somebody threw a magic spiked Molotov cocktail through your window. The damned thing landed in my lap, and I brought it in here and tossed it in the sink. Then all hell broke loose, and Duncan came and fought the green flames." She turned, trembling now in the aftermath, to face her savior. "Thank you, Duncan. I've never seen fire behave that way."

"And so you shouldn't have. This was no earthly fire. It was hellfire."

"Son of a bitch," Dante cursed.

"I'm going to get dressed so I can face our friendly

117

neighborhood fire department with some dignity." Duncan left the kitchen, clutching his towel.

"The fire department is coming?" She turned to ask Dante.

"The house is rigged up to the local station. I had top of the line fire detection equipment installed when I bought the place. Fire has spelled the end of many an incautious immortal." He kissed her once, as if reassuring himself. "I'll meet you in the living room. Go on and let the firemen in before they take a hatchet to my front door."

He grinned at her even though he'd looked so tired she wanted to tell him to go back to sleep and let her handle everything. Of course, she was only a guest in this house. He was the owner, and he would have to answer the firemen's questions and assure them everything was all right.

How he would do it without entering the kitchen, she had no idea. The sun didn't stream in as strongly through the kitchen window as it did in the front, but there were patches of sunlight in the room and no way to cover the window. Both the café curtains and shade had been burned to cinders.

Dante gave her a little push toward the hallway while he retreated into the labyrinth he inhabited beneath the stately home. He closed and locked the door to the "wine cellar" behind him while Megan went to answer the front door.

The firemen were prompt.

Six burly men towered over her as she led them down the hall toward the scorched kitchen. They were huge and imposing and each one sniffed her as he passed.

Dammit! They were *were*. Wolves in fact. The local pack and, if she wasn't much mistaken, their Alpha was bringing up the rear. He paused to stand next to her as the rest of his team inspected the kitchen to be certain all traces of fire had been extinguished.

"You're new," he commented, looking her up and down.

"Just visiting," she said noncommittally.

"Fire's good and out, boss," one of the men reported after a thorough inspection. Some of the others were taking down the burnt curtains and shade and placing them in the empty trashcan. "We'll take the burnt stuff outside, just to be sure. Looks like the thing that started it is in the sink. You'll want to get a look, Alpha. It's not good."

"You don't say?" The big wolf's eyes lit with interest and suspicion as he looked from his subordinate to the scorched sink and back to her. "So this isn't just your ordinary kitchen fire, is it?"

"I'd say definitely not," Duncan answered, finally making an appearance.

He was fully dressed, his hair sexily askew. It was dryer than it had been the last time she had seen him. She realized then that she had to be an absolute mess. Her hair was wet and wild from the sprinkler and the rainstorm Duncan had conjured indoors.

The kitchen floor was wet and slippery and the expensive sprinklers were still deployed from their hidey-holes in the ceiling. Thankfully, they were no longer spitting water in every direction. She looked around at the destruction of what had been a designer-quality kitchen in despair. While she was taking it all in, Duncan and the fire chief walked to the kitchen sink to get a look at the magical Molotov cocktail that had started this whole fiasco.

"Don't touch it," Duncan said sharply when the fire chief reached out to pick up the bottle. "It's more than it seems."

The big fireman turned to look at Duncan as his men positioned themselves around the room in a clearly protective, somewhat combative posture. Duncan didn't back down but seemed, instead, to become bigger as his magic asserted itself. The wolf cocked his head as he took Duncan's measure and finally signaled to his men to stand down.

In fact, he sent them out to the truck, telling them to return to the station while he settled matters here. Megan was surprised, but one look at the Alpha told her he knew what he was about. If he couldn't handle this situation, he didn't deserve to be Alpha of such a big, fierce group of *were*wolves and they all knew it. With nods of respect, his men left.

119

The Alpha looked from her to Duncan and back again. "We need to talk." His tone brooked no argument.

"Why don't we go into the living room?" Megan tried to act the gracious hostess. The sad truth was, she was shaking in her boots. She'd never had any contact with an Alpha male of her kind and this one scared the bejeezus out of her.

Thankfully, Dante was already there when she opened the sliding door that led to the interior, windowless living room. She went in, followed by Duncan. The *were*wolf, however, stopped on the threshold in surprise.

Dante turned to him, holding a glass of burgundy as they took each other's measure.

"Be welcome in my home, Alpha," Dante finally said, breaking the standoff and moving to sit beside Megan. He put his arm over the back of the couch behind her head in a proprietary way that wasn't lost on the fireman. "I am Dante d'Angleterre, owner of this house."

"Kevin McElroy, Alpha of the East Side wolf pack. You must be a really old one to be up and around at this hour of the day." The fireman came into the room and stood a moment more before claiming one of the armchairs for himself.

Dante shrugged offhandedly. "I do what needs to be done when guests are attacked in my domain."

"Then the lone one is your guest?" Kevin nodded his chin in Megan's direction.

"She is, and she is under my protection as well as that of Sir Heathclif Dean."

The *were*wolf sat back in his chair and gave her a speculative glance. "So you're the one who caused such a ruckus at the vampire ball the other night."

Megan was shocked by the knowledge in his eyes.

"And how did a wolf hear about the doings of bloodletters?" Duncan asked. He'd sunk into one of the overstuffed chairs. The *were*wolf's attention turned to scrutinize him again.

"I know one who likes to walk on the wild side. She told

me about the scene Dean made biting a strange *were* and asked me what I knew about the wolf. I don't think she believed me when I said I knew nothing."

"Walk on the wild side?" Megan repeated, confused.

"An immortal who likes to have sex with *weres*," Dante clarified. "There aren't many, and they do it in secret for the most part. There's a stigma attached on both sides, though I remember when such relationships were more accepted."

"So your immortal girlfriend wanted to know about Megan?" Duncan brought the conversation back on track.

"In the normal course of business any wolf who comes into my territory for any length of time would at least have the courtesy of letting me know she was here. You should have checked in with the pack running this territory when you decided to stay for more than a day. It's only polite." Kevin's tone was chastising, and it irked Megan.

"I don't owe you any courtesy. Your kind gave up all rights to dictate my actions when you banished my family." She hadn't meant to get worked up but felt an odd sense of relief once the words were said.

"So you're not just a loner. You're one of the forgotten?" Kevin frowned. "This complicates matters. No wonder you've taken up with a bloodletter and a...uh...what are you? Mage?" he asked Duncan, clearly stumped.

"Half-fey." Duncan inclined his head regally. "I put out the fire when more mundane means did not suffice."

"Which brings us back to the problem at hand. Someone has it in for one or all of you."

Dante sat forward, clearly interested. "How do you know?"

"One of my pack likes to pretend she's a stray so she can keep an eye on some of the more vulnerable homeless who frequent the park across the way. She saw someone lob a Molotov cocktail into your window. She called me right before the alarm came in from your system."

"Did she see the person?"

"Shiny blonde with a bob haircut, she said. Female. Drove

away in a black Porsche."

"Son of a…" Megan swore. "Her again."

"Who is she?" the fireman asked.

"We don't know," Dante replied. "She lobbed a few fireballs at me outside a nightclub the night Megan and I met." He dropped his hand from the back of the couch around her shoulders, squeezing once, bringing her closer to his side. "Megan took a hit meant for me, and I brought her here to recover."

"We can only assume Dante's the target since hellfire is impossible to stop by normal means and fire is one of the few things that can kill his kind," Duncan added. "Plus the timing would have made it next to impossible for Dante to escape a house fire. It's still several hours 'til sunset."

"Hellfire, you say?" Kevin's blue gaze turned thoughtful.

"No doubt about it. I've seen it before, a long time ago. It's not good to see it in use again. It tells me a larger game is afoot." Duncan's tone sounded ominous.

"How so?" Kevin wanted to know.

"For some time now, we've had an idea that the *Venifucus* are back in operation. Or perhaps they never really left. Regardless, they're now ramping up their efforts to return dark magic to this realm. Hellfire is one of the tools they used in ancient days, and it hasn't been seen on this Earth for many generations. To see it now only confirms my worst fears. This, taken in conjunction with the attacks on the *were*lords and their new mate, which Dante and I witnessed firsthand, is very bad news indeed."

"You're *that* Dante?" Kevin asked, blinking in surprise. "We got a safe passage dispatch about you and your friend from the Lords not too long ago. Surprised the heck out of us when we saw a bloodletter had friends in the highest possible places, but I figured our paths would never cross."

Dante raised his glass in salute. "Never say never."

"So what did you do to get on the Lords' good side?" Kevin asked with only a hint of suspicion.

"Betrayed them, switched sides when I figured out what

was going on, then helped save their lives and that of their mate." Dante shrugged as he ticked off the list of events.

"Don't forget how you helped catch the mage responsible," Duncan added helpfully.

"Indeed." Dante grinned at his friend then turned to Kevin. "You know, the usual."

The big *were*wolf actually smiled. "I suspect it's a long story for another time. Right now, I'd like to know how you ended up playing host to one of the forgotten." His expression grew serious, almost apologetic, when he looked at Megan again. "And perhaps more importantly, what did your family do to merit such a terrible sanction. As a rule, our society rarely issues such harsh punishments."

"Having never been part of *were* society, I'm sure I wouldn't know." Megan bristled under Kevin's scrutiny. She didn't have anything to prove to him.

Dante took her hand, squeezing it gently in comfort. "Megan's grandfathers sanctioned the murder of an innocent human firemage named Erik. He was a good friend of mine." Dante paused, and she squeezed his hand this time. "His death sparked the Great Chicago Fire." He paused as Kevin whistled through his teeth. "For their transgressions, they were banished. They passed the burden of redemption to Megan's mother, and thence to her. We've only just discovered the connection ourselves."

"Quite a coincidence, her showing up on your doorstep," Kevin commented.

"It wasn't a coincidence," Duncan stepped in. "She was sent to spy on Dante by someone I believe to be a *Venifucus* mole in the *Altor Custodis* operation."

"I was briefed on the recent trouble with the mage who claimed to be *Venifucus*. The Lords impressed it upon all of the major pack leaders in our last teleconference that the threat was real. Honestly I never expected to see anything in my neck of the woods. At least not so soon."

"Probably my fault, for deciding to visit my place in New York," Dante admitted. "But Duncan's been gone a long time, and he wanted to see the Big Apple again. It was as good a destination as any after our adventure in Montana."

"I tend to believe the Lady guides all our paths. Perhaps She meant for you to be here, in this place, at this time." Kevin surprised Megan with the depth of his faith. She wouldn't have expected such an imposing man to believe so strongly.

"There may be some merit to what you say," Duncan put in. "I don't really believe in coincidence." He looked at Megan with one eyebrow raised. "Someone sent her here to spy on the very man her family had wronged so grievously all those years ago. I'm willing to bet her keeper is based somewhere nearby, though she's been placed under a very strong compulsion not to divulge any information that could help us identify him."

"What makes you think he's nearby?" Kevin leaned forward.

"Timing," Dante said absently, clearly thinking through his answer as he gave it. "We only just got here a few days ago. Even with modern modes of transportation, Megan had to have been pretty close to intercept us when she did."

He looked at her, and she nodded in confirmation even though the compulsion not to answer caused a throbbing pain behind her eyes. She squeezed her eyes closed, trying to control it to no avail. Then a gentle touch on her forehead eased the pain. She opened her eyes to find Duncan leaning over her, a sad smile on his face.

"You see how it hurts her. The bastard who did this to her—" Duncan resumed his seat as he spoke to the fire chief, "—also poisoned her blood. She nearly killed Heathclif Dean last night."

"Son of a bitch!" Kevin seemed all too aware of the potential problems that could have caused. If a *were*wolf had managed to take down the man who was essentially Master of the New York vampires in everything but name, all *weres* could have potentially paid the price.

"He forgave her, and we're keeping this on a need to

know basis for now. Considering your position, I believe you need to know." Duncan nodded toward the astonished Alpha. "If the *Venifucus* mole posing as an *Altor Custodis* leader can do this to a *were* as resistant to magic as she is, none of you is safe."

Kevin seemed to take that in for a moment before he asked another question. "What makes her more resistant than others? You'll excuse me, but she doesn't look all that powerful to me."

"I'm only half *were*," she said belligerently. Who was this man to look down his nose at her? She'd never needed *were* society, and she certainly didn't care to start now.

"And one quarter human," Duncan interjected, surprising her. "And one quarter fey."

"What?" she gasped. Even Dante looked surprised, but Duncan only smiled.

"I noticed it last night and have been mulling over who might have been your sire. You definitely have fey blood somewhere in your line. It had to have been your father, since your mother was a *were*wolf. Of course, her mother was a priestess, since twin Lords always mate priestesses of the Lady, so there is that to consider as well. It might be more accurate to say you're partly fey and not put a numerical value on how much. A little is all it takes, after all."

"How in the world did you arrive at the conclusion that my sire—whoever he is—is part fey?" Megan was truly puzzled.

"When I questioned you, your fey blood responded to my magic. I recognized it then but waited to speak of my suspicions until I'd had time to think this through. I believe your father is a half-fey warrior named Nolan. He always favored the realm where his human family lived and visited them often in centuries past. He watched over them like some kind of benevolent uncle, even after many generations had passed and they'd forgotten his origins entirely."

"If he was so concerned about family ties, then why didn't I know him? I think you're wrong, Duncan. Thanks all the same."

"Ah, but you don't have the entire story yet. About thirty years ago by your reckoning in this realm, he was imprisoned like I was, banished Underhill until such time as his sentence was served."

"What did he do? Why banish him?" Dante wanted to know.

"First you need to know that full fey get very upset when one of their number decides to mate with a non-fey. It's a crime, in fact. Otherwise there would be many more halflings like me running around." Duncan smiled and waggled his eyebrows. "As it is, once the deed is done, the fey will take no action against an innocent child. Of course, the fey boy who couldn't keep it in his pants is another matter. Most of the time it's a male who breaks the rules and gets caught. It's very difficult for a fey female to conceive, so even if they do sleep around outside their species, they're relatively safe unless they get caught in the act somehow."

"So you think this Nolan guy was her mother's lover and got caught when she turned up pregnant?" Kevin asked.

"I'm nearly certain of it. His punishment fits. He was banished to a timeless realm to think about his so-called crime all the while knowing that time was passing in the mortal world, and he would never see his lover again."

"That's so sad." Kevin surprised her with the soft note in his voice. It seemed the big bad Alpha had a tender side as well.

For her part, Megan was having a hard time accepting Duncan's explanation. She didn't want to think her mother had died knowing she'd never see her lover again, knowing they'd been torn apart by his race's prejudice. Then again, perhaps it was better to know he hadn't just been some random stranger who'd forgotten her mother the moment the deed was done.

Megan began to feel compassion for the man she'd never met and had often wondered about. All her life she'd assumed she was the result of a one-night stand or something equally tragic. The real story—if Duncan was right—was much worse. Much more heartbreaking for all concerned.

"Family was always important to Nolan." Duncan sat forward and took one of her hands in his. "If there'd been a way for him to be with you and your mother, he would have done anything in his power to take it. I can only surmise they captured him unawares and banished him before he could even plead his case. Full fey can be somewhat…unfeeling when it comes to human relationships."

Oddly enough, Megan felt tears gathering behind her eyes. She hadn't expected anything like this when she'd set out on this path. She frankly never expected to discover who her father was. She'd given up on him a long time ago. Still, it hurt to find out the truth. She felt pain for him as well as for herself and anger at the powerful beings who had interfered and messed up all their lives.

"For what it's worth, Megan—" Duncan looked deep into her eyes, "—I'm sorry."

She tried to keep her composure. "Not your fault, Duncan. You've been nothing but kind to me and without you, I wouldn't even know this much. Thank you."

"I wish I could do more." He released her hand but not her gaze. "But I've only just escaped my own banishment."

"What did you do?" Megan asked before she could censor herself.

Duncan only smiled. "Pissed off Queen Mab. That's a frequent pastime for me."

"That sounds like another story," Kevin said as he stood. "But I have to be getting back. I'd like to compare notes with you all again if you permit. Perhaps you could join me and my pack for drinks one night this week? I'd like my lieutenants to meet you. If there's going to be any action on our turf, I'd like them to know the players on our team."

Dante stood and shook the fire chief's hand. "That sounds like a good idea, and I thank you for the offer."

"You know Night Shift?" He named one of the hottest trendy downtown clubs.

"Who doesn't?" Megan muttered, surprised he'd want such a public meeting place.

"That one of yours?" Dante sent Kevin a speculative look.

Kevin shrugged nonchalantly. "Keeps the younger ones employed and mostly out of trouble. It also provides good revenue for the pack. We own the whole block. There's a little bar around the corner from the club. It's called Howlies. The entrance is below ground level, down a flight of stairs. We like to keep a low profile. I'll let the bouncers know you're welcome. Someone will show you to the private room. We can talk there. Day after tomorrow, around eleven p.m. all right?"

"Sounds good," Dante agreed, shaking the fireman's hand before he left.

Megan was stunned by recent events. Before she knew it, the fireman was gone and she was alone with Dante and Duncan. Thankfully, they gave her the space she needed.

"I cleaned up the glass in the front sitting room and called a glazier to come tomorrow," Duncan said as they came back into the room after seeing the fireman out. "For now, I taped some cardboard in the window. Luckily, the break is in a small pane that doesn't pose much temptation to would-be burglars. Just in case, I put a little spell of protection on it as well."

"Thanks, Duncan. It's good to have a mage around sometimes." Dante laughed as he poured three glasses of wine, giving one to Duncan, keeping one for himself and placing one in her cold hands.

"So, Megan, where are you from?" Duncan asked unexpectedly as they were all seated.

"I was raised mostly on Long Island, out in Suffolk County. I have a small house in Ronkonkoma that my mother left me."

Duncan sent Dante a triumphant look that she didn't understand until he explained.

"It seems you can't tell us about your keeper, but you can tell us about yourself. I have to surmise that if you're from

128

Long Island, he's somewhere close by—probably in the metro area."

"I knew I kept you around for a reason." Dante toasted his friend.

CHAPTER NINE

"The way I see it, we have two problems." Dante kept himself awake by sheer force of will. He'd have to seek his bed again soon or he'd be a mess tonight. There were things that had to be discussed before he could leave Megan to her own devices. Things he had to discuss with Duncan as well. Dante had joined them in the living room after he'd made a few quick calls and put out some feelers.

"Just two?" Duncan's amusement hid the very real impatience they all felt.

"The more immediate threat is the blonde. We need to figure out who she is and why she's targeting me."

"Then what?" Duncan challenged him. He didn't want to have to speak his deadly intentions in front of Megan, but it couldn't be helped. They were all adults. She had to know he'd killed before and would do so again if it meant keeping himself and those he cared for safe.

"Then we eliminate the threat," he answered succinctly. "I'd also be curious to see if she's somehow connected with Megan's *Altor Custodis* contact. Somehow I get the feeling there could be linkage there. For one thing, the hellfire and the overall level of her magic. She's using stuff not from this realm. Right, Duncan?"

"Yes, you're right," he agreed. "And the *Venifucus* always had linkage to the darker realms through their patroness,

Elspeth. Both the hellfire and the poison in Megan's blood were created using that kind of magic. I strongly suspect they both the blonde and Megan's keeper are in league with the *Venifucus*. I'm not convinced they're acting in concert, yet they both seem to be working toward the same ultimate goals."

"Which brings me to our second problem—Megan's keeper." Dante sighed, hating to bring Megan any more pain. Still, she had a right to know what they were up against. "The blonde is out there in the open, lobbing fireballs and Molotov cocktails. The keeper is working quietly behind the scenes, doing sneaky things like poisoning Megan's blood without her knowledge and putting compulsions on her to hide his identity. Two very different ways of working. To my mind, they are separate entities. I doubt the keeper would let the blonde run amok the way she has been. He's too controlled, too subtle for that. Which leads me to believe they are working independently of each other, though both are, as Duncan said, most likely *Venifucus* followers."

"Good points," Duncan agreed. "So we need to work on each problem separately, yet be aware that they may have common threads."

"Precisely." Dante was about to say more when his cell phone rang. He checked the display and recognized the fire chief's number. They'd exchanged cards when he'd seen the man out. They'd also agreed to keep each other updated should there be any developments, but he hadn't expected contact with the wolf Alpha so soon.

Dante took the call.

"Does the name Siobhan Vabian mean anything to you?" Kevin asked with no preliminaries.

"Vabian?" The surname sent a jolt through Dante's system. "The mage who attacked your Lords and their mate was named Patrick Vabian."

"Looks like he had a sister or maybe a cousin. I spoke to my packmate, and she was able to give me a good description of the black Porsche the blonde was driving as well as a partial license plate. I asked one of my men to track it down, and he came up with the name Siobhan Vabian. Looks like she's the one trying to kill you."

Dante felt his chest tighten. They were one step closer to solving this mystery. He got the woman's address from Kevin before thanking him and ending the call. He had to decide on his next actions though everything in him wanted to go tearing over there to confront the woman.

He had others to consider now and a deeper game to win. He needed to know more about this Siobhan Vabian before he could devise his next move.

*

Dante had gone back to his chamber below ground for what was left of the afternoon, leaving Duncan to investigate the Vabians further while Megan supervised repairs on the kitchen. Dante had a reliable work crew that he used for household repairs and all he'd had to do was place a call and a team of carpenters showed up fifteen minutes later. Duncan left Megan in charge of them while he headed for Dante's home office.

Dante had state of the art computer equipment that Duncan was learning how to operate. Of course, getting information the old fashioned way—by actually speaking to people—was something he had mastered a long time ago.

Back then, there had been no telephones. The modern conveniences made his task much easier.

"It's really amazing how easily you mortals can speak with each other over vast distances. The last time I was in this realm, things were quite different, I assure you."

Megan laughed at his fascination with the cell phone Dante had given him. He was never without it and usually jumped when it decided to ring unexpectedly.

"Without magic, the human race has had to rely on science. Personally, I don't think they've done too bad for themselves."

The carpenters had done a great job of beginning repairs on the kitchen. It wasn't back to the showplace it had been yet, but it was usable and even comfortable. Megan had begun cooking the moment the last carpenter had left and the meal was almost ready when Duncan joined her, pitching in to help her finish. She stirred a heavenly smelling sauce on the stove while he drained perfectly cooked pasta over the sink.

After the excitement of the earlier part of the day, she was glad to have the mundane task of making dinner. She assumed Duncan had been on the phone most of the time she was supervising work on the kitchen. She didn't want to pry into his activities, so she didn't ask. Guilt crept up on her every time she thought about the upsets of the past few days. She had an almost unreasonable feeling that she was at fault for having brought such danger to Dante's doorstep.

It was one thing to be a spy. It was quite another to be an assassin—albeit an unwitting one. She didn't know how she could have lived with herself if the poison in her blood had killed Dante or Heath. It didn't bear thinking about.

They shared a delicious dinner and were cleaning up when Dante appeared in the kitchen doorway. He looked much better than the last time she'd seen him just a few hours ago. In fact, he looked downright delicious.

He came to her and the look in his eyes could have melted stone. His head dipped as he drew her into his arms for a long, hungry kiss.

Dante was the only man in the universe who could make her feel this way. He turned her on with just a look from his dark eyes, a touch of his knowing hands. She was powerless against him even without the added vampire mojo that she knew he could bring to bear. It was a sign of respect that he'd never used his powers on her.

She was dizzy when he let her up from the kiss. He held her while she swayed, an amused smile playing around his sexy mouth.

"Good evening, sweetheart. I like waking to find you in

133

my home. Only one thing would be better."

"What's that?" She was in a daze, under his spell.

"Waking to find you in my bed. That's the only way to improve on this feeling of perfection."

His low voiced words zinged right to her hopeful, foolhardy heart. For a timeless moment, they just stared into each other's eyes, lost.

"*Ahem.*" Duncan banged the last pot he'd been washing in the stainless steel sink, making a noticeable racket.

Megan blushed as Dante released her by slow degrees.

"I hate to break this up, but we've got a battle plan to discuss." Duncan sat at the newly cleaned kitchen table and reached for a notebook he'd been scribbling in earlier.

Dante released her and graciously pulled out her chair for her as she sat. He took the chair next to her and twirled it around, sitting on it backwards, across from Duncan.

"This place looks a lot better," Dante commented, looking around at the kitchen for the first time. "Did the work crew give you any problems?"

"Not a one. They were eager to help for the kind of money you're paying them." She looked once again at the progress that had been made in the kitchen that day. It was amazing how much the group of skilled carpenters had been able to fix in such a short time. "They did a really good job."

"Thank you for overseeing them." Dante touched her hand, drawing her attention back to him.

"It was the least I could do." The silence stretched as she lost herself in his gaze. Only an impatient rustling of papers from Duncan's direction brought her back to her senses. She shook her head, chagrinned as Dante released her hand and turned his attention to Duncan.

"What did you discover today?" Dante rested his forearms along the back of the chair. He was so casually sexy he made her mouth water. Urbane and classy one minute, masculine and tough the next.

She had to focus. She couldn't sit here daydreaming about Dante when they had important plans to discuss. She'd hadn't felt comfortable asking Duncan what he'd learned before Dante rose. Now was her chance to find out, as Dante did, what they might be up against.

Duncan flipped through his notes. "I don't think you'll be surprised to learn Siobhan is our boy Patrick's older sister. In addition to her, there are parents—Viktor and Una. There may be other siblings. The full report hasn't come back yet on that. The Vabian family has a long history of mage craft, going back hundreds of years. They fancy themselves the dynasty. They actually call it that—the Vabian dynasty." Duncan paused to snicker. "Kevin's people got Siobhan's address from her Department of Motor Vehicles registration. Handy thing, making all owners register their vehicles. Finding people seems to be much easier in this age than it was when last I was here."

"Yes and no," Dante said. "You'll find there's a lot more information recorded about each and every person. We're also much more mobile. We can travel vast distances at the drop of a hat and there's no telling whether the addresses are current since it usually takes some time for records to be updated once made."

"I see the difficulty," Duncan allowed, turning to his notes. "Nonetheless, we at least have a place to start in our search for Siobhan. I also have the address of the family compound, though I would caution against laying siege to their castle, so to speak. The mansion and grounds have been in the family for generations. It is their seat of power and liable to be well fortified with magical defenses considering how many Vabians have lived there over the years."

"Good point," Dante agreed, snagging a wine bottle out of the huge wine cooler a few feet from where he was seated. He had to lean out, tipping his chair precariously. He managed to open the frosted glass door with little fuss though secretly, Megan worried about the solidity of the groaning wooden kitchen chair. "How long has Siobhan been at the address you have for her? Were you able to find out?"

"A little under two years, according to title records. Before that, the house was owned by a mortal couple."

"Not mages? You're sure?" Megan couldn't help asking. This entire thing made her nervous.

"As sure as I can be. I used the telephone," Duncan paused to smile at his accomplishment in using the new technology. "Kevin gave me some recommendations. He was able to point me toward a private investigator who is well aware of the supernatural world. She has a bit of mage blood in her and agreed to allow me to test her. She passed my test, and I believe she provided me with good information and will continue to, if needed."

"You did all that in only a few hours? I'm impressed." Dante tilted the bottle and poured a second glass of wine for Duncan when he nodded. He offered to Megan as well, but she declined with a shake of her head.

"It's the telephone you gave me. I've become quite proficient with it and am enjoying it immensely."

"Good. I'm glad." Dante toasted his friend silently, then drank. "Technology is sometimes even better than magic."

"Bite your tongue." Duncan pretended outrage, but Megan saw his grin. "My fey brethren would have your head for speaking such blasphemy."

"Good thing they aren't around then, eh?" Dante sipped his wine, a smile playing about his lips. "So, do you feel up to a road trip tonight? I think we should check out Siobhan's house. What do you say?"

"My thoughts exactly. If we're cautious, we should be able to learn a great deal, whether she's there or not. Of course, I hope she's there. Then maybe we can end this quickly."

The men made a few more plans, and Dante warned her explicitly about taking chances and rushing in where immortals feared to tread. Megan was glad he hadn't decided to leave her behind while the men went off to deal with the sorceress. She wouldn't have put it past him to be a chauvinist. After all, women had only achieved relative equality in the past century or so. He'd no doubt been raised, and had lived most of his life, in much different circumstances.

Not that she'd cut him any slack on that score. She was a capable woman. More than that, she was a shapeshifter, fully able to take care of herself and shielded from most magic by her very nature. If anything, he was probably in more danger from Siobhan's fireballs and hellfire then Megan was.

Dante surprised her by choosing to drive one of his own cars for the hour-plus trip to Long Island. Dante had several vehicles garaged in a mechanic's shop a few blocks over from his brownstone. He paid the owner to care for his sports car, luxury sedan, SUV and even an oversized van of some kind, and bring one of them to him when he called.

A few minutes after Dante placed the call, a shiny black Mercedes pulled up at the curb. The mechanic brought the keys to the door, passing them to Dante. The man left with a smile and a hefty tip in his hand as he sauntered down the street on foot.

The three of them left shortly thereafter. Dante drove and Duncan had chivalrously given her the front passenger seat, while he spread out in the back. They talked sporadically as they left the city, battling traffic here and there on their way out of town toward the suburbs.

"When we get there, let me take the lead," Duncan requested. "If she's got any otherrealm magical traps around the place, I should be able to locate them without setting them off."

Dante looked as if he would argue, but Megan could almost see his thought process reflected in his expression. He wanted to say no. His calmer, rational side saw the merit in Duncan's request.

"It is a sound plan," he finally admitted, taking the curve of the exit ramp. They managed to escape Manhattan in record time by using the 59th Street Bridge and the Long Island Expressway. It was uncharacteristically smooth sailing for early evening, but it looked like the worst of the rush hour was over.

After everything that had come before, the actual house

was a bit of a disappointment. It was set slightly back from the road in a thoroughly middle class community, fenced in with a gate and walkway leading to the front door. Only one light shone through the window, looking more like a night light than an overhead light. Dante parked the car across the street and let Duncan take the lead, though Dante wasn't far behind.

Megan stuck with Dante for a few reasons. First, Duncan was undoubtedly the most magical of them and would more than likely be able to see any traps before they'd been sprung. Second, she had a vague idea of protecting Dante—both with her natural *were* immunity to certain magics and from any ill-advised action he might decide to take. Third, and most troubling, was that she felt safe with him. She wanted to be with him, at his side, to both protect and be protected. It didn't make any sense, but there it was.

Putting aside her thoughts, she tried to focus on the here and now as she and Dante cautiously followed Duncan across the street. They were several yards behind him, moving slowly as he appeared to scan the area.

He paused at the gate, holding up one hand to indicate they should stop. Duncan retreated a few steps to confer with them.

"What is it?" Dante asked in a low, urgent voice.

"There is a protection in front of the gate. It is something...very old and very dangerous."

"The spell is old?" Dante's expression was troubled. "I thought she'd only been living here a couple of years."

"Not the spell," Duncan clarified. "The magic itself. If I'm not much mistaken, what I saw is a variation on the Elspian Ring."

"Son of a..." Megan cursed. Even she had heard of the ancient, deadly spell. It was the stuff of legend. Part of every campfire story meant to frighten children into behaving.

"A variation, you said?" Dante looked thoughtful. "What sort of variation?"

"One I have never seen before. I can only guess what it's

138

meant to do. Stop anyone who might want to intrude, of course, but I have no way of knowing how until the spell is tripped. Moreover, from the little I could See of its patterns, it's keyed to supernaturals, not regular mortals."

"That's one good thing at least," Megan muttered. "The postman won't set it off. Your friendly neighborhood *were*wolf might be toast, though, before he even realizes what is going on."

"I doubt it would be anything visible. After all, she wouldn't want to attract any unnecessary attention from her mortal neighbors. Chances are, despite her use of the Elspian Ring to power it, the consequences of this spell might be a stern warning—or the magical equivalent."

"All right then." Megan squared her shoulders and studied the gate. "I've got the most natural immunity of our little club, so the task falls to me. Otherwise, we'll never even get past the sidewalk." She began walking purposely toward the gate when Dante caught her arm, spinning her around to face him.

"What do you think you're doing?"

"I'm doing my part as a member of this team. What did you think—that I would sit on the sidelines while you brave men did all the heavy lifting?"

Dante cursed. Duncan, surprisingly, came to her rescue. "She's right, you know. Of the three of us, she's got the best chance if this thing does turn out to be nastier than we think. And we can pull her out if it is."

"See?" Megan re-appropriated her arm.

"I don't like this," Dante bit out between clenched teeth.

"Duly noted," she said shortly. "But unless you want to get in the car and go home, this is something I've got to do."

He reeled her in for a lingering kiss, his grip on her strong yet gentle. She was swept under his spell almost immediately, falling into his kiss like a drug addict looking for her fix. He was that powerful.

When he released her, he caught her attention. "Be careful, sweetheart. I'll be here to pull you out if you need me."

"I'm counting on it." She gave him a saucy smile and turned once more to the gate only a few yards away. It looked innocent but could prove to be deadly. She prayed for her sake it turned out to be the former.

Duncan gave her some last minute advice as she stepped up to the gate. "Use only one hand and try to keep one foot outside the circle, just in case. As near as I can tell, the boundaries coincide with the lines in the cement of the sidewalk."

It was awkward. She approached the gate from the side rather than head on. The latch was on the left side, so she stood just left of center, straddling the concrete line. Bracing herself, she took a deep breath and raised her right hand.

"Here goes nothing." She reached for the latch.

A split second later the ground was pulled out from under her, and she was falling. A strong hand gripped her left hand, keeping her from the beckoning abyss. It was Dante. He'd caught her, just as he'd promised.

She realized a few things as she looked up and met his gaze. Her left leg was still on the cement sidewalk, bent at a sharp angle and not holding much of her weight. Her right leg—the one on which she'd had most of her weight—was no longer being supported by the sidewalk. Instead, a hole roughly the size of the sidewalk square had opened, trying to swallow her up.

With Dante's help, she managed to use her left leg to pull herself out of the threatening hole. Her right hand was still on the latch, and she spared a moment to lift it and push open the gate.

Duncan, meanwhile, had his nose to the concrete and was chanting.

"Don't move," he counseled when she was standing again, all her weight on her left foot, her hand in Dante's, and her right foot held above the swirling chasm that had magically opened in the sidewalk. "Hold it open for just a minute longer."

Megan raised her eyebrows as she looked at Dante. He

shrugged and gave her a faint smile of encouragement. His strength was hers in that moment, and she could have kissed him for it.

Duncan made a quick motion with his hands and a sharp crack sounded from beneath her feet. A moment later, the hole was gone and the sidewalk was back. It sported a brand new crack in the cement however, as a byproduct of the magic that had been used on it.

She watched as Duncan picked up a few odd bits of debris—twigs and leaves—snapping and crumbling them into dust. They disintegrated with little pops of magic and left behind an acrid smell.

"Nasty piece of work, that." Duncan sighed as he stepped in front of Megan, taking the lead as they walked into the front yard. "There are bound to be more surprises if that was just the front gate obstruction. Stay sharp."

He didn't need to warn her twice. Megan stepped cautiously, following his path as exactly as she could in the dark. Luckily, as a wolf, she had excellent night vision. Dante stayed close but didn't crowd her. She liked the way they had worked together so far. She wasn't used to having anyone along on the prowls she had sometimes engaged in for her keeper. This was different. This was by her choice and for the first time in her life, she wasn't going it alone.

It felt good. She hadn't expected that, but there it was. She liked being part of a team, having someone to catch her should she fall. They'd already proven they would—quite literally—and now it was her turn to do the same.

She began a deliberate, sniffing appraisal of their surroundings. She had no doubt that Duncan could See magical traps better than anyone. As a shifter, she could *smell* magic. Such skills had stood her in good stead many times in the past and this situation was proving more dangerous than she had expected. Their intrepid group could use all the help it could get.

They were caught between trying to appear normal to anyone who might be watching and doing their best to avoid booby traps. From the looks of the house, Megan didn't think anyone was home. Still, they wouldn't know for sure until they got closer.

Duncan moved quickly up the path seeming more confident. Then, out of nowhere, Megan smelled something. Something bad.

"Duncan, hold up." She tried to keep her voice to a whisper. The half-fey knight stopped, turning slightly to look at her, and that's when it struck.

From a low hanging branch in the tree overhead, a creature out of nightmares jumped onto Duncan's back. He immediately crouched, giving Dante a clear shot at the hideous thing, and that glowing, magical armor suddenly appeared to protect Duncan's back.

Dante move faster than her eyes could track, wrestling with the creature who was about the size of a child but cunningly quick, inhumanly strong and ferociously dangerous. It wasn't any kind of animal that occurred in nature. No, this thing was something dreamed up by a warped and twisted mind.

It had three-inch claws, and it tried to sink its vicious teeth into Duncan's armored neck. Megan finally understood the value of being able to conjure armor out of thin air. It was the only thing protecting Duncan's vulnerable body from this surprise attack.

Dante did a partial shift. Being a bloodletter of advanced years, Dante had the ability to shift into anything he could imagine, including mythical creatures and imaginary monsters like the one he faced. He shifted his hands into fierce claws, using them to rip the creature off of Duncan.

It landed in a crouch, ready to do battle. Dante had its full attention, but Megan wouldn't let him fight it alone. She moved off to the side, taking up a flanking position. Dante gave her a brief nod as she kicked off her shoes, readying herself for a half shift. Her pants were stretchy enough, as was the T-shirt she had chosen to wear this night. With any luck, she would be reasonably clothed when she shifted back to human form after the much larger *were*wolf fighting form she called from within.

The familiar change took only a moment, yet in that moment the nightmare creature charged Dante. A quick look at Duncan told her he was busy conjuring. He now held a glowing silver sword in his hands to match the magical armor. In all likelihood, he was using the blade to focus his spell, but Dante couldn't wait. The monster was already making him bleed.

Megan swiped at it with her clawed hand. It shrieked and jumped away from Dante to face its new attacker. Megan eyed it with both triumph and wariness. She'd succeeded in getting away from Dante, but now she had to deal with it. The thing was small, fast and judging by Dante's wounds, deadly accurate with those wickedly sharp claws.

"Hold its attention," Dante called to her.

She nodded briefly, beginning to dance around the monster, making short feints with her clawed feet and hands. She managed to score a few hits without taking any herself. She knew her luck couldn't hold for long. She had the advantage of reach on the short creature. That was all that was saving her from some nasty gashes.

Dante came in from behind, ramming the monster's unprotected back with claws he had conjured that were like something out of a comic book. The little monster started screeching so loud it hurt Megan's ears. Dante let go, and Megan went in for the kill.

Between the two of them slicing and dicing, they cut the ghastly creature to ribbons. Satisfied it wouldn't be bothering them again, Megan shifted to human form. That's when she noticed a rustling in the trees.

"Oh, crap." Megan eyed the dark canopy overhead with wide eyes.

"I think that thing had friends," Dante observed in a tight voice, also looking upward.

"Get out from under the trees!" Duncan shouted as they made a run for it. The only way to go was forward, toward the house.

They turned on the doorstep to make a stand. Duncan faced the creatures that were massing for an all-out assault. His spell was finally ready. He raised his gleaming magical sword and let loose on them, a jagged bolt of pure power blackening each of the foul creatures it touched. And there were a lot of them. Too many for them to have fought.

Duncan's magic fried each and every one of them, leaving black smudges on the lawn where they'd once stood. Even the one Dante and Megan had torn apart was incinerated in Duncan's cleansing white fire. Megan breathed a sigh of relief.

"Well, if nobody saw that, I'll be amazed," Dante said wryly. "So much for keeping a low profile."

Duncan sheathed his sword, keeping his armor in place for the time being. "I begin to think the entire property is shielded from observation. We can see out, but nobody on the street sees anything out of the ordinary inside the fence. That's why the gate was so well fortified. I think if you get past there, you get what you deserve, in Siobhan's warped mind."

"Nice girl," Dante commented wryly.

"Who is more than likely not at home," Duncan observed. "If she was in there, I think we would've seen her long before now. Either that, or she's bolted through some escape hatch we've yet to discover."

"True. It's best to tread cautiously. If she is in there and waiting to choose her moment to confront us, we've given her ample warning at this point." Dante rolled his eyes and Megan realized this hadn't gone at all the way he'd probably wished.

"Well," Megan said, trying to be positive, "we made it as far as the doorstep. Now what?"

"We've already established that the grounds are dangerous and more than likely, no one's home," Duncan reasoned in a low voice. "I'd prefer to take my chances inside, even though being inside the house may be more hazardous than being out in the open in some ways."

"I concur." Dante nodded. "It's more likely we can pick up good information in the house. Besides, we can always search the yard more thoroughly once we have a peek inside and make certain nobody's around to try and stop us."

"So we're going to do a little breaking and entering?" Megan raised one eyebrow, challenging them.

"No one can see us from the street," Duncan shrugged. "Only the dark mage will have any idea we've been here and personally, I'm not worried about pissing her off."

That startled a short laugh out of Megan.

"We were just lucky she didn't have any surprises for us between the trees and here." Dante's frustration level was easily heard in his voice.

"Thank the Lady for small blessings," Megan intoned, turning to Duncan. He was on point again, taking the lead looking for any more magical traps that might challenge them. "There's little doubt she protected the front door, right? I mean, that's pretty standard, isn't it?"

Duncan shrugged. "It makes sense." He cautioned them to stand back. "Let me have a look."

He waved his hands around in an intricate pattern and even Megan saw the results. Glowing, evil looking glyphs erupted around the portal. They shone an angry red.

"What's that?" Megan breathed. She'd never seen anything like it.

"It's another nasty bit of work, but seeing it is half the battle." A cunning smile spread over his handsome face. "I believe if I just tweak the sequence here..." He did something that gave off the aroma of intense magic to her sensitive nose and the characters moved, reforming into something different. Something tangibly less evil. The glow on that section of the door dissipated, the characters fading into something benign. "...and here." Duncan repeated the process on the other side and even more of the intimidating pattern changed and faded.

"Once more," Duncan spoke to himself as he changed the

last of the glyphs. "Ah. That's it." He stepped back, looking a little worse for wear. "Now it's safe enough. Megan, will you do the honors?"

She was surprised at first, when Duncan asked her to kick down the door. Then she remembered the old stories about bloodletters needing to be invited inside a structure. She did the honors, as he'd called it, with pleasure. Duncan went in first, then turned and gestured to Dante.

"Won't you come in?" Duncan seemed genuinely amused, and Dante scowled as he pushed past the half-fey knight to stand inside the doorway. Megan followed, bemused.

"So that bit about you having to be invited is true?" She couldn't help asking.

"This isn't the time for this discussion, but suffice it to say we are creatures of tradition. While the invitation isn't strictly necessary, it's hard for any of us to go against centuries of custom."

"Wow." She filed the information in her mind for later consideration. She'd love to ask him more, but he was right. This was neither the time nor place.

Megan took a look around as Duncan started moving warily into the house. They were in a small entryway that branched in two directions. The living area was off to the left and a short hallway leading to what looked like the kitchen was to the right. Duncan headed left first, the opening to the living room being larger and more inviting than the other direction. Dante and Megan followed cautiously behind him.

CHAPTER TEN

The first things she noticed were the curtains. They were black and stark against walls that were painted a sickly cobalt blue. Normally, cobalt was one of Megan's favorite colors but whatever they had done—it looked like some weird combination of texture and pattern in the paint—made the color ghastly. The combination with the black curtains gave her the creeps.

"Our girl Siobhan needs some serious decorating advice," she muttered.

There wasn't much furniture and the house had an unused feel to it. Megan couldn't explain exactly why she thought it, but she believed the sorceress didn't spend a lot of time here.

Duncan moved ahead of them checking out a side room. He paused in the doorway, a scowl on his face.

"Damn and blast!" Duncan scooted backward as a dark miasma filled the portal.

It looked like black smoke, billowing and roiling in the room beyond. It didn't spill out into the living room and Megan suspected that was Duncan's doing. He was conjuring something, his hands moving and his voice a low rumble that was just audible to her sensitive ears. He was speaking another language—something she'd never heard before. The cadence of it was lilting and lovely to her senses. It *sounded* magical, if such a thing were possible. In all likelihood, he was speaking the language of the fey.

"What is that?" she asked when he finally turned to them. Looking around she realized Dante hadn't paused in his search of the room, trusting to Duncan's skill. Only Megan had been distracted from the search by a clash of magics she had never seen before.

The living smoke inside that small room had both looked and felt like pure evil. By contrast, the words and motions Duncan had used to prevent it from moving farther felt like the exact opposite. Here was the nature of their conflict in microcosm—good versus evil. If she hadn't realized it before, the point was driven home to her now.

"Whatever it is, it's shielding this room in particular. Give me a few moments to figure out how to counteract it. I suppose whatever it's concealing might be worth looking at."

"Unless it's a true smokescreen—a red herring, if you will," Dante chimed in from the side of the living room where he was searching through an antique bureau.

"There is always that possibility," Duncan allowed. He grimaced and turned back to the smoke filled doorway, looking as if he was ready to do battle.

"Look at this." Dante drew her attention to the other side of the room where he was looking at a photograph displayed in a cheap plastic frame on the mantel. "This is Patrick," he said, something like regret in his dark eyes.

Megan took a closer look. This was the magic user who had conned Dante. She'd heard enough of the story to know that Patrick had played upon Dante's tragic past to coerce him into acting as an unwitting blind for Patrick's own attack on the *were*lords. Even though she'd never been part of *were* society, she did feel sympathy for the twin Alphas and their mate who had almost died because of Patrick Vabian and Dante's willingness to believe him.

"He doesn't look like a monster." Megan spoke softly, putting one hand on Dante's shoulder, offering comfort.

"No, he was very convincing. And I was a fool for believing him. I thought my chance for revenge was at hand

and was so focused on that goal, I nearly forgot about everything else—about fairness and honor and truth."

"From all accounts, you remembered in plenty of time to make up for it. All things considered, it probably worked out for the best. Without your involvement, the *Venifucus* threat might still be hidden. They say the Lady works in mysterious ways."

Dante turned and gathered her in for a quick hug. She was surprised by his actions but went willingly into his arms.

"You're good for me, Megan." He kissed her—just once—a quick buss before releasing her. She felt warm and tingly all over, a sensation of joy bubbling up through her bloodstream.

"I've got you now." Duncan was muttering, his expression one of triumph as the black smoke inside the room began to billow violently, then slowly recede. A moment later, he turned to them with a smug grin on his face. "It's safe. We can go in."

"Good work, my friend." Dante strode forward, confident as always, delivering a pat on Duncan's shoulder as he passed.

Megan followed behind, looking around the small room with interest. It looked like a rather ordinary home office with a cluttered desk and some computer equipment. There were papers scattered around, a filing cabinet and two full bookcases.

Megan scanned the spines of the books finding everything from gardening manuals to travel guides. One shelf held some rather innocuous looking hardcover novels. As she ran her fingers near them a shock ran up her arm, making her gasp. Both men turned to stare at her.

"What is it?" Dante frowned at her.

"I'm not sure. Something's not right here."

Duncan took up a position on her left, Dante on her right as they looked more closely at the books. Both were careful not to touch anything.

"It felt like an electric shock running up my arm and it

hurt," she explained as they retraced her steps. "I think it was right about here." She lifted her hand to point at a cluster of three hardcover books and drew her hand back sharply, grimacing as whatever it was shocked her again.

"Oh, this is good. Megan, you must be more sensitive than I thought." Duncan stepped in front of the rather plain books. Dante drew Megan back a step or two to let Duncan work. "Yes, very good," he seemed to say to himself. "She hid this well. I don't think I would've seen it without your help."

"Is that—?" Dante didn't get to finish his question as Duncan nodded.

"A grimoire. Actually, a set of them." He waved his hand and it looked like the plain covers faded away to reveal ancient looking textured leather bindings with golden letters that glowed under Duncan's influence. "Oh, this is impressive…and very, very dangerous." He took a few more precautions, then pulled the books from the shelf. "These are coming with us."

"Why?" Megan asked. She didn't know what good a few old magic books would do in defeating Siobhan.

Duncan turned to her, and she was struck once again by the gleaming silver armor that encased him. He was an imposing figure at his most intimidating as he met her gaze. "These are books that should never have been written. They specify methods for calling demons from other realms that do not belong here. This knowledge is not for mortal mages. I will take these books and destroy them as I have destroyed other copies I've come across in the past."

"Okay." She held up her hands palms outward, surprised by the vehemence in his tone. "I was just wondering."

Duncan softened then, sending her a small smile. "Sorry, this is something I'm passionate about. Some knowledge is not meant for this mortal realm."

Dante reclaimed their attention as the computer started beeping. He'd started the system while Duncan was working on the books and now had it up and running.

"Most of this is password protected on several levels. However, I did manage to access a few functions including her calendar. Siobhan is out of town. She left yesterday and according to this, will be gone until the day after tomorrow. It says she's gone to visit her parents. I looked in her address book and found a listing for them. It's in Chappaqua, a very expensive, old money neighborhood in upstate New York."

Dante took a sheet of white paper out of the printer and scribbled down the address as he spoke. Duncan, meanwhile, had apparently conjured a satchel from somewhere and put the grimoires within. The fabric of the bag glowed faintly, giving her no doubt as to its magical origin as he fastened it securely to his back. She supposed such magic was necessary to contain—and perhaps to hide—the presence of those ancient and dangerous tomes.

"Does her calendar say anything about appointments after she gets back?" Duncan asked as he continued to search the office.

"Not much. She doesn't seem to plan that far in advance. Instead, she seems to be rather rigorous about accounting for her time after the fact." Dante continued to search the computer files. "Besides, she's going to know we've been here. Chances are, she'll change her plans just in case. I know I would."

"Good point," Duncan agreed. "I think that's all we'll find in here. You two finish up, and I'll go check the rest of the rooms. Meet me at the entrance, and I'll guide you through the rest of the house."

Dante browsed a bit more, then began to shut down the computer system, leaving no trace that he had been scanning it while Megan sorted through some papers and looked at the rest of the bookshelves and cabinets.

"You know, for an old guy, you're surprisingly good with computers." She felt comfortable enough to tease him as he stood. He paused for a moment in front of her.

"I used to have a lot of time on my hands to learn new things before I met a puzzling little *were*wolf." He lifted his hand to caress her cheek as they looked deep into each other's eyes. She wanted him to kiss her.

His head lowered…

A crash sounded from the other end of the house, breaking them apart. The clash of steel against something no doubt equally as hard rang out a split second later. Dante was already in motion, a preternatural blur of speed as he raced to his friend's side. Megan wasn't far behind, but her *were* speed was no match for the vampire.

She discovered Duncan on the threshold of the kitchen, battling against what looked like a dozen heavily armed ghost figures. They were darkly transparent, wearing plate armor of a bygone age. Megan didn't understand how, but she thought she might be looking at the ghosts of dead warriors, somehow held in thrall by the sorceress.

She froze, uncertain what to do. Duncan was holding them off—barely. They came at him one at a time through the kitchen doorway. When they saw Dante arrive on the scene, they started walking through walls.

Megan screamed when one lunged at Dante with his blade, coming right through the paisley wallpaper, taking him by surprise. He grunted with the impact as the ghostly sword stabbed into his abdomen. Blood shone wet and slick against his dark clothing. Megan feared for him and for Duncan. She called on her wolf and halted in half-shift. The quarters were too tight for her to be able to do much. Her half-shift form was just too big. The ghost warriors had no problem maneuvering through walls, but she sure as hell did.

"We have to get out of here!" she roared through elongated teeth. A sword poked through the wall to her left, and she swiped at the ghost's hand with her claws. They went straight through the incorporeal being, much to her dismay. Dante, likewise, was having little effect on the ghost warriors. Only Duncan's magical sword seemed to have any staying power against Siobhan's gruesome army.

"Retreat!" Duncan shouted, covering Dante as they ran for the door. The phantoms weren't far behind.

Megan burst through the door only to find more ghost warriors converging on the path to the gate. Even with all their speed, it would be close. Dante was clutching his side and leaning heavily against Duncan as he did his best to fend off further attacks. Megan bared her teeth, leading the way to the gate that was their only hope.

She took point, moving fast, gauging how quickly she thought Duncan and Dante could follow. She didn't want to get separated from them. These phantoms would take advantage of any mistake. If it came down to it, she would cover Duncan's back as best she could if they had to make a stand.

If it took magic to touch the phantoms, she would call on her own. She'd struck out at that first one using her claws alone. That was usually more than enough. But if she had to confront any others, she'd expend the precious power to put a magical whammy behind her strikes. It would drain her and it wouldn't be much magic compared to what Duncan was throwing around, but it was the best she could do. It would have to be enough.

They ran for the gate, the phantoms gaining on them with every stride. Megan reached it first, hitting the latch with all her half-shift strength. It resisted at first, then slid open as she put her magic behind it. She burst out onto the sidewalk, jumping over the cracked square directly in front of the gate, just in case. She held the door for Duncan and Dante, then slammed it shut behind them once they were clear. Thankfully, the ghost army couldn't get through the fence.

She breathed a sigh of relief until she realized she was on a public street in half-shift. Looking both ways, she leapt into the shadow of some trees and returned to human form. Her stretchy clothes were a little misshapen but still decent as she went to Dante's side, tucking herself under his arm. Together, she and Duncan helped him to the car, assisting him into the back seat.

"Give me the keys," Megan requested. "I'm taking us to my place. He's hurt too badly, and it's too close to dawn. My house isn't far. We can stay there for the day."

Duncan took the keys from Dante's pocket and handed them to her solemnly. He said nothing as he climbed into the back seat beside his friend, applying pressure to the wound that still bled in Dante's side.

They rode in silence for about twenty minutes. Megan was never more thankful to see her small house set in a small patch of trees. The old bungalow was located on a half acre her mother had bought as an investment many years ago. Her family had never lived in this house, but it felt like home because of the family connection.

There were neighbors on either side. Luckily, they were most likely asleep at this late hour. Megan pulled into the gravel drive and parked the car as close as she could to the door. Between the two of them, she and Duncan managed to get Dante out of the car and into the small house.

"Please come in," she invited, remembering Dante's need for tradition as she entered her home. "Bedroom is to the left. I'll get the first aid kit."

Megan rushed around her house gathering supplies. She had a first aid kit under one arm along with a roll of paper towels, a box of wet wipes and one of the few bottles of wine she'd had tucked in the back of her refrigerator. It wasn't anything like the rare vintages Dante kept, but it would do in a pinch.

She brought everything into the bedroom. Duncan helped Dante to the bed, releasing his heavy weight onto the springy mattress. Dante bounced with a groan as he held his side, which had started bleeding again.

He grabbed the bottle of wine without comment and pulled the cork out with his teeth, swigging straight from the half-full bottle. His usually impeccable manners were no doubt on hold due to his injury.

Draining the bottle, he gave a long sigh and rested his head against the padded headboard, closing his eyes as Duncan began cleaning his wounds. He said not a word while Duncan went about the painful business, merely enduring what had to be endured.

"It's not as bad as it looks," Duncan reassured her. "He could probably handle this without my help, but after all the traps we found in and around that house I want to be sure nothing snuck in under our guard when we weren't looking."

"Like what?" Megan was almost afraid to ask.

"Silver, for one thing, though he probably would have had a violent reaction by now. Of course, there are delayed methods of delivery, which is why I'm checking every detail. There's also a possibility of magical contamination. When you're dealing with a dark mage, especially one that dabbles in the black magics of other realms, you can never be too careful."

Duncan continued his work with Megan's occasional assistance. She handed him things and fetched whatever he needed when asked. It didn't really take that long, yet it felt like ages before Dante was patched up and resting comfortably in her bed.

She'd brought him another bottle of wine from her refrigerator and he was drinking it—more slowly this time, which she took as a good sign. Duncan spent a few minutes in the attached bathroom, cleaning the few small cuts on his hands and face. The rest of his body had been protected by that amazing glowing armor.

He reentered the room and sat at the foot of the bed. She was glad she'd opted for the king size. Even so, the two big men dwarfed even that giant piece of furniture. She'd never quite realized how small her bedroom was before seeing these two in it.

She sat on the edge of the bed at Dante's side, glad for a minute of quiet after the crazy night they'd just had. He'd been amazing through it all, steadfast and brave. He'd impressed her even more than before, and Duncan had blown her right out of the water. The armor, the sword, the incredible magics he had wielded. She'd never really seen him in action before, and his capabilities boggled the mind.

"So what are you, really?" She voiced the question

uppermost in her mind. "I mean, what's with the magical armor and that wicked sword? That's like nothing I've ever even heard of before."

Duncan regarded her with serious eyes. He seemed to consider before finally responding.

"I am a *Chevalier de la Lumière*. A Knight of the Light. We are an ancient order sworn to serve the Light and preserve what is just and good against those who would prefer the darkness of evil. We serve the Lady in all her forms in the many realms we inhabit. Most of us are fey and spend our time in many different realms. There are a special, chosen few in each realm who take the oath and serve the Mother Goddess and the cause of good. It is a special honor and a charge that lasts until death."

"Wow. So that's how and why you were able to test Dante when you first saw him again."

"You're quick," Duncan complimented her. "Yes, I had to make absolutely sure he was still on the right side."

Megan looked from Dante to Duncan and back. "You took a big chance."

"He's worth it," Duncan said casually, but she could feel there was nothing truly casual about his words. They made Dante sit up straighter, despite his wounds.

"You're just lucky I didn't turn on you," Dante chided. "In the intervening years I could've become Satan himself for all you knew."

Duncan smiled easily. "I had more faith in you than that, my lad. I was willing to bet my life on it, and you didn't disappoint me at all."

"Thank the Lady," Megan breathed. The extent of the men's relationship was driven home to her.

She'd thought they were close friends, but before tonight she hadn't fully grasped the fact that they were longtime comrades in arms. They'd put their lives on the line for each other many times in the past and would do so again if the situation called for it.

They had a deep bond. They were as close as brothers,

willing to sacrifice themselves for one another. They had each other's backs.

Megan had heard of such deep friendships. Of course, she'd never experienced anything even close in her solitary prowl through life. It was a privilege to observe and an even deeper honor to be included—just for this short time—in their lives and work.

"You should rest." She made to get up, but Dante's hand stilled her.

"Stay," he asked in a rough voice. "There's room enough for all three of us here and as long as you cover that window, it should be safe enough for me for the day."

Megan wasn't sure. She looked from Dante to Duncan, finally giving in. She was bone weary and wasn't looking forward to camping out on her lumpy couch. She wouldn't subject Duncan to that indignity either.

"All right." She sighed heavily, standing and heading for her dresser. "I'll shower quick and get ready for bed. Just give me a sec."

"Don't worry." Dante patted the middle of the bed. "We'll keep your spot open for you. Hurry back."

Megan took a speed shower. She was so tired she couldn't work up the energy to do more than swipe at her arms and legs with a soapy washcloth. She paid a little more attention to the cuts she'd received, but was too weary to fuss. In all likelihood, with her *were* constitution they would be healed in a few hours.

She yawned as she stepped out of the shower and reached for a towel. One was placed in her hands, and her eyes shot open to meet Duncan's amused gaze.

"You didn't think you'd get away without an examination of your injuries, did you?"

"I-I-" She was stuttering and couldn't seem to get a full sentence out. She cut her losses, closed her mouth and held the towel up against her body.

"Come now, lass. Sit here while I patch you up." He patted the vanity top next to the sink, which he'd already covered with a towel.

Seeing little recourse, she jumped up to sit before him. He took the towel she clutched out of her hands and gently began drying her body with long sweeps of the prickly terrycloth against her skin. He stepped between her knees, spreading her legs while he moved closer and she grew warm, but her body was too drained to respond fully. Her eyelids drooped as he made her feel more comfortable.

"I can see you're running on fumes, lass. This will only take a moment and then I'll carry you back to that big bed so we can all sleep off this night's adventure."

He touched her with gentle hands, doing a more thorough job of cleaning her wounds than she had managed. He applied disinfectant he'd brought with him from the first aid kit. She suspected he also did a magical inspection to be sure she hadn't been contaminated by any of the evil things they'd encountered at the sorceress's house.

By the time he was satisfied, she was yawning again. She couldn't help it. She was physically and mentally exhausted. No matter how attractive Duncan was or how provoking his touch, she just couldn't work up enough enthusiasm to make it worth his while. And without Dante, it didn't feel quite right. She would examine that startling thought later—when she wasn't so beat.

From the haggard look of Duncan, he wasn't in much better shape. When he seemed satisfied that her wounds would be all right, he scooped her into his strong arms and carried her into the other room.

He laid her on the bed next to Dante. Dante had removed his shirt and pants while she'd been in the shower and as she watched, Duncan stripped too. He climbed in under the covers on the other side of the bed and turned off the light.

She only gave a passing thought to the fact that she was in the middle of her king-sized bed, flanked on each side by two of the most handsome, magical beings she had ever known. Stranger things had happened, but she didn't know where or when.

＊

"Something must be done. I can't lose another child. Not after Patrick disappeared without a trace!" Una Vabian slammed her hand down on the antique dining table in the family's spacious Chappaqua home.

"Relax my dear," her husband counseled. "I think I have just the plan to rid ourselves of two problems at once. Poferov has threatened us for the last time."

Una's cold eyes turned calculating. "You think we can take him on?"

"Not us. The bloodletter. Let's wrap him up in a bow and deliver him to d'Angleterre. See what happens. Either way, we win. If Poferov prevails, d'Angleterre will be dead. If the vampire wins, the threat of Poferov is removed from our family and we can go after d'Angleterre without concern for repercussions."

"Brilliant!" Una clapped her hands together in glee. "I knew there was a reason I married you. You're a genius, my dear."

"We just need to figure out a way to get them together. I believe the rest will take care of itself."

"I have the perfect solution," Una purred triumphantly. "We'll invite Poferov to the yacht. He was always impressed with opulent vessels. We'll say it's a meeting to discuss how we've reined in Siobhan. He'll think we'll be there to lick his boots but in reality, he'll be confronting the bloodletter."

"An excellent idea. Now we just have to come up with a way to get the vampire to attack. Do you think he's discovered who his pet wolf's keeper is yet? That might be enough motivation given the scene we heard about at the vampire ball. He's kept her with him from all accounts. Perhaps she's ingratiated herself—or perhaps he's discovered she was sent to spy on him and he's keeping her around to get at the one who sent her." The Vabian patriarch shrugged elegantly. "It really doesn't matter. What does matter is that he takes the bait and confronts Poferov once we get him to the yacht."

CHAPTER ELEVEN

When Megan finally woke, it was late afternoon. Dante was wrapped around her in his sleep, his warm body comforting her. After a moment of disorientation, she realized she was in her own bedroom and the events of the night before came back in startling clarity.

Duncan was no longer beside them, and she noticed her bedroom window had been covered with black plastic garbage bags that looked like they were taped together with sturdy packing tape. Not a single sunbeam penetrated. Duncan must've taken care of that, but she couldn't remember when. She'd been too out of it last night.

She figured Dante would sleep a couple more hours until sunset, so she gently extricated herself from his arms. He mounted a faint protest but didn't fully wake as she slid from the bed. As quietly as possible, she gathered a few of her things and went into the bathroom, not turning on the light until she had the door firmly closed.

She cleaned up and dressed, moving slowly, her muscles sore. When she came out of the bathroom, Dante hadn't moved and Duncan was still nowhere to be seen. She tiptoed out of the bedroom, closing the door softly behind her and headed for the kitchen.

Coffee. The heavenly aroma reached her sensitive nose, and she'd bet good money Duncan was responsible for it.

Sure enough, he'd made himself at home in her kitchen. Coffee was ready and waiting for her and it looked like he was gathering ingredients to do some serious cooking.

"What would you like for breakfast, lass? Today, I am your short order cook." He saluted her with a spatula, making her laugh.

"Can you do eggs over easy and some bacon?"

"Your wish is my command." He turned back to the stove with a flourish and began to cook breakfast.

She helped a little, toasting bread and gathering condiments from the cabinets and refrigerator. When she went to set the table she got a surprise. On her battered kitchen table were the three grimoires Duncan had taken from Siobhan's house. She paused, startled by their appearance.

Duncan finished up, turned off the stove and delivered the plate of bacon and eggs into her hands. She looked at him, only then realizing she'd stood motionless for more than a few minutes.

"They feel even uglier now than they did last night, Duncan."

"I don't doubt that." He stacked the books and set them aside some distance from the kitchen table. "They are evil texts from an even less civilized time."

He pulled out her chair and she sat, placing her breakfast plate in front of her. Duncan poured their coffee before taking his place at the table opposite her.

"Our Siobhan had some surprisingly ancient texts. One of them is an original copy of the Munich Manual. I've seen that one only once before. It was written in the fifteenth century, I believe. It deals with demons extensively and unfortunately a few copies remain. I've learned a misguided scholar even republished it, in part, a few years ago. I hope you don't mind—" Duncan gestured with his fork, "—I took the liberty of using your computer to search the web. Dante's been trying to get me to use your modern technology and I will admit, for some things it is very convenient. I learned a great deal about the subsequent history of this book and the other two from a quick search."

Megan chuckled to think of this old world knight surfing the web. Duncan was very intelligent, and she had no doubt he had learned how to make a computer sing for him with only a few lessons from Dante.

"What else did you find out?"

"The second book is the *Pseudomonarchia Daemonum*, which lists the hierarchy of demons and specifies ways to conjure them. And the third is the most surprising of all. It is the *Liber officiorum spirituum de principibus et regibus daemonum*. In short, a book about demons. I thought never to see another copy of that ancient tome. When I was last in this realm, all copies were thought to have been destroyed. In the sixteenth century, a Dutchman named Johannes was thought to have the last copy. He used it as a reference to write his own grimoire. Johannes's copy was destroyed. That I know for certain. Yet somehow, Siobhan had a copy. It must have been handed down in secret from generation to generation, either within her family, or perhaps from teacher to student. I don't know how they managed to hide this one from us, but it will end now."

Duncan's eyes had gone as cold as steel, and Megan could read the determination on his face. This was no doubt important to him, though she didn't really understand why destroying a few old books would matter so much.

"I'm just sorry we didn't get to see the rest of her house." Megan thought about what they might've missed. Whatever those phantom warriors were protecting, it probably was something important.

"I don't think she could've been hiding anything more important than these. Remember, we at first thought the black smoke could be a diversion—a red herring. What if the ghost warriors were the real diversion, and we actually found the prize?"

"Those books are that important?"

"Yes, my dear. They truly are. I take it you haven't had

163

many dealings with magic users before?"

"I've never really mixed with any sort of supernatural before. Not socially, at any rate. I went where I was sent and did what I was told. I tried not to get too involved with the people I was sent to meet, or spy on. And it's not as if I've been doing this for very long. Only a few years, and only a few missions per year."

"Well, in time you'll learn that a magic user's book of spells is something rare and highly valuable. The older the book, the more precious. And if you're a practitioner of dark magic, the books are very rare indeed because of people like me who have made it our task to destroy them wherever we find them."

"Because you're a knight, right?" She thought she understood now why he'd taken it upon himself to destroy the evil books.

Since his revelation of the night before, she had to rethink the motivation behind almost everything he'd done. He was working for a higher power. He was working for the Lady Herself. Megan still couldn't quite grasp the enormity of that. As a *were*, she had great love and respect for the Lady. She was Mother Nature, Gaia, the Earth Spirit all *weres* served.

"Yes, Megan. That is one part of my duties, to prevent the spread of otherrealm magic in places it could do great harm. The mortal realm has few protections against certain dark magics and needs to be protected."

"That's quite a task, Duncan. I'm just glad there are actually beings like you out there doing it. I find it sort of sad that the rest of the world will never know what you sacrifice for them."

"They cannot know. In fact, you must swear your silence on the matter of my identity. I told you because we are comrades in arms in this fight. Generally speaking, we like to keep our identities as quiet as possible since Knights are natural targets for anything or anyone who oppose our mission. If they take us out, what little protection we can give the mortal realm and those beyond will be gone."

"I see your predicament, and I swear I won't reveal your identity, Duncan. I'm honored you would trust me with the knowledge."

"I do trust you, Megan. Even so, I'm going to have to ask you to submit to a binding so you can never be forced to reveal the information." His expression became pained, but he held firm on his request. "I know it's difficult for you. Magic has been worked upon you before without your knowledge or consent. This time, I'm asking you to submit voluntarily. Will you?"

She sat back and considered. "I guess I've already proven that I can be manipulated into doing things I really didn't want to do." She hated it, but there it was. "You're right to want some guarantee other than my word." She gave a hearty sigh, sick of magic. She would have to accept it as part of her life whether she wanted it or not. "What do you want me to do?"

"We'll wait for Dante to rise. I'd like him to witness the binding for your comfort and his. I don't think he'll like the idea of working magic on you at all. Hopefully, he'll see the reason for it or you have, once I get a chance to explain it to him."

"Would you rather I do it?" She saw the grimace on his face and felt heartened that he thought Dante would object. Still, she understood the need.

"No, I'll do it, though you may want to protect yourself from the inevitable bellowing and foul language."

She laughed out loud at his prediction, and they finished their meal in a good mood.

As expected, when Dante rose at sunset, he and Duncan exchanged some rather heated words over Duncan's plan to put yet another layer of magic prohibitions on Megan's thin shoulders. Dante didn't like it. Not one bit.

"Let me get this straight." Dante eyed Duncan across the coffee table in the living room where the men had retired to discuss the situation. "You want to burden her with more magic on top of what's already been done to her and despite the poison circulating in her veins? Duncan, it's too much, I tell you."

"I don't see any other alternative. Look, the prohibition doesn't have to be done the same way her keeper bespelled her. In fact, it would be better to seek another avenue. We could do it while we work to cleanse her of the poison."

"During sex, you mean." Dante spit the words out. They left a bitter taste in his mouth.

"It's the only way I know to weaken the poison. Unless and until we kill the mage who put it in her bloodstream, she'll be a danger to you and everyone else. All we can do is weaken his hold so when the time comes, she's strong enough to fight against it."

"I detest this." Dante stood and paced to the fireplace, idly fingering some of the photos that sat in frames on the polished wood mantle.

"I know, my friend. I can see how you care for her."

Dante looked at Duncan sharply. "She is mortal and shifter. She is not for me."

"I know that and you know that, but does your heart hear and obey? I think not, laddie. I see the way you look at her, the way you make love to her. And that's what it is, lovemaking, not just fucking. Your heart has already claimed her, but even I can't tell if your path will lead to disaster or something more sublime than I have ever witnessed. All I can tell you is that it is a dangerous road, and I don't envy either of you who walk it."

Dante was shocked. He knew Duncan had a touch of the Sight, though it wasn't always informative or conveniently available when they really needed it. The idea that Duncan had seen so much of Dante's motivations—things he hadn't wanted to recognize or come to terms with yet himself—was daunting, to say the least.

And through it all, Duncan was there, helping them. He was the truest of friends and someone Dante could trust. Beyond a doubt, Duncan was on the right side in this whole sordid mess. Dante had known him long enough to know that if Duncan said something had to be done, there was a damned good reason for it.

"Have I been an ungrateful lout?" Dante deflated and sank onto the couch.

"Never that, my old friend. Just blinded by a want and desire so grand it may well overwhelm you in the end. Whether that will be for good or ill, I cannot say."

"I'm on a collision course with fate, Duncan. Have been my whole life. I gave up worrying about it a long time ago. I try to live in the moment as best I can."

"A wise move, but what of your lady? I'm not sure our Megan can do the same. She's much younger than either of us can even remember being, and mortal. She doesn't have the same luxury of time to learn to be as jaded as you, my friend."

Dante barked out a laugh at Duncan's joking insults. Duncan always had a way of putting things in perspective. He'd been a good friend centuries ago and it had been a pleasant surprise to find he still was.

"Megan must be protected as best we can. She is precious, Duncan." Dante felt the ice of resolve flowing through his veins. "Even if she is my end, she must endure."

Duncan seemed to measure his words. "So be it." The half-fey knight held out his hand. "Do you accept my aid or will you go it alone?"

Dante reached for his hand and clasped it tightly. "We're in this together, for better or worse."

Dante was still conflicted, deep in his soul.

On the one hand, he wanted to do all in his power to weaken evil's hold over her. If that meant allowing Duncan into their bed again, he didn't have to like it, but he would allow it.

On the other hand, he'd seen how much pleasure she derived from having both of them at once. He liked giving that to her and while he hated Duncan for making love to the woman he ached to claim fully, he also had to thank Duncan for being careful with her. It was a strange position to be in. The idea that Duncan followed his lead when they were all together like that appealed to Dante's intense need to dominate Megan's pleasure. Of course, he still felt a small, lingering resentment that Duncan *had* to be allowed to make love to her.

And then Dante realized the root of the problem. Without Duncan's help, Dante couldn't protect her. That, which he saw as his own failure, was what irked him most. His inability to take her fully—to claim her body and blood at the same time—was feeding the jealous fire inside him. The reminder of his failure to release her from her keeper's thrall only added fuel to the blaze. It added insult to the injury of not being able to sink his teeth into her neck and sip of her delicate essence. He wanted that simple act more than anything he could ever remember wanting before.

The thought should have bothered him for all the reasons they'd already discussed. She was mortal and had shifter blood. Such beings were all right for occasional amusement, but Dante was thinking of something much more long-term. Permanent—if she'd have him—regardless of how that might be received by both the shifter and immortal communities. He'd have her no matter what anyone said and if she chose to join him in his endless dark, he'd take her there in an instant.

The thought should have been shocking. It wasn't. It was appealing in a forbidden sort of way. Dante was fast approaching the point of no return where Megan was concerned. The idea of turning her—which should have been abhorrent considering that she was *were* and therefore forbidden to turn—preyed upon his mind.

"So what's on the agenda for this evening?" Megan bounced into the room with a smile that brought an echo of sunshine to his dark existence. She plopped onto the sofa and looked at them with an expectant smile.

Dante couldn't resist her. Slowly, he stalked forward, cornering her on the soft sofa between his outstretched arms.

She looked up at him with no fear, only sexy expectation. He growled and dipped his lips to claim hers in a quick, hard kiss.

He let her up but didn't let go. "We'll go back to my place...eventually."

"Mmm. I think I like the sound of that." She grinned at him. "So what did you have in mind to pass the time before then?"

"You know sexual pleasure is sustenance to my kind, right?" He waited until she nodded. "Well, you've eaten. Now it's my turn." Dante rose with her in his arms and headed toward her bedroom.

There was also the little matter of allowing Duncan to use the energy released in the sex act to loosen the hold her keeper had over her and bind her from revealing Duncan's true identity. Dante wouldn't speak of it. She'd agreed. Duncan would do the magic. All she had to do was enjoy. If all went well, she wouldn't feel anything except pleasure as Duncan did his thing.

Dante stood at the side of her bed, grateful she had opted for a large size and jealous at the same time. Why would a lone woman have such a large bed unless she shared it frequently? Of course, she was a *were*wolf and they were known to like their space, so perhaps the existence of the decadent bed wasn't so sinister after all.

He wouldn't ask. Not now. He knew enough about women to know she'd take offense. His jealousy would only ruin the mood and derail his plans. That was the last thing he wanted to do, but the thought lingered in his mind. He vowed he would make her forget all who had come before him. He'd give her more pleasure than any of those shadows in her past. It was his mission and his goal.

The lamp beside the bed switched on, bathing the room in a soft golden glow. Dante looked over to find Duncan had followed them into the room and was regarding him with solemn eyes.

A nod was all it took to make Duncan aware of Dante's intent. Duncan came up behind Megan, joining them.

Four strong hands caressed her body as Dante seduced her senses once again. Duncan was his able assistant and willing accomplice. Both men were focused on her pleasure, and she knew without a doubt they would bring her passion as she'd only imagined before meeting them.

Dante alone was potent, but when he directed Duncan in their little love drama, he was unparalleled. He was always a dominant sort of man. When they came together like this, his dominant streak went full throttle. And she loved it.

She loved the way he ordered her around. The way he told Duncan what he wanted him to do her. What he orchestrated for them to do together to her. The passion, the pleasure, the purity of their time together was something she couldn't have imagined or anticipated. It was something totally outside her prior experience.

Had she thought about actually living the fantasy of being with two men at once, she never could have come up with such a scenario. She never would have expected the way she felt. There was nothing tawdry about the way they were together. Nothing sleazy. Instead, she felt honored and cherished. Totally respected by both men.

The only thing she could have wished for was love. She knew in her heart of hearts that such a thing was impossible between her and a vampire, much less a half-fey Knight of the Light. She had to enjoy this moment while it lasted because she knew all too soon, it could be over. They were involved in a dangerous situation and any one of them could be killed easily.

More than likely it would be her. She was the weakest link of their little chain. Very little could damage a being as magical as Duncan, and Dante hadn't lasted for so many centuries by being weak. No, if there was a vulnerable party in this group, it was her. Young, only half-shifter and under the compulsion of a sinister mage who'd tricked her and her family into doing heaven-knew-what for him, she was the one who'd be the easiest target for their enemies.

But such thoughts were for later. For now, there was pleasure to be had and two men devoted to bringing her the greatest passion she'd ever known. She'd be a fool to ruin this moment with fearful thoughts of an unknown and nebulous future. No, this moment was for savoring.

Dante demanded her full attention with his dark gaze. He leaned down to graze her skin with his mouth, working his way toward her lips. As he kissed her deeply, Duncan's hands were at her waist, removing her jeans and skimming them over her legs. She shivered as his hands lingered on her calves, working their way slowly back up her thighs and then to her panties. He dragged them down too, allowing them to pool at her feet with the denim of her blue jeans.

Dante lifted her out of the wad of fabric, placing her on the bed with gentle hands. He sat at her side, caressing her shirt up and off over her shoulders. The bra followed, and she was bare to his gaze and his roaming, arousing hands.

The bed dipped and Duncan joined them, sitting on her other side. She was surrounded by them, but not overwhelmed. Not yet. She figured that would come later, and she was really looking forward to it.

"Take off your shirts," she requested with a purr. Dante looked at her slyly, and she wasn't sure he'd comply. He gave in after a moment's consideration.

Both of them shrugged out of their shirts, and she was rewarded with the vision of two of the most perfect male chests she'd ever seen. Both men were built on the muscular side and she loved the way they looked, one on either side of her, ready to make love to her. How did a girl get so lucky? She didn't know, but she wasn't going to argue with her good fortune.

They were hers for as long as it lasted, and she would enjoy every moment she had with Dante and Duncan while she could. Dante was the most compelling man she'd ever known and his half-fey friend wasn't bad either. To her mind though, it was clearly Dante who made this encounter so special.

She was very much afraid that she was in love with the vampire.

It couldn't come to anything, of course, but there it was. She'd never have given herself so freely to him and his desires if she wasn't already a little in love with him. She may be *were*, but she wasn't a bitch in heat to do anything a man asked. She was more discriminating than that.

It was *this* man. When he came to her, all bets were off. She'd do anything for him, and she was afraid he knew it. She was all too transparent where he was concerned.

She stroked her fingers over his chest, loving the warm, hard feel of him. Rising to her knees, she went into his embrace, kissing him, needing him to hold her and make her feel alive.

She'd never felt this way with anyone. She doubted she ever would again.

"Dante, I—"

He silenced her with a finger over her lips. "Ssh, *ma petite*." He looked deep into her eyes, and she almost felt as if he were reading her mind. "Turn around, sweet, and give Duncan some of that. Kiss him as you just kissed me."

She sent him a questioning look, her heart in her eyes. How could he ask her to turn to his friend when she really wanted only him? Didn't he want her too? Or was this all a game to him?

It was delicious, of course. No woman was immune to having two handsome men so totally focused on her pleasure, but she wanted more. Somehow... she wanted a sign this meant more to Dante than just a momentary pleasure.

He seemed to see the pain in her eyes. His gaze softened as he stroked her hair away from her face.

"It must be this way. For now." His eyes held promises of which he refused to speak. "Duncan's magic will touch you, help you, protect you from what's coming."

She realized in that moment, he really did care. He wasn't sharing her with his friend out of some bored ennui, but rather out of concern for her welfare. Duncan was the most magical being she had ever encountered, and she'd seen firsthand his care and friendship for Dante. This act was one of love. The love of a friend for a friend, a brother in arms for his fellow, a guardian for those he was sworn to protect.

She was a little frightened of Duncan's power. She knew he was going to use it to bind her, just as her keeper had done without her knowledge. This was different. Duncan had explained the necessity, asked her permission and more than that, she trusted him. He had her best interests at heart. She'd always fancied herself an avenger—someone working for the greater good. She'd seen her work for the *Altor Custodis* in that light and only now realized she'd been duped.

There was no doubt in her mind that Duncan was on the right side. She'd seen for herself the way he wielded his magical sword and wore that stunning armor of light and goodness. He was the real deal. He was sworn to protect this realm and others from the encroaching darkness. There was no higher calling than that to her mind. For that alone she loved him. It was a different kind of love from the all-encompassing, consuming sort of feelings she did her best to suppress when in Dante's presence.

"Come now, sweetheart," Dante coaxed as he held her loosely by her shoulders. "I promise you, we'll bring you more pleasure than ever before. All I ask is that you trust me. This must be done."

She read what looked like regret in his eyes, and it comforted her in a strange way.

"I do trust you, Dante." Her words were a whisper against his lips as she leaned up for one last kiss.

She turned in his arms to face Duncan, and her heart was touched by the tender, compassionate expression on his face. He reached for her, and she went willingly. Duncan held her for a moment, hugging her close to his muscular chest, rubbing her back in comforting circles.

"I would never harm you, Megan. I only mean to help you."

"I know," she whispered to him. "But I'm wary of your

magic. Just lately, I've learned to fear mages."

"With good reason," he agreed. "Trust that my aim is to undo what has been done to you."

"And to prevent me from speaking of your true identity." She looked at him, trying to reconcile the necessity of what he had to do with her dislike for what had already been done. She hated that she couldn't speak of her keeper. She hated the pain that even the attempt to tell Dante and Duncan about her *Altor Custodis* contact generated. More than anything, she hated that the choice to speak or not had been taken away from her.

Duncan looked pained. That was the difference between him and the other mage who had worked his magic upon her without her knowledge. Duncan cared.

"I'm sorry, Megan. For now, it has to be this way."

She placed her finger over his lips and smiled gently. "It's all right. At least you asked, and you've never lied to me."

"It's not in my nature to lie," Duncan agreed, pulling her closer so her breasts rubbed against his muscular chest. "Especially not to such a beautiful woman."

She laughed as he swooped in to place a tickling row of kisses down her neck. Dante growled behind them, and she could feel Duncan looking at the bloodletter as he chuckled.

"Our friend is jealous that I can nibble your neck, but he's been banned from the pleasure." Duncan moved back, facing her. "That's one of the things we'll work on tonight. I don't think I can destroy the poison in your blood, but I can weaken it, and the hold your keeper has on you."

"I'm all for that," she agreed.

"Good. Then unzip my pants."

The playful tone switched to seduction in the blink of an eye, leaving her senses spinning. Duncan hadn't led the dance since that first time with Heath. He'd deferred to Dante since then, and she'd assumed it was because Dante was the more dominant of the two. She quickly reevaluated her assessment of Duncan. He was a warrior after all. Perhaps he'd been taking a lesser role because he sensed Megan's growing attachment to the bloodletter.

Whatever the reason, she was suddenly faced with two dominant men. Rather than put her off, the idea made her tingle as she lowered her hands to do his bidding.

Dante tugged at her hips, and she scooted back to accommodate him. She ended up on her hands and knees between the two men, a provocative position to be sure. Unbuttoning Duncan's pants with slow deliberation, she teased him as she lowered the zipper, tooth by tooth.

"Did you know our little Megan was such a tease, Dante?" Duncan asked over her head.

A growl and a smack to her ass was his immediate answer. Megan jumped but found the little spank more exciting than painful. He wasn't swatting to hurt. Instead, it tantalized, and her body was taking notice in a big way. Fire raced along her veins as her heart beat a quickening tattoo.

"Get on with it, Megan. I want to see your lips wrapped around his dick while I fuck you."

He'd never really spoken so bluntly to her before, and she was surprised to find it made her even hotter. She liked the picture he painted with his words. And she liked even more the way his hands molded her ass. His long fingers delved into the crease of her ass and lowered to tease the folds of her pussy.

"She's wet and ready for us, Duncan. I wonder if she'd like to take us both at once?"

Dante's deceptively casual question made her jump as she freed Duncan's long cock and pushed his pants out of the way.

"I think she likes the idea." Duncan took hold of his cock and guided it toward her waiting lips. "Open wide, lass. I want to feel your lips around me."

With little ado, Duncan pushed between her lips, stuffing her mouth while Dante's fingers slid into her wet channel. They both pulsed within her a few times before withdrawing. Duncan didn't go far. He retreated to let her tongue the tip of his cock while Dante's fingers dragged the moisture from her pussy up a few inches, to play around her ass. She sucked in a breath.

"You like having a cock up your ass, Megan?" Dante asked behind her. She could hear the teasing amusement in his voice, but she couldn't answer. Her mouth was otherwise occupied. She moaned as he pushed one finger inside her ass, just the tiniest bit.

"I think that's a yes," Duncan said on a laugh as he stroked into her mouth. He was letting her take what she could of him in small increments. She liked his thoughtful movements as much as she liked him.

Dante pushed deeper. "I'll make it so good for you, Megan. You know I can."

Everything Dante did to her felt better than anything she'd ever experienced before. He had more sexual skill in his finger—the one that was delving even deeper—than any of her past lovers.

Duncan eased out of her mouth and cupped her cheek with one big hand. "You know you want it."

He held her gaze with his encouraging, mesmerizing blue eyes. Slowly, she nodded.

Duncan smiled at her, his touch gentle, his gaze approving. "I won't use my magic to lull you into it this time. We'll take it slow. I think you'll enjoy this even more than that first night with Heath."

"If you say so," she panted as Dante began to move his finger around inside her. "How often have you done this before?"

"Many times." Duncan grinned wickedly. "We fey are highly sexual creatures, lass. This kind of encounter is delicious for all concerned when done correctly and one of the most powerful unions that can be made."

"So it's for the magic? That's why?" She was having a hard time stringing words together into coherent sentences.

"That's only one reason, Megan," he was quick to assure her. "I've only known you a short time, but already you're special to me, as I know you are to Dante. Let us show you how special."

She looked over her shoulder at the man whose opinion meant more than it should have. Dante's expression was shuttered, but his eyes lit with desire as he gazed at her.

"Everything he said goes double for me." Dante's roughly stated words surprised her, and from the quirk of his masculine lips, surprised himself as well.

She shut her eyes, drinking in their attention and coming to what felt like a fateful decision.

"All right then. Do your worst." The dramatic phrase was followed by a husky laugh as she put herself completely at their mercy.

CHAPTER TWELVE

Duncan scooted off the bed and disappeared into the attached bathroom. Dante positioned her to his liking, as if she were a rag doll. His strength impressed her again as he lifted her easily, placing her on her stomach with her knees pulled up under her. Her ass was presented and spread for him as he sat back. She could feel him looking at her, a low rumble sounding from his chest that felt like approval. It warmed her and sent the fire in her belly up another notch.

She knew a lot of wolves liked to use the backdoor with their lovers. It was a dominance thing. She was an independent woman—a lone wolf—and she liked it that way. Getting mixed up with a dominant shifter male had always seemed like more trouble than it was worth. So she'd only had human lovers and not many of them. None had delved into the kinkier side of sex.

Dante and Duncan were more than making up for her lack of experience in that area. She was discovering new facets of her personality and new desires she'd never even imagined.

Duncan returned and the bed dipped as he knelt on the side opposite Dante. She peeked around her shoulder and saw a tube of something passing from Duncan to Dante. No doubt he'd found something suitable in her bathroom to use as lube.

"Easy," Duncan counseled as he rubbed her back. No

doubt, he could feel the tension in her muscles. Without the drugging magic touch he'd used on her that first time, she was tense. He leaned down to whisper in her ear, nuzzling her neck and shoulder while Dante began a gentle but firm penetration.

It felt...weird. At first. Different than the last time. She was more aware of every sensation, sensitive all the way around. He touched something inside her that made her want to howl. No wonder shifter women put up with this act of dominance by their males. Holy Mother, that felt *good*.

She began to move with him and heard his rumble of approval as he added another finger, stretching her. The sensations grew and multiplied. Suddenly she craved his possession like nothing else.

"Now, my little wolf, let's see how you like the real thing." Dante's voice was an intoxicating growl as he positioned himself behind her. Duncan massaged her back and shoulders. She could see him watching Dante—or more likely, the place where Dante began to join with her—with rapt attention.

She couldn't see much with her head turned at an odd angle. It was enough to know that both men found this act to be utterly fascinating. Or perhaps arousing would be a better word. Duncan's cock was standing at full attention just a foot from her eager mouth. Whatever nerve Dante had hit with his probing had made her suddenly voracious. She wanted them both, and she wanted them now.

She reached out and took hold of Duncan's cock with single-minded determination. He jumped in her hand and when she looked up, she knew she had his full attention once more. She smiled and licked her lips.

"Oh, my beauty." Duncan moved closer, a cunning grin on his handsome face. "You like it even better without your senses dulled, don't you?"

She couldn't speak as Dante chose that moment to push inside her. She felt the ring of muscle give and the slight invasion of the tip of his hard cock. She wanted it all. She craved it with everything that was within her.

"More!" she cried, and Dante answered by pushing deeper. She gripped Duncan's cock, moving on him as her pleasure rose. Dante shoved inward once again until he was in full possession, claiming her in every way. "Oh Goddess!"

Duncan laughed at her reaction. "She approves, I'm sure. After all, my brethren believe She made us to enjoy each other in all ways."

Megan had never heard that said of the Goddess she had worshiped all her life. Then again the Goddess was at times one of plenty and fertility. She had other seasons, of course, but this was by far one of the most enjoyable for her followers. Shifters, in general, followed the Goddess and, until mated, weren't stingy with their sexual favors. Megan was perhaps, more fastidious than most, but then, she hadn't been raised in a typical shifter household.

Dante used his immense strength to roll, taking her with him as he shifted positions, maintaining his possession of her bottom at all times. They ended up on their sides, her top leg bent backward over his thigh, her legs spread wide to accommodate him. Dante's hand cupped her breast, squeezing her nipple as his mouth moved to nuzzle her neck.

Duncan intervened, earning a growl from the bloodletter. Yet he would not be deterred.

"No biting, my old friend."

Dante backed off grudgingly. "Move your skinny ass and join us or we're liable to end this without you." He sounded grumpy, but he felt wonderful within her as he began to pulse in short little digs that drove her wild.

Duncan moved close, rolling onto his side so he was facing her. He positioned his cock and paused, looking deep into her eyes.

"I've yet to take you this way, Megan. Will you give yourself to me like this?"

"It's a little late to start asking now," Dante griped from behind, making her giggle.

"Do it, Duncan. Do *me*." She'd never said something so

sleazy before in her life. Yet somehow it seemed to fit with the moment. Rather than breathless, all too serious passion, she was feeling lighthearted and...loved. If not loved, then cared for in a deeply touching way. It was enough to make her sheltered heart sing, and her body craved the feeling of their possession.

"Mm, I like it when a woman knows what she wants." Duncan complimented her as he moved even closer, lining himself up with her pussy. Dante's hands came around to help, spreading her so Duncan could support himself with one arm and use his other hand to help guide himself into her.

He penetrated her with just the tip, his cock filling her with Dante firmly in her ass. She felt a growl of desire rumble up through her chest, shocking her with the primal feelings these two men stirred. She'd never been closer to her wolf then at this very moment. Her animal nature joined with her mortal self, reveling in the males dominating her.

"Goddess, you're tight," Duncan said as he pushed deeper. The tone of his voice made it clear it was a compliment. When he was fully sheathed, he stayed motionless for a long moment, looking deep into her eyes.

Dante was the one who shattered the moment. He began a small, pulsing movement inside her that made her want to scream...or howl. She held the impulse in check as long as she could. When Duncan joined him in the motion and they increased both the tempo and depth of their thrusts, her wolf began to sing.

Luckily for her—not to mention her neighbors—in human form, her throat couldn't reproduce the sounds accurately or with nearly as much volume. As Megan moaned, her inner wolf did the same, joined with her completely at that moment in a way they seldom were.

The pace increased yet again and she was dimly aware of Duncan reaching over her shoulder, offering his wrist to Dante. She felt Dante's breath on her skin as he struck deep into Duncan's vein, pushing his arm down to rest on her shoulder. For the first time, she felt part of the sensuous act of Dante's feeding. She felt the small movements of Duncan's wrist against her arm. Dante's teeth and mouth moved as he sucked and swallowed, causing the small motions.

It took only a moment of this for blinding pleasure to hit her like lightning, striking her every nerve and sending her into orbit. She screamed as she felt the shock of magic striking her at the same time. Duncan's no doubt, cuddling her close and making her feel safe in a way she'd never felt before.

His magic tasted like honey on her tongue. His body pleasured her as his magic bathed her senses. She lost consciousness for a short time—so intense was the feeling.

Dante came inside her, and Duncan followed soon after. It felt as if he were watching over them. Duncan was more guardian and protector in that moment than he had ever been, encasing them in his magic and sharing himself with her on the most basic level. She thought she finally understood why the fey were such sexual creatures. If this was a taste of the way they interacted with each other, she finally understood why they shared themselves so freely.

She cried out as Dante released Duncan's wrist, the wounds healed by their combined magics. Dante's head rested in the hollow of her neck, safe from the temptation of her blood now that he'd been sated.

"You are so beautiful in every way," he whispered near her ear. The aftershocks of passion were still riding her, and his tender words caused the glow to linger.

She must have slept, for the next time she opened her eyes, Dante was standing beside the bed, fully dressed. She blinked at him and was gratified to see his satisfied smile. She felt like a goddess under his eyes and the appreciation she saw in his expression turned what could've been an awkward moment into something sublime.

"What time is it? Did I sleep long?"

"Not too long." He sat on the edge of her bed, leaning in

for a quick kiss. "I'd let you sleep, but we have things to do."

As the fog of sleep cleared, she remembered they were supposed to go back to his place. Being a bloodletter, he didn't have the luxury of being able to travel whenever he wanted. The move had to be accomplished at night.

"I just need a quick shower, and I'll be ready. Where's Duncan?"

A strange look passed over Dante's face. "He's securing the house in preparation for our departure." He stood, towering over her. She sensed him drawing back but didn't understand why.

"Pack a bag, Megan," Dante instructed on his way out of the room. He knew he was being irrational, but he didn't like the way she'd immediately asked about the half-fey knight. He hadn't liked the idea of sharing her either. It had to be done, of course, so he'd allowed it.

Funny that. He hadn't felt so possessive of a female in recent memory. Normally, he wouldn't have minded sharing at all. There was something special about Megan though. Something that called to his more primitive nature, that brought out the caveman in him. He didn't understand it and didn't like it, but there it was. He'd have to deal with it and whatever the fallout might be.

"Don't expect to come back here for a couple of days," he told her as he approached the doorway. "And don't forget, we're going to meet the wolf pack leader at that shifter bar tonight. You probably won't have time to change when we get back to Manhattan."

"I hear and obey, master." She gave him her best Jeanie nod, complete with crossed arms and a saucy grin.

He chuckled, his mood restored just that easily, as he made his way down the hall to meet Duncan. He heard the shower switch on and knew she needed a few minutes to recuperate from the sexual gymnastics they'd put her through. In this case, her *were* constitution was a blessing. If they'd fucked a mortal woman like that, she'd no doubt be awfully upset to have to go out for a business meeting just a few hours later. His little wolf was full of surprises and more than able to keep up with him, which was a new and exciting experience for a man who'd lived centuries and never had a liaison where he could totally let himself go sexually.

"I put a few telltale spells in place," Duncan said in a brisk voice as Dante entered the living room. The half-fey warrior indicated the window he was standing in front of with a nod. "This way, if anybody comes around here while Megan's gone, we'll know. It's nothing major and nothing traceable, but it should do the trick."

"Sometimes simpler is better," Dante agreed.

They took a few more precautions while Megan packed. It didn't take her long at all, and they were on the road inside of an hour. That left them just enough time to make their meeting.

When they arrived at Howlies, the bouncer recognized them immediately. They were directed to a private room in the back of the rather unassuming bar. Dante felt the eyes of everyone in the place following them as they made their way to the back room. The vast majority of the patrons had to be *were*. For one thing, most of them were big and muscular, as such creatures often were. Handsome too, by human standards, though none of the females present could hold a candle to Megan, in his opinion.

The private room was bigger and quieter than he'd expected. The moment they entered, the ambient noise from the bar receded. The room had to be soundproofed, which Dante realized was probably a necessity with a bar full of shifters right outside. Many shifters had the keenest hearing of all supernaturals, so if the Alpha wanted to meet with some guarantee of privacy, he needed a place where his people could guard the perimeter but not overhear what was said inside. He'd achieved both with this private room that was in a very public place, yet protected both by the bar full of shifters outside and the superior soundproofing in the walls.

"Welcome," Kevin spoke from one end of the long room. There was a big conference table in the center and plenty of room to move around between it and the walls. There were also long, thin tables along the sides that held everything from blank notepads, pencils and pens, what looked like a teleconferencing setup, flip charts and office supplies, to refreshments.

Kevin McElroy wasn't alone in the room. Dante recognized two of the firefighters who had been in his home. The other two men were unfamiliar and there was a female as well. All wolves. Most likely all members of the hierarchy of Kevin's pack.

"Please be seated," Kevin invited. "Can I offer you some refreshments?" He indicated the platters of food, an arrangement of soda and water bottles, as well as liquor on one long table.

Dante was surprised to see a few bottles of wine as well. He could tell at a glance they were not cheap vintages either. The Alpha wolf was pulling out all the stops, making quite a show of hospitality. Dante only hoped it was more than just a show. So far, the pack leader had been very helpful indeed. Dante hoped that would continue.

Duncan snagged a bottle of wine and some glasses, pouring for himself and Dante while Megan opted for a soft drink and some munchies. She smiled at the pack leader in thanks and just that small gesture annoyed Dante to no end. If she was going to smile at any male, it would be him, not some mangy dog.

Dante breathed deep to settle his turbulent emotions. He hadn't been this out of control since the great fire. He was off balance, and he didn't like it. Duncan's steadying presence helped as the half-fey knight handed him a full glass of burgundy.

They sat around the table as the wolves did, each side eying the other.

"Thank you for meeting with us." Dante figured he'd start the conversation on a polite footing. Where it would go from there was up to the dogs.

"Thank you for coming." Kevin met Dante's gaze with what he read as sincerity. So far, so good. "I've asked some guests to sit in. You may remember Bob and John from the visit we paid you after the fire." The two burly firemen nodded in his direction and Dante did the same. "Stacy is head of our community outreach program, such as it is. She's the one who saw Siobhan Vabian lob that firebomb into your window and called me."

"I am in your debt for your quick action." Dante made a point of thanking the chestnut-haired beauty.

She was tall for a woman with the figure of a bombshell and the angular features of a model. He'd bet she was a nice looking wolf when she shifted, but found himself put off by her size. Megan was petite, and he found her smaller lines more attractive. The brunette smiled and nodded, but her smile was tight. He'd bet she'd had no idea she was coming to a bloodletter's rescue when she had called the fire house.

"Clarence and Dominic are sitting in on behalf of their packs, whose territories adjoin ours." He indicated the other two wolves with a wave in their direction. Clarence was a burly blond, and Dominic looked like his countenance could have graced the head of a Roman coin back in the day. Dark hair, skin and eyes shouted his heritage, yet he was taller than most people from that part of the world and thickly muscled, as most shifters were.

Dante noted that except for the female, Kevin didn't specify the ranks or roles of the so-called *guests*.

"I am Dante d'Angleterre. It's good to meet you all," he said formally. He went on to introduce his companions, taking the lead and acting as Alpha for his own tiny pack. "Duncan le Fey is newly returned to this realm." That one sentence let the shifters know who they were dealing with without revealing too much. "And Megan is a lone wolf whose family owed me a blood debt."

"How does a wolf bitch end up owing a bloodletter a blood debt?" Dominic wanted to know.

"My grandfathers sanctioned the death of Dante's ward, a firemage named Erik. It was unjustified and for their mistake, you banished them."

"The last twin wolf lords? Those were your ancestors?" Clarence seemed stunned, his blond brows rising in surprise.

"They were. They had one daughter, my mother. All of them are now gone and it has been my task to restore the family honor."

"And how did you think to do that without the backing of a pack?" Stacy asked. Her tone was condescending, and Dante didn't like it. He bared his teeth in her direction, but subtly. He had to tread lightly for now. Still, if the wolf bitch didn't play nice with Megan, he'd put her in her place.

"I've never needed to lean on a pack," Megan shot back. Dante liked the way she stood up to the other woman. "I make my own way."

"As it happens," Duncan broke in, helping defuse the tension somewhat. "Megan's ancestors were recruited by the *Altor Custodis*. One in particular told them they could work off their debt to society by performing certain tasks for him."

"What kind of tasks?" Kevin asked, leaning forward, clearly interested.

Megan shrugged. "I spied for him, delivered messages, ran errands when asked. That sort of thing."

"She was placed under a compulsion never to speak of her keeper's identity and had some of her memories altered to conceal the fact that her keeper was a follower of Elspeth, Destroyer of Worlds." Gasps sounded around the room as Duncan continued. "We believe the *Altor Custodis* have been infiltrated at the highest levels."

"You can't be serious," Clarence objected.

"Deadly serious, Alpha." Dante was gratified to see the man's eyes widen again as Dante correctly guessed his position in the neighboring pack. "If you don't believe us, I suggest you talk to Rafe, Tim and Allie again. We all had a run in with Patrick Vabian—the brother of the woman you saw—" he nodded toward Stacy, "—attacking my home."

"I put a call in to the Lords yesterday." Kevin drew all their attention with his announcement. "They wanted us to give you our full cooperation. They also had a message for Megan. They asked me to tell you that all is forgiven. Banishment of your grandfathers was never meant to extend to their descendants. You should never have had to pay for their mistake. You're welcome to petition any pack for membership, just like any other *were*. The prohibition on your family is at an end."

Dante had mixed feelings about the announcement. On the one hand, he felt vindicated on Megan's behalf. On the other, he disliked the idea that she was now free to join *were* society. She could easily seek membership in any pack— including Kevin's. While he was glad for her, he also selfishly didn't want to give her up to any of the wolves. She was his.

Oddly, the possessive thought didn't disturb him as much as it should have. He was coming to accept the idea that some things just happened, whether he wanted them to or not. His attachment to Megan was one of those things. He didn't question it. He just knew in his heart that she was meant to be with him—at least for the moment. What came after they dealt with this crisis, he had no idea.

He sought Megan's gaze, gratified when she reached for his hand under the table. She looked so lost he wanted to hug her and hold her close, protecting her from all others. The grasp of his hand would have to do while they dealt with this development.

"While I appreciate the gesture." Megan squeezed his hand as she spoke. "I'm not ready to make any decisions. There are still a lot of problems I need to face and dispense with before I can consider ending my lone existence. All in all, it hasn't worked out too bad. I was raised a lone wolf and right now I can't even contemplate living within a pack structure."

Kevin sat back, watching her with sad eyes. "I don't expect it will be easy for you, but your options are open, should you wish to return to the fold."

"Thank you, Alpha. It was kind of you to speak to the Lords on my behalf." Megan was polite if distant, and her grip on Dante's hand never let up.

"Now, as to our current problem," Dante deftly turned the subject. "The three of us paid a visit to Siobhan's address last night. She wasn't home, but she left some rather nasty surprises for any who might call on her."

"I don't doubt it," Stacy said with a grimace. "That bitch was laughing when she bombed your house. She's *loco*."

"I found no less than three very ancient books on demonology in her home," Duncan revealed, much to the surprise of all gathered. "They will, of course, be destroyed. However, their presence in her house is proof positive that Siobhan, and perhaps all the Vabians, are seeking power from realms forbidden to this mortal plane."

"Why do you include her family? What proof is there?" Dominic spoke for the first time.

"Such ancient texts have long been hunted by the guardians of this realm. Surely you are aware of that." Duncan turned to the dark wolf. "I have always been interested in magical tomes. The last time I walked in this realm, I became acquainted with one whom I knew to be a guardian. I helped her search for certain titles, aiding her in finding them when possible. Siobhan Vabian had one of the titles I believed to be completely eradicated. The only way a copy of that book could still be in existence, and in her possession, was if her teachers or her family—and I suspect they are one and the same—have kept the book hidden and passed it down through the generations."

"Then the problem may be even larger than we first suspected." Kevin had a grim expression on his face as he summed up their situation.

"All too true," Duncan agreed. "And we may need some of you to act as backup. Such evil must be contained and cannot be allowed to escape. If we fail..."

"Have no fear." Kevin held up one hand, palm outward. "The Lords asked us to assist in whatever way we can. You two must've impressed them. They've given you *carte blanche* with us and that's good enough for me."

"Me too," Clarence seconded.

Dominic eyed them once more before also agreeing. "My pack will assist as well."

"So what's your next move?" Kevin asked before Dante could thank them for their pledges of support.

He thought it significant that Kevin had called in not one but two of his neighboring pack Alphas for this discussion. That was a good sign. It meant Kevin was taking this as seriously as he needed to. Either the Lords had done a good job impressing upon Kevin how important the Vabians were, or Kevin had arrived at the conclusion all by himself. Either way, the all-important cooperation of his pack was now more or less guaranteed.

"Siobhan wasn't home, but we know where her family lives. Before we even think of storming their castle, we need a little more information about them and their holdings. I was hoping you'd be able to help with some of the legwork. I know your kind is generally good at that kind of thing and well connected." Dante looked around at the gathered wolves.

Kevin chuckled. "You'll have to tell me sometime how you know so much about us, but you're right. It just so happens I have some law enforcement connections within my pack that might be able to help us dig up further information on the Vabians."

Dante smiled. "I thought you might. What I'm interested in now is whether or not they have any secondary holdings closer to the city. If we have to, we can lay siege to their Chappaqua compound. I'd rather not go that route if I don't have to."

"Roger that," Kevin agreed.

"I suspect if Siobhan has gone to ground, it's somewhere nearby. She has a hard on for you, Dante," Stacy said. "If you could've seen her face when she attacked your house, you'd know she was motivated by hatred. It was written all over her. She wants you dead, and I doubt that kind of anger will be satisfied by a near miss or two. She'll keep going after you until she's killed you."

"Not if we get her first," Duncan put in with a challenging lift of his brow.

"Good point," Kevin agreed. "Now, let's figure out how we can do that."

The meeting lasted another few hours, during which time the men discussed plans and contingency plans. Kevin took the opportunity to make a phone call to one of his pack members who was with the FBI. They put her on the speakerphone while they discussed what kind of information they needed her to look for. She promised to get right on it and have a preliminary report ready for Kevin by close of business the next day.

Dante was pleased with the level of support the wolves were giving him. He figured they owed it to Megan, at least, for all those years of shunning her and her family. Moreover, he was just as glad to have backup in this hazardous situation. It wasn't only his neck on the line this time. No, this time Duncan and Megan were along for the dangerous ride.

If he only had to worry about himself, he wouldn't care. And Duncan could probably take care of himself. Megan, though, was a whole different story. He wanted to protect her and feared that if he was taken out, she wouldn't survive. At least with the wolves' involvement, the chances of her survival were considerably better than if they went it alone, and he had some hope that if he died in this pursuit, Megan wouldn't be so alone anymore. He hoped if he didn't make it, one of the wolf packs would take her in.

The meeting finally broke up somewhere in the wee hours of the morning. They took their leave of the wolves on a much stronger footing than they had entered. The relationship was building slowly, but it was building. That was a positive sign as far as Dante was concerned.

He, Megan and Duncan headed uptown to his home. All three were tired after their adventures. They spared a moment to convene in the living room, to go over the night's events. Dante pulled Megan down to sit next to him on the couch. He didn't examine why, but he wanted her close. Much to his delight, she snuggled into him without a word, as if she belonged there.

"All in all, I think the meeting went well." Duncan sat in an overstuffed chair facing them. "They were better prepared for us than I gave them credit for. Kevin doesn't let any grass grow under his feet. That's for sure. He had not only verified our story with his Lords, but brought in two of the neighboring Alphas to look us over as well. He's as cunning a wolf as I've ever met."

"Yes," Dante agreed. "I think we can work with him. What was your take on Dominic and Clarence?" He squeezed Megan's shoulders, asking her opinion.

She started sleepily and turned her pretty face up to his. "I was surprised by them. They were Alphas in their own right. Yet they seemed to defer to Kevin. Of the three, he's not the eldest, but he's somehow superior. Probably by right of challenge. I'd guess either Clarence or Dominic, or maybe someone else of a higher rank we don't know about, challenged Kevin and was defeated by him. That would have given Kevin the superior rank in the hierarchy. It's a little different here in the city than it would be elsewhere. The individual packs probably interact often because of their close proximity. I could smell the way both Dominic and Clarence deferred to Kevin, though it wasn't obvious. I also liked that he didn't lord it over them. He included them more or less as equals in the discussion. From my understanding of *were* society, he could have easily pulled rank but didn't. That says something for him."

Her level of insight amazed him. She was a keen observer of people, and her *were* senses and instincts told her things Dante had almost missed. He thought she was dead on in her assessment of the situation, but he still didn't like the hint of admiration in her voice when she talked about the Alpha wolf.

"Very astute of you to notice all that," Duncan complimented her. "There's something else about Kevin that I wondered about the first time we met, and confirmed tonight. He's got something—almost like a Glamour—around him. I'd lay odds it has something to do with his job. I think, although I can't be sure unless I see it in action, that he's impervious to fire. Or at least has some natural magical protection from ordinary flame."

"Makes sense that someone with that kind of ability would become a firefighter," Dante allowed. "He's also an Alpha wolf. I know *weres* have some natural resistance to magic. I've never actually met any that had this kind of magic of their own."

"Neither have I, actually." Duncan scratched his chin thoughtfully. "It could be something that's developed since I've been away. Or it could be something special—something specific to Kevin alone, or perhaps to his family line. Perhaps a mating with a human mage somewhere in his ancestry that passed the ability to him. I really can't say without further investigation, though I doubt he'd just come out and tell me if I asked."

"That ability could be why he's superior to the other Alphas," Megan said, nestling into Dante's side.

He could feel her fatigue. It had been a long night for all of them. Especially for her, since she couldn't feed off the energies they'd released earlier like he could, and didn't have a nearly unlimited supply of magic at her disposal like Duncan. She was mortal and subject to the rules that governed most mortals, though her strong *were* constitution helped a great deal.

"Good point," Duncan said, yawning. "I, for one, am going to sleep on it." He stood from the chair. "I'll let you know tomorrow if I think of anything else. For now, I wish you both good rest."

Duncan leaned down to give Megan a gentle kiss, then took himself from the room.

Megan yawned. "I think I'll turn in, myself."

She tried to get up, but Dante held her back with gentle insistence. She turned to look at him, surprise lighting her eyes.

"Stay with me tonight, Megan. Sleep in my arms." He didn't know where the request came from but knew the moment he spoke the words they felt right. He wanted her with him. He wanted to watch her sleep until daylight drained him and when he woke at dusk he wanted to smell the scent of her shampoo on the pillow next to his head.

She smiled at him and this time when she tried to stand, he let her, following close behind. She took his hand as she led him toward the hallway.

"I'd like that too." Her whispered words were a balm to his soul.

He lifted her hand to his lips for a tender caress before sweeping her into his arms. He carried her to his room and laid her on the bed, coming down beside her. He would have done more, but the lines of weariness on her lovely face stilled his ardor. She was tired and needed rest. It would be selfish of him to make any more demands on her this night. She'd already gone above and beyond for him. The least he could do was allow her time to recover before he made love to her again.

He tucked her next to his heart and stroked her arms in a gentle caress.

"Rest now, my love. Allow me to watch over your slumber." He wasn't sure if she heard him or not, for the next moment she was sleeping peacefully in his arms.

CHAPTER THIRTEEN

Megan woke two hours before sunset, still held close in Dante's warm arms. She loved waking to feel him next to her. It was something she'd love to get used to, even though she knew a relationship between them was impossible. Still, it was a nice fantasy, while it lasted.

With a sigh, she left the bed to start her day. For one thing, she was famished. After the tumult of the last few days she'd missed a few meals. Shifters needed to eat more than the average person. Their high metabolism aided them when they shifted and helped them heal faster than humans. It just required a lot of fuel to keep their bodies running efficiently.

After she cleaned up and dressed, she joined Duncan in the kitchen. He was already cooking.

"Oh, you read my mind." She joined him by the stove and peered over his shoulder to see what he was making. "Fettuccini Alfredo with chicken? That smells good."

"I spent a lot of time in Italy in the past. I prefer their cuisine to most others and pasta is simple enough to cook in this day and age when it's all pre-made for you." He snagged a towel off his shoulder to grab the hot frying pan handle. He tossed the chicken pieces, then flipped them expertly into the sauce pot. "This should be ready momentarily. Would you mind setting the table?"

"Not at all." Her mouth watered as she grabbed plates and

utensils from the cupboards and placed them on the table.

They ate in a companionable silence. Megan was focused on her hunger to the exclusion of all else, and she was thankful Duncan didn't say anything about her wolfish appetite. Her table manners weren't up to her usual standards. Then again, she usually wasn't starving when she sat down with company either. She figured he'd cope.

From the quantity of food he'd made, she knew he'd realized how hungry she would be and was thankful for his thoughtfulness.

"How are you feeling? Aside from the giant hole in your stomach that we've just filled?" Duncan asked as he took another bite of the delicious pasta he had prepared.

His teasing warmed her and set her at ease. "I'm all right. I was really tired last night—or should I say this morning—after we got in. I totally conked out and slept straight through, which is abnormal for me. Usually, the slightest noise wakes me. I'm a light sleeper."

"I think most *were* are the same. It's all those innate animal instincts. They keep you on guard, even when you're asleep. Not a bad defense mechanism actually."

"True." She would have said more, but the ringing phone interrupted her.

Duncan wiped his mouth with his napkin and rose to answer the phone. His expression was one of mild puzzlement. He knew as well as she did that any friend of Dante's had to realize he wouldn't rise for another hour at least. So whoever was calling either had the wrong number or wanted to speak to one of them, not Dante.

"Hello?"

Were hearing was sharp and Megan could easily pick up the other side of the conversation in the quiet house. She was only mildly surprised to recognize Kevin's voice on the other end of the line.

"Duncan. I have some information for you."

"That was fast." Duncan carried the handset to the table and sat, shooting Megan a questioning look. She nodded, telling him without words that she could hear what was going on.

"Yeah, I realize that and it does raise my hackles a bit. I figured you could use your own judgment. We turned up information about a yacht owned by the Vabians that's currently moored out on Long Island. Port Washington to be exact. I called in a favor from some affiliated shifters that are water based out that way. They took a sniff around the boat this afternoon. A blonde matching Siobhan's description was seen there about an hour ago. She was bringing supplies aboard. It smelled like food and probably some clothing. My friends think she was moving in for an extended stay."

"That would make sense if she's been to her house. After what went on there, she had to know somebody had tripped the traps. Not to mention the fact that I took her books. She's either running scared or really pissed off. Probably a little of both." Duncan chuckled at his own observation.

"My friends are there and will report back any movement to me. I thought I'd make you aware of the situation so you could discuss it with Dante when he gets up. If you're going to make a move on the boat, let me know so I can warn my people."

"Do you think they'll stick around to give us a hand?"

"Hard to say. They're not wolves. I can't order them around. I can only request. They're talented people and unparalleled in the water. To be honest, I haven't had a lot of dealings with them. They keep to themselves for the most part. I can tell you they have a stellar reputation among our people. If they agree to help you, you'll be lucky to have them on your side."

"I see." Duncan looked thoughtful. "Well, I'll give you a call back once we decide what to do. I'm pretty certain we'll be taking a drive out to Long Island tonight."

"It could be a trap. In fact, I'd bet good money on it. The information was too easily obtained."

"Oh, I have no illusions on that score. It most likely is some sort of trap, but we must take our opportunities where we can find them. Dante is a man of action who prefers to do battle head on rather than wait for a better opportunity. I'm of a mind to be the same way in this case. Like I said, we'll let you know. Probably in an hour or two."

"I'll wait for your call. And I'll be in touch if anything else dovelops."

"Thanks for your help, Alpha. It is more than I expected and greatly appreciated."

"No problem, but if this works out for you, I hope you'll explain to me sometime how you got so tight with the Lords so fast. That's a story I would love to hear."

Duncan laughed and assured the pack leader he'd be happy to regale him with the story over a pint of beer at the earliest opportunity. They chatted briefly about beer of all things, then hung up with a friendly goodbye. It sounded like the beginning of a friendship from where Megan sat. She'd never interacted much with other shifters and was unprepared for how congenial the wolf Alpha appeared to be.

"You heard?" Duncan asked.

She nodded. "It could very well be a trap, but I agree with you. I think we can handle her between the three of us. I'd rather go out and face her than wait for her to attack again."

Duncan agreed with her and they finished their meal in pensive silence, waiting for Dante to rise.

*

When Dante entered the kitchen, he found a subdued wolf and grim-faced half-fey knight waiting for him.

"What's wrong?" He was expecting the worst.

"Kevin called." Duncan's words were clipped, but he tried to put on a brave face. "His people found Siobhan, possibly hiding out on a yacht owned by her family."

"So what's the problem?" Dante breathed easier, pouring himself a glass of wine.

"It's most likely a trap."

"Why do you think that?"

"Kevin said the information came too easily."

"I see." Dante took a sip, thinking hard. "So at least we're forewarned."

"Damn, I knew you were going to say that." Duncan shook his head, laughing softly.

"Am I so predictable then? I'm not sure I like that," Dante mused, sipping his wine as he stepped over to Megan.

She looked at him with those worried wide hazel eyes he couldn't resist. He bent down to kiss her, glad when she responded warmly to him. She was a beautiful thing to wake up to, and he liked having her in his home. Probably too much. He would have to deal with that when the time came.

"What do you say, sweetheart?"

"I'm with you, whatever you decide. I should tell you that we already assumed you'd want to check it out tonight. The wolf Alpha is waiting by the phone for your decision."

Dante laughed out loud at that. "Why does he need to be involved?"

"It's all very mysterious." Duncan's eyebrow rose as he grinned. "Kevin called in some help from water *were* of some kind. He didn't say what kind, but they're still there, watching the yacht. He wanted a heads up if we decided to move in and indicated if those water shifters decided to help us, we'd be glad to have their help."

"I wonder what kind of shifters are so good in the water?" Dante mused.

"Tigers, certainly, but the *tigre* clans probably don't interact much with the likes of Kevin. It's more likely some obscure tribe of *were*folk, but I didn't think there were any polar bears or orca around Long Island, except their animal brethren imprisoned in zoos. Of course..." Duncan's eyes narrowed as he thought, "...it could be selkies."

"Selkies? Like the Irish myths about people who turned into seals? They're real?" Megan asked. The old fairy tales had always appealed to her, though she didn't understand why people thought the shifters had to put on and take off their seal skins in order to shift. Because of that aspect of the story,

BIANCA D'ARC

she hadn't believed such creatures really existed.

"Aye, they're real enough but rare. Very rare indeed," Duncan confirmed. "I didn't realize they'd made it to the new world and settled here. The last time I was in this realm, most of their leaders were convinced they should isolate themselves from humanity. The last I knew, they were hiding out in enclaves in the most inaccessible areas of the Irish coast."

"Maybe they moved?" Megan puzzled it out. "They could probably blend in on Long Island. Although the area isn't known for seals, there are miles and miles of coastline— much of it privately owned. If they struck it rich and were able to buy a place along the shore, they could come and go as they pleased and no one would be the wiser."

"Very likely," Dante agreed. "Myself, I've never met a seal shifter. According to legend, they're supposed to be among the most handsome of beings. Yet I don't know how good they'd be in a fight."

"Kevin seemed to think they could more than hold their own. He said, in fact, we'd be lucky if they agreed to help us," Megan offered.

"All right then." Dante polished off his wine and put down his glass. "Give Kevin a call and tell him to let those water *were* know we're on our way. If they want to help us, they're welcome."

Duncan picked up the phone as Dante tugged on Megan's hand. She stood and followed him from the room. Once he had her in the living room, he pulled her into his arms and kissed her the way he'd wanted to since the moment he rose.

She was breathless by the time he let her go. Breathless but smiling. He loved the way she responded to him.

"Now that's what I call the right way to start my evening." He rubbed her lower back with long strokes of his hands. He wanted to make love to her, but they had things to do and villains to catch. "After we take care of this business, tonight you're mine. All right?"

She nodded, her eyes wide and so innocent-looking he

could almost cry. She was so young compared to him. Young and vital. She was like catnip to a *tigre*. Irresistible and seductive. And he would have her again tonight. No Duncan. Not if he could help it. Just him…and her. Poisoned blood be damned.

But they had work to do first.

They took Dante's car to the north shore of Nassau County, following the coast to the quaint and bustling town of Port Washington. There wasn't much cover as they approached the marina, but that couldn't be helped.

Dante went first with Megan. He didn't want her in the path of danger, but he needed her nose. If there were explosives on the boat, she'd be able to smell them. Likewise, she would be able to sniff out anything else he might miss, and she did have a natural defense to most magic. If Siobhan got the drop on them, Megan would probably be okay. She had fast reflexes and knew how to handle herself if fireballs started raining down.

Duncan was acting as backup. They hadn't gotten a straight answer from the wolf Alpha about the supposed water *were* who had been on site. If they were still there, Dante didn't see them.

"The yacht is the last one in this row, way at the end." Megan reported after checking a diagram at the main entrance and walking a short way to the right arm of the complex docking system.

He didn't like this setup at all. They'd be too exposed on the final approach to the boat, which was moored at the very tip of one of the marina's spindly arms. It was a prime location that must've cost a pretty penny. Not only was access to the open water achieved more easily from that location, but it was quieter away from shore without a lot of foot traffic on the small ramps that connected the boats to land.

They would have some cover until they got near the end of the arm of floating planking to which the yacht was moored. The last few yards would leave them out in the open and very vulnerable. Still they had little choice. They'd have to approach cautiously and keep to cover as much as they could until that final stretch. That would be the most dangerous part of this plan. If any surprises had been set for them that would be the place.

Keeping that in mind, Dante set out with Megan, taking the lead and keeping to the shadows between the smaller boats as much as possible. They had quite a distance to traverse. Boats of many sizes were all connected by a network of skinny pathways that bounced up and down on the water as they walked.

There was no direct route to the yacht. Instead, they had to make their way over a series of connected walkways that led like a maze toward their goal. There was some advantage to the circuitous route, providing them darkened spaces between smaller boats for cover and places where they could stop and observe their destination.

Dante called a halt when they were nearing their goal. He wanted to take a minute to scout out the area. Chances were, there was something foul waiting for them in their not too distant future. Siobhan wouldn't have left her hiding place unguarded. Not after the things they had encountered at her home.

Megan grabbed his hand as he saw movement on the deck of the boat they were heading for. Someone had come up from below and was doing something on deck. It was a man. An older fellow. Definitely not Siobhan. Maybe her father?

Megan pulled at his arm as he moved forward. "This smells bad," she muttered, sniffing the air. "It smells like..."

"What?" Dante asked while in motion. He was heading for the boat more quickly now, intent on his target.

"Dante, stop!" She tugged at him urgently, her voice pitched low so only he could hear it.

"What's the matter?"

"That's—" She broke off as a blinding pain crashed

through her skull. The heel of her hand ground against the pain between her eyes. "Oh Goddess!"

"What is it?" Dante crouched to next to her as she doubled over in pain. "You know him?"

It was all she could do to nod her head as the magical prohibition did everything it could to stop her. Dante must've realized what was going on. He supported her by the elbows and dragged her into a shadowed aisle between two boats where no one could see them.

"It's your keeper, isn't it?" Dante's expression was grim. "That's the only thing that could be causing you such pain."

She tried to nod again, but wasn't sure if she actually made any movement. The malevolent magic held her in its grip, denying her the ability to identify the man she'd seen on the deck of the yacht.

"Dammit! I hope Duncan is watching. If that man is the one who did this to you, we'll need Duncan's special touch to overpower him." Dante stood, peering over the top of the boat they were crouched behind, though Megan tried desperately to draw him back.

Fear rose within her, choking her. It was like nothing she'd ever felt before—a cold dread that seeped into her very bones. She, who feared little in life, was deathly afraid now, facing a man she'd known for many years. She knew how cold Poferov could be. She'd experienced his frigid demeanor and soulless cunning many times.

She'd never dared to go against him. She wasn't sure she had the courage to do so now. She was nearly paralyzed with fear on Dante's behalf should he confront Poferov in any way.

"Don't!" she whispered, fighting with all her might against the compulsion not to speak. "He's too dangerous."

Dante crouched down beside her once more, cupping her cheek in one powerful hand. The look in his eyes told her much. She read sympathy, caring and a ghost of something that could have been love, were they both free to feel such things for each other. It warmed her to think this brave man could be so gentle with her when faced with such danger. She hated the fact that she'd ushered such evil to his doorstep and involved him in her problems.

That Poferov was involved in this at all was her fault. Megan felt the weight of it in her heart and on her conscience. She felt like she had brought this upon them. Her mistake, her vulnerability, her stupidity in believing the lie the *Altor Custodis* agent had perpetrated upon her and her family. Why hadn't she questioned it before? Why had she blindly believed? Simply because her mother had?

"Will you be all right here, Megan? I don't think you should go any closer. Let me handle this."

His voice was a balm to her bleeding soul. "I'm sorry. I'm so sorry, Dante." Her broken whisper sounded painful even to her own ears.

He shushed her gently, drawing her close for a short moment. "Stay here. Stay hidden. I will slay your dragon, sweetheart, and then we can celebrate together—just us two."

The promise in his eyes was nearly her undoing. If she could be free from Poferov's control—if Dante could kill him—her blood would be cleansed of his evil magic. She would be free to be with Dante as she knew he desperately wanted and needed. She wanted it too. She wanted to feel the bite of his fangs into her skin, the reward of his passion as he took her essence into himself. She wanted to share everything she was with him—if only for as long as it could last.

She didn't delude herself with dreams of forever. She and Dante could only have a short time together, but she vowed to make the best of it.

"Will you be all right?" he asked tenderly.

A single tear trickled down her cheek as she nodded. He kissed it away and gave her a soft smile.

"Stay alert and stay here. I'll come for you when it's done."

"Be careful," she managed to whisper, though Poferov's tainted magic tried to silence her.

Dante grinned devilishly as he moved away, heading toward danger. She realized he was in his element, the warrior in him reveling in the fight to come. She watched him make his way between the boats in the row they had taken shelter in. There was an open space and then another row of boats before he reached the final approach to the yacht.

Unencumbered by her presence, Dante shifted form into a black-coated leopard, prowling silently toward his objective. Because he used a different sort of magic to shift than a *were*, his clothes went with him, absorbed in the shift. She couldn't manage that and often lamented the need to undress and stash her clothes somewhere before she shifted to wolf form.

Dante's power was different. The big cat form he'd chosen tonight was both lethal and sexy. Megan admired his skill in shifting and the way he moved in the cat's skin as she watched him edge closer to their objective.

Poferov was no longer visible on deck, but she didn't take comfort in that. Instead, she worried more. Had the bastard seen them? Was he just waiting to spring some trap or launch a strike against Dante? The thought made her queasy.

"Oh, Goddess!" she whispered, followed by a deeply felt prayer for Dante's safety. "Please watch over him, Lady." Another tear rolled down her cheek, the chilly night air stinging her eyes as she watched his progress.

"Does he really mean so much to you?" a strange voice sounded from below.

Megan gasped and started violently. Thankfully, she was hidden between the smaller boats. Looking around wildly, she realized the voice had come from the water. A wet hand rose to the wooden dock from between it and the nearest boat.

She would have screamed if her vocal cords weren't already frozen with fear. Megan scooted away from the ghostly hand as fast as she could, crab-walking on her hands and feet backward, away from the apparition.

She hit something and could go no further, ready to scream when another wet hand clamped over her mouth and a man's hard arm clutched her around the middle, dragging her back into his embrace. Her back was to the stranger's chest, and she could feel he was soaking wet and massive. He had muscles on his muscles, and his voice was a dark whisper at her ear.

"Calm down, little wolf. We're here to help."

She struggled as the hand still on the dock was joined by a second one. A moment later, a naked man propelled himself out of the water to land on the dock. She'd sensed the magic thick in the air around them.

They were shifters. She stilled. Perhaps these were the water *were* Kevin had mentioned.

"Ah, you begin to understand."

The one behind her eased his grip and took his hand from her mouth slowly, no doubt ready to act if she started to scream.

"You're *were*?" she asked, needing confirmation to calm her racing heart.

"Sorry we scared you." The one in front of her spoke in low tones that didn't carry over the water. "We've been watching the yacht. Nasty fellow on board. I hope your bloodletter friend is armed for bear."

"Dante," she whispered, her gaze seeking him. The black cat was just visible as it slunk toward the last of the smaller boats that provided cover. She turned to the water shifters. "Please, you have to help him. I-I can't. There's a binding on me." Even to speak the words was difficult as the pain returned. "The man on the boat…he did this to me…without my consent or knowledge." Daggers stabbed into her skull as she fought against the compulsion. "Please, help Dante. Please." She subsided and huddled on the deck, pain slicing through her head as the evil magic had its way with her.

She watched the water shifters as they looked at each other, then at the boat where Dante was headed.

"Be at ease, little sister of the land," the one behind her said as he touched her temple. In a flash, the pain was reduced to manageable levels, but it wasn't completely gone.

"Must be a powerful mage to do this to a young wolf in her prime," the other one muttered.

Megan nodded through her tears. They were leaking out

of her eyes uncontrollably now, both in pain and fear for Dante. She absolutely hated being helpless. But these men could help. She just knew it. She just needed to convince them.

There was one thing she could say that would both convince them to help and warn them of what they were up against. She didn't know if she could speak the word without passing out, yet she had to try. For Dante's sake.

She grabbed the arm of the man behind her, struggling to speak. "He's...evil. He's... he's... *Venifucus.*"

She saw the man's face darken as his eyes narrowed. As she'd suspected, these were men of integrity. They recognized the threat.

"Goodmorrow, gents."

Duncan chose that moment to reveal himself. His armor was in place but darkened to a gleaming midnight glow to conceal him in the dark. The two water *were* were startled by his quick appearance. They didn't seem afraid even as they flinched. Rather, they seemed impressed. And once they got a good look at Duncan in his ethereal armor, their whole manner changed.

A low-voiced conversation ensued between the three men. It was in a language Megan didn't understand. It was hushed and quick. Rapid fire. It sounded faintly like Gaelic, but she couldn't be sure.

The two men seemed to defer to Duncan in some indefinable way, yet treated him as an equal. Megan didn't completely understand the dynamics of the situation. Yet it was clear to her that Duncan had their respect. Now, if only he could convince them to help Dante.

They spoke for less than a minute. All the while Dante was putting himself closer to danger. Megan watched him as best she could from behind the boat, but his black-furred body and the docked boats made it hard to see him. She thought he was in the last row of boats by now, preparing to make the final leap through the open space of the walkway that led to their target.

The urgency of the situation made her blood run cold.

"Duncan," she whispered. "He needs you now. He's almost to the yacht."

The fey knight looked up sharply, assessing the situation for himself. Immediately he turned to the water *were* and spoke a few short sentences. The two men shifted as they slipped silently into the water, and Megan got a quick glimpse of what looked like giant seals as they cut into the depths and disappeared below. They shifted form like other *were*, but she'd never seen anything like them in her life.

She knew now the myths and legends that had sprung up over the centuries about their kind were wrong. Selkies didn't need to put on and take off their seal skins like a coat. They shifted form just like other *were*, but even she could tell, they were a lot more magical.

"They're going to help him?" she asked Duncan as he too, headed toward the yacht.

"Stay put, lass. We'll take care of this." He winked at her before heading away from her, toward danger.

CHAPTER FOURTEEN

Dante crouched low in the concealment of the second to last boat in the row. The man was no longer visible on the deck of the yacht. In this form however, Dante could smell him. He smelled foul to the cat's senses. Evil.

After seeing the way his presence affected Megan, he wasn't surprised by the odor. He was taken aback by its intensity though. Perhaps he shouldn't have been, but there it was. Megan had to be even stronger than he'd thought to have faced this kind of evil and still retained her self. A lesser soul would have succumbed a long time ago.

He watched, using the stalking skills of the cat. Crouching lower to the deck, he sensed a disturbance in the water beneath him. Unsure, he didn't know what to make of the currents he could feel through the thin wood of the walkway.

He backed off a second before a dark face broke the water. It was a seal. And if he wasn't much mistaken, a magical one at that.

One advantage to Dante's type of shifting was his ability to speak while in animal form. It wasn't always pretty, but for the most part it was understandable, depending on what form he chose to take. He regarded the dark face, his whiskers twitching, taking in information.

"Sssselkie?" he asked, the cat's mouth making the sibilants ring, even in a whisper.

The head bobbed up and down, and the nose pointed to his left. As Dante watched, a human hand rose from the water, followed quickly by a man's head.

"We'll help." His voice was pitched low and terse. "The wolf is in pain. She knows we're here, as does the fey. He's coming. We'll cover the water. There were some nasty things set beneath the yacht. We took care of most of it when we first arrived. Whoever did the work was not a true watermage."

"Thanksssss," Dante said as the two selkies disappeared soundlessly below the surface of the dark water. When this was all over, he'd like to talk with these seal shifters. They were good at disappearing. In all his years, he'd never seen the like.

Dante sensed Duncan's approach and decided to wait for him. Their original plan had been for Duncan to hang back in reserve while Dante and Megan confronted Siobhan if she was on the yacht. The presence of Megan's *Altor Custodis* keeper changed everything.

Megan was out of the action until her keeper could be stopped. Killed preferably. Dante wasn't entirely sure he would have enough power to neutralize such a potent mage all by himself. With Duncan's help though, the scales tipped in their favor—or so he hoped.

Duncan sidled up beside him. Dante's focus was on the yacht, but he was aware of Duncan's presence. He spared him only a quick glance, pleasantly surprised by the dim glow of his armor—now black steel for night work. It had been a long time since Dante had seen that particular talent of Duncan's. Fighting side by side with the half-fey knight brought back memories of a time long past.

Here they were, centuries later, still facing evil together. And the evil hadn't changed much either. The *Venifucus* may have hidden, but they'd never been completely annihilated. They'd been foolish to believe otherwise.

"Megan is laying low. You and I should do this together, my friend. And we have friends in the water."

Dante shifted back to human form, making a quick decision to face this on two legs rather than four. His black clothing returned to his body in the magical shift that took only a small fraction of his power.

"We've met. They said they would guard from below and intercept anything that's been set in the water."

"There are no finer warriors in such situations. I believe we'll have no trouble from below."

Dante nodded quickly. Duncan was more knowledgeable about selkies than he was.

"Then I suppose we must lay siege to the yacht. Any preference as to how?" Dante raised one eyebrow in challenge.

"I follow your lead, my friend. Challenge the mage and while he is busy with you, I will take his measure and counterstrike."

"It's a good plan." Dante had a few skills. Hopefully he'd be able to fend off the mage until Duncan could join the fray. "All right. I'm ready when you are."

"No time like the present."

The two old comrades shared a smile. They'd done this many times before but not often in recent memory. Dire as the situation was, it felt good to be taking action. Dante knew without asking that Duncan understood. Both of them were old campaigners. They'd fought many battles together, laid siege to castles, taken strategic positions and stormed the gates many times.

Each time could have been their last. Somehow, they had always prevailed. They'd taken their share of lumps, but they had always ended as the victors. Dante sent a quick prayer skyward for a similar good result.

This time a woman's life hung in the balance. Megan had been sent to spy on Dante, so if he showed up in a battle against her keeper, there was no doubt the mage would know his spy had turned. Megan's life would be forfeit if Dante failed.

Regardless, she couldn't go on this way. The poison in her

blood, the magical prohibitions placed on her mind—that was no way to live. For her sake and his own, Dante had to free her from the control of the man on the yacht. He prayed to the Goddess to give him the strength to do so quickly and with as little damage as possible to Megan.

Standing tall, Dante strode out from between the boats, heading directly for the yacht. He didn't see the man at the rail. He could be on deck. It was a large boat, after all. Dante's purpose was to draw the mage out so Duncan could get a good look at him both physically and magically. This would be no sneak attack on Dante's part. No, that honor went to Duncan. With any luck, the mage would think Dante was alone and wouldn't expect Duncan's immense magical power.

As Dante approached the yacht, he noticed ripples in the water. For a brief second, he thought he saw one of the selkies, but he couldn't be sure. He took it as a good sign anyway, taking the water shifters at their word that they would guard the depths. Dante moved steadily forward, watching the luxury boat with alert attention.

In the shadows toward the back of the deck, he sensed movement. A moment later, a wall of energy rose in front of him on the dock, sparking and sputtering with painful electrical jolts as it advanced toward him. Dante stopped in his tracks, seeking a way around it. There was only a thin wooden walkway leading to the yacht.

There was water all around, of course. With the selkies protecting the depths, Dante could make use of that. He'd bet the mage was counting on it. The wall of energy was most likely being used to herd him into—or perhaps above—the water.

But the mage didn't know about the selkies—their ace in the hole.

Dante shifted form to that of a giant, gray owl. Owls had special adaptations for stealth and could fly almost silently, unlike other raptors. Flapping massive wings over the water, he tried desperately to gain altitude in case something got by the seals. He needn't have worried. Nothing sprang out of the murky water to ensnare him as he rose into the dark night. Instead, he heard the distant bark of a seal amidst the muttering curses of the man who now stood openly on the deck of the yacht.

From his vantage point above, Dante saw Duncan move into position at the same time the mage raised his hands, aiming directly for Dante. Pouring on the speed, Dante called on the instincts of the owl, hoping like hell that Duncan could neutralize the mage before he blasted Dante out of the sky.

A dark stream of sparkling, malevolent energy burst from the deck of the yacht toward Dante. He dove and swooped as best he could but still managed to get his feathers singed. Duncan, however, wasn't idle. He launched a counterattack on the mage, and the stream of deadly energy ceased. The mage turned his attack on Duncan instead. His power merely sparked harmlessly off Duncan's black armor.

Duncan was in his element, fighting the fight he was best equipped to handle. Magic against magic. Dark against light. Evil could not stand in the face of Duncan's goodness.

The massive amounts of magical power being thrown caused the lights of the marina to dim. Then, one by one, the light bulbs began to pop, raining shards of glass and sparks everywhere as the fight escalated.

Since it was the middle of the night, the marina was mostly deserted. Only one or two brave souls popped out to try to see what was causing the disturbance. No one looked in the direction of the yacht. Such was the magic of Duncan's calling. It protected the innocent even as it smote the guilty.

Dante made wide circles, looking for his opening. He could help Duncan end this quickly. All it took was one moment of inattention on the mage's part.

There!

Dante stooped and dove, aiming his three-inch talons at the last second. He went for the man's throat. Too late, the mage realized the danger. Dante had him in his clutches and tore through skin and tissue, ripping the man's throat out as he took once more to the air.

The mage clutched at the wound that would kill him. He had little time left. There was no way he could recover from such damage, but until he was dead, he could still hurl his vile magico.

Duncan moved closer, encasing the evil mage in a protective bubble of light his final acts of magic could not penetrate, and so he could not curse those who remained in this realm while he crossed over. His magics would fade with him, never to return.

Dante had seen Duncan do this before, but it had been too many years to count. It was good to see that Duncan's power had only increased with age. Dante flew to his old friend's side, shifting as he alighted to stand beside Duncan. They watched the mage breathe his last on the deck of the yacht.

Duncan held the shield in place until he was certain no further harm could be done by the mage. He then released his magic with a weary sigh.

"That should do it."

"Glad I am to hear it. That one was as foul a being as I have ever run across."

"You'll get no argument from me on that score," Duncan agreed.

"I must check on Megan."

"Your lady is well and on her way to you," a man's voice said from below.

Dante looked down to see one of the seal shifters in human form, bobbing in the water. He knelt to speak with him.

"Thank you for your help. If you should ever need anything of me, please do not hesitate to ask. I definitely owe you for your assistance here tonight."

"We'll remember that," the man eyed him shrewdly. "I think, after what we just saw, that you and your friend are on the side of light. We are sworn to that cause and glad to help eliminate such nasty pieces of work as the one on the wooden whale."

Dante chuckled at the man's nickname for the ostentatious luxury yacht. "Be that as it may, I consider myself in your debt and would welcome the chance to further our acquaintance."

The man tilted his head. "We'll see. So far, you have us intrigued, I'll grant you that, but further contact will have to be decided upon. Most likely, we'll be in touch. If not for you, then for your friend, the knight."

Duncan bowed to the man in the water. "I am at your disposal whenever you wish to talk. There are things I believe your people should be made aware of."

The man nodded. "It's good to see the likes of you in our world again. Good—and troubling, if you get my meaning."

Duncan laughed outright. "I understand and take no offense." He spoke a few more words with the selkie in a dialect of Gaelic Dante had never learned. It was old. Far older than Dante himself if he was any judge.

He would've tried to listen, but he heard Megan approaching and turned to meet her.

She flew into his arms looking drained and relieved.

"How are you feeling?" He held her, supporting her weight as she sagged toward the deck.

"The pain is subsiding. Give me a minute or two, and I'll be okay. You got him?" She looked hopeful.

"We got him," he assured her. "He's dead, and his magic with him. You should be free of the effects shortly. It takes a while to fade completely, from what I recall."

"You've done this sort of thing before?" She looked at him sideways.

"In the distant past. Not often, but often enough to remember how it works for the most part." He smiled at her because he couldn't help himself. She would be free and that meant he'd be free as well...to feast on her.

Dante noted absently when the selkie slid under the water and disappeared. Duncan seemed to have had a lot to say to the man, but Dante wouldn't pry. Duncan had a higher calling and many secrets to which Dante was not privy. It was the nature of his race to be secretive, and Dante would have long ago lost him as a friend if he let such things bother him. It was enough to know what Duncan was and who he served. All the rest were just details he could easily do without.

Megan pushed away, able to stand on her own. She looked tired. Some sleep would help restore her. A lot of sleep. First, however, they had a yacht to search.

"Are you up to looking around a bit? We should take this opportunity to search the yacht." He studied her beautiful face, concern for her wellbeing foremost in his mind.

"I'm feeling better with every passing moment, as a matter of fact. I'd like to see what's left of him. Just so I know... So I can be sure."

"I understand." Dante tucked her under his arm as he led the way toward the boat. Duncan joined them, seeking to board first.

"Everything magical in the vicinity should have been obliterated by that final blast, but just in case..." Duncan hopped over the railing, climbing nimbly aboard the huge boat. The gangplank had been stowed, but Duncan set it out for them after taking a quick look around.

Dante allowed Megan to precede him aboard, bringing up the rear as he kept an eye out for any signs of possible trouble. There were none. As Duncan had predicted, very little magic had survived the battle. The area had been cleansed by the clash of energies and was as close to pure as possible given what had taken place here only moments ago. Duncan was a better judge of such things, of course, but Dante had seen his share of magical battles in the past and had learned what to look for.

"Thank the Lady," Megan whispered. She stood looking down on the sightless eyes of her keeper. "He's really dead."

"That he is," Dante agreed. He wasn't too worried about Megan's sensibilities. Shifters were used to the hunt and to killing their prey. She wouldn't be shocked by what was left

216

of her keeper. In fact, he realized, she *needed* to see it, to know for certain he no longer had any power over her.

"His name was Igor Poferov," she said, looking at the corpse. She smiled faintly as she looked up at Dante. "I can actually say it without any pain. His hold is broken. Thank the Goddess!"

"And Duncan," Dante added with a grin.

"And a certain sharp-taloned owl," Duncan said with fierce approval. "Couldn't have done it without you, brother." Duncan patted him on the back as he passed, heading toward the hatch that led below. "I'm going to have a look around. Will you keep watch above?"

Dante agreed quickly, knowing Megan needed a little time to recover and take it all in. Duncan could search the mage's domain more thoroughly than he could anyway and it wasn't *that* large a boat. The search wouldn't take long.

"Poferov is—was—the top man in the *AC* for the metro New York region. There will be some turmoil when they learn of his death."

"The real *Altor Custodis* won't do anything about it. It's the wolves hiding in sheep's clothing, if you'll forgive the metaphor that we have to be worried about. If this man had other *Venifucus* agents under him, or even above him, they'll be on the lookout for us, though I doubt we'll be the first ones they seek for his death."

"What do you mean?"

"This tub belongs to the Vabians."

"Ah..." He could see the wheels turning in her mind. If Poferov died on Vabian turf, it would be the Vabians who'd be sought first in connection with his death.

"Are we just going to leave him here then?" Megan asked.

"I think it best." Dante shrugged carelessly. "He certainly deserves no better and I wouldn't like to taint any other place with his evil, even in death. This is a fitting place for him until his fellows discover him. Then they can do with him what they will."

"Dammit!" Duncan walked back onto the deck, a dead

snake in one hand. "The bastard had a pet on board and it bit me."

Megan and Dante both went to him. Dante grabbed the snake, made certain it was dead and ascertained it was of the non-poisonous variety. He threw it onto the dock after securing its mouth with a spare piece of line to prevent any of Duncan's blood from tainting the wooden planks. They'd take the snake with them when they left and dispose of it properly so it couldn't lead anyone back to them. Megan, meanwhile, was looking at Duncan's wound.

"There should be a first aid kit on this boat somewhere," she muttered, looking around.

"I'll get it," Dante said. "Don't touch anything if you can help it and if you do touch something, wipe it off. Good old fashioned fingerprints could lead them to us even more quickly than Duncan's magical signature."

Megan nodded as she opened Duncan's sleeve, wiping at the slow trickle of blood. Dante was pleased to see they were both careful about leaving any behind. So far, they hadn't left anything on the boat that could lead back to them, but this complicated matters. Dante knew better than anyone that blood was a powerful marker for all kinds of beings.

He found a small first aid kit stowed within easy reach of the deck and brought it to Megan. She'd ripped through Duncan's sleeve to expose the wound and was examining it. It didn't look too bad to Dante's eyes. Still it had to hurt like the dickens.

"I'd offer to lick that closed, but I hesitate given the snake's involvement. For all we know, some residual magic could have resided in it."

"Your caution is warranted, my friend." Duncan cringed as Megan began to bathe the wound, carefully keeping track of every item she used, putting the bloody gauze in the top tray of the plastic first aid kit. They would take that with them too when they left. "I felt it zap me with a good dose of black magic when it struck, yet not enough to do me harm. It probably would've killed anyone else though, so it's not to be trifled with."

"Poferov used to keep that thing in a big aquarium behind his desk," Megan reported. "Gave me the creeps every time he called me into his office."

"Probably his familiar," Dante murmured. "Some mages still invest part of their magic in a pet, keeping it handy to call on as a reserve should need arise."

"That was definitely the case here. Because the creature had been given the mage's energy to keep as its own until it was needed, it survived its master's death," Duncan reasoned. "Just my luck to come across it."

"I'm sorry. I didn't think he'd travel with it." Megan cringed. "And I couldn't tell you anything. Not even about the damned snake."

"It's all right, lass." Duncan soothed her as she began applying antiseptic to his wound. "None of this was your fault."

"Then why do I feel like I brought all of this to your door?" She shook her head, clearly exhausted. "I'm sorry."

"Did you find anything below besides the snake?" Dante asked. He figured a change of subject was in order.

"Nothing useful." Duncan looked grim. "The mage wasn't staying here. It looked as if he had just arrived, and he had none of his personal effects except the snake, of course."

Something smelled bad about this whole setup. They'd come here to hunt Siobhan and had ended up with much bigger prey. It didn't add up to Dante's way of thinking.

"This was too easy." Duncan spoke Dante's thoughts, fatigue in every line of his body.

"Easy?" Megan bandaged the wound on his arm. "You call this easy?"

"If you'd have asked me how this was going to go down, I'd have said Siobhan Vabian would be the first to fall. She seemed like the easier target, all things considered." Dante shrugged. "She has no discipline. So far she's acted out of a surplus of emotion with little success. Whereas this Poferov fellow, by his very nature, is a planner, a deep player."

"Someone served him to us on a silver platter," Duncan concluded.

"I wouldn't be surprised to find that there are others involved in this." Dante shifted his weight uncomfortably. "Perhaps there's someone close to Siobhan who's a little more experienced than she's shown herself to be. Could be they didn't want to see her fall and decided to distract us with another target instead."

"It's a likely possibility. Then again, getting Poferov was a good day's work." Dante leaned down to stroke Megan's hair. "You're free of him now. However it happened, the result is something to be thankful for."

They didn't take long to leave the yacht, leaving Poferov's corpse behind for the Vabians to discover. Dante used his own brand of magic to blur their presence from anyone who might still be looking. Only two people in the marina had poked their heads out when the light bulbs blew and both were long gone, but Dante wasn't taking any chances. Without the lights, the marina was pitch dark. All three of them had good night vision and could easily see where they were going.

They reached the car, which he'd parked out of sight a block away, and drove off without further ado.

"Where to now?" Megan asked.

"My place," Dante said firmly. "The Vabians will likely check tomorrow morning to see who survived this encounter. They wouldn't chance coming in the night, in case things unfolded as they have. They wouldn't want to face us after we'd just dispatched their pawn and if Poferov had survived, they'd be able to come up with some excuse for not arriving before daybreak. We should be safe enough at my home for the rest of the night and most of the day. I doubt they're prepared to strike at me again so soon, considering they had to believe Poferov might've done the job for them."

The ride to Manhattan was accomplished quickly, with little traffic at this time of the morning. While it was true that New York was the city that never sleeps, it did snooze every once in a while and the wee hours of the night was one of those times.

"I'm sorry I was so useless back there," Megan said as they headed toward the bridge that would take them off Long Island. "I was no help at all."

Dante reached for her hand, steering the car with his other hand. "Don't be so hard on yourself. We had it under control."

"You did the best you could, given the circumstances," Duncan said helpfully from the back seat. "Poferov was one hell of a mage. I'm surprised you were able to defy his compulsion as much as you did. Look on the bright side— you're free of it now. You can tell us everything you know about his operation and I'll take a final look at your blood, just to be certain the poison died with Poferov. I feel certain it did, but it pays to be cautious in cases like this."

"Why? What do you think might happen?" Megan turned in her seat to look at Duncan worriedly.

"Well, we've been operating under the assumption that Poferov was the one who poisoned your blood. It's a good assumption, but before anyone does any biting—" he looked significantly at Dante, "—we need to be certain. You don't remember being put under his compulsion or having the poison put into your bloodstream, do you?"

"No." Megan's brow wrinkled in a frown.

"It's more than likely he clouded your mind. I just want to make sure he was the only mage involved. If there's another one out there, the poison could still be active. If not, you're probably clean."

"I hadn't thought of that. Let's check as soon as possible, okay?" Megan sounded eager, and Dante took that as a good sign. She knew as well as he did that if her blood was clean, he'd be drinking it as soon as could be arranged. He'd fuck her and feed from her as he'd wanted to do since the moment he first saw her.

She sent him a shy look as she turned back to the front of the car and it touched him deeply. He could tell from that

221

one guarded look that she was on the same page. She wanted him. She was charmingly shy about it for some reason, but she definitely wanted him.

He would be more than happy to accommodate her. In fact, he'd be downright thrilled to do so. It was exactly what he wanted too.

After they got home and Duncan did his test, the waiting would be over. Finally. He would have her. Body, blood, heart and soul. She would be his.

At Dante's townhouse, Duncan burned the snake's carcass with magical flames in Dante's fireplace. It sparked blue and green as it disappeared, leaving not even an ash behind. They patched up Duncan's arm in clean bandages. The horrible gashes were nearly closed already.

"And now for you, my dear." Duncan motioned for Megan to sit beside him on the couch. He placed a flat glass plate on the coffee table, then produced a gleaming dagger from somewhere near his waist. He hadn't been wearing it. He had produced it from the same magical plane his armor existed on, waiting for him to call it forth when needed.

He quickly nicked his own finger and allowed a drop of his blood to fall onto the plate before the wound closed. Duncan beckoned to Dante, and he offered his hand with a raised brow.

"I chose the steel dagger just for you, my friend," Duncan teased, showing off the gleaming blade in the soft light. "The silver one remains hidden Underhill."

Dante grinned. "I thank you for your discretion." He placed his hand over the plate as Duncan inflicted a tiny nick that allowed a single drop of his blood to fall to the glass below. Then Duncan turned to her.

"The reaction of your blood to mine will alert me to the presence of magic—especially that which should not be there. The reaction of your blood to Dante's will tell us if the poison is, indeed, completely gone."

She offered her hand and Duncan took it in gentle fingers.

"It will not hurt. One of the blessings of my calling is my weaponry. It is charmed to kill—or in this case, injure—with no pain." He nicked her finger and held it over the plate, allowing a single drop to fall right next to the drop of his blood. He moved her hand quickly, placing a second drop next to Dante's blood before her wound closed.

Duncan closed his eyes, and it looked like he was fighting fatigue. He rallied and let her hand go, refocusing his attention on the plate. Using one finger, he made a stirring motion and Megan felt the prickle of magic rise in the air as the two drops of blood—his and hers—began a twining, spinning dance before joining together with an audible tinkling sound.

Megan shivered as something inside her tingled along. Duncan watched the droplets of blood intently. At length, he stilled his finger and breathed a sigh.

"So far, so good. I can detect no evil energies. If any remain, the next test will bring them out, even if they are hiding."

He raised his hand again, this time above the drops of Dante's and her blood, stirring counter-clockwise this time, joining the two droplets into one larger pool. Megan felt her entire body flush when the drops joined, followed by an intense arousal. She'd never felt such a thing—and neither man was even touching her.

She gasped as Dante's gaze locked with hers across the low coffee table. His dark eyes held intent, promises and desires that made her even more breathless. She looked away redirecting her attention to the plate and Duncan's test. Their mingled drops of blood were bubbling gently. It didn't look malevolent. She didn't know exactly what it meant, but the magic of it was potent.

Duncan watched carefully and she knew he was using all his senses, both mundane and magical, to assess the reaction. At length, he sat back, a relieved smile lighting his face.

"The poison is well and truly gone. You are free, my dear."

Relief washed over her. She'd been half afraid the death of Poferov hadn't been enough. It looked like she'd worried for nothing. Poferov was gone and so was his control over her. She felt liberated, free in a way she hadn't felt since her mother had first introduced her to Poferov years ago.

"Thank you, Duncan." She clutched his hands, smiling broadly. "I can never thank you enough."

"It is my pleasure to see you so happy, Megan. Ever since we first met, I've thought you don't smile enough. It's good to see you this way, though I fear this development marks the end of our time together." He leaned close and kissed her sweetly, though she didn't understand. He moved back with a wistful smile just as her head began to spin.

"What do you mean?" she asked, puzzled.

"Now that you are no longer a danger to our friend here, I doubt he will tolerate my presence in your bed. It was sweet while it lasted, Megan." Dante watched them with impatient, glowering eyes as Duncan kissed her hand and finally let her go. "Now I need to rest. All the excitement tonight has left me fatigued." He walked toward the hallway, turning to look at them before he exited. "Be good to each other. From the way your blood reacted...well...it should be an interesting night." He winked at her. "Leave the plate. I will dispose of the blood properly in the morning. Such things are best done in the full light of day."

She didn't understand what he meant by that. He was the magician here, not her. Not for the first time, she was grateful of that fact.

Free of the mage's compulsion with the poison gone from her bloodstream, she was finally whole and healthy again. Ripe for the plucking. And she had no doubt Dante was more than ready to pluck.

"Alone at last," Dante said with a trace of humor that made her smile. He claimed the place next to her on the couch and sat, looking at her with those mysterious dark eyes.

The way he watched her made her want to squirm, but she held her ground. This was an Alpha male at his most intimidating. It didn't matter that he wasn't a shifter. He had that dominant, Alpha way about him. It frightened her. At the same time it made her mouth water in anticipation.

He didn't move forward. He didn't come closer. He only watched her. The intensity of his gaze sharpened, and his relaxed stance was only for show. She was certain of it. Beneath the façade of calm urbanity lurked a predator just waiting for an opportunity to strike.

"Nothing is inevitable, you know," Dante said at last, breaking the silence. "You're free of the poison. If you want, you can also be free of me. I don't hold you under any obligation. If you come to me now, it's of your own volition. You're not a spy anymore."

"I never wanted to spy on you," she admitted. "I haven't had a lot of control over my life in recent years."

"I know." He reached out with one hand to stroke the hair back from her face. His touch was gentle, caring and all too seductive. "What I'm trying to impress upon you here is that you're free to make your own choices now. The big question is, do you want me the way I hunger for you? Contrary to all my prior experience, I would find it nearly impossible to take you if your answer to that question is no."

"Really?" She searched his eyes.

His intensity didn't waver. "Yes, Megan. I don't understand it myself. I've never felt this way before."

She moved toward him, drawn to him and the honesty in his words. "I haven't either. I thought it was just me." She was in his arms, drawing ever closer.

"It's not just you. I feel it too." His words drifted over her as his head lowered and his lips met hers in what felt like their first kiss. Perhaps it was, in a way. The first of many, now that she was free to choose her own path.

She flowed into him, loving the way he made her feel. His mouth possessed hers, his body so much larger than her own, but she didn't feel threatened in any way. Instead, she felt protected, cherished and...loved. It was a heady feeling.

As heady as the feeling he gave her when he lifted her into

his arms and rose from the couch. He was incredibly strong, dominantly masculine. He lit her senses on fire. He strode toward his bedroom, kissing her, drawing back only to shove open doors with the power of his mind.

He truly was a force to be reckoned with. He had abilities, power and skills beyond any mortal. While she was a shifter, she couldn't compete with the things he'd learned to do over his centuries of existence. Rather than frighten her, the thought made her feel warm and cosseted. She knew he would never use his power against her. He would never harm her in any way. In fact, he'd done nothing other than protect her, fight on her behalf and free her from the moment she'd first met him.

He laid her on the bed and came over her, stripping off his shirt as he went. She was already struggling out of her clothing. They'd waited too long to go slow. She was starved for him, and she wanted him now. No more delays.

"I've been dreaming of this for days." Dante stripped off his pants. He was glorious in the buff, all strong muscles, dips and valleys of masculine perfection. She'd dreamed of him too. Scandalous dreams where he made her come from a simple bite on the neck, or the thigh, or anyplace he damned well pleased. She was up for it all.

She was wet and wanting already. She didn't want to wait. She tugged at his shoulders and wrestled him down onto the bed, using her *were* strength to get him to move, though she suspected nothing would have made him move if he didn't want to.

He smiled up at her when she straddled his nude body. She'd done away with her own clothing, and they were skin on skin. Every inch of him was enticing, and she wanted to rub all over him like some kind of cat. But she was a wolf and her baser instincts were telling her to devour him in every way possible.

She mounted him, preparing to push down so he'd be within her body, just where she wanted him. She made the mistake of looking into his eyes. It wasn't a mistake really. It was more of a reward, for when she met his gaze, she saw the same vulnerability that hid in her own heart shining out from his.

"Dante, I…" She poised, the tip of him parting her folds as she held herself above him.

He laid a finger over her lips, stilling her words.

"This is a beginning, Megan. A fresh start. It all begins right here, right now, with just us two."

"I feel it too." She felt a wistful smile bloom over her face. "I thought it was just me."

"It's not just you. Now…" He thrust his hips upward in a slow arch, sliding deeper as he held her gaze. She caught on quickly and moved downward to meet him until he was sheathed completely within her. She stilled, holding him firmly within her depths. "Now it begins anew."

She moaned as they began to move together in rhythm. They'd learned each other's bodies over the past days. They knew how to complement each other's desires, but this felt different. For the first time, they were alone in their pleasure, just the two of them. It felt right. Better than right. It felt good. Perfect, in fact.

Not that she hadn't appreciated her time with Duncan. Those wicked threesomes were something she would never forget. But she'd wanted Dante since the first moment she laid eyes on him and it was with a sense of homecoming that she took him. Alone at last as he'd said earlier.

They moved together, totally in synch. It was as if they were made for one another. She used her thighs to press upward as Dante moved marginally downward. When they came together, he guided her hips, adding his strength as he pushed into her and she spread her legs to their widest angle to take as much of him as possible. All of him. That's what she wanted. In every way.

Her fever rose sharply as their rhythm increased. She panted for breath, her climax dangerously close. Dante tossed her beneath him, never leaving her body, using his incredible strength to reverse their places so he could claim her fully.

His head lowered to hers as he came over her. He held her gaze for a moment, his expression as earnest, hot and open as she'd ever seen it.

"I'm going to drink of you as we come, Megan. I've wanted to taste you, to savor you, to bask in your essence. Will you allow it?"

"Oh, Dante. Was there ever any doubt?" She stroked his muscular shoulders, smiling up at him. "I would never deny you. I've wanted to share this with you for just as long. Bite me, Dante. Make me yours."

He growled as he lowered his head, kissing her first, then sweeping his lips to her neck in a warm, wet path of kisses that grew progressively hotter as he neared his target. His hips resumed their pounding cadence as he drew near the source of her lifeblood. She felt the scrape of his fangs against her sensitive skin a moment before he struck.

She was desperate. Desperate to come and desperate to make him come with her. She felt the sting of his bite a moment before she screamed her pleasure to the stars, experiencing the most intense orgasm of her life.

She felt her blood flow into him, joining them, coalescing their essences to produce a new, single entity. As she climaxed, she felt Dante join her, reaching with her toward a distant star. She felt more than that, she felt his wants and desires, his needs and hopes, his dreams.

In a blinding second of clarity, his mind was open to hers. Their blood mingled...as did their minds.

"We are One." Dante's voice sounded through her head, though she knew he could not speak with his mouth. His lips still drew on her neck, drinking her blood, joining them together. No, the words had come directly from his soul to hers.

Incredibly, she heard his thoughts. A flash of insight followed, and she suddenly understood. They were truly *One*.

For each bloodletter, there was One person who could join with them fully. Who could complete them. They searched their whole lives for their One. Many never found their perfect mate. For the few lucky souls who did, the blessing of perfect union—of hearts, minds and souls—was the ultimate reward.

They had achieved this rare honor and nothing or no one would ever part them again. She saw the love in his heart, and he saw her love just as she saw his. No words were necessary. Words were, in fact, totally superfluous. They were communicating on a much deeper level.

They were One.

Megan smiled blissfully as she came back to Earth from the most intense experience of her life. She was utterly exhausted, but a grateful smile graced her lips as she sank into the oblivion of sleep.

"I love you, Dante."

"I love you, too, my One."

CHAPTER FIFTEEN

Megan woke in the late afternoon, wrapped in Dante's arms. She never felt more safe and secure than when she was with him.

In a rush, the events of the night before came back to her. While she was alone in her thoughts with Dante asleep, she could feel that place in her mind where they were connected. That magical place that made them One.

She couldn't quite believe it. She had once heard the legend about how bloodletters searched through their entire lengthy existence to find one special person created just for them. She'd thought of it as a simple romantic tale. She never really believed it could be true.

Here she was though, living the fairy tale. It didn't seem possible that she could be Dante's perfect mate. The One for whom he had been searching for so long.

She kissed his cheek before she left the bed, gratified when he smiled even in deep sleep. She felt truly alive for the first time in years. The curse was lifted—both the compulsion placed on her by Poferov and the debt owed to Dante for the tragic death of Erik. She was free, yet not. Her life was tied irrevocably to Dante, for better or worse. They no doubt had many things to work out, but she felt certain with love, many things were possible.

She dressed quickly and bounced down the hall toward the

kitchen to find Duncan there ahead of her. As usual, he was cooking.

"I don't think I've made one single meal since I've known you," she said by way of greeting.

Duncan turned from the stove and saluted her with his spatula. It was an action she was quickly becoming familiar with. His smile turned questioning as he met her eyes.

"Something's different." His head tilted, considering her.

Megan felt her face heat under his perusal. She felt different, but she didn't know if such deep changes would actually show on her face. Then again, this was Duncan. He had a way of seeing to the heart of the matter. If anyone could sense the differences in her, it would be him.

"Dante and I…" She didn't quite know how to phrase it. "We…uh…we joined…sort of. Last night."

A broad smile broke over Duncan's face. He leaned back against the counter with a knowing look.

"It's as I suspected then. Congratulations are in order. I have long despaired for Dante, hoping he would find the balance to his life. You're it, Megan. As I'd hoped."

She could feel his happiness. "You wanted this to happen?"

"Oh, I've wanted Dante to find his One for a long time. He's had too much tragedy in his life. I always hoped he'd be one of the lucky ones. I hoped he'd find that perfect someone to share his life and his troubles. After I got to know you, Megan, I started thinking you might be the answer to his prayers. I'm only glad my suspicions were true. You need each other. Both of you have been so alone for so long. I think you'll make a magnificent team now and into the future."

"But for how long?" Her thoughts turned depressing, and she finally allowed herself to think about some of the big questions surrounding their relationship. "It's just not done for a bloodletter to turn a shifter."

She sat at the table, wallowing in her thoughts as Duncan turned off the stove and served up giant hamburgers. He sat with her at the table as they began to eat.

"There's another complication, Megan."

"Oh?" She looked up at him, pausing as she lifted her burger from the plate.

"You're part fey." His eyes twinkled at her.

"You know, I still don't really believe that."

"You should." Duncan continued his meal as if they were merely discussing the weather. "Half-fey and bloodletters have been forbidden to mix for centuries, though it was not always so. It was believed that such a union would give too much power to those individuals. I have existed long enough to be certain of the truth of the adage that absolute power corrupts absolutely."

"You're saying that Dante and I can't be together?"

"I'm not saying that at all. Merely that you shouldn't be together, given past precedent. The prohibition against half-fey and bloodletter unions is longstanding and with good reason. However, times are changing and new threats are emerging. I've been around long enough to remember the last couple who were like you, of mixed blood."

"There have been couples like us in the past?" Now she was confused. He'd just said it was forbidden.

"Not many and not often," he confirmed. "When last we faced Elspeth, such things did occur every now and again. The nature and strength of the magic she had at her disposal—and that she passed to her followers—necessitated equal strength to fight it. Once she was banished to the Farthest Realms, the need for such power diminished and was eventually forbidden."

"I remember, Duncan." Dante's voice came from the doorway. Night had fallen and he had risen without Megan being aware. She checked the place in her mind where he was joined to her and found a passageway blocked from his side. It hurt to think he didn't want to keep the connection open. It felt like a refusal of her love.

"Don't ever think that, my love." Dante came into the kitchen and knelt before her, cupping her cheek in one strong hand. "I blocked the connection because I thought it would be more comfortable for you. Neither of us is used to this yet and I, particularly, have some memories that I prefer you didn't see—at least not until you're ready to see them."

Understanding dawned. "You want to take it slow?" She offered him a shaky smile.

"Just so. I think we both need to acclimate to being in each other's minds." He placed a gentle kiss on her lips, speaking in her mind through the small trickle of connection that still flowed between them. *"Good morrow, my love."*

"I'm truly happy for you both," Duncan said as they pulled apart. He watched them with a sappy grin on his face. "Congratulations, my friends."

"Thank you," Dante replied. "I never thought I could be so blessed."

"The Lady knows what She is doing. Her ways are mysterious, but She never gives anyone more than they can handle. Those with the purest hearts sometimes suffer the most on their journeys. You, Dante, have been proven a man of honor time and time again though you suffered greatly. Perhaps this is your reward." He gave Megan a teasingly speculative look.

Dante rose and headed for the cooler to select a bottle. "I believe this calls for a toast." He lifted a fat, dark bottle from the back of the refrigeration unit. "How about some champagne? I've been saving this for a special occasion and there is nothing more special than the gift of finding my perfect mate."

The look he sent her melted her heart and held the promise of many happy times to come. She tried not to think about the problems they faced as a couple. This moment was too special, too happy to ruin with questions about tomorrow.

They all raised their glasses for a joyous toast. The champagne was the finest vintage she had ever tasted. It rolled over her tongue in gleeful bursts of tiny bubbles. She savored the drink and the company. These two men were the best friends she'd ever had. Of course, Dante was much more than a friend, but the basis of their relationship was a mutual respect, liking and camaraderie. That was rare in her experience.

It was a while before they returned full circle to the troubling subject of their mixed heritage mating. She could feel Dante's concern when he thought on the subject. It had a different flavor than her own panic that somehow someone was going to forbid them to be together. His worry felt more long term while hers was immediate.

"No one will come between us, Megan." He took her hand and squeezed it reassuringly. "What concerns me is the fact of our mating at all. If bloodletters are finding mates among *were* and part-fey once again, it bodes ill for our world. Your blood powers me like no other. I will be one of the strongest of my kind to walk this Earth in many centuries." He looked from her to Duncan's serious face and back again. "If you decide to join me in the darkness, you will be the first shifter made bloodletter in just as long. Your fey blood will only increase your power. Together, we will be mighty, but I have to ask why the Goddess would grant us such power, unless…"

"…unless She is preparing this realm to face a dire threat," Duncan finished the thought in ominous tones. Megan felt her stomach clench at the implications. She was finally free of her family's debt and her keeper only to be thrust into an even more dangerous situation.

"So you can turn me? I thought it was forbidden." She clutched at the part of his words that gave her hope for them as a couple.

"It can be done." Dante brought her hand to his lips for a gentle salute. "Such a thing has not been done in a very long time. If you chose to spend eternity with me, I would turn you in a heartbeat. Or if you chose not to become as I am, I would join you in the next realm when you eventually die. I would not continue here, in this life, without you, Megan. We are One."

234

"That's the most beautiful thing anyone has ever said to me, Dante." She held his gaze, hope coursing through her. "I want you to turn me."

"Don't forget, my love, I can see into your heart. I know you love the sun and I know you fear the change. We have a lot of time to make this decision. Let's just enjoy learning each other for now and let tomorrow's big decisions wait until we're more comfortable. There is no rush."

"Not to mention," Duncan interjected, "that having one of you able to operate in the daylight could be very beneficial as a tactic."

"It's good to see old campaigners like you never really lose their edge," Dante chided his friend.

Now that Megan was One with Dante, she could feel things directly from his mind. He had constricted the connection but was not able to close it completely. Images still made it through from time to time. Things from Dante's past. She saw the image of Duncan, looking much the same as he did now, only clothed in the rough fabric of a bygone age. She also saw him shrouded in chainmail, a cunning grin on his face as he sharpened a sword.

These were memories of times past. Good times shared between the two men in another century. Megan was awed by the thought and feeling of friendship that was so strong between them. They were more like brothers than mere comrades.

And now she was part of their small circle. Through Dante, she was brought into the select group. Warriors and comrades in arms with a *Chevalier de la Lumiere*. Stranger things had happened, but she wasn't sure where or when.

"The way I see it, last night we took care of a huge problem. Of course, we still have Siobhan to deal with." Duncan brought them back to their current mission.

"The more I think about it, the more I believe Poferov was positioned there, just for us. Kevin said he thought the information came too easily. He warned of a trap, but the trap wasn't for us. It was for Poferov."

BIANCA D'ARC

"He was the highest ranking *Altor Custodis* agent in the metro area. He controlled a multitude of agents," Megan recalled. "Usually *AC* field agents move around a lot, going from place to place. It helps keep their covers intact. The administrators—the ones like Poferov who keep the records and don't engage in fieldwork—they're assigned to different locations and often live there for years. Poferov has been the section head for New York Metro for a long time. Forty years at least."

"Convenient if he was also the local *Venifucus* leader," Duncan commented with a sneer. "I can easily imagine a scenario where the Vabians wanted him out of the way and used us to help them do it."

Dante looked pensive, then nodded. "It's likely. He was too much out in the open last night. Too ripe for the picking. I think either way it turned out last night, the Vabians gained. If Poferov had defeated us, Siobhan would be thrilled. On the other hand, if we offed Poferov, he would no longer be around to object to anything the Vabians did. The *Venifucus* have been keeping a very low profile. I can't think that Siobhan's antics would have sat well with Poferov if he was the head honcho."

"That makes a lot of sense. I wonder if our *were* friends have any news for us. In particular, I'd love a chance to talk more with those selkies. I haven't dealt with their kind in far too long," Duncan said with a thoughtful arch to his eyebrow. "They were always a complex, thorough people. I think those two we met last night could be of great help to our cause if they are willing to help us more."

"Do you expect further action on the water?" Megan didn't really understand what help water shifters could be unless it had something to do with the ocean.

"Selkies are more than just seals, my dear," Duncan said kindly. "They are superb fighters both on land and on the sea. They are the ultimate warriors. Smart, quick and multi-talented. If you had a selkie on your team in the old days, you were almost certain of victory."

236

"They're really that good?" she asked, awed by Duncan's praise. He wasn't one to lavish such praise on just anyone.

"Better."

"That's it then." Dante slapped his thighs as he stood. "I'm going to call Kevin. If for nothing else than to thank him for the help last night. Want to listen in?"

Dante led the way to his office toward the back of the house. It was more of a library, really, with a large desk at one end and a fireplace with the requisite leather wing chairs at the other. Duncan pointed at the logs that had been laid in the fireplace, and they burst into cheerful flame.

"Handy to have you around." Megan gave him a playful smile.

"I try my humble best," Duncan replied with patently false modesty. He pulled the two heavy wing chairs around to face the desk where Dante sat organizing the call.

Dante moved the phone to the center of the desk so they could all participate. First he called Kevin's number and told the Alpha he was putting him on speaker. Duncan and Megan said hello, and they got down to business.

"Our watery friends got in touch with me this morning and let me know what happened last night. They were impressed with you three and wanted me to pass on their compliments. They said the man you took out was someone they'd had their eye on for a long time."

"No kidding?" Dante asked, surprise showing on his face. Megan could feel his satisfaction through their bond, even if she didn't understand the full ramifications. "As it turns out, we knew him to be a highly ranked *Altor Custodis* agent, in charge of the New York Metro area. We suspect he also played a similar role in the *Venifucus* hierarchy."

Kevin's low whistle met the pronouncement. "The water *were* already had him under surveillance. They didn't say why. I should tell you, they don't share much with me as a general rule. They're sort of the spooks of the *were* world."

Duncan spoke. "I suspected as much. Even centuries ago, they were always in the thick of things when stealth was called for. I would very much like to speak with them further if they are willing."

Kevin paused as if considering. "I think they'd be willing, but I'll have to ask."

"I understand." Duncan's tone was respectful. "Thank you for passing on the request."

Dante took the reins of the conversation back. "Regardless of the outcome, I have to agree with your suspicion that we were set up last night. For one thing, Siobhan was nowhere to be found. The yacht was empty except for Poferov and his familiar. It clearly wasn't his home base. I think the Vabians sent him there for us to take care of, wrapped up in a bright, shiny red bow."

"Igor Poferov?" Kevin sounded shocked even through the speaker.

"You know him?" Megan asked quickly, sending her companions suspicious looks.

"The pack had some dealings with him, though I had no idea he was a mage. I ended the business relationship because he just rubbed me the wrong way. Every time I got near him, my hackles rose. I've been Alpha too long to ignore that sort of feeling."

"Good thing too. The man was a mage to be reckoned with. He was the one who poisoned Megan's blood, and he placed her under one of the most powerful compulsions I have ever seen. Any mage who can, and would, do that to a *were*—even a half-*were*—without them knowing, is someone to steer clear of," Duncan said with finality.

"How'd he managed that?" Kevin wanted to know.

"I worked for him." Even now, free of his taint, Megan felt grimy just thinking about the man. "I didn't know he had worked magic on me until it was too late. Heathclif Dean bit me and almost died. Then the compulsion rose to prevent me from even speaking Poferov's name or disclosing anything that might lead to him."

Again, Kevin sounded warily impressed. "So now that he's gone, I assume you're free of his influence?"

Megan sighed. "Thankfully, yes." She knew it was too soon to disclose to the Alpha what had happened last night between her and Dante. Their mating was going to make enough waves as soon as it was discovered. No need to borrow trouble by speaking of it now.

"I'm glad for you," Kevin said in a kind tone. For a big, bad Alpha, he could be as sweet as a puppy when the occasion called for it. "So what next? With Poferov gone, there's going to be quite a shakeup within the *AC*. Probably within the *Venifucus* too if your theories are correct."

"Exactly. We need to monitor what happens in both organizations if there's any way to do so. My more immediate concern is the Vabians." Dante stared at the speakerphone as if the machine itself could provide the answers he needed. "They apparently wanted Poferov out of the way. We did their dirty work for them last night. In this case I don't mind because it solved a big problem for us as well. Siobhan remains a difficulty we have yet to address. If Poferov was holding her leash, she is well and truly off it now. Until another keeper steps into his place, she will most likely be running amuck and I fear she will redouble her efforts to make my life difficult. The biggest problem is that when she comes after me, she invariably puts everyone around me in danger as well."

"I see your problem," Kevin spoke in measured tones. "I have a few calls out to my people that haven't been returned yet. Let me check with them, and I'll call you in about a half an hour."

He signed off quickly, a man with a task, leaving the three of them alone in Dante's office, looking at each other as they sat around his desk. Megan didn't like the feeling of not knowing what to expect next. Dante was right. Siobhan was likely to attack again given half a chance. They needed to go back on offense. They needed to get her before she got them.

Her new relationship with Dante only increased the feeling of urgency. She couldn't lose him. Not when they'd only just found each other.

Dante got up and poured wine from a decanter on a side table. He served all three of them, passing the glasses around.

"I don't like waiting." Duncan picked up a pencil and threw it back down in frustration.

Megan almost laughed at his annoyance but knew Dante felt the same way. She was able to glean that much from their constricted connection.

"It is hard to wait when you've been bred to action," Duncan admitted, saluting them both with his glass before drinking deeply.

Before the conversation had a chance to degrade further, the phone rang. She was as surprised as both of the men. Dante went around his desk and sat before hitting the button to pick up on the speakerphone. It was Kevin on the other end, sooner than expected.

"The seals want to meet with you as soon as possible. Given the compromised nature of your home they suggested you meet them at Howlies. Same room as before."

"When?" Dante asked. Megan knew both men were eager to further their acquaintance with the water *were*.

"As soon as possible. They won't tell me, but I suspect they know a lot about the inner workings of the *AC*. When I mentioned Megan's involvement with Poferov, they jumped at the chance to discuss it in more depth with you all."

"We can be there in half an hour. Will that work?" Dante consulted his watch.

"I'll tell them. They'll be here. See you then." Kevin rang off with a quick farewell and Megan stood. If she was going out to that *were* bar again, she had to change into something a little snazzier.

Seeing them in the light for the first time, Dante got a very different impression of the two selkies he'd met under cover of darkness the night before. They were older than they seemed, though guessing the ages of *were*creatures was never a precise calculation. Depending on the animal that shared their soul, different shifters aged differently. According to what little Duncan had been able to tell them on the ride over, selkies were some of the most long-lived of the many shifter tribes.

Still, something about these two men indicated maturity. Combined with the steely look in their blue eyes, their appearance gave Dante even more confidence in their abilities. These were hardened warriors who had seen and done much in their lives, if he was any judge. He knew the warrior breed well.

One of the selkie males was slightly taller than the other, though both were heavily muscled. They had short haircuts and an overall clean cut look that spoke of a military background. They wore dark utility pants and well-worn combat boots with their plain, close fitting T-shirts. They weren't identical, but they definitely had the same ideas about fashion—or rather, about how to dress to be ready for anything.

The older one greeted Duncan with an outstretched hand as they entered the back room at Howlies. Kevin was also there, but none of the others from the previous meeting. This, then, was to be a private session.

Duncan and the two selkies exchanged greetings in a language Dante had heard once or twice in the distant past. He regretted he'd never taken time to learn that ancient tongue. It was pretty clear they asked Duncan a few questions about Dante and Megan before turning to greet them as well, seamlessly switching to English.

"I'm Nathan and this is Gunnar," the taller one said as he shook Dante's hand.

"I'm Dante," he replied politely. "You've met Duncan and Megan, of course. Thanks once again for your help last night."

They all moved farther into the room and took seats around the big table. Megan sat on Dante's left, the taller of the selkies, Nathan, on his right. They arranged themselves around one corner of the oblong table, the *weres* on one side, Dante, Megan and Duncan along the other.

"It's good to see you looking better, Megan." Nathan nodded toward her.

"Once Poferov was gone, his hold over me dissipated."

"We recognized his magic but not the man," Gunnar spoke in a gravelly voice. "We didn't realize it was actually Poferov until Kevin told us. We could sense the evil. Unfortunately, neither of us got a good enough look at him to be sure of his identity."

Nathan picked up the narrative. "We've had people watching Poferov for a while now. We've had suspicions about his activities unrelated to his position in the *Altor Custodis*. He's been doing a lot of moonlighting according to our sources. We just weren't able to pin down all the details of exactly what he was doing, with whom, or why."

"He's been my *AC* contact—my keeper—since my mother's death," Megan offered. "Before that, both my mother and my grandfathers were used by him in the same capacity."

"The Alpha filled us in on your background." Nathan nodded toward Kevin. "We're sorry for what happened to your family after your grandfathers' banishment. From what we were able to learn today, your grandfathers disappeared off the map after their disgrace. Nobody knew they had a daughter or granddaughter. I like to think some Alpha somewhere would've taken you into his pack, had any of us known about you."

Megan shrugged but Dante knew, through their connection, the selkie's words touched her deeply. "We did all right on our own. Except for the *Altor Custodis* interference, of course."

"Well, thanks to the sharing of information, we've been able to piece together some of the puzzle we've been working on for a few years." Nathan stood and went to a whiteboard setup that was folded shut on the wall. He opened it up to reveal a flow chart of sorts, with the names, rankings and positions of a network Dante had only begun to guess at. "This is as much as we have for the New York Metro area.

As you can see, Poferov was the kingpin. The Vabians figure prominently in the hierarchy and may even be poised to take over that top slot now that Poferov's out of the picture."

"Son of a bitch." Dante had known they'd been used the night before. He hadn't minded too much at the time, since by killing Poferov they'd managed to free Megan, but this information put a new spin on the situation. The Vabians had gained far more than Dante had imagined. He didn't like being used. "How does Siobhan figure into this? I assume it's her father or mother who would step into Poferov's shoes, right?"

"Exactly," Gunnar spoke again, his harsh voice driving home the point. "Viktor and Una Vabian. Both are, from all accounts, very gifted magic users. For sheer ambition, my money's on Una. She seems to wear the pants in the family."

"They both pretend to be regular mortals. Some of our people have gotten close enough to them to detect their level of magical ability. It's intense, according to our reports. They also both hold minor administrative positions in the *AC*. Ostensibly, they were members of Poferov's extended staff. Either could be selected to fill his position once his disappearance has been noticed by higher ups at the *AC*."

"I always heard the *Altor Custodis* was supposed to be an organization free from magic of any kind. They're supposed to be regular mortals who watch and record but don't become involved in supernatural doings." Kevin looked askance at the two seals.

"Yes, that's the way it's supposed to be. However, we began noticing some time ago that certain key positions within the *AC* had been awarded to magic users. We don't think the mortals who originally appointed them knew about their hidden talents. Once one mage infiltrated the higher levels of the organization, he brought in others. Over the years, it's been a challenge to find any non-magical humans in the upper ranks of the *AC* at all." Nathan sighed and ran one hand through his short hair. "We've been watching the watchers for a long time. It seems the time has come to share the information we've managed to gather. The prophesied time may be upon us."

"Prophecy?" Megan asked in surprise.

"Magic runs strong in our clan and every once in a while, a seer is born," Gunnar explained. "The strongest seer of our generation is my baby sister. She foresaw the coming of evil, the return of the *Venifucus*, a time when things that had not happened for centuries would come to pass. In fact, she spoke of a lone wolf bitch who was not fully wolf." His eyes swiveled to pin Megan. "And her bloodletter mate." The dark eyes turned to Dante as the room fell silent.

"Is this true?" Kevin asked finally.

Dante saw no need to lie, though it might ruin any chance of more help from the Alpha. Prejudices and traditions ran deep, after all.

"It is." Dante reached for Megan's hand, glad when she gave it into his keeping without comment, presenting a unified front for all to see. "We discovered the truth last night. We are One."

"Blessed Lady!" Kevin swore, sitting back heavily in his chair as he watched them. "I never thought I'd live to see such a thing."

"I did," Gunnar said with a knowing grin. "You are the ones my sister foresaw. You are the ones we're meant to help with the knowledge we've gathered and with the skills we can provide."

Nathan, still standing by the whiteboard, inclined his head in a gesture of respect. "Gunnar's right. Our people have been waiting for a sign, and this is it. Congratulations on your mating."

"Thank you," Megan murmured. Dante could feel her confusion through their link. It was a reflection of his own.

"Yes, thank you for your good wishes. To be honest, Megan and I aren't quite sure what to make of this yet ourselves. We're taking it slow and learning our way." He squeezed her hand, sending comfort through their link, which was quickly reciprocated.

"The first order of business has to be getting Siobhan Vabian off your back." Gunnar brought them back to the main issue they'd come here to discuss. "You two are key. You need to survive. Any threat to either of you must be eliminated."

That sounded serious to Dante. While he agreed with the idea of them surviving, he was a little put off by the vehemence in Gunnar's words.

"Excuse me, but why are we key? What else did your sister say about us?" Dante's brows drew together in a frown.

"Your union was foretold. It is the first but not the last, my sister said. All will be needed to defeat the coming storm. There's a reason things that have been forbidden since the last time evil threatened are happening now. Forbidden, powerful unions like yours will help defeat the enemy that has grown stronger in exile. Our duty is to protect you and others like you so you'll be ready to fight against an even stronger enemy, should Elspeth's forces manage to free her and bring her back."

"Holy shit." Kevin was white faced as he listened. "You guys aren't kidding, are you?"

"Unfortunately not, Alpha." Nathan breathed deeply. "We've been quietly preparing for this for a long time. There's a reason our people have kept separate from the other *were* tribes. We're more magical than most *were*. We've never shied away from taking human mates who had magical ability or breeding with idle fey lads who wanted a fling with a pretty selkie lass. As a tribe, we took on the responsibility of historians, caretakers, observers and warriors a long time ago. Now's the payoff. Now's our time to come forward and reveal the things we've learned, trained for and prepared over the years."

"Such as?" Kevin challenged.

Gunnar grinned. "Such as a majority of the elite fighting forces of the U.S. Navy. There's a reason they're called SEALs, Alpha."

Kevin's jaw went slack. "Holy shit."

CHAPTER SIXTEEN

"Back during the Vietnam War, a few of our brethren signed on for duty in the Underwater Demolition Teams. The UDTs were the precursors to the SEALs. There were a bunch of humans in the original teams, and there still are some that make it through the intense training, but a lot of Navy SEALs nowadays are shifters."

"They're all selkies?" Megan asked, clearly astounded.

"No," Gunnar chuckled. "We just started the tradition. Remember, there are a lot of shifter varieties that enjoy the water. Tigers are one example. There are quite a few of them in the Teams today, as well as other kinds of big cats."

"The thing is," Nathan spoke up, "we have a lot of men with a lot of training. SEAL shifters have to retire from the Teams at some point to discourage questions about why they don't age like normal people. That's why we got out close to thirty years ago. Since then, we've collected a lot of former SEALs and other special operatives into a loose organization."

"How many men are we talking about?" Duncan asked, speaking for the first time.

"Hundreds," Gunnar answered. "All aware of our mission and working to collect data for just this kind of thing. They're all over the country and the world. And they all report back to Nate." Gunnar hooked his thumb toward his comrade in a familiar gesture.

"They've prepared an army of highly trained warriors with specialized skills," Dante mused, and Megan jumped. He'd unconsciously shared that thought with her in the privacy of their minds.

"Navy, if I heard him correctly," came her tentative, joking reply in his mind. He loved the feeling of her thoughts. It was a new and exciting experience. Something they would share together for years to come if they were lucky.

"Thank heaven they're on our side," he said. *"I feel marginally better knowing men like these are looking out for you."*

"You too, Dante. Thank the Goddess. But I fear what it means for our future."

"I will do all in my power to keep us both alive and together for many years to come."

"Right back atcha." She squeezed his hand as they shared this private moment out of time.

"Forgive them." Dante became aware of Duncan's teasing voice, pulling him away from the magnificent reverie of their silent communication. "They're newlyweds, after all."

Duncan's grin was echoed around the room as Dante cleared his throat and shifted in his chair. Megan blushed beautifully, but fierce as always, she refused to flinch under the scrutiny. By the Goddess, he loved her.

"I love you too." Her voice touched his mind with warmth even as she stared down the men who snickered at them.

"You're at the very beginning of your relationship." Nathan leaned against the table. "It's the most vulnerable time for you. As you learn how to work together and share your minds, you'll acquire skills most of us can only dream about. It's our mission to help you live long enough to develop those abilities."

"While I appreciate your enthusiasm for keeping us alive to serve a higher purpose,—" Dante felt compelled to say, "—we're not exactly helpless. As you saw last night."

"Even the fey knight would have had some trouble with the things we found under that tub," Gunnar muttered.

"And we were glad of your assistance," Duncan put in. "Dante merely points out that while you and your brethren have been warriors of some renown for several decades, he and I were fighting side by side when the sword was still the most advanced personal protection device available." Duncan laughed self consciously "I don't claim that because we've been at it longer, we're necessarily better than you who know modern weaponry and tactics, but we are not novices either."

"I'll grant you that," Nathan allowed. "And I mean no disrespect. We're here to help you. It's what we've been preparing for. And now that you have Megan to consider..."

Dante firmed his grip on her hand. "She is as capable a woman as I've ever known. Truth be told, she saved my life the night we first met. She also helped save my house from being torched with us all inside. She can hold the half-shift longer than any wolf I've ever seen, and it doesn't drain her."

She squeezed his hand, and he knew he was embarrassing her, but he didn't want these newcomers counting her out of the action or dismissing her entirely. She would be by his side, no matter what. Right where he could keep a close eye on her. Where he could defend her with his life.

"While I appreciate the thought," she whispered in his mind, *"it goes both ways, lover. We'll be watching out for each other."*

"I wouldn't have it any other way." He raised her hand to his lips for a gentle salute.

Duncan cut in once more. "As best I can tell, in addition to being the granddaughter of a Priestess, Megan is also part fey, part human and half wolf. The mixture appears to have made a formidable combination." He sent her a kindly smile that Dante knew made her feel better. She knew as well as he did that Duncan didn't praise lightly.

"I also have a personal dislike for Siobhan Vabian. She's tried to kill us twice. Three times if you count those shadow warriors at her house. And then she or her family set us up for last night's fun and games." Megan was getting angry, and it came through in her tone. "I want a piece of her."

"Spoken like a true Alpha bitch." Kevin gave her the

highest compliment a *were*wolf Alpha could give a female of his kind. The fire chief had a gleam of admiration in his eye if Dante wasn't much mistaken. It didn't bother him. After all was said and done, Megan would be going home with him. She was his as much as he was hers and the joining of their minds had made him as sure of that as he was of the sun setting every evening.

"All right then." Nathan nodded to her respectfully. "We'll tell you what we know about the Vabians and provide assistance, but I can see you want to call the shots." He grinned at them. "Frankly, I'd have been disappointed if you were weaker willed."

Dante understood then that much of the posturing of the past few minutes had been a test of sorts. Nathan was craftier than he looked, as was his comrade, Gunnar. Dante doubted Kevin had been in on it because the Alpha wolf's expression wasn't as guarded as he probably thought it was. Dante could easily see that the seals had surprised the wolf Alpha with their deceptively tough talk.

"Now that we've got that cleared away—" Dante sat forward, " let's get down to business."

Smiles from the selkies indicated their approval of his straightforward manner. These men played a deep game. Dante would have to be on his toes around them. It was good to be challenged by such warriors as these. It had been a long time since he had enjoyed the company of comrades in arms, excepting Duncan, of course.

"All right." Nathan opened the other side of the whiteboard, which had a list of addresses on it. He must have written it beforehand, indicating again that they'd planned for this entire scenario. "All of these locations have something to do with either the Vabians or Poferov. We've included Poferov's haunts operating under the assumption that it'll take a while before others realize he's gone and during that time, the Vabians should be clear to use his properties as they wish. In fact, it would be to their advantage to do this on his land so that even in death, he could take the fall if something went wrong. Viktor and Una like to have their bases covered and in this case, I believe they are doing their best to keep their daughter out of trouble with the more powerful members of their sect. We have intel that suggests Poferov already spoke to the parents about keeping Siobhan in line. Shortly after that meeting, they set him up for death. Their playing field is clear for a time, if they handle it right, to do what they like without repercussions from above."

"Then it is as we suspect," Duncan spoke into the tense silence following Nathan's words. "Poferov was the head of not only the *Altor Custodis* contingent here in the New York area, but the *Venifucus* as well?"

"Aye," Gunnar spoke with a steely look in his gray eyes. "We've been watching them for some time. Poferov kept the New York *Venifucus* under control and working toward the organization's goals. The Vabians appear to be highly placed, but as soon as certain others learn that Poferov is dead, there will likely be a huge turf war to decide the succession. I'd bet good money Una and Viktor will be at the head of the line of magic users contending to fill Poferov's shoes."

"So Siobhan—and her family, if they're involved in the vendetta against me—has only a short time to operate freely," Dante observed.

Nathan nodded. "Once Poferov's absence is noted, the elder Vabians will most likely be too wrapped up in their own fight for power to continue, or assist with, Siobhan's plans. Once the succession is settled, if you haven't taken care of the problem already, it will most likely come back to haunt you. My advice, for what it's worth, is to take care of the situation now, before the Vabians gain even more power."

"Then you think they'll succeed in claiming Poferov's position?" Duncan watched them with an assessing gaze.

Nathan looked to Gunnar who nodded. "Highly likely given the family background and skills. There are few in the metro area who can compete with Viktor and Una acting as a team."

Megan leaned forward in her chair to make her point.

"The way I see it, we have two options. We can either find where Siobhan is hiding and attack her on her own ground, or let her come to us in a place of our choosing, a position fortified with our power."

"So you'd wait and let her attack first?" Gunnar challenged her strategy, watching her with measuring gray eyes.

Megan stood firm. "I would." All eyes turned to her. "For one thing, we already know she likes to set booby traps, and they're nasty. I imagine she learned to do so from her parents so any property they own would most likely pose some problems for us just getting in. Second, on our own ground, or in a place of our choosing, we could set our own traps and fortifications to make Siobhan's life difficult. Third, I doubt the Vabians would come *en masse* to attack Dante. More likely, it would be Siobhan alone or at most, with a helper or two. If we go to them, we won't really be certain how many we'll face until we get there. Fourth, we know she has a limited time to act. We probably won't have to wait long for her to take action. And finally, the idea of going after her when she's not actively engaging us first just doesn't sit well. Oh, my inner wolf is all for hunting her as prey, but my human side thinks it's just a little too much like assassination or murder. We're supposed to be the good guys."

Silence reigned for a long moment as her words sank in. It was Duncan who spoke at last as the men regarded her with varying expressions of respect, surprise—and from Dante— pride.

"The youngest of us speaks wisdom," Duncan complimented her. "I like the idea of acting in defense rather than offense in this case and all of Megan's reasons are valid. By choosing the place of battle, we can better prepare for it. After seeing the protections Siobhan had on her home, I wasn't looking forward to battling through another army of ghost warriors or sickening black fog."

"Not to mention the bottomless pit that opened beneath my feet or the little monsters in her front yard," Megan put in.

The selkies seemed impressed as they shot each other an indecipherable look. Dante decided to add his viewpoint and finalize the plan.

"We'll do this at my place uptown. It's one of many homes I own, and it already has a decent amount of magical protection laid on the place. Duncan has already added more. It would be a simple matter to place some more booby traps—both mundane and magical. Further, Siobhan knows the location and has attacked there before. She probably thinks she left a way in with her hellfire." He looked over at Duncan with a raised eyebrow.

"The hellfire was designed to leave a path into the building she could later exploit, but I destroyed it," Duncan said. "It would be easy enough for me to simulate the path and add my own little whammy to it, should she take the bait."

"That's what we'll do then." Dante was satisfied they had a plan at last. "We'll set the stage. Invite her in. And when she enters our domain, on our terms, we'll be ready to deal with her."

"We stand ready to help," Nathan said at once. "We can stand guard with you—either inside or on the perimeter. Whichever you prefer. And perhaps we can assist with some of the magical preparations as well."

Kevin braced his elbows on the table. "Some of my Pack can prowl the perimeter to be sure she doesn't escape. We can also help keep civilians away and relay information to you from the outside if necessary."

Dante considered the plan. "That's a good idea. You have my thanks, Alpha, and we'll gladly take you up on the offer of assistance."

"Time is short," Duncan put in. "We need to work fast."

"I'll put together a rotation," Kevin volunteered. "I'll put a team of wolves on your block day and night until this is over."

"And if you permit, we'll follow you home." Nathan erased the whiteboard, leaving no trace of the information he'd shared with them.

"Sounds like a plan." Dante rose, feeling better about the situation already.

They left with little fanfare. Kevin promised his people would be in place within minutes—even before they made it home. The selkies followed behind in a dark car. Their tail wasn't obvious and if Dante hadn't known they'd be back there, he would have been hard pressed to spot their presence on his own. They were that good.

When they pulled up outside the brownstone there was a wolf nosing around the doorstep. It wasn't behaving in a blatantly obvious way and the small creature could have easily been mistaken for a stray dog. It was female, and Dante suspected it was the woman they'd met the first time they'd gone to Howlies.

Dante nodded discreetly to the wolf as they entered the house. A baring of teeth was the only answer as the wolf moved off down the street at a slow amble. They went inside and found the house undisturbed in their absence.

"Much as I hate to say this, I think you ought to get some sleep, Megan." They paused in the living room to discuss plans for the immediate future.

"Why?"

He cupped her cheek and leaned down to place a quick kiss on the crown of her head. "Because we should probably take shifts. I need to take the night shift, obviously, and Duncan can do days and part of the night. He needs less sleep than you or I. I propose you take the part of the night Duncan sleeps and days as well. This way, there's always two of us on guard."

"Makes sense, but I'd rather stay with you." She rubbed her cheek against his shoulder in an unconscious gesture of affection that touched him deeply.

"I'd rather have you with me at all times, sweetheart, but we need to stay on guard until this is settled."

"I know. You're right, of course. I…" She turned into his arms. "*I wanted to be with you, Dante.*"

He loved the way she slipped her thoughts into his mind.

They had a definite naughty flavor that made him want to take her to his lair right that moment, but they had to secure the house first.

"Tell you what," he answered in the intimacy of their minds. *"I'll tuck you in, then come back here and help Duncan make the place safer."*

"You think we have time for a quickie?" The breathless need in her tone made him hard as a rock. Just like that.

"We'll make time, vixen." He bussed her lips with a silent promise of more.

Duncan cleared his throat. Megan jumped in Dante's arms, but he didn't let her go far. She blushed so beautifully. He loved to tease her just to see it.

"I'll start laying some groundwork for a few magical traps. Take your time." He left them with a knowing grin as Dante scooped Megan into his arms and headed for the nearest bed.

Hell, he probably wouldn't even make it to the bed. Not in this condition. He'd woken up wanting her and the need hadn't subsided in the few hours since. He *needed* her. Like he needed his next breath. She was vital to his existence.

Dante kicked the door to their bedroom open with a crash, pushing her up against it. She didn't protest. In fact, she helped him tear her clothes off. She then moved his out of the way in record time.

They were in perfect synch, even better than before. They'd been good together since the very beginning of their relationship, but now that they were joined, they were utterly attuned to each other. Dante knew what she was feeling. The connection with her provided sensory information from her mind directly to his. He felt her urgency as if it were his own. And it was. He needed her bad.

The connection was amazing, though he tried to hold it to a controlled flow. It was hard to taper the flow of information. Still, it was necessary for both of them until they got used to it. The sensation was dizzying and divine at the same time.

He intended to regulate the bond as much as possible until

they'd been together longer. He was afraid she'd learn things from his memories that would repulse her. He wasn't proud of some of the things he'd done in his past.

"Don't ever feel that way, Dante. I love you. I know you're not a saint. Believe me, a saint wouldn't be half this much fun." She bit his earlobe with just the right pressure as she spoke into his mind.

It was one of the sexiest things he'd ever experienced, and they weren't even physically joined yet. Of course, they were getting awfully close. He knew she was ready and heaven knew he was. This would have to be fast. They didn't have a whole lot of time.

"Don't wait!" Megan urged him on, reading his thoughts as easily as he read hers. His control over the connection was slipping. The union was so utterly enthralling, he didn't care. He felt her urgency reflected in his own state of mind.

Neither one of them wanted to wait. He spared only a moment to reach between her bare thighs, searching for the moisture that would ease his way. He wanted to be certain her body was as ready as her mind when he took her. Never would he cause her pain of any kind. Not if he could help it.

His fingers slid in her folds and her anxiety rose another notch as he toyed with her clit. Dante looked deep into her eyes, penetrating her with two fingers to be absolutely certain she could take him hard and fast. There was no time to take things slow. Not when they were at a fever pitch.

He pulled out, and she growled low in her throat in protest. She jumped up and wrapped her legs around his waist when he bent to catch her thighs in his big hands. She climbed all over him, and he loved every move of her sinuous body. He didn't have to tell her how to move. His thoughts were hers and vice versa. For the first time, Dante understood how different lovemaking would be for them from now on. It had been good before, but now it was sublime.

He pushed upward as she came down over him, sliding deep and hard on the first thrust. She fit around him like a warm, wet haven, an extension of his new self—the one that existed only when they were joined together in body, mind and soul. They moved together in an undulating motion until that became too much, too soon, in the very best possible way.

Dante gripped her thighs and pushed her harder against the door, pounding into her as she screamed his name. She growled and clawed his back in her passion, and it drove him higher. For the first time, he let go completely with a lover, taking her hard, fast and without worry that he was being too rough. He knew she loved the way he was doing her. He tasted the satisfaction and greed for more in her thoughts, mingled so intimately with his.

"Now, Dante! Bite me now!" she cried, offering up her delectable throat. She knew what he wanted, and he knew she wanted it too. It was a tricky business, this sharing of minds, but in passion there was no him, no her. There was only them.

He held that thought firmly in their mind as he pumped into her in short digs, driving them toward the pinnacle. There was no time for finesse. No need for it. They both wanted it hard and fast and that was exactly what he gave her.

Sinking his fangs into her neck, her blood bathed his tongue in her essence, her magic and that special sensation that was hers alone. The fey aspect of her ancestry was more noticeable in her blood. The magic of the shifter and the special oomph of the fey was tempered by her mortality, mixing together to send him into a state of orgasmic bliss. He took only a small taste of her essence. He didn't need much from his One to feed him unlike any other in his past.

He lost control of the connection between them. He was in her mind fully—as she was in his. It was glorious. Magnificent. Better than anything that had come before. Ever.

The power of her climax rolled over him, firing his senses. If he'd had any doubts, this would have blown them all away. *He* was blown away by the experience. Everything was new again—with her.

"Mmm. I'm glad you feel that way." Her sexy tone whispered through his mind. *"I feel the same."*

"I know, my love." He eased away after licking the wounds on her neck closed with a little zap of his magic. *"You are my light, Megan. My sun. My world."*

Her breath caught, and he knew she was as touched by what they shared as he was. All was finally right with his world. She was the center of his universe, and he'd never be alone again. *They'd* never be alone again. It was a calming, sustaining thought.

He left her because he had to. Not because he wanted to. He had work to do. Things had to be done to ensure their safety and their future together.

He tucked her into the big bed and lingered only a moment until she'd fallen asleep. He wished he could join her, but Duncan was waiting.

Siobhan, on the other hand, wouldn't wait. She would be coming for them, and they had to be ready.

With that thought firmly in mind, he closed the door behind him and headed off to work.

Megan woke hours later, when Dante went to his belowground chambers to sleep for the day. She felt his surprise through their link. It was much later in the morning than he usually sought his bed. He'd lost track of time while working with Duncan to lay magical traps within the house.

Normally, his energy, both physical and magical, would have drained away with the sun. Today, for the first time in centuries, he hadn't noticed any real change once the sun rose outside. He was aware of it in a peripheral way but had none of the usual urgency to finish up and seek his bed. That in itself was odd. When he thought about the high-level magics he'd been able to produce long into the daylight, Dante was somewhat astounded.

"I didn't mean to wake you, love," came his voice in her mind. She lay in the aboveground bedroom they'd used the past few

nights. She knew he'd sought shelter in the underground room that was more secure for him.

"It's all right. I should be up helping Duncan anyway. Did he manage to catch any sleep at all last night?"

"He is not of this realm. He doesn't need as much sleep as we do."

"He must need some sleep," she protested. Sometimes her maternal instincts came out where these men were concerned, even though she knew them to be fully capable and fierce warriors.

"He's fine. You'll see. I'm immortal and that man makes me tired. He's got more energy than any five normal people. I bet he's peculiar even among the half-fey. Some kind of freak of nature."

She chuckled as she knew he'd intended. They said goodnight after a few more traded quips and a whole bunch of sweet nothings passed between them. She wanted to be in his arms, but life was interfering. They had an enemy to deal with, and they couldn't rest easy until the matter with Siobhan was settled one way or another.

Megan found Duncan in the living room. He didn't seem to see her at first. He looked involved in casting some kind of complex spell. His fingers waved around in complex patterns, and he was muttering in some ancient language under his breath. Megan could actually feel the gathering magic in the air.

The fine hairs on the backs of her arms stood on end as if she were caught in a wave of static electricity. She'd felt the sensation before. Mostly when magic was flying around her.

At length, the wave of energy subsided and Duncan looked somewhat drained.

"Are you all right?" She moved into the room to stand in front of him.

Duncan looked at her, a lopsided smile on his handsome face. "Good morrow, Megan. I'll be fine in a minute or two."

"Even fey need to sleep once in a while." She took the seat next to him, concerned for his welfare.

Duncan had become dear to her in the time they'd spent

together. She also had the flavor of his long-standing friendship with Dante in her mind. She had no doubt the two of them had gotten into and out of more scrapes together than she could even imagine. She suspected when she and Dante were ready to fully share their minds, she'd learn more about the mischief he and Duncan had caused together than she really wanted.

"You, on the other hand, look bright eyed and bushy tailed, if you'll pardon the expression." His twinkling blue gaze teased her.

She stretched a little in her seat. "I feel great. You can rest a bit if you like. Or if you tell me what you want done, I'll do some of your legwork this morning while you take it easy."

"I may be old, but I'm not decrepit," he groused good-naturedly. Still, he sat on the couch, watching her. "You don't sleep much, even for a *were*."

She shrugged. "A couple of hours is all I need. All I've ever needed."

"I suspect your mother and grandfathers slept more than you did. Am I right?"

"Yeah, I suppose that's true." She wondered where he was going with this.

"Could be your fey nature is stronger than I suspected. I noticed some things as I worked with Dante earlier. He's either jumped another notch in power or..."

"Or what?"

"Or it's you. My blood gives him the same kind of elevation, but the flavor of the resulting magic is slightly different. Perhaps your fey/*were* mix is having a strange effect on our friend, Dante."

"Strange?" She didn't like the sound of that. "He's not in any danger, is he?"

"How could he be when you are destined mates?" Duncan looked calm, so she tried to relax. "The Goddess would not pair you if it was a bad thing. There is reason in all She does."

"You have the strongest faith of anyone I know." She truly did marvel at his deep belief.

"That's because I serve Her, Megan. I've felt Her presence in my soul, guiding my sword and influencing my actions. To be a Knight of the Light is to be directly in Her service, for in many ways She *is* Light."

"I never quite thought of it that way." Megan was humbled by his words and his deep and true conviction.

"So I have to wonder about your mating. She, no doubt, has plans for you both. I think it would be wise to test the boundaries of your bond as much as you can. You'll want to go slow, I'm sure. Just remember, the more you explore what the bond means for each of you, the better prepared you'll be for whatever comes." Duncan tempered his intense words by sitting back, though his gaze didn't waver. "You two are unique. There hasn't been a mating such as yours in a very long time. The selkies were right to want to guard you during this period of vulnerability. But coddling would never sit well with Dante. Or you, I believe. You're both creatures of action, needing to be in the thick of it."

"You've got that right. I think it's good to have friends helping us, but neither of us would be comfortable sitting back while others take action."

"Just so." Duncan stood, looking better than he had. "Perhaps we should have a bite to eat before we tackle anything else."

They shared a meal in companionable quiet. Duncan seemed tired but able to function at a reasonable level. Megan worried silently about what Siobhan had planned for them. So much had happened in such a short time. It was a lot to take in.

CHAPTER SEVENTEEN

When the attack came, it was without warning.

Breaking glass was heard from every room. Megan and Duncan jumped to their feet, not knowing which way to go. The tinkle of deadly shards of sharp glass sounded throughout the house. It was as if every window had shattered simultaneously.

"Be ready for anything!" Duncan shouted. She could feel him gathering his magic, an intense vibration in the air around him.

She sniffed and listened closely, hoping her *were* senses would tell her what direction to take. After that ear-splitting shattering of glass, all was silent. Eerily so.

Then, from below she heard the sounds of movement.

"Dante." She breathed his name in a whisper of dread even as she took flight toward the secret entrance to his underground lair. Duncan was right behind her.

She leapt down the flight of stairs, only bothering to bounce off one or two on the way down. Megan harnessed all of her *were* agility and strength to get to the room she had never visited but knew from the sharing of Dante's mind.

He was awake. Thank the Goddess. He was awake. She could feel that from the connection, held tightly closed on his end. If he had enough strength to maintain the compression of their link, then he was either unharmed or protecting her from something much worse.

She prayed as she had never prayed before that he was all right, even as she tore through the rooms that made up his lair, heading for his bedroom. She felt his presence there. His presence—and one other.

One other that most definitely did not belong. An incongruous abomination. A blank hole of evil magic where there should only be Dante's warrior spirit.

"She's in there with him," Megan whispered back to Duncan in warning as she finally slowed. He wasn't far behind, but he was still no match for her *were* speed. She was in front of the door, and she wouldn't wait to help her lover.

Megan kicked open the door and ducked low, expecting the sorceress would aim high if she was lobbing fireballs. The scene Megan interrupted was far worse.

Dante was covered in blood. A quick look at Siobhan told Megan it wasn't her blood. Dante was bleeding. Far too freely from the looks of it.

Megan half-shifted, growling as Siobhan turned to face her, a bloody silver knife in her hand.

"So it's true. D'Angleterre's got himself a wolf bitch," Siobhan spat. "No doubt she was your reward for murdering my brother."

"I didn't kill your brother."

Megan could feel Dante's regret through their link. He knew what it was to lose a brother all too well.

"He left with you," Siobhan accused. "You returned. He's nowhere to be found. Nowhere in this realm! I've looked and looked. He's dead, and you're responsible."

"Your brother brought about his own demise when he attacked an innocent woman. To my great regret, I helped him—until I understood what his true mission entailed. When he tried to kill a Priestess, I realized what he was."

Siobhan seemed to grow in height as her outrage sizzled in the room. "He should have killed you when he had the chance, vampire!" She struck out with her silver blade. Thankfully, Dante was no longer within reach.

Silver was deadly to immortals and dangerous to shifters too. Megan didn't care. This bitch was going down. Megan advanced on the sorceress, the gleam of death in her eyes. Megan's clothes were in tatters over her half-shifted body, but that barely registered through the battle haze engaging her senses, except as a nuisance. Her claws extended, ready to rend the sorceress from end to end if only she could get close enough.

Duncan registered in the back of her mind. He was in the doorway, standing firm. He wouldn't let Siobhan escape, even if Megan failed. But there was no way she was going to fail.

"Why are you awake?" Siobhan accused, probably to gain time as she tried to corner Dante again. "It's high noon. You should be dead to the world. Weak. Vulnerable. Pathetic. Yet here you stand, defying me. Did you steal my brother's magic when you killed him?"

No, Megan thought. Dante had enough of his own. It was a good question though. Dante should probably be a lot weaker than he appeared. Even bloody and bludgeoned, he stood his ground and moved quickly when needed. He was strong, even with the sun streaming over the house outside.

"You brother's evil was dispersed," Dante said. He kept the woman talking to gain time so Megan could get closer. They made a good team. She could feel his intent from the connection that joined them. She'd take him up on his useful ploy so he could get close to the sorceress and take her out.

The bitch wasn't going to make it easy. Megan got in range and made one long arcing swipe with her clawed hand. Her razor sharp nails skittered along an energy barrier, causing sparks to fly in every direction, igniting little fires along the rug, furnishings and bedclothes. Shit!

Duncan's magic swept into the room, dousing the flames, much to her relief. Fire was just as deadly to vampires as it was to any other being. Dante sagged, but he stood behind Siobhan, ready to engage. Megan read his intent through their bond.

"*She's mine,*" Megan growled through their link. "*I want her blood.*"

It didn't happen often, but every once in a while her beast demanded blood. For what Siobhan had done, Megan's wolf wanted her dead.

"*She's crafty,*" Dante warned in their shared mind. He allowed the connection to open a little more, sharing information easily between them. In a flash, Megan saw how Siobhan had taken Dante by surprise. She sent back images of what had happened above stairs. Siobhan had taken them all by surprise. "*Her shield is strong. We might find a weakness if we work together.*"

It was a sound plan. "*Good. We do this together. My wolf needs her blood, and you're injured. I'll take point. You hang back.*"

"*Never let it be said I argued with my lady,*" Dante answered gallantly. "*However, if she puts even a toe wrong, all bets are off.*"

Even in this dire situation, he had the power to charm her. She sent him a feral grin through her elongated teeth as she rolled out of the way of a small fireball. It was a good thing Dante believed in luxurious simplicity. His bedroom was huge and uncluttered enough for her to have room to maneuver.

Duncan remained in the doorway. Dante stood on the far side of the room, near the bed that filled one corner. Siobhan was between them, holding them both at bay with outstretched hands crackling with evil fire.

"So you admit it," Siobhan screamed. "You killed him!"

"He's gone," Dante said quietly, "but not by my hand. I'm sorry for your loss, Siobhan. However, this is no way to honor his memory."

"Avenging his death with yours is the perfect way," she countered. "My Order has wanted you dead for centuries. Patrick could have done it, but he wanted to use you first. I'll have my pick of honors for killing you."

"Among the *Venifucus?*" Dante asked shrewdly. Siobhan jumped visibly, surprise written on her features. "Oh, yes, I know of them. I know they were never fully eradicated. And I know they're working to bring Elspeth back. Just as I'm working to keep her banished."

"You'll never succeed. I'll kill you and unlike the fools who've tried before, I won't try to turn you to our side. I'll just end you. After all this time, they'll have to realize you won't be turned. You can't be allowed to continue and fulfill your destiny."

"Destiny?" Dante repeated quietly, surprise showing on his face.

"Don't say you didn't know?" Siobhan laughed. It wasn't a pleasant sound. "A seer spoke at your birth. You're to be a knight."

"I was a knight," Dante said, still clearly confused. "I fulfilled the seer's words. I served my king and country."

"Fool." Siobhan was gathering her power. Megan could feel the crackle of it in the air. "Not that kind of knight."

Dante's eyebrows rose in surprise. He said not a word as Siobhan prepared another volley. She sent little licks of flame out around the room, a warning to keep back.

Megan could feel Duncan's magic rising to meet it, tamping it down, controlling any stray bits of flame that might escape. The feel of his power a tingle along her nerve endings—gave her an idea.

Though Megan was no mage, Duncan insisted she was part fey. If that was truly the case, she should be able to use the innate magic of the fey race, coupled with her natural *were* ability to withstand most human magic, to her advantage.

She advanced on Siobhan, drawing her attention.

"When I get close enough, distract her."

"How?"

"I don't care. Throw something. All I need is a split second."

"I hope you know what you're doing."

"Don't worry. I think I can get her. I need to get close enough—jam her up so she can't lob any fireballs."

"What about her shield?"

"I'm betting I can slice through it like butter if I really put my mind to it."

"You sparked off it before. What makes you think you can get

265

through it now?"

"I sparked off her perimeter. I'm willing to bet that I can walk right through the perimeter to use my claws. Close in, she can't throw fire and she can't use that perimeter unless she knows some way to magically armor bare flesh."

Dante was silent a moment, most likely thinking through her plan. *"It's worth a try, but stay clear of her blade. It's pure silver, and it's magically enhanced."*

The reminder of what had caused his injury only heightened her desire to end this quickly. Dante was still bleeding. He needed care and healing as soon as possible. Until Siobhan was out of the picture, Dante was in danger. No doubt, he was fighting against the poison of the silver just to remain standing.

Megan advanced quickly, holding Siobhan's attention.

"Do it now. Distract her!"

An object flew through the air behind Siobhan, sparking off her perimeter shield to fall harmlessly to the floor. Siobhan fell for the ploy, spinning her head to see what had hit her shield.

It was only a split second, but that was all Megan needed. She was through the perimeter, her hide only slightly singed, and on the sorceress in the blink of an eye. Megan's claws dug into Siobhan's pale skin.

She made one last attempt to slice Megan with the blade. Megan clamped one hand over Siobhan's wrist until it crunched. The blood covered blade fell to the floor, thumping against the plush carpet harmlessly.

"Do you yield?" Megan ground out between elongated teeth. She had to give Siobhan a chance, regardless of her bloodthirsty words to Dante. Megan wasn't a cold-blooded killer.

"Never!" Siobhan spat, dragging out a small dagger that must've been hidden at her waist with her free hand. She swiped at Megan's head. Only a quick dodge saved her from losing an ear. The reflexive counterstrike to Siobhan's exposed throat was the killing blow that ended the sorceress's life.

Siobhan dropped to the carpet as Megan released her, lifeless.

Megan looked down at her with satisfaction as her wolf retreated, happy now that the threat to its mate was ended. In human form, Megan went to Dante, leaving Duncan to deal with Siobhan's residual magic.

Dante sagged in her arms as she helped him to the bed. He was weak and bloody, but rallying now that Siobhan's magic was dissipating. Megan ripped off his shirt to expose the slashing wounds on his chest and arms. There was also a deep puncture wound very near his heart. Her fingers paused as she touched the skin above his beating heart.

"So close…"

Dante's hand covered hers, drawing her gaze to his.

"She missed. I woke up a scant second before she struck and was able to flinch just enough to make her miss."

"Thank the Goddess." Megan leaned in to kiss his damaged chest. "I couldn't live without you, Dante."

"It's the same for me, my love."

Duncan appeared at Dante's side. Megan took a quick look back and saw that he'd sent Siobhan's body…elsewhere. Probably Underhill, until he could get a chance to deal with it properly. That was the least of Megan's worries now though. Dante was in bad shape.

"The silver blade burned as it sliced," Duncan said after a quick examination. "Luckily, there is no silver in the wounds. They will heal in time." He sat back on the bedside as he looked from him to Megan and back again. "How do you feel?"

"I've been better, but I'll live."

"How about your strength? As Siobhan reminded us, it's high noon outside. You seem rather perky for this time of day, my friend."

Dante laughed. It turned into a wheeze punctuated by a dribble of blood from the corner of his mouth. No doubt the knife had hit his lung, but with his immortal constitution, he was already on the mend. Still, the silver of the blade would make it a comparatively long and painful healing process.

"I feel good, actually. Better than I have in a long time while the sun is high."

"And what do you attribute that to?" Duncan's raised eyebrow went from Dante to her.

"My lady, I'm sure. She gives me strength." Dante's hand clasped hers tightly as his gaze shifted to her. She felt the love behind his words and echoed it right back to him.

"More than you know, my friend," Duncan murmured, drawing their attention.

"What do you mean?" Dante asked.

"Megan is part fey, among other things. I believe her unique blood will give you abilities few of your brethren can claim." Megan looked at Dante hopefully. She loved the idea that he'd be stronger for their love. "There's more, and I believe you are finally ready to hear it." Duncan's strange words drew their attention back to him. "Siobhan knew of the seer's words at your birth, Dante. Apparently the *Venifucus* took those words to heart and that's why you've been targeted these many years."

"I don't understand why, Duncan. I was a knight of the realm. I fulfilled the midwife's vision. Why should the *Venifucus* care?"

"Because you did not fulfill the vision." Duncan's words were weighty and deliberate. "You were meant for greater things than serving your king, Dante. You were meant to serve the Light, to be my brother, my comrade in arms, a fellow *Chevalier de la Lumiere*."

Shock rode Dante's handsome features as he sat up, clutching his wounds. His full attention was on Duncan and his startling words.

"Don't toy with me, Duncan." Dante looked at his old friend sideways, as if not entirely sure if he was kidding or not.

"I never joke about the Order." Duncan stood at the bedside, a shimmering glow suffusing his being as he called his power. Megan felt the surge in magical energy. When her eyes adjusted to Duncan's glow, he wasn't clothed in the armor she'd expected. Instead, he wore a tabard and coat of arms she'd never seen before.

The symbol of the eternal flame and the all-seeing eye were prominent, as well as some sacred geometry in the design. It stretched the limits of her arcane knowledge. All she could really tell was that it was immensely powerful. She could feel it first hand. It shimmered in white and gold, as did his entire being. This was a Knight of the Light in full, formal regalia.

Dante tried to rise, but Duncan's hand stayed him. "Many Knights have been made in their hospital beds after proving themselves in battle. I see no reason to alter the tradition in your case, my old friend."

"You would make me a Knight?" Dante was clearly stunned. "I'm not worthy of the honor, Duncan, as you know firsthand."

"I beg to differ." Duncan stood tall at the bedside, his expression full of compassion and care for his friend, "I've watched over you for many years, Dante d'Angleterre. Since returning to this realm, it's been my honor to discover that you are more worthy than ever for the space reserved in your name since the moment of your birth. That old wise woman saw far more than I'd realized, and it took our enemies to make it come clear."

"Think before you act, old man. This cannot be undone," Dante warned.

Duncan only smiled. "Spoken like a true Knight. I should have seen it sooner. My only excuse is that we had been parted so long, I was afraid you'd changed too much. Or perhaps the world had changed too much for me to deal with so quickly. Forgive me for taking time to see the truth."

"What truth?"

"That you are—and always have been—on the side of Light, Dante. Now, with Megan by your side, you are even stronger. The Goddess would not have trusted you with such a mate if she did not believe in the goodness of your soul through and through. You are a Knight of the Light. It only needs Naming, and you will gain the power you were born to wield."

"Duncan…" Dante was at a loss for words. Megan could feel his worry, his wonder and his brimming hope. He wanted to believe Duncan's words but felt unworthy. She sent her love to him through their connection. She knew his heart and if any man was worthy of such an honor, it was Dante. He was the best of men.

"I name you, Dante d'Angleterre, *Chevalier de la Lumiere.*" Megan felt the same white and gold power coalescing around Dante as Duncan spoke. "Your compassion, even for your enemy, your strength of will and character. Your unfailing honor and willingness to do what's right even when tempted beyond reason. Your steadfast belief in the Light. These are the things that make you a Knight, Dante. Do you vow to fight for all that is right and good for the rest of your days?"

"I do."

"Then welcome, brother." Duncan made a glowing sigil in the air that floated between them before sailing toward Dante to be absorbed into his chest. The wound closed before Megan's eyes as a tear tracked down her face.

A glimmer of light in the background caught her eye, and she turned to see the ghostly outlines of several men—all clad in similar white and gold tabards—as they flickered into existence, filling the room.

"They project their images here to welcome you, Dante. Our newest brother in the Order. Others will come in time, to teach and train, though I will begin your initial instruction as soon as you are fit." One by one, the men nodded or raised a hand in an informal salute, then winked out of existence. Megan had witnessed more than a few fey faces in the mix of solemn men.

"None of them were bloodletters," Dante observed when the last presence had left and the glow around Duncan eased. His formal wear went back to wherever it had come from, leaving him clad in his normal clothing.

"You are the first of your kind to join us in many centuries. In fact, you are the first Knight created in the mortal realm since the last time Elspeth threatened this place."

"That's sobering news." Dante reached for Megan's hand. "I'm concerned by what it might mean for our future."

"As you should be," Duncan agreed. "Lately all the signs point to preparation for the worst. Hopefully, with your help, we'll be able to avert that disaster from happening. I think, with you on board, we'll be able to do it."

"I'm honored by your confidence in me." Dante looked at Megan and squeezed her hand. "But what about my lady? We're joined. What I know, she also will know. There are no secrets between mates among bloodletters."

Duncan looked at her with kind eyes. "Women cannot be Knights. However, they too can serve the Light. It is not for me to induct a *Dame de la Lumiere*, however. I leave that to my counterparts in that even more secretive organization." Duncan winked at her. "If I'm any judge, they are already aware of you, Megan, and will be watching your progress closely."

"I've never heard of them," she whispered, suddenly wary of more spectral people visiting them.

"As it is meant to be. They are the best of spies. The most covert of operatives. They are our counterparts and our better halves, though by no means are they all mated to Knights. Many of us remain single. But the Dames are special women who work behind the scenes to aid us." Duncan's voice held his utter belief in their service. "I think, however, inducting someone like you will change their Order significantly. I can't blame them for thinking it over before they take that final step." He chuckled to soften his words, and she joined in.

"It doesn't matter, Duncan," she said honestly. "I am Dante's mate. I'm done spying for bad guys, even though I didn't know I was doing it at the time. From now on, we're both on the right side of things."

"I know," Duncan said with gentle respect. "And I finally understand why the *Venifucus* targeted you both. Nothing is more powerful to them than a good person gone bad. If they could have manipulated Dante—or you, Megan—to their side, they would have gained a powerful weapon. Left to follow your destinies, you are weapons for good. They either wanted to control you or kill you. Thank the Lady, they've managed to do neither. My guess is, now that you're joined and you have the strength of the Order behind you, they'll scale back their overt attacks on you. They failed to stop you. You've already achieved that which they wanted to subvert."

"That's some good news, at least," Dante muttered, bringing her hand to his lips for a kiss. "I wonder if the Vabians will cut their losses as well?"

"Only time will tell," Duncan said as he headed for the door. "If they're wise—and I have to believe they wouldn't have risen so far in their organization if they weren't—they'll know when to quit." Duncan turned when he entered the doorway. "I'm going to see what happened to the *were* who were supposed to be guarding us outside. I fear the worst for them since we received no warning before Siobhan's attack."

Megan recalled the wolves and selkies who were supposed to be on watch, and her heart clenched. She'd hate it if one of them was hurt or killed in this mess.

Dante stood, healed of the worst of his wounds, and tugged her in for a quick hug as Duncan left the room. He kissed her lightly, reassuringly as he allowed his love for her to bathe her senses through their link.

"Go help him, sweetheart. I'll start putting the indoors to rights while you assist with the shifters. He might need your help, and I can feel your concern for them."

She leaned up to kiss him softly. "You're the best of mates." She kissed him once more, then drew back. "I just want to be sure they're okay. I can let you know what happened through our link, so you won't have to wonder."

"Handy thing, this link," Dante smiled at her, holding her

272

close. He also sent images of what he wanted to do with her as soon as they had some time to spend alone.

"I like the way your mind works." She moved out of his arms as he let her go. "Hold that thought. I'll be back as soon as possible."

*

They discovered the *were* who had been stationed on guard outside the brownstone and treated their injuries. Siobhan had attacked them first, putting them out of commission. In fact, one of them nearly died, but with Duncan's help, he was expected to make a full recovery as well.

The selkies weren't easy to find. They'd stationed themselves in well-hidden places —one on a rooftop across the street, the other in the sewer. Both were unconscious when Duncan finally located them. They'd been taken out by the same spell that had shattered every window in Dante's home. Blood trailed down their ears, and Megan feared they'd been permanently damaged.

Duncan worked his magic, placing his hands over their heads, one by one, cupping their ears and chanting in a low, melodic voice for over an hour. The selkies were semiconscious during the treatment, obviously in great pain. Duncan soothed them, restoring them at great cost to himself.

Megan tucked Duncan into a guest bedroom when he'd finished, and he slept for two days. He slept right through the muted hammering of the construction crews who replaced every single window in record time. He slept through visits from three *were* Alphas, including Kevin and a number of his pack members. He slept through a visit from the Master and Mistress of the New York vampires. And he slept through the vigil held by the recovering selkies, who refused to leave his side. They guarded him day and night, which Megan found oddly touching.

*

Days later, when Duncan was better, the selkies had left and things were as back to normal, or as normal, as they were going to get, Duncan broached a subject that had been preying on Megan's mind. She loved Dante, but he was still holding their connection closed. He also refused to talk about turning her.

Duncan was telling her about her fey heritage. He'd also begun teaching her about magic.

"Fey magic resides in the fey realm. However, being half-fey, I can call it forth in any realm. My half-fey blood connects me to the fey realm at all times. I've been wondering if it does the same for you, or if your *were* side somehow interferes?"

"During the battle, I felt your magic. I've felt it every time you've called it. It buzzes along my skin and reverberates through my bones," she admitted. "I wondered if I could use it to break through Siobhan's shield. I figured between being part fey and my *were* blood, I could get through. Thankfully, it worked."

"Lucky for you. I doubt even a full-blooded *were* could have walked through that shield so easily. It was your mixed heritage that helped you again, I have no doubt." Duncan nodded knowingly. "There's only one thing that will make you even more powerful, although it will weaken you at times too. It's a tradeoff." Duncan shrugged.

"Turning me." Megan supplied the topic that had been preying on her mind.

"Have you and Dante discussed it at all?"

"Not much. He says we have plenty of time to think things through."

"And you do. There is no need to take this step hastily," Duncan agreed. "You should think about the ramifications. You would be the first *were* bloodletter in centuries, Megan. No doubt both shifters and bloodletters would have something to say to you about it. Most would condemn you both for taking such a huge leap. Many would fear the kind of power you would have in such a state."

"As long as our enemies fear me too, I have no problem with it."

Duncan laughed out loud at her challenging words. She snapped her teeth in a mocking snarl as she laughed along with him.

"Dante's a lucky son of a gun." Duncan smiled at her. "I like your style, Megan. You match him well."

*

Megan woke Dante just before sunset. She hadn't meant to disturb his sleep as she slid into bed beside him. She'd just wanted to be there when he woke, but he woke more easily and stayed awake during the daylight hours without the expected debilitating fatigue now that they'd joined. He sent her a sexy smile as he tugged her in close to his warm, hard body.

"Now this is my idea of the perfect way to wake up." He nuzzled her neck as she sank into his embrace.

"Guess you'll have to keep me around for a while, then," she quipped.

"For eternity." He rolled with her in his arms until she lay under him, her legs spread and wrapped around his hips in blatant invitation.

"Do you really mean that?"

He stilled. "You mean that bit about eternity?"

Slowly, she nodded. "I love you, Dante. I don't want a few decades with you. I want as long as possible."

"Life—even immortal life—is uncertain. If Duncan's right, we'll be facing some fierce enemies in the near future. Would you really punish yourself by giving up the sun so soon? If we make it through the coming trial, there's plenty of time to think about the rest of our years together."

"True," she allowed. "But all the sunshine in the world won't mean diddly squat without you."

"Oh, my love, you say the sweetest things." He kissed her. "I never thought to have something so special with anyone. You're a miracle, Megan. *My* miracle."

"I feel the same." She cupped his broad shoulders in his palms. "And since we agree on that, there's one other thing I'd like to try."

"What's that?"

"I want you to open the channel between our minds. Completely." She spoke the daring words directly into his mind using the small trickle of communication he allowed except when they were in the throes of passion and he lost control. That was the only time the connection was fully open. She thought they should probably start experimenting more if they were ever going to share their minds fully, the way true mates were supposed to share.

"Are you certain?" Dante looked apprehensive. It was the first time she could ever recall seeing that expression on his face.

"Yes, my love. It's time. I've already seen inside your memories when we lose control in passion. It's time to start sharing other memories. Other thoughts. Other feelings."

"Some of the things you'll see in my mind might change your opinion of me."

"Is that what you're worried about?" She smiled at him and moved her hand to his cheek, stroking him with compassion. "You can forget it, Dante. I love you just as you are. Nothing I could learn from your memories would ever change that. All that you've done—all that's led you to this point—that's what made you who you are. The man I love. Nothing can alter my love for you."

He kissed her, allowing the trickle in their minds to open more. She understood he would do this slowly and was glad of his consideration. It was a lot to get used to, but she wanted to do this for him. For *them.*

She pushed at his shoulder, wanting him to roll them over so she could be on top. He complied, and she straddled him as she undressed atop his muscular body. Her shirt went first, sailing off across the room as she flung it from her. Dante wore only soft pajama pants with a drawstring closure. She untied them and pushed them downward, laughing when he raised his hips to help, rocking her perch as well.

He kicked the pajamas off and away while his fingers toyed with her nipples. She pushed her own lounge pants and panties downward, readjusting over his thighs to accommodate their removal. He helped marginally, seeming to be more interested in her breasts than in actually helping her get naked.

"No, baby. I want you naked. I'm just a little...distracted at the moment." He raised his head, licking one nipple into his mouth. She felt the scratch of his fangs against her tender flesh. It didn't hurt exactly. It tantalized.

She didn't need preliminaries. She needed him. Now.

She was wet and ready for him, so she lifted up and placed his thick, hard cock inside, pushing downward inch by inch, savoring the feel of claiming him with her body. He was hers, and she was his.

"Oh, yeah." His voice rumbled through her mind. She could feel his pleasure at their joining, his desire, his passion. It matched her own. *"Ride me, baby. Show me what you want."*

"I only want you, Dante. Inside me. Biting me while I clench on you."

The image her words spawned in their shared minds made them both gasp.

He moved from one breast to the other, sucking deep, making her move faster on him as her desire rose fast. Faster than ever as they shared their minds more fully. Her thighs worked as she slid up and down on his cock, grinding her hips in a way guaranteed to bring them both the ultimate pleasure.

He bit, striking without warning as he licked the soft skin above her nipple. He bit the fleshy part of her breast, making her jump, but not causing a great deal of pain. It was just a little bite, more of a nip, really. It made her sit up and take notice and brought her to a small climax as she rode him.

There was more to come. He swirled his tongue around the pinpricks in her skin, licking at her blood—playing, in a purely vampire way.

"Tease," she accused in their minds.

"Come down here and I'll give you what you want. Naughty girl." His voice curled her toes, low, rumbly and intimate in their shared minds.

"Make me." The dare aroused them both.

Dante growled aloud as he rolled, pinning her beneath him, his cock spearing into her. He stilled, holding her gaze.

"Do you truly want this?"

The pathway between them was open more fully than it had ever been. She could feel he still held a little back. She was afraid, but she wanted it all. With him. For him. She gathered her courage. She could do this. She must do this. If she loved him enough—and she certainly did—she could be brave.

"Do it, Dante."

He held her gaze as he let go of his conscious control over the flow of information from his mind to hers and back again. The floodgates opened and she was immediately immersed in his thoughts, knowing he was feeling the same kind of thing.

Her thoughts were magnified by their duality, reflected back at her from his mind. Dizziness assailed her for a moment, but Dante was there to steady her, to ground her, to be her anchor in times of peril.

"As you are for me, my love."

Their thoughts were mingling, caressing each other from within the confines of their minds as their bodies stayed joined in the physical world. It was more intimate than she'd thought, and nothing to be feared.

It would take a lifetime to learn him. To see all that had made him who he was today. Immersing herself in him, she finally understood that this new closeness wasn't as scary as she'd thought. It was beautiful, in its way. Pure, good and as close as two people could get.

Only one thing could bring them closer, and she wanted it with all her heart. She saw how he wanted her to join him—to be willing to forsake the sun for him—to give herself into his keeping in all ways as he did for her.

But he would never ask.

"Is this why you held back? I mean, you didn't mind that I was afraid of sharing our thoughts because you also wanted to hide how badly you wanted to turn me?" There was no accusation in her tone, merely curiosity and an undying love.

She felt his inner shame. "I would never ask it of you. It was to have been your choice to make."

"You don't need to ask." She stroked his hair, holding his gaze as he hovered over her, their bodies still joined. "I want to give you this gift. This final thing that holds us apart. Any separation from you now is unbearable. I want to be with you always, Dante. For all time."

"My love." He was beyond words, easing down to kiss her sweetly, as if it was the first kiss of the rest of their lives.

He tried to hold still. She felt his inner struggle. Eventually, the emotions, the sensations, were too much. He began to stroke into her in long, satisfying sweeps that made them both moan. Then even that wasn't enough as he continued to devour her mouth with his. His tongue stabbed into her, mimicking his cock, digging into her, touching off little spasms within her core. She mewled in need, gasping as he released her mouth, his lips working their way to her throat with tiny, biting kisses.

She couldn't wait any longer. Her body wanted to explode. Her mind was so intertwined with his, she didn't know where she left off and he began. She felt his climax build and build until the pressure pounding through them both was unbearable. They needed release…but he needed one more thing.

He bit into her throat, accessing the vein. She felt it both physically and mentally, feeling it from his point of view as well as her own. The utter surrender, the complete claiming. The drain as he sucked on her blood and her psychic energy, replenished by his spike in power and strength as he fed from her and gave it all back.

She climaxed, but he needed the ultimate rush. He sealed the small wounds on her neck with his tongue and transformed one finger into a sharp claw, slicing deep into his chest. Blood welled up and his hunger became hers as he cradled her head and drew her mouth to his body.

The first coppery taste bathed her senses in his aura, his power, his indefinable essence. Never had she tasted something so heady and strong. She wanted more.

His hunger fed her new desires as she drank deeply from his life giving force. He climaxed as she sucked at his skin, sloppy in her haste, driven by needs she'd never known she had. She would never quite know if they were his needs now become hers, or if they'd been buried inside her all this time. It didn't really matter.

All that mattered was this moment out of time. This spark of eternal life passing from him to her in the most beautiful, passionate and sacred way.

The sharing of blood. The sharing of life. The sharing of love.

Now and forever.

*

Despite making love all night and sleeping more deeply than she had in ages, Megan woke at her normal time in the afternoon of the next day. Dante rolled over when she left the bed, closer to the surface of sleep than he normally was at this hour. She thought nothing of it until she got to the kitchen.

Sunlight streamed in through the windows, making her squint. Aside from that small inconvenience, the sunlight felt good on the bare skin of her arms. Then she remembered. She was a vampire. Sunlight should burn—not feel pleasantly warm. Something very strange was going on here.

Duncan turned from the stove, as he had many times since

she'd come to stay in Dante's house. When he saw her, the plate full of eggs slid out of his hand to crash on the floor in a million pieces. He didn't even notice.

"Sweet, blessed Lady." His voice was a whisper of shock, his eyes wide as he looked at her. "He changed you last night, didn't he?"

Mutely she nodded. She didn't understand what was going on here and Duncan's reaction had her worried. She clutched at her arms, rubbing one hand over her opposite forearm.

"And the sunlight here doesn't bother you?"

"No." After her eyes adjusted, she was okay.

Duncan considered her as if she were a germ under a microscope. "Are you hungry?"

The question was so commonplace, it put her more at ease. "Now that you mention it. I could go for some steak and eggs."

"Fascinating." Duncan stepped over the shards of ceramic and globs of egg decorating the floor. "Don't you want blood?"

At mention of the word, fangs erupted in her watering mouth, but not just any blood would do. She wanted Dante's blood and his lovemaking. With her fangs also came a wave of lust for her mate. She didn't want any other—not in any way. Only Dante.

"Not yours," she answered Duncan's question as he stood facing her. His gaze measured her, noting the slight bulge of her dainty fangs and following them as she spoke around her new dentition.

"Dante's? You want Dante's blood?"

"Yes!" The word was torn from her lips as her body heated.

A second later, the door behind her swung open and Dante's arms came around her from behind, pulling her into the dark hallway. She turned willingly in his arms, sealing her lips to his as he kissed the breath from her body.

This was what she craved. What she needed.

"I know," he answered in her mind. *"It's what I need too. You.*

Only you, my love. Forever."

EPILOGUE

Far away, a mage sat up straight in his chair.

"Poferov, the old fool, is dead," the mage said to his companion.

"Are you certain?"

"I bespelled his familiar to send me an alarm should anything happen to Igor. He is dead. As is the snake."

"It is a loss for our cause."

"He can be replaced. I'm more concerned about how he was caught and who ended him. The first question could cause problems for us if he was betrayed from within."

"And the second question?"

"Not to worry. The snake tagged its killer. If they didn't kill Poferov, they were close enough to see who did. We will find them and...ask."

"Ask?" The companion smiled evilly.

"With all due prejudice, of course. If you're good, I'll let you have the honor of torturing the being who bested Poferov. No doubt such a one will make good sport for you."

# # #

ABOUT THE AUTHOR

Bianca D'Arc has run a laboratory, climbed the corporate ladder in the shark-infested streets of lower Manhattan, studied and taught martial arts, and earned the right to put a whole bunch of letters after her name, but she's always enjoyed writing more than any of her other pursuits. She grew up and still lives on Long Island, where she keeps busy with an extensive garden, several aquariums full of very demanding fish, and writing her favorite genres of paranormal, fantasy and sci-fi romance.

Bianca loves to hear from readers and can be reached through Facebook (BiancaDArcAuthor) or through the various links on her website.

WELCOME TO THE D'ARC SIDE…
WWW.BIANCADARC.COM

BOOKS BY BIANCA D'ARC

The *Tales of the Were* branches out into several different related sub-series. *The Others* is the first sub-series and begins with…

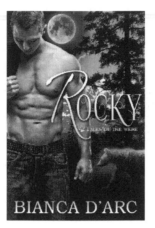

TALES OF THE WERE ~ THE OTHERS
ROCKY

On the run from her husband's killers, there is only one man who can help her now… her Rock.

Maggie is on the run from those who killed her husband nine months ago. She knows the only one who can help her is Rocco, a grizzly shifter she knew in her youth. She arrives on his doorstep in labor with twins. Magical, shapeshifting, bear cub twins destined to lead the next generation of werecreatures in North America.

Rocky is devastated by the news of his Clan brother's death, but he cannot deny the attraction that has never waned for the small human woman who stole his heart a long time ago. Rocky absented himself from her life when she chose to marry his childhood friend, but the years haven't changed the way he feels for her.

And now there are two young lives to protect. Rocky will do everything in his power to end the threat to the small family and claim them for himself. He knows he is the perfect Alpha to teach the cubs as they grow into their power… if their mother will let him love her as he has always longed to do.

The *Redstone Clan* sub-series follows the story of five cougar-shifter brothers who own a construction company and starts with…

USA TODAY BESTSELLING AUTHOR
BIANCA D'ARC

TALES OF THE WERE ~ REDSTONE CLAN 1
GRIF

Griffon Redstone is the eldest of five brothers and the leader of one of the most influential shifter Clans in North America. He seeks solace in the mountains, away from the horrific events of the past months, for both himself and his young sister. The deaths of their older sister and mother have hit them both very hard.

Lindsey Tate is human, but very aware of the werewolf Pack that lives near her grandfather's old cabin. She's come to right a wrong her grandfather committed against the Pack and salvage what's left of her family's honor—if the wolves will let her. Mostly, they seem intent on running her out of town on a rail.

But the golden haired stranger, Grif, comes to her rescue more than once. He stands up for her against the wolf Pack and then helps her fix the old generator at the cabin. When she performs a ceremony she expects will end in her death, the shifter deity has other ideas. Thrown together by fate, neither of them can deny their deep attraction, but will an old enemy tear them apart?

Warning: Frisky cats get up to all sorts of naughtiness, including a frenzy-induced multi-partner situation that might be a little intense for some readers.

The newest *Tales of the Were* sub-series is the story of *Grizzly Cove*, a settlement of bear shifters in the Pacific Northwest. They're available separately or in this money-saving bundle...

TALES OF THE WERE ~ GRIZZLY COVE

Welcome to Grizzly Cove, where there's wild magic, unexpected allies, and a conflagration of sorcery and shifter magic the likes of which has not been seen in centuries. That's what awaits the peaceful town of Grizzly Cove. That, and love. Lots and lots of love. This three-story collection contains:

All About the Bear - The sheriff has more than the peace to protect. The proprietor of the new bakery in town is clueless about the dual nature of her nearest neighbors, but not for long. It'll be up to Sheriff Brody to clue her in and convince her to stay calm—and in his bed—for the next fifty years or so.

Mating Dance - Tom, Grizzly Cove's only lawyer, is also a badass grizzly bear, but he's met his match in Ashley, the woman he just can't get out of his mind. She's got a dark secret, that only he knows. When ugliness from her past tracks her to her new home, can Tom protect the woman he is fast coming to believe is his mate?

Night Shift - Sheriff's Deputy Zak is one of the few black bear shifters in a colony of grizzlies. When his job takes him into closer proximity to the lovely Tina, though, he finds he can't resist her. Could it be he's finally found his mate? And when adversity strikes, will she turn to him, or run into the night? Zak will do all he can to make sure she chooses him.

Or, if you like vampires and weres mixing it up, check out the related series, *Brotherhood of Blood.*

One & Only - Atticus is a vampire on the edge, ready to greet the dawn and end his immortal existence, until...he hears the faint heartbeat of a woman in need. A woman who might just be his One. Saving her life gives him reason to go on, but will the fates allow them to be together forever?

Rare Vintage – Marc LaTour is the Master vampire. Kelly is the new Gal Friday at the winery her best friend and her new husband own. Marc is obsessed with Kelly, though he doubts he could be so lucky as to finally find his One after over six hundred years of searching. Still, he reacts with jealousy when his old friend and fellow Master comes for a visit. When upstart vampire in Marc's territory issues a challenge to Marc's leadership, it will be a fight to the death, but Marc knows he has much to live for... if Kelly turns out to be his One.

Phantom Desires - Computer expert Carly is tired, and ready to downgrade her hectic lifestyle to something simpler. Her solution - pull up stakes and move to an old farm house in the middle of Wyoming. Dmitri, a Master Vampire, lives beneath Carly's new house, in his hidden lair. Even if Carly can't deny the attraction arcing between them, loving him will force her to make a choice. Life in the sun without him - or an eternity in darkness.